Prais
White Man'

"A fascinating picture of early 18c ....ugh the story of one family tossed and turned by the waves of change in their world and within themselves. Slavery, abolitionism, emerging feminism, the founding of the colony of freed slaves in Liberia—this very human story shows us all the different movements and attitudes roiling together at this time in history through its characters' struggles, losses, and loves."

—Nancy Kilgore, author of *Bitter Magic*

"Drawing on her own family's history, Sarah Angleton has crafted a compelling, well-written novel that encompasses two key anti-slavery forces of the mid-19th century. The young Annie Goheen is a committed Abolitionist, while her brother Sylvanus works on behalf of the Liberia Colony for freed Blacks in west Africa. The story of Liberia, the White Man's Graveyard of the title, is almost forgotten today and the novel brings to light both the ideals on which it was founded and the difficulties encountered by the people who settled there. It is eloquent not only of the period in which the story is set but also resonates as we grapple today with the history of slavery in America."

—Ann Marti Friedman,
author of *A Fine Tapestry of Murder*

"In S. Angleton's *White Man's Graveyard*, the question of abolition and emancipation as a solution for slavery versus the "back to Africa" movement is explored. Annie and her family, particularly her little brother, Sylvanus, suffer various trials, and operate as a station on the Underground Railroad for a time. They take in an escaped enslaved woman, Esther, and treat her like a member of their own family. Sylvanus joins the back to Africa contingent, as a physician in Liberia—but is he doing more harm than good? Which is the better path to freedom and equality—abolition, or Africa? The white man's graveyard, Liberia, puts ideals and family relationships to the test. This largely true story from the author's family will keep you reading, and pondering the issues."

—Michael L. Ross,
Amazon bestselling author of the *Across the Divide* series

Praise for
Gentleman of Misfortune

"Quality fiction and real history make a great match, and Sarah Angleton's *Gentleman of Misfortune* offers the best of both. This is an engaging story with surprises on every page."

—Jeff Guinn, *New York Times* bestselling
author of *The Last Gunfight* and *Manson*

Gentleman of Misfortune is and intricately constructed historical novel inspired by a lesser-known part of Mormon Scripture. Mormon prophet and founder Joseph Smith appears as a black market buyer of Egyptian goods in this suspenseful, ominous, and captivating saga."

—Midwest Book Review

Praise for
Smoke Rose to Heaven

"An intriguing exploration of an oft-ignored part of U. S. History. Angleton's lush prose and realistic characters are sure to cast a spell on readers and history buffs alike."

—Nicole Evelina, *USA Today* bestselling author of *The Guinevere's Tale Trilogy*

"A clever page-turner sprinkled with twists and turns of fate that kept me engaged to the end. I love it."

—Pat Wahler, author of Western Fictioneers' Best First Novel of 2018, *I Am Mrs. Jesse James*

White Man's Graveyard

Sarah Angleton

Sarah Angleton
Nov. 2021

bright
button
press

ST. LOUIS, MISSOURI

Cover Design by Steven Varble
Author photo by Karen Anderson Designs, Inc.
Book Layout © 2017 BookDesignTemplates.com
Book Design by JeanneFelfe.com

Published by Bright Button Press:
PO Box 203
Foristell, Missouri 63348 (United States of America)

This is a work of fiction. All names, places, and incidents are either products of the author's imagination or used factiously. Any resemblance to actual incidents or persons, living or dead, is coincidental.

Publisher's Cataloging-in-Publication Data
provided by Five Rainbows Cataloging Services

Names: Angleton, Sarah, author.
Title: White man's graveyard / Sarah Angleton.
Description: St. Louis : Bright Button Press, 2021.
Identifiers: LCCN 2021917516 (print) | ISBN 978-0-9987853-7-0
    (paperback) | ISBN 978-0-9987853-8-7 (ebook)
Subjects: LCSH: Abolitionists--Fiction. | Slavery--Fiction. | Brothers and
    sisters--Fiction. | Missionaries--Fiction. | Liberia--Fiction. |
    Pennsylvania--Fiction. | Historical fiction. | BISAC: FICTION /
    Historical / General. | FICTION / Christian / Historical. | FICTION /
    Sagas. | GSAFD: Historical fiction.
Classification: LCC PS3601.N55441 W55 2021 (print) | LCC PS3601.N55441
(ebook) | DDC 813/.6--dc23.

In Loving Memory
of
Pat Goheen
&
R. J. H. Goheen

Prologue

August 13, 1837

Even the buzz of the insects hushed as the final preacher of the Sabbath day stepped onto the stage to claim the pulpit. It was this man they'd come to see—the farmers and the merchants, the ladies in their finest silks, the young lawyer who, at the request of his friends, had left piles of work in his office six miles away in Springfield only to hear the renowned speaker.

Peter Akers didn't disappoint. He was a giant of a man. More than six feet tall and broad with long limbs and large hands that animated his speech, he loomed above the crowd. They leaned into his words in the slick heat of the Illinois summer.

He began his sermon with a text from Zechariah 9:9: *Rejoice greatly, O daughter of Zion; shout, O daughter of Jerusalem; behold thy King cometh unto thee.* Akers favored the Old Testament prophets, often preaching from these strange and ancient texts sometimes for hours, diving without hesitation into high-minded allegory and apocalyptic language, inviting his congregation to ascend with him to new intellectual heights.

His were not the emotionally exhilarating sermons of his colleagues. He neither condemned nor flattered. His words did not inspire the quaking and contorting otherwise common at camp meeting revivals, yet he held his audience rapt and eager.

Like Jacob of old, Akers wrestled with God, and all who listened came away changed. His sermon danced among the words of God's prophets, from Zechariah to Isaiah, from Ezekiel's proclamations of the unrighteous overturned, to the book of Revelation and Babylon's inevitable fall.

And the merchants of the earth shall weep and mourn over her; for no man buyeth their merchandise anymore: the merchandise of silver and gold and precious stone, of wine and oil and fine flour, of sheep and horses and chariots and slaves and the souls of men.

Akers paused here, his eyes raised to heaven and at the same time locked into the hearts of each silent person awaiting the forthcoming conclusion, breaths held in anticipation.

"If we interpret the prophecies of this Book correctly. . ." Though the preacher's commanding voice lowered to nearly a whisper, not a word could be missed. "There will soon come a time when the head and front of this offending shall be broken; a time when slave-ships, like beasts of prey, will no longer steal along the coast of defenseless Africa. When we shall cease to trade in the flesh and souls of men but will instead expel forever from this land the manacle and the whip.

"I am not a prophet," Akers explained to a congregation that did not believe him. "But a student of the Prophets. American slavery will come to an end in some near decade."

At these words, shifting and murmuring rose in the crowd, some perhaps angry but most filled with hope and awe at the sheer audacity of the assertion. Undaunted by the excitement, Akers carried on, saying, "Who can tell but that the man who shall lead us through this strife might be standing in this presence."

This was a pronouncement rather than a question. The preacher paused, giving space for the seed of prophetic vision to find fertile soil.

At the edge of the crowd, the young lawyer drew a long breath, rubbed his weary eyes, and reflected on the preacher's powerful words.

One of his friends clapped him on the back. "What do you think, Mr. Lincoln? Are you glad you came with us?"

"As odd as it seems," he answered with only slight hesitation, "When the preacher described those changes and revolutions, I was deeply impressed that I should somehow strangely mix up with them."

He did not wait for a response from his dumbfounded friend, but stood tall and stretched the stiffness from his shoulders and limbs as he thought of the many tasks awaiting him on his desk, and of the much greater work he'd yet to begin.

1

Annie

September 12, 1814

Twenty-one days shy of the age of seven, Miss Mary Ann Goheen became a mama for the first time. Others might not see it that way, but Annie felt it the moment her mother placed Baby Sylvanus in her arms—the day their father died.

When the doctor pronounced Father's death, Annie's strong-backed, proud mother, giver of comfort and all things good, wilted in the exhaustion of defeat. At the age of thirty, Elizabeth Goheen had become a widow with five sons under the age of eleven and an only daughter, who looked on, helpless, as her mother folded in on herself. Ten-year-old Mayberry placed a hand on their mother's shoulder, eliciting a shudder that made Annie's stomach churn.

Silence blanketed the farmhouse, muffling the sharp pang of grief, the stillness broken after several long minutes by the innocent wriggling of the little boy in Mother's grasp.

"Take him." Mother handed the squirming, pudgy-cheeked sixteen-month-old to Annie.

The baby protested with a loud, "No!" His usual babble made up of more sounds than words was rarely so clear, but there could be no mistaking him.

"Shh," Annie whispered to the tot and brushed back a curl of silky hair that had fallen across his forehead. "Smee, Mama can't take you right now. You have to be a good boy." She shifted him to her jutted hip.

He continued to protest, twisting against her as tears squeezed from his eyes and he hollered the one word that made it feel as though time stopped: "Dada."

Mother turned toward him, her face drained of color. The baby hushed in the tension, shrinking into Annie's embrace, the solid weight of him the only thing grounding her to the moment from which she wished more than anything she could flee.

"Take him!"

That's when Annie understood. The command wasn't to take care of her littlest brother for a few minutes, but to remove him from this unfolding picture of grief. The baby was a problem Mother could not solve and could not face.

Annie squeezed him tightly and envied his innocence, his underdeveloped cognizance. The next youngest, John Wesley, was nearly four and, though his memories would fade, he was old enough to have had at least a foundation of a relationship with Samuel Goheen, the man who had given him his dimpled chin.

The baby didn't even understand Father was dead.

Sadness seeped through Annie at the realization. The youngest Goheen would never know how funny his father had been—how warm and strong and kind.

She kissed her brother's cheek and stepped out of the house into the bright fall afternoon. He didn't make another sound until they crossed the threshold. Then he began to cry.

Annie bounced him on her hip to no avail. This was not the whine of dissatisfaction, but the guttural swell of some inconsolable sorrow. He buried his chubby, wet face in her neck. Perhaps the baby understood more than she'd believed. He grew heavy for her slight frame, and she sat on a lush patch of grass, arranging him on her lap.

"Hush now, Smee," she soothed. He paused at the sound of the name only she used. When Mother and Father had announced the name of their fifth son, Annie was appalled. By boy number five, in an extended family of more uncles and male cousins than Annie could count, her parents' creativity had run to the end of desperation. And so, this youngest son, named for his mother's father, became Sylvanus McIntyre E. Goheen, the biggest name for the smallest of them.

She'd begun calling him Smee. Mother detested the nickname, but Father had found it endearing and Annie had flushed with pleasure at the implication that he'd found her endearing as well. It remained a small piece of Father the two of them could share, this name that would be a private tribute.

Annie hugged Smee close, the weight of a large responsibility settling into her as the baby released a hot, halting breath, dropped his head onto her shoulder, and hiccupped.

The chill of November gave way to the outright cold of a Pennsylvania winter, matching the mood in Annie's home. Her brothers Mayberry and Davis trudged through the biting wind to care for the horses and milking cow. Though the tasks were the same as they had long been for the stoic ten and eight year old, Annie could see the weight of extra burden of their grief in the seriousness of their expressions. Without Father to supervise and guide their work, it was up to them to see the crucial tasks completed. When Mother insisted, they dragged along five-year-old William.

"He slows us down," Mayberry complained. "He's not strong enough to help and he dances around, startling the animals."

"And so did you when you were his age." Mother would offer no sympathy to her eldest sons. She placed a plate of biscuits on the table in front of the hungry children. When the ever-famished Davis reached for the plate, the sharp downturn in the corners of his mother's mouth was enough to stall him. Sheepish, the boy folded his hands onto his lap while enduring a smirk from Mayberry.

Annie sat at the long table between her youngest brothers with whom she shared a bedroom. John Wesley existed in his own world, his dark hair tousled despite her earlier effort to tame it. He rubbed his tired eyes after a sleepless night with the gusts of a winter storm howling against their windows. Little Smee was the only one of the three of them to have gotten any sleep at all, and now the tot glanced between his mother and the older boys, seeming to follow every word in a way Annie, exhausted, could not have done even if she'd wanted to.

Mother placed a small bowl of jam beside the biscuits and settled into her chair at the head of the table, the place vacated by Father.

"When you were small, your patient father brought you along on chores and taught you the skills you needed to complete them yourselves. Now that he's gone, it's your job to do the same for your brothers. We all must do our part."

"Yes, Mother." The response came from both of Annie's biggest brothers, who had uttered the phrase at least ten times a day over the past few months.

"Look at your sister. She's not complaining about extra responsibilities."

Annie's eyes grew wide at the attention called to her. Mother's praise earned a swift kick from Davis sitting across from her. Mayberry didn't so much as look at her. He wouldn't. As the man of the house, he took himself too seriously to outwardly express jealousy.

Annie hadn't complained, not out loud anyway, but she did long for the days of the previous summer when she'd found time between chores to play with her doll and read in the meadow by herself, away from the noise and bustle of a house full of children. The winter trapped her necessarily inside, but it was the now constant task of caring for the littlest boys that kept her running, without a moment to herself. She, for one, was grateful when William accompanied Mayberry and Davis, and had been exceptionally pleased when Mother decided the five year old would move into the room the older boys shared, leaving her with only the two littlest requiring her comfort during the long nights.

Mother gazed over her seated and well-mannered household, a graceful queen atop an uncomfortable throne, and bowed her head to pray over their breakfast.

"Amen," the children chorused. Even the baby lent his voice with a sweet "a-ma."

Annie reached for a biscuit to give to John Wesley. When he immediately cried for jam, she obliged him before handing a torn piece of biscuit to Smee, who shoved in into his mouth with an already slobbery hand. His other fist reached and smacked down onto the bowl of jam, flinging a sticky glop onto the table and coating his fingers, which happily replaced the other hand in his mouth.

With barely a thought, Annie righted the bowl and scooted it from his reach. He would need a wash after breakfast.

She poured a small amount of fresh milk into two cups, handing one to John Wesley and supervising as he took a careful gulp. She pressed the edge of the other to Smee's lips, inspiring him to turn away and squeal. He always refused milk at first, but when she persisted, he would oblige her by swallowing some. This morning instead, he knocked the cup loose from her hand and it clanged to the floor in a foamy, white puddle. The baby giggled, as did John Wesley, his sister wrenching the cup from his hands before he could mimic the action.

The event might have triggered chaos had it not been for a knock at the door demanding everyone's attention.

Mother stood, her own plate still as empty as her daughter's. "Annie," she said as she moved toward the door, "clean up the spill and make sure you eat."

The moment Mother rounded the corner, Mayberry jumped up to follow behind her. He stopped and peeked into the hallway from which Annie could hear her mother greeting their visitor.

"It's Uncle Leon." Mayberry slunk back to his chair, uninterested. "They're going into the sitting room."

One of four of their mother's brothers, Leon had emerged as the most recent spokesman urging Mother to lay out plans for the family's future. Over the summer and into the autumn when Father had fallen ill, an army of uncles and cousins from both sides of the family helped see to the farm, ensuring their ability to survive through the winter, but now those same family members pressured Mother to take the next steps.

Annie could imagine the thin line of Elizabeth Goheen's lips as she endured her brother's wisdom, words she would angrily reproduce in front of Annie later. This was the biggest change she'd seen in her mother these last months: her tendency to speak to Annie and to the older boys as if they were adults. It both thrilled and frightened her.

She finished cleaning up the spill, wiped Smee's sticky hands and face with a wet cloth, and set a tray with biscuits, jam, and two cups of steaming coffee.

"I wouldn't go in there, Annie. Mother wasn't happy to see him." Mayberry spoke with an edge of confidence that might almost have made her listen, except she wouldn't give him the satisfaction of bossing her around.

He might like to claim to be the man of the house, but as the only daughter, she held a special place in her mother's attentions and could decide for herself how to fulfil her role in the family.

Despite her brother's warning, she carefully balanced the tray and headed down the front hall to the sitting room, the muffled tones of her uncle reaching her ears.

"The boys need a father."

"Samuel is barely cold." The venom in her mother's response caused Annie to hesitate in the hallway, her presence still undetected. "My boys have everything they need—the legacy of a wonderful father, a fine farm, and a Heavenly Father. Let's not forget, too, they are surrounded by a full family of uncles and grown cousins who can provide any necessary male guidance."

"It's not the same, Elizabeth, and you know it."

"Of course it's not." She spit the words at him, this fierce woman who had held her family together in their grief, reserving her own tears for times when no one could see. Annie had heard the muffled sobs behind the closed door of the bedroom her parents once shared. Her brothers must have heard it, too, but the siblings maintained an unspoken pact to keep their mother's secret.

"It would be better if they still had their father, if I still had my husband. But we don't have him. They don't need a poor substitute. I don't need some man to claim my property as his own. And I certainly don't need any more children!"

Annie's hands began to shake as her mother's temper flared. Fearing she would spill the tray, she announced her presence by clearing her throat and leaning into the room.

"Mary Ann, why are you lurking in the hallway?"

Annie stepped into the room and placed the tray on the side table. "I thought you and Uncle might want some breakfast."

"That was very thoughtful, young lady." Uncle Leon smiled at her through tensed jaw muscles.

Mother's lips formed a frown, but the crinkles at the corners of her eyes communicated gratitude. "Thank you, dear. Go see to the little ones, please."

Annie nodded and spun to leave as Leon offered some excuse to depart rather than eating.

"I've said my piece, dear sister. I know I'm not the first. I beg you to consider your options."

Annie did not hear her mother's response, but as she rounded the corner into the kitchen, the front door shut loudly behind Uncle Leon.

Father had died in 1814 and nearly twelve years later, Annie still recalled every detail of that terrible day—the hushed sobs of her mother, the silent helplessness of Mayberry and Davis, the inappropriate jittery energy of the two younger boys, and the audacity of the brilliant sun to warm the Pennsylvania countryside on a day that could only ever seem dark and cold.

But what stood out more than all the rest was the sensation of clutching tightly to the sweet, innocent babe who had somehow become the arrogant teenager standing arms crossed in her bedroom doorway.

"She's going to sell you off."

"Don't be rude." Annie reprimanded the thirteen year old. "I'm not a slave. Mother will not be selling me like one."

Her brother ran his fingers through his hair, sweeping the dark curls from his forehead. He was an attractive boy with chiseled cheek bones and expressive eyes that balanced out the ears he'd not grown into yet. The shadow of the man he would become hid just beneath the awkward surface of adolescence. Sometimes she glimpsed it out of the corner of her eye and it made her breath catch. She had loved him above all others for these many years, and now she would be tormented by him as he aged with a mixture of pride at seeing him grown and a deep longing for the baby she'd snuggled.

"She's presenting you like a prize cow."

"I am not a cow." She smoothed her dress and rolled her eyes. "And perhaps I want to be presented."

She almost believed it. She'd been excited when her mother first mentioned the church picnic and the newly licensed young preacher who would be in attendance. Now she felt faintly ill at the prospect.

Their own circuit preacher Reverend Franks had known Annie all her life. He had baptized her and all her brothers and offered words of comfort over her father's grave, making him perhaps the man most responsible for her spiritual development. She wasn't sure, however, that lent him any authority when it came to match-making.

When he'd spoken to Mother about the upcoming church social, he mentioned without subtlety that his incoming protégé would have difficulty carrying out the duties of his own circuit without a comfortable home and a sturdy and competent wife to maintain it. The name Mary Ann Goheen was on his heart, he'd told Mother.

Perhaps a perfect match.

"You do not want to be presented. How would some poor preacher be of any interest to you?"

"First of all, you don't know what is of interest to me." She pointed an accusatory finger at him. "Secondly, preachers make fine husbands. Their wives must be smart and hardworking and educated. They must be prepared to become leaders in the churches they serve and in the efficient homes they run."

"You sound like you're quoting from a ladies' handbook. Or Mother."

"What do you know of ladies' handbooks?"

"Or Mother."

"You don't know much about Mother, either. Not in this instance anyway. She wants the best for me."

"And marrying a stuffy minister who's going to give you a dozen children and never be home is what's best for you?"

His words stunned her. She opened her mouth and then closed it again, not sure how to respond. A small part of her did doubt she would want that kind of life, one of much toil, little support, and so many children to break her heart when they grew into mouthy youth. At eighteen she was, according to Mother, in the full blush of her beauty, the implication being what few advantages she possessed—the smooth skin and optimism of girlhood—would soon give way to her undeniable plainness.

"Look here," she said, bottom lip quivering. "This is what young ladies do. We look for husbands. We establish homes of our own." She stopped short of saying *we place ourselves at the mercy of whatever man will have us.*

"Besides," she added, pinching at her cheeks, "he may not like me."

"He'll like you fine."

"Yes, well, thank you for that." She pulled in her stomach and ran her fingers along the silky ribbon of her dress. "It has always been my fondest dream to be liked fine."

"He might find you a little overly sensitive. And vain." He ducked the shove that came his way. "And not much good in a fight."

She laughed. "If he's the kind of man who needs his lady to back him up in a fight, I'm not much interested."

"That is a relief to hear," Sylvanus said. Then added, "I bet he's a monster."

She appraised him and swelled with gratitude at his misguided protectiveness. "He's a man of God, Smee."

Sylvanus straightened and crossed his arms, his head nearly even with hers. He had grown tall in recent months. "That doesn't mean he's not a monster."

Annie was in a state when the wagon rolled up to the churchyard, her skin blotched and red from stress as much as from the hot sun. Parishioners had turned out from all over the countryside on a beautiful day to greet the newcomer.

Among them were several other eligible young women near her age—girls she'd been acquainted with long enough to know none was likely to make a suitable wife for a circuit rider. It was not surprising that Reverend Franks had singled her out, but still she felt herself overwhelmed by nerves as she took in the appearance of each of their pretty dresses, carefully styled hair, and fresh smiles hiding vacuousness.

Making her way to the food table to set out her pies, Annie warmly acknowledged each person she passed. Most had been part of the church as long as her mother had been.

When she walked back to her family, Annie found Mother speaking with the reverend. With him stood a thick-necked man in a worn coat who swept his hat from his head at her approach and revealed a flop of straw-colored hair. Annie had to bite back a giggle. He looked like the scarecrow standing watch over their kitchen garden. Reverend Franks introduced the man as Gregory Whitcomb.

Mother presented her family, scrubbed clean and freshly instructed in their good manners. "These are my sons, William, John Wesley, and Sylvanus. I have two older boys as well, studying in Philadelphia. My eldest, Mayberry, hopes to become a circuit rider himself one day. And this," she nodded toward Annie and gave her a nudge of encouragement. "Is my daughter Miss Mary Ann Goheen."

Annie tipped her head in the semblance of a curtsy, an expression of humility and gentleness. Her brothers fidgeted behind her, no doubt struggling to ward off humiliating giggles.

Reverend Franks frowned in their direction. The scarecrow had eyes only for Annie. She thought of her uncomfortably displayed womanly qualities and shivered slightly under his scrutiny.

"Mr. Whitcomb recently completed an examination of his gifts and usefulness in which he expressed a deep knowledge of both Scripture and Doctrine." The reverend addressed Mother as he spouted Mr. Whitcomb's many fine attributes, but his gaze shifted occasionally to her, his eyes searching her face for a reaction to the recitation of his pupil's many husbandly qualifications.

"He was awarded his license to preach and is now entering a preparatory term before becoming a candidate for ordination. We are fortunate to have him on our circuit for a time."

"Yes," Mother interjected, "I'm sure we'll all learn much from a fresh, young perspective."

The preacher hesitated at the barbed words, which brought a much-appreciated pause to his sales pitch. Perhaps Mother was as unimpressed with the supposed match as Annie was. Mother could be a powerful opponent in conversation when she chose to be and had often wrestled with Reverend Franks, who'd long counseled her to remarry.

Annie settled into an awkward silence with the younger preacher likely only a few years older than she. He wasn't bad looking, she supposed. His eyes were a little beady, and his hair was ridiculous, but his brow furrowed pleasantly when he spoke. He might have been less scarecrow than she'd first thought. There was also a gentle resonance to his speech when he commented politely on the beautiful weather.

In the meantime, Reverend Franks had extricated himself from Mother and moved to address the gathered crowd. He thanked everyone for coming, for bringing food enough to feed the 5000, and introduced Mr. Whitcomb. Annie watched some of the other women assess the young man with open stares. None lingered for long.

"Miss Goheen," Mr. Whitcomb said to her after the Elder blessed the meal. "Reverend Franks tells me you teach the local farm children." He smiled kindly as he spoke to her, and the nervous energy in her body began to calm.

"I do. I have seventeen students between the ages of six and thirteen, including my youngest brother Sylvanus."

Smee's attention flicked to her at the mention of his name, causing Annie to momentarily lose her train of thought. She wished he would go away, perhaps take this opportunity to gather a plate of food, but he showed no signs of leaving and she thought it might signal much too forward intentions were she to shoo her brother away.

Mr. Whitcomb nodded, encouraging her to continue.

"They are intelligent young things, all of them, though not always highly motivated to learn."

"I'm sure most rural children have more provincial goals when it comes to education."

"That may be true for some," Annie admitted, not caring for his condescending tone. "But that's why I find it's so important to encourage them to learn of the world and its possibilities."

"Noble," he said, as though he thought it was anything but.

She raised her chin. "I'm grateful to be their teacher and to guide them when I can in more spiritual pursuits as well."

At the mention of spiritual teaching, the young man sparked, but before he could speak, Mother interjected from behind him. "Mary Ann began teaching at an early age as my assistant, and now as the woman in charge of her own school, she works tirelessly in her efforts to both instruct the young ones in her care and to rouse the community to minister to its families whenever the need or opportunity arises."

Annie shifted, not entirely comfortable under the intense and scrutinizing gaze of the young preacher as her mother continued.

"Last year she joined the Ladies' Benevolent Society of Columbia and, at their request, she's begun working with a Sunday School program for the local colored children. The ladies teach Bible lessons, reading, and basic skills." Mother put an arm around Annie's waist in a surprising gesture of maternal pride. "My daughter has a great gift for mission and organization of charitable efforts."

Annie's cheeks burned at her mother's praise. The words were not ones she would often hear directly from her mother, but while highlighting her daughter's appropriateness as a preacher's wife, Elizabeth Goheen held nothing back.

Mr. Whitcomb's face darkened. He addressed his next remarks more to Reverend Franks approaching with a plate of food in hand than to either Mother or Annie. "It sounds like Miss Goheen is involved in much worthy work, but I do wonder at the wisdom of teaching coloreds, especially when there are so many sinners in need living among God's holy people."

Reverend Franks responded only with a subtle shake of his head, a warning the younger preacher either didn't notice or refused to heed. Annie felt a stab of betrayal at her minister's silence, and she read a similar emotion on the faces of her mother and youngest brother.

"We are all sinners, are we not? All in need of Jesus?" Annie's voice quivered more than she'd have liked, but the questions stood, demanding to be answered. She added, "And are we not all recipients of grace and keepers of the Divine breath of life?"

"Surely some more than others, Miss Goheen." The large blond preacher fixed her in his intense gaze. "I only meant it might be viewed by some as inappropriate to elevate the Blacks in such a way, with their role in American society causing such controversy even within our own churches."

She didn't like the way her name slipped from his lips, as though he were testing the worthiness of her soul. She began to perspire.

Smee saved her from forming another response. "That's not good theology. 'All have sinned and come short of the glory of God' and there is 'neither Jew nor Greek, neither bond nor free.' There's no room for interpretation."

Annie glanced in appreciation at her brother, though he didn't seem to notice. The downturn in his expression suggested he instead caught sight of their mother who was probably less pleased with his performance. Beside him, William was focused on the table lined with food, while John Wesley, the namesake of the very theologian likely to agree with Smee, stared with determination at his shoes.

"We have a young scholar among us," Reverend Franks proclaimed boldly. "Will you take what your sister has been good enough to teach you and become a man of the cloth someday?"

"I believe in serving with other skills, in meeting God's people where they are."

"That is precisely what a minister does," Mr. Whitcomb said. "He preaches to the people so they might have guidance through their sinful lives, navigating them through dangerous and controversial theological trends."

Annie didn't know whether to scold Smee or praise him for his impertinence. Her brother, emboldened by the verbal sparring, continued. None of the rest of her family seemed to know either, but Smee did not wait to see whether they approved.

"You can't tell people they are living sinful lives until you have given them some reason to both trust you and to trust Scripture. Jesus fed the five thousand as he preached to them. And He spoke of living water with the woman at the well even though she was an unworthy Samaritan..." Smee's eyes darted toward Mother. The guilt of defiance flitted across his features before he added, "and a harlot."

With the experience of many years on the circuit preaching to practical and hardworking farmers—imperfect men and women struggling to hold onto their faith in a shifting world—

Reverend Franks nodded in recognition of the truth Smee spoke.

Mr. Whitcomb, his theological training untested among the toiling sinners of the land, hardened the tight lines of his jaw as if steeling himself for battle. "Jesus may do as He wishes, of course. But the word of God does not require our assistance, young man."

Smee clasped his hands together in challenging defiance, his gangly form taking on an authority reminiscent of a child David staring down Goliath. "God may not need our assistance to reach people, but He has asked us for it, commanded us even to love our neighbor as ourselves. You can't do that while you're preaching at him or judging him for the color of his skin. First give people what they need physically, then you can meet their spiritual needs."

"Are you suggesting that, in order to minister to people, we must dilute the truths of scripture to make them more palatable?" The scarecrow's face had grown red with barely controlled anger.

Reverend Franks cleared his throat in his obvious discomfort. Mother glared at Smee. The boy didn't back down. Annie's heart warmed.

"The Bible is not palatable to all people yet. If they are to comprehend it then yes, we must first teach them to read it, to come to the truth of it from wherever they began."

"It sounds to me like your sister's lessons lack somewhat in Biblical truth."

Finally, it was Annie's turn to speak, and she did so with gusto. "Mr. Whitcomb, when I serve food to the poor of our community, when I teach a young Black child his letters, what I am doing is making the Biblical truths I share more understandable, more visual. How can someone possibly seek spiritual food when their belly is grumbling for physical sustenance or their mind craving too long denied knowledge? My brother is wise far beyond his years."

The new preacher had nothing more to say to her. He turned instead to Mother. "Mrs. Goheen, thank you for your kind welcome. And," he said with a frown directed at Smee, "the stimulating conversation. If you'll excuse me, I need to make myself available to mingle with the other parishioners."

Annie watched him walk away, thinking she'd never appreciated her youngest brother more in her life.

"Well, I suppose that opportunity's gone." Mother collapsed into a chair after they'd all piled into the house.

"There was no opportunity there, Mother." Annie should have regretted her flat tone that carried a decidedly nonbiblical disrespect for her mother, but she did not. Instead, she felt her words weren't strong enough. "Honestly, that was one of the most insolent men I have ever met."

"All men are arrogant, daughter of mine. You'd better get used to it."

"But he's a servant of God, a man tasked with sharing the Gospel. His position must require some small bit of humility."

"In my experience, preachers can be the worst among men." Mother sighed and leaned forward as her daughter sat across from her. "They feel assured they've been handpicked by God to be His representative in the world."

Annie's eyes widened.

"Don't look so shocked. I won't pretend you'll find a perfect man among the clergy, but what you will find is the stability of a good name, a husband who is frequently away, and the opportunity to use your God-given gifts to preach and teach and serve."

Annie fumbled for her next words. "T-thank you, Mother. I don't know what to say."

"You're my daughter. And you've been faithfully serving me and this family since your father died. I could not have raised your brothers without you. Especially Sylvanus. And to hear him speak the way he did today—"

"I'm sorry for his behavior." More than any of her younger brothers, Annie always felt responsible when headstrong Smee stepped out of line.

"Don't be. You should be proud of that boy. I certainly am. He spoke with the confidence and wisdom of a man."

"You didn't seem to appreciate it this afternoon."

Mother sighed. "Because confident and wise thirteen year olds filled with the fire of the Spirit easily become arrogant men full of the Devil."

"Mother, I cannot marry a man like Mr. Whitcomb."

The corners of her mother's mouth turned down, but she reached out and took Annie's hand in her own. "You will marry a man like Mr. Whitcomb, at least something like him. The life of a preacher's wife would suit you, give you the intellectual stimulation you deserve. There is much to recommend such a match. But I agree he's not the one."

Annie was quiet for a moment, a question rattling in her mind as she sought the courage to speak it aloud. "Why have you never remarried?" she'd long wanted to ask but had never found the right time.

Mother dropped Annie's hand and waited a beat before answering. "Make no mistake. Marriage is the best of few opportunities for a young woman, but also the riskiest. Not all men are good like your father was."

Annie remembered little about her father, but she did know in her heart he had been a good man, a knowledge reinforced by the recollections shared of him by those who had known him longer. She nodded encouragement for her mother to continue.

"In the eyes of the law, a married woman might as well be as helpless as a dark-skinned slave." Mother fixed Annie in her gaze, perhaps expecting her to find the words shocking. She did, but also recognized a terrible truth in them.

"I was fortunate in my marriage," her mother said. "And in your father's wisdom when he willed his property into my hands. Such a man may be difficult to find, but he is worth the searching. Mr. Whitcomb proved he was not the man I want for you, but there's a fine husband out there for you."

"If I want him," she said.

"You do, Annie. A husband who will cherish and encourage you is worth finding." The older woman slumped back once again in her chair. "Now you should go and scold your brother for happily ruining the day."

2

Sylvanus

1830

Riding beside Dr. Thompson, Sylvanus guided his horse past Lamb Tavern and up Locust Street toward the northeast part of town known as Tow Hill. He'd not been up this way, though Annie came weekly with her ladies' benevolent society to deliver food, clothing, and lessons.

He admired his sister's generous spirit, but she behaved carelessly at times. A quarter of Columbia's population consisted of free Blacks, and among those at any time were rumored to be large numbers of escaped slaves who had made the dangerous journey from Virginia and Maryland toward freedom. With such violence and pain in their own past lives, he doubted they could all be trusted not to lash out at any whites who ventured into their midst.

The city's free colored citizens provided cheap labor for the thriving lumber businesses along the Susquehanna River where most were employed by wealthy Black business owner Stephen Smith, himself once a slave and manumitted upon his master's death. This was both a boon for the local economy and a source of resentment for much of the town's white population.

Sylvanus's imagination painted tension in the air around the haphazard rows of log cabins and crudely built shanties on the Hill. It was quiet with most of the men at the river separating and washing boards in the stifling August heat.

"Where do we need to go?" Dr. Thompson's voice pulled Sylvanus from his thoughts and into the moment. All was not silent after all. A nearby chickadee whistled and chirped *dee dee dee*. Dark-skinned children shrieked and scampered about the collections of rough homes.

"Annie said to look for the largest house on the right side of the main road. There." He pointed to a cabin a few buildings in front of them. It appeared better built than most with a large front window, its shutters open to catch the slightest breeze. Beneath the window someone had transplanted a wild patch of cardinal flowers. Their red petals perched on tall, feathery stems resembled a swarm of fragrant moths standing vigil over the house and the ailing within in.

"You are familiar with the symptoms of cholera?" Dr. Thompson pulled up on his horse's reins and slid off the saddle.

Sylvanus did the same with a nod. He knew of cholera from the books in the physician's office where he'd served as an assistant for the past year. He'd been drawn to medicine since he'd been rescued from a near drowning as a child and cared for by the man who now questioned him.

"You'll notice the smell," the doctor said. "Take only shallow breaths. Avoid direct contact with any fluids in the home, bodily or otherwise. Drink nothing that might be offered."

The two men approached the door which swung open before either got close enough to knock.

"Oh, Doctor, thank the Lord you come. Miss Annie said you would." The woman who answered had such light-colored skin she might have been white. Short and trim, she wore a long apron and had tucked her hair into a kerchief.

Sylvanus held his forearm to his nose as the foul odor of feces wafted through the open door. He suppressed a gag.

"How many are sick?" Dr. Thompson asked.

"Seven. I tell everyone bring 'em here. Two are mine, the others from other homes, but all the same. One man already die before sunup."

Dr. Thompson uttered a low curse. "Where's the body?"

"Still here. Don't have a man to carry him out. Those that can are working. I tell 'em keep away. If they here, they dyin'."

"Why aren't you ill?" Sylvanus asked.

The woman shrugged. "The Lord need a nurse for the sick."

Dr. Thompson moved toward the door and the woman backed out of his way. Sylvanus reluctantly followed.

The foul air in the cabin was inescapable. Sylvanus fought the urge to run back outside. He was in little danger of drawing the deep breaths Dr. Thompson had warned against. Sunlight streamed through the windows illuminating two rooms connected by a doorway. One clearly served as the home's kitchen with a wide fireplace taking up most of one wall and a rough wooden table. The other served as a makeshift hospital.

The patients wore little clothing. They lay upon mats slick with the filth of human waste. In a display of greater fortitude than his young apprentice could muster, Dr. Thompson squatted beside the nearest mat and surveyed its occupant, a man who stared back with yellowed, sunken, fear-filled eyes.

Sylvanus turned away, focusing his attention instead on the woman who had let them into the cabin. Eyes closed and lips moving in silent words, she remained composed amid the suffering before her. After a moment she lifted her head and stared back at him.

"You're Ellen?" Sylvanus asked.

Her expression softened. "Yes, sir. And you must be young Master Sylvanus. Your sister said you learnin' to doctor. God bless both of you for comin' here."

"I don't dare but listen to the requests of my sister."

A smile might have graced Ellen's otherwise sober face, but the hint of it faded the moment Dr. Thompson stood again. Sylvanus's gut clenched.

"Feel the skin, Mr. Goheen."

He obeyed, biting back his revulsion. The patient's sunken eyes barely tracked the movement of Sylvanus's hand reaching toward his stubbled cheek. Despite the stifling heat of the cabin, the man's skin felt cool. When Sylvanus pulled back, the dent of his fingers remained in the loose skin of the jowl.

"He's nearly gone." The doctor spoke with authority Sylvanus would not dare question. "They're all nearly gone."

Sylvanus stood up behind Dr. Thompson, who signaled for Ellen and him to step outside into the fresher air.

"Will they take anything to drink?" the doctor asked.

Ellen shook her head. "Not that one. Not for a day at least. Some will."

Dr. Thompson gently touched the woman's elbow—a tender, almost fatherly gesture. "You have given them good care. You were right to keep them isolated."

Much of the tension she carried in her muscles visibly released at his words.

"Mr. Goheen," he addressed Sylvanus, "there's a packet of powdered opium in my saddle bag. Bring it to me."

Grateful for an opportunity to move away from the stench of the cabin and the sight of the dying people within it, Sylvanus took his time retrieving the medicine while the physician explained to Ellen how much to dissolve into hot tea.

"Give them nothing cold—those who will drink at all. The medicine will slow the bowels and will offer some relief from their misery, but I'm afraid there's nothing more to be done.

When the time comes, which it soon will, the bodies must be covered in a tarpaulin and buried away from any home using the utmost care."

Ellen seemed to shrink under the words, but she thanked them both for their time. Her humble words, emerging from the depths of sorrow, haunted Sylvanus as he and Dr. Thompson rode away from her, leaving her alone to tend the dying.

They continued in silence until they reached the bottom of the hill.

"Your first brush with so much death, I assume?" Dr. Thompson asked.

"Yes." Sylvanus swallowed. "Cholera is far worse to see than to read about."

"As are most diseases. Are you determined to pursue medical training?"

"I think so," he said, aware it was an inadequate answer.

"You're smart. You're compassionate. But you have to know you won't always be able to save them."

"How can you stand it?" Sylvanus feared his question was rude, but the physician had always been honest and plain with him. When Sylvanus first expressed his desire to study medicine, his family had been surprised and less than thrilled. He'd be forever grateful to the influence of Dr. Thompson who suggested Sylvanus work with him in his medical practice for a time before making a commitment to further medical training. His elder brothers were pursuing careers in business and the ministry. No one before him had ever been a physician. "Why do you continue to practice?"

Dr. Thompson looked sideways at his companion. "On days like this it's hard. But I do it because God continues to call."

He frequently spoke this way, with an absolute conviction Sylvanus had admired since they'd met, when he was only a soaking wet child pulled from the river and grasped from the clutches of death. That boy had never thought about being specially called by God for any purpose.

Sylvanus didn't know if he belonged in the practice of medicine, but he liked Dr. Thompson, appreciated that the man saw potential in him, and believed this was something he could be good at.

Sylvanus learned a great deal in the four years since his first brush with serious illness during the cholera outbreak on the Hill. In the scraps of time between farm work and study, he'd shadowed his mentor through the grind of running a small-town medical practice.

Dr. Thompson was a patient and deliberate teacher, but what Sylvanus valued most was his mentor's stubborn opinions and the intellectual sparring matches the two occasionally shared. He never failed to challenge his young assistant, and Sylvanus was anxious to broach a difficult subject.

He set to work on the menial tasks of sweeping floors, washing out the basins used for catching blood, and tidying the shelves of tools and supplies as Dr. Thompson penned notes and observations from the day's constant parade of patients. At last, the gray-haired man set aside his work and stored the ledger on a shelf lined with the careful records of a long career. "A good day's work, Mr. Goheen."

"It was a good day's work," Sylvanus agreed, leaning the broom against the corner of the exam room. He rubbed his hands together and took a deep breath, sensing the moment had arrived to share some important news with his mentor. "I want to thank you," he began. "for the opportunity to learn by your side and to practice my skills on your patients."

"*Our* patients, Sylvanus. They see you that way."

"Yes, sir, they do, but I'm not a physician."

Dr. Thompson grumbled, "You might as well be." The doctor had begun his career in the time of apprenticeships and did not embrace the change now sweeping his profession. Under the tutelage of this experienced physician, Sylvanus had treated a wide range of illnesses and injuries, he'd borne witness to miraculous healing and wept alongside those who grieved a life lost, but there was more he longed to learn.

Natural scientists had been making great progress in understanding not just the world man inhabited, but the world inhabiting man—that universe of organs and tissues and dynamic systems perfectly designed.

To be a part of the journey, to share with curious colleagues in the adventure of discovery, unchaining the potential of the human body in balance with the world around it was his fondest wish. Despite his admiration for Dr. Thompson, Sylvanus believed greater standardization of medical training was required to reach such a goal.

"I'm not a young man," Dr. Thompson continued. "I intend for you to take over my practice."

"Once I have a degree."

"Yes." He threw up his hands in exasperation. "Once you have that fancy degree our great Commonwealth thinks you need."

"I'm honored, sir. Thank you."

"You're a skilled physician, Sylvanus. I don't need some self-important medical college to tell me that."

"You may not need it, but Pennsylvania does." Sylvanus cleared his throat. "In fact, I wanted you to be the first to know. I've been accepted at Jefferson Medical College. My classes begin in October."

"Well, I suppose congratulations are in order, then." The doctor stood and clasped his student's hand in a congratulatory shake. "You'll teach them a thing or two, I'd wager."

Sylvanus began to form a witty retort when a series of heavy, desperate thuds at the door brought a sharp end to the conversation. He crossed the room in three long strides and flung open the door to find two Black men standing on the doorstep. One leaned into the other with his eyes clenched tight in an expression of pain. Blood soaked the man's shirt and ran down one leg of his trousers—a lot of blood which had begun to pool on the step.

Dr. Thompson appeared by Sylvanus's side and together they helped the injured man's companion pick up the patient and place him on the exam table.

"What happened?" Sylvanus asked. The healthy man, familiar to Sylvanus though he could not recall his name, shrank from the bloody scene playing out in front of him. Dr. Thompson ripped off the patient's ruined shirt and began his examination.

The sight of the physician in action shook Sylvanus from his immediate curiosity to the more pressing situation at hand. He retrieved clean rags from a cabinet and applied pressure to the bleeding wound after Dr. Thompson sloshed a good portion of whiskey over the gash. The patient writhed on the exam table, his expression frozen in a voiceless scream.

"He was stabbed," said the second man. His identity clicked into place in Sylvanus's mind.

"Bennet. Your name is Bennett."

"Yes, sir."

Annie had introduced Sylvanus to this man. He had often repaid her kindness to the people of Tow Hill by doing odd jobs around the schoolhouse. Annie spoke of Bennett as highly skilled and uncommonly kind.

"How did it happen?"

"There's rioters on the Hill. We was holding prayer meeting at the African Zion Church and a stone come flying through, breaking a window. Then another and another. A bunch of us men went out to see about the ruckus and was ambushed."

"At the church?" A blinding fear replaced Sylvanus's professional focus.

Prayer meeting was the code his sister used for the lessons she taught to the Black children and any willing adults—lessons that had little to do with praying and everything to do with improving the colored man's lot in life. Not all citizens of Columbia looked kindly upon her work.

"My sister?" As he spoke, Sylvanus let off the pressure he'd been applying to the patient's wound. Warm blood seeped around his fingers, impeding the view of the gash the doctor attempted to suture.

"Mr. Goheen!" Dr. Thompson's sharp reprimand drew him back to the task at hand. Bile burned Sylvanus's throat in anticipation of Bennett's answer.

"She hid with the children and the other women. I think they safe."

Sylvanus exhaled, realizing only then he'd been holding his breath. "I have to go." He motioned with his head for Bennett to step forward and take his place at the exam table. "Press as hard as you can right here."

Bennett's eyes grew wide and he shook his head, but Sylvanus continued to insist, and the man finally took a few tentative steps forward to slide into position beside the exam table and place his hands where Sylvanus's had been.

The patient moaned at the jostling—a good sign. At least he was conscious.

"Mr. Goheen!" Dr. Thompson's voice had become a threatening growl. "Your patient needs *you*, not some ignorant fool who couldn't tell a blood vessel from a pitchfork."

"But Annie—"

"Your sister is strong and resourceful and *white*." He emphasized the last word with a pointed look to the inadequate assistant now shrinking from the duty Sylvanus had attempted to give him. "Do your job, Mr. Goheen, and this man may yet live."

3
Annie

In the middle of a sentence, haltingly read aloud by a bright young girl with braided pigtails, dark brown skin, and dimpled cheeks, a tall window shattered.

Annie screamed.

Only later did she pause to wonder whether those around her had done the same.

The girl's mother grabbed her child's wrist, and with the other Black women hustled the children away from the windows. With practiced efficiency and little discussion, they tucked themselves beneath wooden pews. The few men present rushed to the front doors, their eyes wild, preparing to meet any threat attempting to force its way through.

By the time the second stone crashed into the church building, Annie remained one of four—the white women who had been leading the lessons—sitting stunned in the middle of the sanctuary. The other teachers seemed to have been struck dumb, a reaction Annie understood but fought against and called out, "Find safety!"

The words had barely escaped her lips when a sharp pain exploded. Her vision filled with vivid splashes of color fading slowly to black.

Annie awoke to a tremendous pain in her head that pounded to a terrifying rhythm. Disoriented, she couldn't move freely, held in place by something, or someone—arms, she realized with a jolt of panic. Strong arms cradled her. She was moving swiftly. The throbbing in her head mimicked the thumping of her captor's feet. She tried to summon another scream, to shake off her confusion, to open her eyes. With all her might, she twisted. The arms released and she tumbled to the ground. A man—the man who had carried her—fell to his knees beside her.

In the gloom of the summer evening, he was difficult to make out, but he was white, and he possessed well-muscled shoulders and a square jaw. He fell forward onto his hands and drew great gulps of the hot, sticky air. Annie scrambled away from him across the ground. She tried to push herself upward to gain her footing, but as she stood, nausea overwhelmed her, and she collapsed again beside the stranger who had made no move to stop her.

"Who are you?" she demanded. Her voice trembled.

"Jonas Edwards," he said between gasps. "We need to keep moving."

"What?" She'd have articulated a better protest if she could summon the strength, but even through his obvious exhaustion, the man's rich voice imbued her with a sense of calm. Fearing she should, Annie did not struggle when he helped her to stand.

Her head and stomach protested, but this time she managed to remain upright.

"Can you run?" he asked as he caught her hand.

"I'll try."

She managed no more than ten steps before he once again scooped her up. This time she encircled her arms around his neck, held tightly, and began to pray for deliverance from these strange circumstances.

Branches brushed her dangling feet as they moved, the air cooled slightly, and an earthy scent tickled her nose. Her captor slowed, then stopped, setting her gently onto the soft ground of the woods on the outskirts of Columbia.

Annie tried again to stand, but dizziness overwhelmed her, and by the time she regained a sense of balance, the man's breathing had slowed. There would be no escape.

Instead of running she balled her fists, prepared to defend herself if necessary, forced down her fear, and demanded an explanation. "What on earth is happening?"

"Rioters on the Hill." Once again, his voice injected her with a sense of peace and safety she couldn't have explained. She lowered her fists and regained a seat on the ground beside him.

"I don't understand, Mr.—" her mind searched for the name he'd given her.

"Edwards. Jonas Edwards."

In the shelter of the trees, the falling dark of the evening took on a new depth. She could barely see the outline of him now, and when his hand reached up to touch her head, she shrank from him in surprise.

"I apologize." He pulled back. "You were struck."

"In the church," she added. She grappled with the memories—the little girl, the children gathered around for lessons in reading and arithmetic. She pictured their faces and those of the adults who had brought them to church to learn from the Ladies' Benevolent Society of Columbia. The white women had been there to instruct, to offer hope to the sweet colored children forced, even in their freedom, to grow and live in a world that viewed them as less than human rather than as precious children of God. Other faces came back to her, too. Several of Columbia's Black women had come to the church to help, or in some cases, to learn skills previously denied them. Men, too—those same men who had rushed to the door at the sound of breaking glass.

"A rock through the window. There were others, too."

"Yes," he said. "Most escaped and fled to the woods. They started with the church, but they'll not stop until they've terrorized the whole Hill."

Flames flickered in the distance. At least one building was on fire, to the west of the church if she had her bearings. Someone's home.

Suddenly infuriated, she asked, "Who are they?"

"The most dangerous people in the world—small-minded men so afraid of another man's humanity they'd make him out to be an animal and punish him for rising above their expectations."

Annie's heart thumped viciously. "Columbia is a friend to free people of color," she insisted, though she knew that to be only a partial truth.

Edwards crouched beside her. "Lately it's also become a good friend to those escaping bondage in the south. There are some who won't abide that."

She'd heard the rumors, even seen evidence, though she'd not allow herself to dwell on it. Columbia's large and successful population of free Blacks had been playing host to runaways fleeing to the northern free states or into Canada.

"Thank you for helping me."

"It is my privilege, Miss Goheen. I'm honored to have been of assistance."

Perplexed, she asked, "Do we know one another?"

"I know you by reputation. I wouldn't dare presume that to be mutual."

"I'm sorry."

"Don't be. It's better you haven't heard of me. I have an aunt and uncle who farm here, but I myself hail from Virginia where I practice law and help people gain their God-given freedom—by whatever means necessary."

"You run escaped slaves from Virginia to Pennsylvania?"

There was a long pause in his speech, but he answered her. "I do."

"What will happen in town, with the rioters?"

"I imagine they'll work out their anger as the drink wears off. Some might spend a night or two in jail, though I doubt any real justice will come of it. Pennsylvania may be a free state, but there's a large gap between free and fair."

Annie agreed. She'd heard enough people say in one breath that all human lives were equally cherished by God and, with the next, promote peaceful tolerance of southern slaveholders, to know the human capacity for duplicity and injustice.

"How are you feeling?" A gentleness not present only a moment before crept into his tone. She wanted to cry.

"Angry," she whispered.

"That's good, Miss Goheen. Stay angry." His head tilted, and he brought a fist to his mouth. "But I was asking about your head injury."

"Oh." She couldn't help but smile. "Better, I think. It hurts, but I feel more like myself again."

"If you think you could walk, we can make our way along the edge of the woods back into town. It would be best not to get any closer to the rioters tonight. I have a carriage. I'll get you home safely. I suppose it wouldn't be proper to linger alone in the woods longer than necessary."

"No," Annie said, shocked as the meaning of his concern formed in her sluggish thoughts and curious at what might happen were the two of them to linger.

"Oh no." She groaned as reality crashed into her scandalous musings. "Smee."

"Pardon me?"

"It's my brother, Smee. Sylvanus." Annie felt weak with dread at the thought of how he would fear for her. "I was supposed to meet him. He'll have heard about the riots. He'll be worried."

"I'm sure he will be."

Annie felt the pressure of Mr. Edwards's hand on her back as he helped her to her feet, and imagined that in his touch she might also sense disappointment.

"Let's go find him."

4

Sylvanus

Something was burning. He smelled smoke from blocks away and pictured the small, tightly spaced houses, most barely more than shacks, engulfed in flames, those who dwelled in them forced unsheltered into the night.

Annie.

Panicked, he urged his horse into a gallop toward the Hill, screams of terror mingling with shouts of sick glee. When he arrived, no houses actively burned, but he passed two smoldering front porches and several bonfires in the road fed by furnishings snatched from homes abandoned, he hoped, for the relative safety of the nearby woods. He couldn't make himself look into the faces of the men stoking the flames, the air so thick with their whiskey breath that it stung his nose as he passed by.

No one questioned his presence, a realization that landed like lead in his stomach. Either they were too drunk to notice him or, worse, they weren't bothered by the presence of a white man they assumed supported their cause. He shivered and continued toward the church where the unholy glow of a nearby fire revealed broken windows and a gaping door barely clinging to its hinges.

He dismounted and stepped into the dim sanctuary, careful to avoid the rocks and broken glass that littered the floor.

"Annie." His urgent whisper filled the space, as did the pounding of his heart that longed to hear an answer that didn't come.

He spoke more loudly. "Annie, are you here?"

Again, his query met silence broken only by the faint rasp of a labored breath. He eased around upended pews and followed the noise to the chancel where he was met by two wide eyes peering around the corner of the pulpit.

The eyes were set in a dark, round face and when they met his own, a squeak escaped the throat of their frightened owner. A boy, maybe twelve or thirteen years old, pulled his head behind the pulpit again.

Sylvanus crouched low and exposed his empty palms. "I won't hurt you," he said to the place the eyes had occupied. "I'm looking for my sister, Annie. She was leading Bible study here tonight. Do you know where she is?"

The boy peeked at him again, his head tilted. Sylvanus was being appraised. He hoped he would be found trustworthy.

Slowly, the boy's eyes closed, and Sylvanus saw the hint of a nod. "You Miss Annie's brother?"

As he spoke, he scooted a few inches from behind the pulpit.

Sylvanus released a breath and dropped back on his haunches. "Yes," he said. "Sylvanus Goheen, very worried brother of Miss Annie. Pleased to meet you."

The boy didn't volunteer his name, but he didn't retreat into his hiding place, either. Sylvanus was making progress.

"I need to find her," he prompted. "Do you know where she went?"

"The church folk ran off to the woods." He licked at the corner of his lip and winced.

"Are you hurt?" Sylvanus reached out toward him and pulled up short when the boy scooted out of reach.

"Took a beating, is all."

"Is that why you're hiding in the church and not making a run for the woods? I'm a doctor." He hoped the partial untruth might instill confidence and inspire more sharing of information.

"Don't need no doctor." Mistrust once again edged his words.

The quiet of the night was broken by the drunken whoop of several white revelers celebrating the terror and chaos they had caused. Sylvanus could smell the young man's fear, a mixture of sweat and the tang of blood.

"I want to help." It was true, or at least partly so. He wanted to find Annie and this boy could help, but also true was the fact that Sylvanus's white skin, his presence in this place, the blood of another Black man who had taken a beating still clinging to his clothes garnered little trust, even if he had helped save that other man's life.

The stranger in the church could not know all that was wrapped up in Sylvanus's motives, but he did appear to know Annie, and her goodness would have to serve as a bridge to trust.

"Were the people who escaped the church hurt?"

"Don't know." The boy shook his head. "There was a white man yelling orders, helping them out. He wasn't with the others."

"Who was he? Where is he?"

"Don't know that either."

Sylvanus clenched his fist in frustration, the heat rising in his temples as he fought to keep his voice calm and nonthreatening. "Can you show me where they might have gone?"

"Mama said to meet here." His voice trembled. "I'm staying."

Sylvanus glanced over his shoulder at the damaged church door and back to the injured stranger. "It might not be safe," he said.

"Ain't no safe place for me." The young man shifted again, scooting back around the edge of the pulpit until he was almost gone from Sylvanus's view. "You find your sister, doctor. Take care of your own."

The image of those wide eyes haunted Sylvanus as he made his way toward the woods to discover nothing more than frightened faces ducking behind undergrowth and avoiding his gaze. None were white. None belonged to his sister.

The hour had grown late by the time he returned to Dr. Thompson's office where lamps still burned, their lights spilling through the windows. The door opened at his approach and in the doorway stood Annie, apparently unharmed. He flew to her when he saw her and pulled her into a tight hug.

"I went to find you. Someone said you'd been helped to the woods?" He led her into the light, studying her as though she might burst into flames and disappear. He brushed his thumb lightly over a bruise on her head and she winced.

Dr. Thompson, seated at his desk, held up a hand in greeting. "She showed up not thirty minutes after you left."

The Black man Bennet sat on a chair beside the cot where his injured friend lay bandaged and resting, his chest rising and falling in even breaths, a testament to at least something having gone well in the evening.

Seated across from Dr. Thompson on the other side of the desk was a man Sylvanus did not know. White and thick-muscled, the stranger was probably in his late twenties. He stood, touched the bridge of his crooked nose, and held his hand out toward Sylvanus.

"Mr. Goheen, my name is Jonas Edwards. It was my pleasure to assist Miss Goheen. I was near the Hill on some business when violence broke out. I saw the initial attack upon the church and rushed to help where I could."

Sylvanus took the man's offered hand in a firm grip. "I owe you thanks, Mr. Edwards."

"I'm grateful to have been in the right place at the right time." The man flashed a smile toward Annie. Sylvanus watched as a blush rose in his sister's cheeks and with it, he felt the heat of his own suspicion rise.

"Are you well?" Sylvanus asked Annie, thinking less about the riot than about the man who had ordered his sister into the dark woods.

It was Edwards who answered. "She took a blow to the head, but Dr. Thompson seems to think she'll be fine."

"Is that what Dr. Thompson said?" Sylvanus responded, rolling his eyes toward his mentor. "And what does Annie say?"

"I'm perfectly well, Smee." She stepped toward him and placed her hand on his arm. "I'm sorry you were worried."

He placed his other hand on top of hers and squeezed her fingers. He fixed her rescuer with the narrow-eyed glare of a protective brother.

"Well." Edwards brought his hands together with a sharp clap. "I should be going." He looked toward Bennet, who hadn't said a word since Sylvanus's return. "I'd be happy to help you settle your friend into a place where you'll both be safe tonight."

"I appreciate it." Bennet nodded his thanks and leaned toward his friend to gently rouse him.

"Miss Goheen," Edwards said, waiting a beat for her attention. "I'm glad to have met you. I believe you are a great friend to the cause. And I hope as we become acquainted, perhaps a great friend to me as well."

Annie's fingers slid out of Sylvanus's grasp as she stepped toward the man he wasn't as prepared to trust. "I'm glad to have met you, too, Mr. Edwards. Will you be in Columbia long?"

"I'm afraid not." He cleared his throat. "But I would like to call on you when next I'm here, if you wouldn't mind."

Sylvanus noted a waver in her balance and when he reached out to offer support, she accepted it.

"I would like that," she said. She shrank into her brother's side, but her eyes remained only on Mr. Edwards and his crooked nose.

5

Annie

For days after her encounter with the mysterious Mr. Edwards, Annie found herself inexplicably happy at the oddest moments. Her students had never been cleverer, Mother never more kindhearted, her brothers never more endearing to her, as though the world itself celebrated a momentous occasion it had been anticipating for many long years. Miss Mary Ann Goheen had met a man.

Eligible bachelors dotted Columbia and the surrounding countryside, but few had ever shown much interest in her. The feeling, or lack of one, had always been mutual, and through the years from the height of her marriage potential until her near attainment of old maid status, she'd not found reason to dwell overly long on the notion of the opposite sex.

Now she appraised herself with new eyes. The bloom of her youth had not yet faded entirely. She possessed creamy, smooth skin and a serious chin that narrowed into a sensible point. Her neck did not yet sag as her mother's and, despite her overlarge nose, there was nothing particularly unpleasant about her features. Mr. Edwards had gazed at her with what she imagined might have been appreciation of her appearance, and he could certainly look that way at any woman who caught his fancy without fear of rebuff.

Annie tried not to spend her time in foolish fantasy, but she couldn't help but imagine. He would write. They would be enchanted with one another's wit. She would become his perfect wife and the mother to healthy children who would inherit their father's good looks.

The first letter from Jonas arrived exactly two weeks after they first met.

"I think it's from your young hero," Mother said as she handed Annie the neatly folded letter bearing steady, masculine script. "He certainly didn't take long, did he?"

Annie did not share her mother's assessment. Two weeks had been an eternity, but slipping her trembling finger beneath the wax seal, Annie returned the almost girlish grin. Mother turned to her own correspondences, graciously offering her daughter a moment to read over her mail in privacy.

Dear Miss Goheen,

It was a great pleasure to make your acquaintance, though I do regret the circumstances. I pray you are well recovered from the bump on the head and the fright you received on that terrible night. Your bravery and calm in the face of a great difficulty speaks volumes of the high quality of your character. I regret I am unable to visit with you in person yet. My law practice in Richmond keeps me busy, as does my work advocating for the end of what Southerners call "the peculiar institution" of slavery, but as you and I know it is in reality the darkest stain of sin upon the soul of America. Here I stare into the face of this evil every day, but I must do it, for it is only in acknowledging our sin that we may be truly repentant. I am strengthened when I think of your bold work in reaching out to those in need. I ask that you pray for me, and for an end to this horror, until we may meet again.

Humbly Yours,
Jonas Edwards

Her heart dropped into her stomach. She read the letter through three times before her mother came to stand behind her, evidently no longer able to resist the call of a potential lover's note. Annie held the page out and Mother snatched it from her, scanning it with eager eyes.

"Well," Mother said at last. "He thinks of you. That's good."

"I suppose it is." Annie attempted to smile, to capture the enthusiasm with which she had opened the sterile words. This was not the gushing profession of love she had hoped it would be.

Mother dropped the letter back onto Annie's lap. "The letter is polite and proper and extremely complimentary of you."

"I'd hoped he might also mention my loveliness and grace or how he sees a vision of me when he closes his eyes to sleep at night."

A snort of laughter bubbled out of Mother. Annie's face grew hot, and her limbs turned to ice.

"Mary Ann Goheen, you're not a little girl anymore."

"I'm aware that I'm an old maid, Mother."

"Well," Elizabeth lowered herself onto the sofa beside her daughter. "I hardly think twenty-six is old."

"You were married with five children by the time you were my age."

"I don't know that I would recommend it."

"You've done so plenty of times."

The older woman patted the back of Annie's hand resting on Jonas's folded letter. "Yes, I should have married you off when you were eighteen. By now you could have six or seven children, a much thicker waist, and no time for anything outside of snotty noses and soiled clothes."

"Are you telling me, your daughter, there is no joy in motherhood?"

Elizabeth sighed. "That's not what I'm saying. But by not marrying young and following that path, look at what you've had the opportunity to do. I always wanted you to marry a preacher not so you could have his children, but so you could use your gifts to teach and to spread the message of the Gospel. You do that now. I'm proud of you."

"You are?" Annie blinked.

"I am. Truly. And if instead of a preacher you end up marrying a lawyer who chooses to focus not on your sparkling eyes, but on the beautiful soul behind them, then I will remain proud of you."

Annie looked down and brushed a piece of lint from her skirt. "I don't think he wants to marry me."

"Not yet." Mother raised one eyebrow. "But a man doesn't take time to write to a woman that he hopes to see her again soon if he doesn't mean it."

Jonas turned out to be a meticulous correspondent. Letters arrived for Annie every two weeks with only minor variations to their regularity, depending on their origin. He did travel a great deal, and though the substance of his letters remained maddeningly focused on the abolition movement, Annie sensed his tone softening.

She wrote to him of her students—charming stories that demonstrated her benevolence yet remained light in nature. Her mother proofread each one whether her daughter wished it or not.

"He's a serious man, isn't he?"

"Yes." Annie clipped a maddening article from the latest edition of the *Columbia Spy* to include with her next letter to the man she hoped was her suitor. Her messages had taken a darker turn as she shared in his frustrations at the mistreatment of their colored brethren. "That's what I appreciate most about him: his serious mind and his tireless pursuit of right."

Her mother scowled at the clipping. "Righteousness is a noble quality, but are you sure you shouldn't shift the conversation back to more pleasant things? You could write more of your students, or your gardening."

Annie smoothed precise folds into her letter and looked up from the table. "You think I should play the fool? Shall I show Jonas I can be a woman of no substance, without a care for the injustices of the world or anything beyond growing cabbages? Like a good little wife?"

"Mary Ann, watch your words." Mother reddened and sat beside her. "You know very well that's not what I mean, but a man as hardworking as Jonas might appreciate some happy distraction, perhaps a bit of the mundane and domestic. It's good to demonstrate your support and passion for his cause, but it can't hurt to remind him you're a woman. Men don't marry political activists."

"Good men do."

"And you know this because. . .?" Mother slipped the newspaper clipping from between the folds of the letter and smoothed it on the table. It described a recent town meeting in which the chief burgess read a proclamation responding to the riots and detailing the institution of a curfew on the colored people of Columbia, as though they had been responsible for the chaos. The article had soured Annie's stomach.

"I don't know what kind of women men want to marry, but this is who I am. I'm a woman who is concerned for her community, for her country, and for her fellow man. If that isn't what Jonas wants, then I will wish him all the best as he finds a silly little fool who thinks of nothing more than how fashionable ladies are wearing their hair." She snatched the article from her mother, tucked it safely back into the folds of her letter, and dripped sealing wax onto the edge. "And I'll thank you to mind your own business."

"I can see you don't need my help." Mother stood, her mouth a thin line and her hands folded neatly in front of her. "I suppose we can expect a proposal any day."

Annie felt a twinge of regret. She did value her mother's advice, might even have shared a small amount of the woman's concern that Jonas might see her as too hardened and political to become proper wife, that he might not know the color of her eyes or long to feel the way an errant wisp of her hair felt silky between his fingers.

But that was foolishness, and the fire inside her demanded she address the injustices of her community. She longed for Jonas to know it.

This was not her mother's courtship. It mightn't be courtship at all, yet she had found much to admire in this man.

6

Sylvanus

1835

Sylvanus gazed out the window of the shop, sipping coffee as he awaited the arrival of his friends and worrying over his performance on his evaluation. He'd seen seven patients that morning, each presenting with a wide range of complex symptoms. The only feedback the attending physician offered was a nod when Sylvanus explained his findings and treatment plans. Such a nod could convey many different meanings.

"Is that worry I see etched upon the face of the great Mr. Goheen?" Wilson pushed into the café and nudged Sylvanus, causing him to choke on his coffee and splash some onto the table. "You seem in a dark mood."

"I am now," he sputtered.

"It couldn't have been so terrible. Was it?" Wilson used his handkerchief to dab at the wayward drops.

Sydney James walked in behind him and answered. "Leave the man alone. It was a tough exam. Even I thought so."

"Oh, even the mighty Mr. James thought so. Well, then, perhaps I ought to worry, too." Wilson lowered himself onto a chair and snapped up a newspaper Sylvanus had brought in but not yet read.

"Don't listen to him, Sy." James settled on the other side of Sylvanus. "We all know you did well. You're the best student among us."

"I'm not, but I can see how you might think so given that I'm better than all of you in every other way."

"Much humbler at least." James grabbed Sylvanus's cup and lifted it in a mock toast. "But seriously, if I had to put my life into the hands of any member of this class, it's you I'd choose."

Sylvanus grabbed back his cup. "If you have to trust your life in the hands of any of your barely trained colleagues, I think your life will have gone terribly wrong somewhere."

Despite the banter, his friend's confidence in him did more than the coffee to warm Sylvanus. It had been a difficult four months since his arrival in Philadelphia. Everything was different, more intense than the comparatively sleepy rural practice in which he'd shadowed his mentor.

Few of his fellow students could claim such experiences, and the apprenticeship had provided him a great deal of insight difficult to gain from a city lecture hall alone. Before arriving at Jefferson Medical College, Sylvanus had already mastered the art of collecting a patient's history and performing a basic exam. Regardless, the medicine practiced in the city, and the techniques employed for teaching it, reached beyond the scope of what he'd seen in Columbia.

More than once, he'd balked at the gruesomeness of dissecting a human body and run from the room and the stench. The sick, too, appeared so often beyond his help, weak and sad and pitiful. His heart ached at the memory of the first houseful of cholera victims he'd visited back home, at his inability to alleviate the misery of so many. Such a situation had not grown easier, only more frequent. Sylvanus lost many hours of sleep to a parade of ghostly figures of sick and injured patients tripping mercilessly through his mind.

But then there were also triumphs, like the mother who had been sure to die on the birthing table, whose bleeding he'd managed to stop and would now live to raise her child. There was the young girl saved from the clutches of diphtheria, comforted during the darkest hours of the night, who awakened to a breaking fever and a chance at long life. Though not yet infallible, Sylvanus was a clever, confident student and could believe he would one day be a talented physician.

For now, he was grateful for his classmates. He'd never have made it through the difficult cases, or the long hours, without his friends. Garnet Wilson and Sidney James were as unlikely a pair as he'd ever encountered. Wilson was the son of a staunch abolitionist in New York; James, a devoted son of the South from Georgia, full of graceful manners, a tender heart, but also a darkness Sylvanus couldn't comprehend.

His third friend, the one who shared his living space as the second boarder in the home of Mrs. Francis Dane—a widow who clothed herself in false kindness—was Richard Grimes. Like Sylvanus, he hailed from Pennsylvania, from another small town on the other end of the state similar to Columbia. From a large family, Richard was the middle son of five, with three sisters. He often teased Sylvanus that he would introduce him to his sisters and let him have his pick.

Outside of such jests, Grimes was a quiet spirit who often kept to himself. Sylvanus suspected that, without his friendship, young Grimes would have disappeared into himself at the medical college and may not have reemerged. Instead, with Sylvanus at his side, the young man had thrived despite a dangerous secret the other students could never be allowed to know.

The bell above the door tinkled as Grimes stepped inside.

"There he is. The last of us to finish!" Wilson stood and pantomimed dusting off his chair to prepare the way for the newcomer. "Madame," he bellowed to the shopkeeper. "My friend needs a cup of your finest black coffee, strong as can be after that ordeal, I imagine."

Grimes dropped onto the offered seat.

"How was it?" Sylvanus asked him.

"Not bad. I think I performed as well as I could have. The student before me took a long time or I'd have been here much sooner."

"I'm sure you did us proud," James drawled in his friendly way and did not seem to notice Grimes shrink from the attention.

Sylvanus saw and understood. He liked James, this friendly, up-beat young man who oozed charm and gentility, if only he didn't carry the shadow of his ugly politics.

A half hour later, Sylvanus and Grimes had finished their coffee and managed to extricate themselves from the others to walk the three blocks to their rooms in a narrow brick house with polished marble steps. It stood neat and trim like all the others in the row, yet somehow stiffer and more unyielding than any of them.

Sylvanus took out his key but held it in his fist and did not slide it into the lock. The two had said little as they walked, and now a question burned too brightly to ignore.

"What truly took you so long today?"

Richard Grimes was by far the best student among the four of them, despite what James might claim. He'd have likely finished his exam a good twenty minutes faster than anyone else. Sylvanus suspected his friend had been up to something.

"Did your late arrival at the shop have anything to do with a woman?"

Richard colored a deep scarlet as he placed his own key in the door. He tugged at Sylvanus's sleeve and pulled him into the house. Mrs. Dane was not there to greet them, but Grimes hurried up the stairs to the platform between their bedroom doors which stood across from one another. He motioned for Sylvanus to follow him into his room.

The space was practically bare, much more than Sylvanus's homier, more welcoming room sporting a painting by his brother William of the farmhouse where they'd grown up, a quilt made by his eldest brother's wife, and a desk scattered with books and with letters from home.

Richard's space included an impeccably neat bed, no evidence of clutter, and a spotless chamber set that might never have been used.

"You live like a monk," Sylvanus teased.

His friend finally smiled. "I assure you, I do not."

Sylvanus chuckled uncomfortably and took a seat in the wooden desk chair.

Grimes sat across from him on the corner of the bed. "When I stepped out of the medical college building today, I spotted Helena at the edge of the tree line, waiting. She catches me there if we need to speak outside of our prearranged meetings."

Sylvanus leaned forward, elbows resting on his knees and, mouth dry with dread. Grimes walked a dangerous path. "What did she need to talk to you about?"

"Her brother."

Sylvanus sagged, relieved. In the back of his mind, he'd expected Grimes to reveal Helena was with child, Sylvanus's greatest fear for his unwise friend who'd fallen in love with a free colored woman. "She has a brother?"

He hadn't been aware that Helena had family in Philadelphia, or anywhere as far as he knew, and it would be better if she didn't as far as he was concerned. It was difficult enough for Grimes to hide the affair that would ruin his reputation and bright future without adding more people to the secret.

"I haven't met him. He just arrived from North Carolina. He's an escaped slave."

"And he sought out his sister?" Sylvanus asked, indignant on the young lady's behalf for the danger her brother's presence placed on her.

"Of course. Who would you go to if you were running for your life?"

The answer was obvious. Sylvanus would run to the only person in the world he knew beyond a doubt he could trust to welcome him: his sister Annie.

"Where's he staying?"

"She smuggled him into her boarding house, but obviously he can't remain there. She was hoping I could find a place for him. I don't know where to turn. He can't stay here. Mrs. Dane would never allow it. I'd be placing him in more danger just by asking."

"I assume he has a name?"

Grimes rubbed his temples. "Taylor."

Sylvanus conjured a picture of a proud man with Helena's high cheekbones and dark skin. Now that he had a name, he could make himself feel a kinship with this Taylor. Helena was a good woman—warm, generous, and beautiful. Sylvanus had no trouble seeing why his friend loved her, as unwise as it may have been to allow romance to blossom. He had little doubt her brother demanded a similar sympathy.

"Wilson will help," Sylvanus said.

Grimes shook his head. "I knew you'd say something stupid. Wilson is a jackass."

"Maybe. But he's also an abolitionist."

"His father's an abolitionist. He's a spoiled, selfish jackass."

"You underestimate him. He is part of the Pennsylvania Abolition Society."

"Only because of who his father is. He wants the contacts. He doesn't believe a word of it, I'd wager."

"Let's find out, then. There's a meeting tonight. He's always inviting us to them. Maybe Taylor could come, too. He could appeal to better men who may be in a position to help. Do you have a way to get a message to Helena?"

"I do. But I don't like this. I don't attend those meetings because I'm afraid to cast suspicion on myself and endanger Helena."

"I don't think you need to worry about that."

"I do nothing but worry about that."

Sylvanus pulled his coat tight to block the growing chill as he and Grimes made their way along the streets that blessedly dark evening. Seven knocks in a distinct pattern yielded an open door and a hurried invitation through the side entrance of a tavern neither had been inside before.

A handful of men greeted them inside, including their friend Wilson. Sylvanus was relieved to see him, as he and Grimes were as newcomers to the society. Abolition was fashionable among the Philadelphia elite, but still they valued discretion and guarded their meetings from the public eye. Wilson's presence made theirs less awkward.

Wilson spoke the moment he saw them. "Goheen and Grimes, my good men. Glad you've come." More quietly, he added, "These men will help your colored friend."

Behind him, Sylvanus heard seven raps on the door and two new figures shuffled through, one slight and hooded, the other tall and thick with skin the color of rich earth.

Wilson, with a welcome on his lips, pushed past Sylvanus and Grimes to greet the newcomers, the first of whom took down her hood to reveal her identity. Helena was more striking than Sylvanus remembered. Shapely beneath the cloak, she had the face of a dark, forbidden angel.

Wilson hesitated slightly before he clasped Helena's hand and flashed a warm smile. To Taylor, he absolutely beamed as he introduced him around the room.

Sylvanus remained close to Grimes who shrunk under the scrutiny of those curious at Helena's presence. Her eyes, too, darted about, betraying her discomfort, and her hand clutched her brother's sleeve as he explained his situation to a concerned gentleman with a thick, white mustache.

Mingling continued as men kept arriving. The total in the tight back room reached more than two dozen before a mustached man broke from Taylor and called the meeting to order.

"Welcome, gentlemen. We have some new business to deal with tonight." He indicated Taylor standing among mostly white faces. "Our guest here has made a long and dangerous journey and needs our help. He wishes to head north but must find shelter in the city before moving on. Can anyone offer him safe accommodations?"

A gentleman in the front row raised his hand. "I can provide shelter for a week or two while he determines what his next move will be."

"I thank you, as does our guest, I'm sure."

Taylor nodded his thanks.

"Now, gentlemen, we must address the recent move within the United States Congress to table all discussion of anti-slavery petitions as supported by the Southerners and Northern Democrats. Our noble cause has great support among the Northern Whigs, but their voices have been temporarily stymied by this so-called 'Gag Rule.'"

The speaker, whose name Sylvanus never heard, continued for at least an hour, his impassioned speech accompanied by bursts of supportive outrage. Sylvanus lost the pieces of the argument, his brain fogged over from too much study and too little sleep.

Though Sylvanus detested slavery and considered himself an abolitionist, politics held little interest for him. His brothers, especially the eldest two who had already entered the ministry, were the political voices in the family. Perhaps also his sister, whose actions in helping the Black community of Columbia, spoke even more loudly.

Sylvanus hated the peculiar institution as much as anyone in this gathering, but he remained practical. Slavery would not end in the United States until it became repugnant to society as a whole. Even then, he wasn't convinced Black men would ever be fairly integrated into society.

After the speech ended, Sylvanus turned to Taylor. "What are your plans, then, exactly?"

"I'm gonna leave this place. As soon as I have a way out of the country, I'll head to Canada." He placed a large arm around his sister's tiny frame. "We'll work to buy a farm, live a quiet life as free people."

"You mean to take Helena with you?" Grimes asked the question, his voice edged in panic. He looked to the lady in question. Her gaze did not meet his. "She's free. Why would she leave her home?"

Taylor shook his head. "There's no freedom for a Negro in the United States, not even with good folks. You been good to my sister, Mr. Grimes, and to me. I thank you, but if she gonna have any kind a life, it won't be here."

Helena did not meet her secret lover's eyes, and Sylvanus felt a sharp stab of sympathy for his friend. But Taylor's words resonated with him, too. The dark-skinned man, though unsophisticated after a lifetime of oppression, made a valid point. Sylvanus couldn't help but agree with him. No colored person would ever find fairness or be allowed to build any kind of free life for themselves while remaining in a country that refused to believe he was human. He'd need to find a new place, a home away from the shadow cast by the evil of slavery. Perhaps Canada was a good solution.

Grimes barely spoke the rest of the evening, or for days after. Sylvanus attempted to engage him in conversation over a dissection. Thankfully, Wilson left him alone. After Grimes had attended the society meeting, a new kind of respect developed between the two men.

James, the only one oblivious to the tension, continued in his own obnoxious way, making light of every shared moment spent hovering above the carefully removed intestines of a rotting corpse. Sylvanus wondered how his demeanor might change if he knew the secret held between the other three.

When Sylvanus arrived at the boarding house that evening, Grimes hadn't yet returned from the college. The reason had to be Helena. Grimes continued his appeals to her to remain in the country. He wouldn't succeed. Determination shone in those big, dark eyes, even if Grimes had refused to see it. Love was a beautiful thing, but if he couldn't let her go, to have a chance at a better life, then Sylvanus suspected his friend might not love her after all. Love couldn't be allowed to become a form of shackles.

Such thoughts swirled through Sylvanus's head as he let himself into the boarding house. Mrs. Dane greeted him with her hands on her hips. "Mr. Goheen, where have you been? Dinner has been waiting for you more than an hour. You'll have to eat it cold."

"I apologize, Mrs. Dane. I was kept late at the school."

She crinkled her nose, unappealing on a woman of her age, which he suspected to be near the same as his fifty-two-year-old mother. The landlady certainly carried herself with the same cranky, uncompromising dignity as Elizabeth Goheen. The two women shared an identical scowl when cross, which for both of them seemed, without exception, to be in the presence of Sylvanus.

"You smell like the dead." She turned on her heel, leaving him standing in the hallway with only his stench to keep him company. She was right, of course. Beneath his coat, his shirtsleeves bore spattered blood that had also found its way to his shoes. Hungry as he may be, his cold supper would have to wait until he changed.

Before he climbed the stairs, he looked to the table beside the door where Mrs. Dane separated the mail. A letter brought a smile to his face, his name and address scrawled in the spidery hand he associated with home. He picked up Annie's letter and sprang up the stairs.

Once inside his bedroom, he stripped off both coat and offending shirt, but before crossing to water basin to wash, he broke the seal and gently unfolded the message.

My Dearest Brother,

I trust this letter find you well and hard at work learning to use your God-given gifts to save the sick in body. The soul will not be saved if the sick cannot see beyond their physical needs to the spiritual ones, which are far more important. You, then, are on the front lines of God's great work among the lost. I am proud to call you my brother.

Mother is well, as are our brothers. We miss you and pray for you daily and are hopeful you might be able to travel home soon. I have continued to correspond with the Virginia lawyer Jonas Edwards, the man who delivered me safely to you the night of the terrible riots. He has a powerful love for God and for service. It would please me if the two of you might come to know one another better.

Be well, dear brother. I will see you in my prayers and, I hope soon, in the flesh.

Your loving sister,
Annie

Sylvanus set the page on his desk. Annie's letter had little to do with how well his brothers and mother fared and everything to do with the Virginia lawyer. There was a man in his sister's life. The thought should please him, but as he watched the water turn a dull pink and then gray from blood and filth, he only hoped this Edwards deserved her.

7
Annie

Flustered at the thought of seeing Jonas again, Annie scanned the letter once more.

Dearest Ann,

It is with a great deal of joy and anticipation that I let you know I will soon be once again in Lancaster County. I wish I could tell you I was coming for a longer period, as my heart could surely use the rest, but this will necessarily be a brief visit. I long to see you and present you with a request of the utmost seriousness. I have come to so appreciate your kind and generous spirit through the precious words you write to me. I believe I might anticipate your answer but am anxious to make my plea in person. Expect me within the week.

Your Humble Servant,
Jonas

She refolded the brief note and slipped it into her pocket, conjuring an image of the man she most admired—the once she might even love.

Their meeting had been brief, but he'd made an impression. He was as tall as her brothers and his arms were thick with the strength to carry her from harm's way. She wished she could picture the color of his eyes. She clung to what details she could conjure. In her memory, he loomed large, his face in need of a shave, his hair in want of a trim. He'd absentmindedly run his hands through it when he addressed her, like he was trying to put himself together in a way wholly unnecessary but unquestionably appreciated.

She could barely contain her joy at the prospect of seeing him again. Jonas spent much of his time working in support of an end to slavery, raising money for abolitionist societies, seeing to the welfare of enslaved people however he could. It was important but dangerous work. As a Southern son from a well-regarded family, he had access to circles of likeminded people, but also frequent encounters with those who did not want his message spread. His work demanded vigilance.

He had written to her a dozen times in the months since they'd met, and in each letter his words were kind and honest and full of promise. He wrote of his work, of both his successes and his failures. He wrote of the sorrow he found along the way in the eyes and hearts of slaves—families separated, women abused, children with no understanding of freedom.

Never did Jonas shy from relaying difficult or unpleasant things, but he showed concern for her in the tender ways in which he addressed her, considered her feelings in all things and claimed she had enchanted him with her enthusiasm for the cause.

Enchanted! He'd said enchanted! Annie read every word with both dread and hope. Her heart raced at the tales of his adventures, the details of which were necessarily sparse. As she read, her heart raced with both fear for his safety and pride in his righteous determination. Though not a preacher, he'd make a fine husband. Even Mother had said as much.

Annie eagerly replied to him with long letters of encouragement, both for his work in pursuing freedom for the enslaved and, she hoped subtly, in pursuit of his own contentment.

With each loop and swirl of her pen, she was keenly aware her twenty-seven years placed her well past the ideal age for a bride. Even fairly fresh-faced and appealing, as her mother insisted she was, Annie knew time to find a husband had run out. Jonas was a perfect candidate. Not much older than she, he was in every way respectable.

And, at last, he would return—*with a serious request.*

Four days after receiving his letter, she saw him coming from a long way off not on horseback, but driving a small wagon. She grabbed a broom and busied herself brushing imaginary dirt from the front porch. She called for Mother and tried to calm her nerves as she watched his approach.

"Is that your Mr. Edwards?" Mother stepped onto the porch.

"He's not *my* Mr. Edwards." Annie had not shared all of the contents of Jonas's letter—nor her hopes at their meaning—but her mother could not be innocent of speculation.

"Not yet," her mother replied with a knowing smile.

Annie's heart thudded in her chest and she waved. Jonas drew back the horse's reins and stepped down from the driver's seat, but instead of moving toward Annie as she'd anticipated, he stepped back and tugged at the edge of the tarp-covered wagon. As he lifted, it a pair of eyes peeked from beneath.

"You're safe here," Jonas said to the eyes. "You can come out."

The form of a woman rose from the tarp as a spirit from a grave—a ghost as brown as the earth, wearing a wrinkled dress and a dingy head rag.

Only then did Jonas greet Annie.

"Good day, Miss Goheen!" Jonas called to the porch. He removed his hat and tipped his head as he helped the young Black woman from the wagon where she had been hidden. "Mrs. Goheen. How wonderful to see you both."

"Mr. Edwards," Annie's mother replied, her tone skeptical.

Annie managed no words at all, so shocked was she at Jonas's revelation. Her heart fluttered in her delight to see him at her home, but to find him in the company of another woman, even a wretched one, came as a shock. She had ached for him while he was away, dreamt of this moment of reunion. She just hadn't pictured it quite like this.

"I've brought a surprise for you—one I sincerely hope your heart will allow you to welcome."

The woman, perhaps more of a girl, stood beside the wagon, rubbing life back into her limbs. The dark color of her skin created the illusion that the whites of her eyes glowed. She did not look directly at Annie but focused on the ground as she gave a small curtsy, dipping her head and saying slowly, as though it was a practiced recitation, "It's a pleasure to make your acquaintance, Miss Goheen."

"This is Esther," Jonas said, clutching her gently by the elbow to steady the tiny thing as she rose from her curtsy.

Annie didn't know quite what to say. She took in the sight of this newcomer, whose small frame might have been made of glass, so fragile was she compared to the man beside her, but whose bones might have borne more pain and misery than Annie could imagine.

"You are a slave?" It was barely a question. The woman would not look at her. She lacked a confidence innate in the free Blacks Annie knew.

The young woman was filthy and far too thin. Something about her expression struck Annie as hollow, and a pang of guilt shot through her. Regardless of her jealous desire for Jonas's attentions, the woman before her was deserving of Annie's pity.

Jonas answered for her. "She was a slave, but now she is free." He locked eyes with Annie and her insides melted. *Green*. His eyes were green and vivid. "She needs a home for a time, and I was hoping she might find it here with you."

Annie's heart jumped into her throat. The pathetic creature before her made the maternal instinct in her swell and she felt keenly her Christian duty to this fellow human being. But she also hesitated, motioning for Jonas to join her aside for a conversation outside the earshot of Esther.

He smiled brightly to the woman and followed to the shade of a tree several paces away.

"Is she an escaped slave?" Annie asked in an urgent whisper.

Jonas sighed, and Annie sensed his disappointment in her question. "She is a liberated slave."

"Liberated by whom, exactly?"

"By God the Father her creator, who bought freedom for all His sons and daughters, from bondage to sin and man." A hard edge of impatience permeated his response and stung her. Annie remained silent, waiting for him to continue, hoping he would offer her more confidence than what she currently felt with a fugitive slave at her home.

Jonas took her hands in his and spoke quietly. "Look, Ann, you needn't be frightened of this sweet woman. She's quite docile."

"I'm not frightened of her!" Her eyes narrowed in an attempt to communicate the indignation she found difficult to retain while his warm hands covered hers, his calloused thumb running across her knuckles in a terrifying and exhilarating way. She lowered her voice. "I'm not frightened at all, not really. I just wonder what you could be thinking bringing a fugitive here without any prior consultation with my family. There is a certain amount of risk."

Esther had turned nonchalantly to examine a nearby tree trunk, though Annie suspected the move had more to do with turning an ear toward the two of them to better discern their conversation.

"And there is the burden of another mouth to feed."

"I think she hardly eats." His levity eased the knots in her stomach, and she smiled.

"No," she said. "I suppose she doesn't eat much."

She wished she could wrap her arms around him and soak in his courage. Had they not been under the watchful eyes of Mother and the wretched interloper, she might have done it.

"And she will gladly work to earn her keep."

Annie sighed. "I have no doubt of that."

"Then what, dearheart, is your hesitation? I took you to be a fellow crusader in the great cause of abolition. Was I mistaken?"

"Of course not." She chanced another glimpse of the former slave, currently engaged in scrutinizing her own fingers. "I am. I just don't know what I can offer her."

"She only needs a friend, an advocate who can help her to navigate a new home with a new identity as a free woman."

"And how are we to convince people she belongs here?"

"Columbia has long seen its share of those seeking freedom, and of those willing to help them achieve it. You must have known."

Annie shook her head, though of course she knew.

"Well, it has. Concoct a story. Claim she is a friend visiting from the North."

"Will people believe it? She doesn't look anyone in the eye, and I've barely heard her speak."

"My dear, I have been traveling with this young woman for days. She is grieving over the loss of her people, sold into the deep South when their master passed away. Before the family could come in to evaluate the assets, I managed to steal Esther away. It's likely they believe she was transported with the others and their primary interest is in unloading the estate. They are not going to come looking for her as long as she remains obscure. And if they do, she has been given forged documents. Good ones."

Jonas seemed so sincere it was difficult not to accept his confidence, but Annie remained doubtful. "Will she move on from here to someplace farther north?"

He shook his head. "She's not strong enough to travel on, and there may be no need. It's too dangerous for her to stay with my relatives, as I possess something of a reputation. Her best protection will be that you are above suspicion as you have no discernible relationship to me."

Annie's throat closed at his words at the casual way he cast her aside and proclaimed her insignificance in his life. The humiliation of his statement washed over her, and she'd have liked to slap his square jaw and scream at him, but the earnestness in his eyes and his utter lack of malice or awareness of his own insensitivity melted her resolve.

Though her heart rejected that this had been the request he wished to make of her, she respected him for asking the question, for caring about Esther, and for trusting in her to keep safe a cherished child of God.

"I must speak with Mother, but tentatively I agree. Esther will remain with us, and we will teach her how to be a freewoman from the North so no one might threaten her."

Jonas pulled her into a brief embrace, as highly inappropriate as it was completely wonderful.

"Thank you, Annie." She thrilled to hear her familiar name fall from his lips. "Speak to your mother."

Though she had just as fierce a sense of injustice as her daughter, Mother had always been a law-abiding woman and, as a widow with children, she'd generally avoided engaging in controversy. This would be a difficult sell. Annie offered a shy smile to Esther as she passed by her on her way to the porch where her mother waited with wide eyes.

Mother said not a word but only waited for an explanation.

"That's Esther. She's a runaway who needs a place to stay."

"And why did he bring her here?"

"Because Jonas knows we are good people, and it would be too risky to take her to town where things continue to be unsettled. Her whereabouts could be too easily traced."

Mother's mouth opened in what Annie assumed was a protest and she quickly added, "He doesn't think she'll be pursued."

"Those Southerners will pursue their slaves to the end of God's green earth."

With the pronouncement, Annie felt her face drain of color, along with her hopes of ever becoming Mrs. Jonas Edwards. She studied her mother's expression, hard and serious, then a hint of softening.

"Of course, she'll stay here."

Annie couldn't help herself. She hugged her mother, who braced herself against the edge of the doorway to prevent injury to them both.

Elizabeth Goheen had always possessed a great deal of warmth and love, but it was sometimes hidden so deeply at her core it wasn't apparent to others. Annie had seen it in the way Mother cared for her family, protected them as best she could from the evils of the world and dangers that might befall them. Often, she displayed her devotion to those she loved in her determination to shield them and prevent them from becoming involved in risky ventures.

But now she had thrown aside such caution. If this young woman was in danger and they were in a position to help, then Elizabeth Goheen would do what she could. Annie loved her tremendously for it, and despite her disappointment, she loved Jonas for seeing the potential of it.

"Thank you, Mother!"

"Stop smothering me, Mary Ann. Invite our guests inside and let's meet this young lady who is to be a part of our family."

Annie warmed with sudden delight and a calm sense that this would work. She had thought this day to gain a groom, but for a lone daughter among sons, to gain a sister would do almost as well.

After the initial shock of her presence had passed, Esther struck Annie as a quiet and gentle soul. She'd said little as Annie spoke with Jonas and then saw him off to his family's farm from which he would leave again the next morning. With the visit officially ended, Annie turned her attention to the newcomer she had determined would be her friend.

"What is your surname, Esther?"

She looked toward the wall and Annie thought perhaps she mightn't answer at all before she finally said, "Seddon was the family name, ma'am. I don't have another."

"Do you wish to be referred to as Miss Seddon?"

"No, ma'am."

Annie thought for a moment. "We have to call you something. Goheen won't do, as you're clearly not a blood relative."

Mother placed a hand on Esther's shoulder. "Mr. Edwards provided papers with the name Smith. You were born free in New York. I have distant relatives there, and one could hardly question a Miss Smith from New York."

Annie mouthed a thank you to her mother and gave Esther what she hoped was an encouraging smile.

The Black woman responded with a subtle nod and it was decided. Annie's heart ached at the thought of a woman without a name and uttered a silent prayer that Miss Smith could look forward to a long, happier life filled with love.

"Mary Ann." Mother's commanding voice pulled her from her thoughts. "Go find something more suitable for Esther to wear. There must be a dress or two from when you were younger. We can go into town for new fabric next week and make her something all her own. For now, I'll help her set up a bath so she can be refreshed by the time John Wesley comes home."

A bath and a clean dress had transformed Esther, whose shy smile spoke to a growing spark of hope in her new freedom. John Wesley returned home as the sun began to set. He hid his surprise at Esther's presence well and when, at Mother's invitation, Esther sat beside him at the long table, he put forth a great effort to include her in the dinner table conversation. She had little to say, and no one pushed her, but by the end of the meal, her shifting, suspicious eyes held a subtle hint of new light.

After supper, Mother asked John Wesley to read to the family as they gathered in the sitting room, the soft lamps ablaze, the windows open to the evening breeze.

"Has the new serial arrived?" he asked.

Mother shook her head. "Choose an old favorite from William's collection. I assume he left a few behind." She settled onto her favorite wingback chair in the corner of the room.

Annie chose a space on the long sofa and invited Esther to sit beside her. The young woman obliged, moving timidly, her gaze focused on the floor. Once perched on the edge of the sofa, her ankles crossed beneath the full skirt, she might have made the image of a well-bred lady if only she projected the fearlessness of one. Esther had clearly not been a field hand. Perhaps a household servant, even a lady's maid. Annie wanted to ask her but feared the question would cause the woman to retreat further into herself. Annie hoped one day her new friend might be comfortable enough to open up about her past.

John Wesley returned from his upstairs bedroom with a well-worn book in hand and took his place beside the hearth. The night was far too warm to light a fire, which Annie regretted. The glow from the dancing flames had a way of making such evenings cozier. She feared they might need the extra warmth when she saw her brother's choice.

His melodious voice rang out:

Found among the papers of the late Diedrich Knickerbocker.

> *In the bosom of one of those spacious coves which indent the eastern shore of the Hudson, at that broad expansion of the river dominated by the ancient Dutch navigators the Tappan Zee, and where they always prudently shortened sail and implored the protection of St. Nicholas when they crossed, there lies a small market town or rural port, which by some is called Greensburgh, but which is more generally and properly known by the name of Tarry Town. . .*

Annie could have recited the opening lines of Washington Irving's *The Legend of Sleepy Hollow* by memory had she a need, as John Wesley could have done. It was one of the family's most beloved and most often read books, so much so that her brother knew which parts to skip to make the novella fit into a single evening's entertainment. Still, Annie wondered if the book were a ghastly choice to share with a newcomer who herself had survived such unimaginably frightening ordeals.

Beside her on the sofa, Esther perched like an attentive statue with wonder painted on her face. The woman didn't seem the least bit perturbed by the mention of spirits, or witches, or a headless Hessian. She did draw closer to Annie as the story progressed, and when Gunpowder the horse galloped madly across the bridge, his saddle cast aside and his bumbling rider barely holding on, Esther gasped and thrust her hand through the crook of Annie's arm.

This closeness with another woman, the proper age of a longed-for little sister, touched Annie more deeply than a proposal might have done. Her heart swelled at the thought of the wonderful gift her beloved had given her, forgiveness replacing some of the anger at the embarrassment he had caused.

Her brother was in great form, the swells of his voice matching Irving's vivid descriptions of the picturesque setting to the caricature of the hopelessly awkward Ichabod Crane. When John Wesley read of the schoolteacher singing from his tattered hymn book, Annie closed her eyes and pictured the ridiculous man who would never catch the eye of a pretty heiress and nearly heard a throaty warble rising above the words.

At the suggestion that rival suitor Brom Bones concocted the entire encounter, pumpkin and all, Esther produced the kind of laughter that bursts forth from the depth of a suddenly awakened soul. The sound of it filled Annie's ears and heart with gladness that carried the two of them off to bed.

"Did you enjoy the story, Esther?" Annie pulled a nightgown from her bureau and handed it to her.

"Yes, ma'am, I did. That old Ichabod Crane reminded me of a man used to come to the house to call on my old mistress's granddaughter. I'd a hit him in the head with a pumpkin if I could've. So would the young miss, before she married another man, not much better." Esther tucked the nightgown beneath an arm and covered her grin with both hands.

"Please call me Annie." Annie sat on the edge of the wide bed the two women would now share. "I suppose it never occurred to me how funny the story is. I've always found it frightening."

Esther, so slight and insubstantial she might herself have been ghost, shook the nightgown open and held it in front of her. It was old and worn, with small blue flowers embroidered at the neckline. "Oh, Miss Annie, sometimes you just have to laugh at a man getting knocked off his horse with a pumpkin. Besides, there's much scarier things in this world than ghost stories."

"There are indeed." She stood and began to undo the clasps at the nape of her dress, a task made easier when Esther began to help. Annie returned the favor and asked the question burning foremost in her mind. "What do you want to do now that you are free and safe?"

Esther shuddered under her dress, but she did not hesitate to answer. "I want to read stories, like your brother read tonight. Do you think I could?"

"Yes." The answer flew out of Annie's mouth with more enthusiasm than she had intended, but Esther's response had been the one she's most longed to hear. "I know you could. I will teach you."

Annie took advantage of the warmth of the late afternoon to finish reviewing the next day's lessons on the steps of the church. Esther's cheerful humming reached her from the schoolhouse next door and filled her with a contentment further fueled by the day's successes.

Annie's class contained several bright students, and she enjoyed the challenge of finding new ways to encourage them in their academic pursuits, yet no sense of accomplishment teaching at the school could compare to the delight she felt at seeing Esther flourish.

After only a couple weeks, she identified all the letters with sounds and could recognize many simple words. Mother lent her own teaching skills to the project as well, and during the days when Annie taught the farm children, Mother and Esther spent a good deal of their time together in reading practice.

In fact, Esther's presence had done much to soften Mother who, for as long as Annie could remember, had been stern and serious, a dictator directing her children's lives. This had been the reality of life as a widow with six children, but now, the presence of this new young woman in their lives, another daughter on whom Mother need not so heavily rely, had rejuvenated her. Annie might have been jealous except she so appreciated coming to know this more relaxed version of her mother, in whom she could more easily glimpse herself.

Some things, however, had not changed. It had been Mother who insisted Esther meet Annie at the schoolhouse one afternoon to select a new book for the family to read aloud. Annie grinned broadly as she saw a distant approaching figure and recognized the deviousness of Elizabeth Goheen. Bennett Miller, the school's most dedicated repairman, had arrived in time to escort the two ladies home on nice autumn day.

"Esther," she called as she stood and approached the schoolhouse door. "There's someone I'd like you to meet."

Esther leaned her head out of the doorway, her gaze following Annie's to the man walking toward them. "Who is that?" she called softly, her words betraying the familiar timidity Annie hoped she'd lose in time.

"A friend." Annie beckoned to the young woman who stepped out of the schoolhouse.

With a dubious expression she asked, "A friend?"

"Yes. And I think you'll find him charming. Remember to look him in the eye and address him as though you expect the same courtesy. You are a proud, free woman of the North."

Esther released a slow breath and ran her hands down the front of her skirt. In addition to reading, Annie had been working with Esther to smooth out the diction and mannerisms that might set her apart, even advertise her as an escaped slave. Bennett would be the perfect candidate for a bit of practice, and maybe a bit of something else.

Annie had no intention of giving into her mother's scheme and playing the matchmaker, but Bennett Miller was one of the most honorable men she knew, a hard worker who dedicated his free time not only to the betterment of the colored citizens of Columbia, but to her own school full of white farm children as well. He was a man of God who wore his freedom well. If not a love interest, he would at least make a fine example for Esther.

"Good afternoon, Miss Annie." He doffed his cap and smiled. "I have a little free time today. Mrs. Goheen mentioned you had some rotted boards in the schoolhouse. Thought I might take a look."

The boards he referred to had been repaired by John Wesley more than a week ago, which Mother well knew.

"That's kind of you, Bennett. My brother replaced them already." She watched his face fall slightly before adding, "But I'd be honored if you'd walk us home."

Annie reached for Esther's hand and pulled her forward. "Mr. Bennett Miller, I'd like you to meet Miss Esther Smith."

"Miss Smith." Bennett bowed his head toward her, his eyes drinking in the sight of her. He shook his head as if unsure what to say.

Annie rescued him. "Esther arrived last week from New York. She's a dear family friend come to stay with us." She saw the dawning light on the man's face. "Mr. Edwards was kind enough to escort her."

"A pleasure, Miss Smith. Welcome to Lancaster County." He placed his cap back on his head and extended his arm toward the timid young Black woman. Annie couldn't help but grin as Esther took his arm.

She might not have much success making a match for her daughter, but perhaps Mother had picked this one just right. Annie sensed a spark. The two would make a handsome couple, and connection to a respectable free man would provide Esther a level of security.

As she locked the schoolhouse doors and followed behind them, Annie prayed that despite her mother's well-intentioned meddling, the introduction might result in love for her new friend.

8
Sylvanus

Sylvanus faced the end of his studies with both hope and dread. He'd completed many months of training and, while intellectually he knew he possessed the skills of a physician, there remained the inkling that he might prove incapable of holding lives in his hands without the crush of self-doubt.

He believed he'd not caused death during the year of his training. Not directly anyway. But his schooling had been supervised medicine. His careful notes, his knowledge of the human body, met up against the same limitations as his colleagues. It was only enough until it wasn't.

All he knew for certain was that he had no plan for his next steps in life. Dr. Thompson hoped for his to return to Columbia, to join and eventually take over the medical practice there, but the thought of his hometown, of the long years ahead of him surrounded by a large extended family and his opinionated mother, did not wholly appeal to him.

He'd considered remaining in Philadelphia to set up medical practice but suspected he could not compete in such a well-established medical community. Even if he possessed the talent, he lacked the necessary experience.

He supposed his return to Columbia was inevitable. He'd be close to his brothers and sister. Of course, he'd also be close to his mother. He could take over Dr. Thompson's practice, perhaps move it to the countryside where his patients might be fewer and simpler in their presentations, and where the general mistrust of medicine might lower expectations.

"You should come with me to South Carolina." James always said this when he'd had a drink or two. He'd invited each of them at one time or another, giving the impression that he, too, was reluctant to pursue a life separate from the bubble of the medical college and his closest friends of the past year. They'd been through much together—late nights of study and foul-smelling days elbows deep in the gore of human cadavers—experiences that produced strong bonds.

"I can't do it, which you well know," Sylvanus slurred. He'd drunk little. In fact, he rarely drank, but found it easiest to speak of serious things when those around him assumed he'd been in his cups. "My conscience will not allow it. I could never live in a state that supports the condition of human slavery."

"Bah, always so serious, Goheen. What about you, Wilson?"

"I confess myself an ardent abolitionist, as you well know, James. I couldn't see myself at home in the Carolinas. Besides, my uncle has a practice in New York I'll be joining. I'm afraid you'll have to count me out."

"What about you, Grimes? Are you a champion of the darkies, too, or do you have more berries than these flapdoodles?"

Richard said nothing, though he shot James a look that might have landed as hard as a slap across the face had James been paying attention. Already he'd moved on to a new topic. Then Grimes seemed to think better of just letting it go. "You could do with a lesson in manners."

"What did you say?" James gazed at the young doctor, curiosity and perhaps delight etching his face. "Do you think I need to be kinder to the coloreds? Is that what you think?"

Grimes moved his mug from the edge of the table and stood. "I think you'd better learn how to treat people, whatever color they may be. Your words may be acceptable in South Carolina, but here they are not taken kindly."

"Settle down. I didn't mean anything by it. I didn't know you were in love with the nig—"

That's when Richard Grimes punched Sydney James square in the jaw and sent him sprawling on the floor.

"Time to sober up and be educated." Wilson's smug attitude was almost more than Sylvanus could handle, but James had upset him, too. For the duration of their entire medical education the four men had managed to avoid angry confrontations about their differing political views. One thing Sylvanus had always tried to keep in mind was that he'd not spent a great deal of time with Black men and those he had, as far as he knew, might have been exceptional.

Sydney James, on the other hand, would have spent little time with exceptional Black men and so perhaps he had a better perspective on the capabilities of American slaves were they to gain their freedom. But then Sylvanus had also borne witness to the riots in Columbia in which enraged white men attacked their Black neighbors for committing the crime of performing capably in jobs usually filled by white workers. He'd seen the ugliness hidden inside the hearts of the white man who would rather his Black counterpart never existed at all.

Sylvanus's perceptions had been challenged, too, when he came to know Richard Grimes and met his Helena, pretty and industrious but not of some outstanding, exceptional nature. She was just a woman like any other, and it made him suspect all Black people might simply be men and women, different from whites only in the circumstances of their births.

Always among God's creation would there rise up those who were especially gifted, and always among God's creation would be those who were made to provide a backdrop. All races, to some extent, must be made up of these two types of individuals.

Tonight's exercise might be a futile one, dragging Sydney James along to hear a lecture from a Black speaker, but this mattered absolutely to Grimes and was equally encouraged by Wilson. Sylvanus was, at the least, curious what might come of it.

They arrived at the Saint James Methodist Episcopal Church a half hour before the scheduled speech and already it was difficult to find places along the hard benches. Against James's will, Grimes dragged the young man toward the front to claim the last of those oft neglected seats.

Wilson pushed into the middle of one of the center pews. Sylvanus remained standing in back and surveyed the crowd. The attendees were all white men and women, most of them probably the regular worshippers of the church in which they now gathered. They chatted, some polite and subdued, others animated in the anxious environment.

At last, the regular preacher made his way down the aisle, greeting those on the ends of the pews as he went. In his wake followed two men, one white and distinguished in appearance, one Black, his clothing shabbier but tidy and respectable. The latter held his head high and appeared neither nervous nor uncomfortable in the slightest as he stood beside the other two, positioned as their equal.

"Welcome, all of you." The regular preacher spoke first, raising his hands to call the attention of the quieting crowd. Sylvanus had seen him a handful of times when he'd had time to attend Sunday service. He'd have not admitted to his mother or sister how infrequently that had become, nor that he couldn't recall the preacher's name.

"It is a wonderful thing to see so many of you here on this fine evening. The speakers we have with us tonight are prominent men, both of them." He indicated the two gentlemen beside him, lingering particularly in his gaze on the Black man.

Pointing to the white man, he said, "Reverend John Seys is a member of the Methodist Episcopal Missionary Society, is representing the American Colonization Society, and is currently serving as the Superintendent for the Methodist Episcopal Church in Liberia."

He indicated the other speaker. "And Mr. George Brown here is a licensed preacher under the tutelage of the Methodist Episcopal Church for which he has served faithfully, preaching before both colored and white congregations throughout the Northern states. He will be among the emigrants to Liberia where he will serve in a missionary role. It is an honor to have them both here with us tonight and to hear what they have to say."

The crowd applauded politely as George Brown stepped first into the pulpit. "Thank you for allowing me to speak to you tonight." From his pocket, the preacher pulled a worn leather book and opened it in front of himself. "I'll be speaking from the twenty-fifth chapter of Matthew."

When his speech began, a mouse might have made itself heard scurrying between the pews, as attentive as the congregation became to the eloquent sermon. He read the familiar verses in which the King separates the sheep from the goats and fails to recognize those who did not serve their fellows, expounding on the Scripture passage to suggest colonization could be a way provide for the personal dignity of Black men and women who were denied this basic human need in the United States.

As he finished, Sylvanus fought the urge to break into inappropriate applause. Not often had he felt so moved by the powerful words of another man, and this a Black man, a surprising but effective vessel through whom God chose to speak.

Brown nodded at some of the people in front who whispered words of appreciation to him. He then slid aside and took the seat of John Seys after the latter vacated it to approach the pulpit.

"Thank you, Brother Brown, for those inspired words. And thank you all for giving Brother Brown the opportunity to speak, preach, and teach in your midst. He preaches with the leading of the Holy Spirit and with great conviction, but while it is a pleasure to hear him wrestle with and illuminate the Scriptures, you must all, dear brothers and sisters, also realize that to do so, to even be allowed to walk into this building and be treated with the respect deserved by all men, is a struggle for him. Our America, even the parts of it most filled with enlightened people such as yourselves, who wish to embrace the colored man as their brother, is a difficult place, an uncomfortable place, and even a dangerous place for our dark-skinned brothers in Christ to become the men God has called them to be." He paused to survey the congregation.

"It is the belief and the goal of the American Colonization Society to provide an opportunity for those of our Black brothers and sisters who desire it to establish themselves in a land that is hospitable to them, that affords them the luxury of opportunity, which remains unattainable in these United States.

"There is a new land, a colony, established and prepared for men such as George Brown, and those who share his great spirit, to flourish. This land is Liberia in Western Africa where missionaries, both Black and white, carry the message of the Gospel to those poor African wretches who have been living in the darkness of sin. Will you help us to be luminaries in this land so all children of God may shine His light and gain access to prosperity?"

The pitch didn't last long. It didn't need to. George Brown had inflamed the passions of the congregation already with his powerful message. Reverend Seys had only to pass a basket, which was soon filled.

The cool night air was a relief after the stuffy, packed church.

"Did you donate, James?" Sylvanus asked the question with a smirk as the four friends walked out into the night.

James perked up and smiled, a ghastly expression given the mess of his blackened and swollen eye. "As a matter of fact, I did."

Wilson slapped him on the back. "Old Grimes scare you that bad?"

"No," James said. "Well, maybe. But I donated because I think it's a great idea."

"You do?" Sylvanus said, taken by his arrogant friend's admission of a change of heart.

"Look, I know some Black men are exceptions, that not all are well suited for slavery. Clearly this man Brown is one such example. But the problem is free Black men cause trouble for their lesser brothers who are incapable of the kind of advancement these men spoke of tonight. The slaves of the South are like children, really. They cannot survive the world on their own. If the ACS wants to ship all the troublesome free Blacks to Africa, I'm in favor of it. Slavery will be a happier, gentler institution for it."

Wilson shook his head. "You know, you're a real ass, James."

His smirk indicated that James did know.

"Gentlemen," Sylvanus said, heading off the brewing trouble. "You go on. I need to return to the church. I'd like to say a few words to Reverend Seys and Mr. Brown."

Before his friends could ask questions, Sylvanus sprang up the stairs and into the church, now largely empty though a few people had remained to speak to the two missionaries. Sylvanus waited his turn, mulling over James's words. His dichotomy of Blacks held some validity, but then reason dictated the more highly educated would have more intelligence at their disposal. If that were the case, those in slavery would not appear as capable as those outside of it. The hypothesis could not be adequately tested as long as the institution of slavery continued. And, he reasoned, it mattered little if Southern slaveowners were enthusiastic about recolonization if it provided a good opportunity for America's free Black men and for the furthering of God's kingdom throughout the world.

"Reverend Seys." Sylvanus reached out to shake the superintendent's hand and found the minister's grip firm and sturdy. "My name is Dr. Sylvanus Goheen. I would like to hear more about your mission."

"Doctor?" John Seys was older than Sylvanus by more than a decade, but young for one so accomplished. His short-clipped hair clung to the rich brown of youth with only a hint of silver at his temples. The enthusiasm with which he now appraised the man whose hand he'd shaken revealed a youthful exuberance undampened by long years. "Are you a physician, then?"

Before this moment, Sylvanus had yet to introduce himself in such a way, nervous to claim the title, but now he was eager to do so. "Yes, sir. I have only just completed my course of study at Jefferson Medical College."

Seys relaxed back on his heels. "Recently completed? Have you established a practice?"

"Not yet. I'm considering my options." As an afterthought, he added, "Praying, actually, for God's guidance. I leave for my home in rural Pennsylvania in a few days, hopefully to discern whether I will practice there or return to a larger city."

"Certainly you should consider your options carefully. Pray about them, too. You are a young man, ready for adventure, I would imagine."

"I do love adventure."

The minister's right eyebrow quirked. "Married?"

"No sir," Sylvanus said, heat rising in his cheeks. "No prospects on that front yet, I'm afraid."

"All in good time, I'm sure." Seys crossed his arms and looked Sylvanus in the eye. "Have you considered joining the foreign missionary service? We are currently seeking to include a physician in our ranks."

Sylvanus felt in him a tug. It might have been a calling, not the literal voice of God, but perhaps a nudge in a direction he'd not considered before, a spark of something warm and inviting accompanied by a swell of confidence.

"Reverend Seys," he said, "would you like to meet my mother?"

Supper at the Goheen farm was rarely such a festive occasion, but there was much to celebrate. For the first time in two years, Mayberry graced their table with his presence, along with his wife Mariah, flush with the glow of her first pregnancy.

Sylvanus, the newly minted physician, felt welcomed even by his mother who had never struck him as a welcoming soul. She was a good sort of woman, he supposed—sturdy and reliable, the kind who could raise a large brood on her own, which was no small task. Of course, Annie had a lot to do with his upbringing, too, and it was she he was most anxious to see upon his return home.

He was proud, too, to be coming home with the distinguished Reverend Seys. His mother's expression reflected a similar emotion when she greeted the reverend, and Sylvanus enjoyed the glow of her pleasure.

"Reverend John Seys, this is my mother Mrs. Elizabeth Goheen."

Seys took her hand warmly in his. "It is a pleasure to meet you, Mrs. Goheen. Thank you for so graciously welcoming me into your home. Your son speaks highly of you. He's quite an extraordinary young man. You must be proud."

Mother's eyes widened slightly. "We are honored to have you with us." Mother performed beautifully, smoothly hiding from Seys the surprise her son could see clearly. "Please come in. We have another minister as well. My son Mayberry is visiting from Baltimore where he serves a congregation. And joining us from Virginia is Mr. Jonas Edwards, a dear family friend."

Seys shook the other visitor's hand and the group exchanged pleasantries. Sylvanus took his turn as well, formally reintroducing himself to the man who had captured his beloved sister's affections. He seemed genial enough. His nose was still crooked, but one couldn't hold that against the man.

As they talked, two more people slid into the sitting room, and Sylvanus's heart soared to catch sight of Annie. She was now twenty-seven, an old maid by anyone's accounting, but she wore it with grace, wisdom shining through a clear complexion the years had yet to dull. She was pretty, he decided, as far as sisters could be pretty. She had fashionable milky skin and her features were well proportioned. She also possessed a bright blue gaze that had a way of cutting through a person as though she could see the thoughts inside a man. What unnerved him when he was young made him grateful now. No one could fool her or dare try. She would be a lovely bride if this lawyer had the sense to snatch her up.

Behind Sylvanus's sister, half hidden by timidity, stood a petite woman with dark skin and large eyes. Annie had written often of Esther, the former slave delivered into their lives by Jonas Edwards. She'd become his sister's project as she taught the woman to read and encouraged her in womanly pursuits. She'd become a living doll of sorts, perhaps a replacement for himself, the previous recipient of Annie's enthusiastic sisterly attention.

Mother introduced the ladies and invited everyone to the table. Sylvanus stole a glance at Annie as she turned to speak to her Mr. Edwards. She appeared happy, more so than Sylvanus could recall seeing her in some time.

He breathed in the scents of comfort and home. The clean country air mingled with the savory smells of roasted chicken, fresh bread, and warm apples. All settled into place—family, strangers, and friends, both Black and white, a great contentment seeped into Sylvanus as he ate, listening to elevated men speak of elevated things.

"You are a missionary, sir? What is your field?" Mr. Edwards took command of the conversation and turned it to Reverend Seys.

"I am." Seys set down his fork. "I serve in Liberia where I coordinate the efforts of many small mission settlements among the natives as well as recruit both Black and white missionaries from the United States. And, of course, freed men who wish to emigrate."

"I see." Mr. Edwards touched the side of his nose and frowned. "And do you feel your efforts are worthwhile?"

"Oh, yes. It's the most important work of my life."

"How is that, Reverend Seys?" Mother asked as she placed her water glass on the table.

"It's a wonderful concept, recruiting and training Black men who lack not intellect nor drive, but only opportunity. We provide them with tools so they might spread the Good News of the Gospel to their African brethren."

"I think it sounds like a wonderful program," Mother said, but the countenance of Annie's Mr. Edwards darkened as Reverend Seys spoke.

"Yes," Edwards said with barely the flicker of a look at Mother. "It does on the surface sound like a wonderful idea. I'm sure the natives appreciate the attention." He shifted in his chair. "Certainly, there is a great need on the darkest of continents for the message of Christ. But do you not find you are performing a terrible disservice to your own countrymen?"

"What do you mean by that?" Sylvanus asked the question, shocked at the audacity and disrespect coming from Edwards whose presence suddenly felt like an intrusion.

"There is a far greater cause here in the United States." Edwards stared directly at Esther as he spoke these words. The young woman shrank under his scrutiny. "One that must be the priority of all men of God."

A blush rose on Annie's porcelain cheeks. Sylvanus could almost physically feel the heat of her discomfort but resisted the urge to comment. He recalled keenly another meal with a different young suitor. He didn't want to receive the blame for another budding romance soured.

Seys, however, didn't wait a beat to respond with steady tone to the concerns raised. "You must refer to the call for abolition. I assure you, the American Colonization Society and the Methodist Episcopal Mission Board both heartily support and pray for that great cause. Slavery is a terrible sin on the conscience of America, and it will one day be reckoned."

"Here, here," added Mayberry, raising his glass to a point of agreement on which to end a contentious conversation.

Edwards proceeded without acknowledging the blatant hint. "Then how can you propose removing from our shores the very people whose presence might most effectively serve to bring it to a swift and decisive end?"

Sylvanus's pulse quickened with a flash of anger, but John Seys calmly finished chewing before answering the accusatory question.

"I don't deny abolition is a necessary and noble cause, nor that its success will depend on the extraordinary efforts of extraordinary individuals, both Black and white. We can and should allow space for God's calling to work upon individuals. Both causes are just and in need of souls to carry them out."

Jonas Edwards responded only by shaking his head.

Seys followed up his argument with a question of his own. "Can we not offer Black men and women in this country the opportunity to live the lives they desire? They can remain in the United States and work for change, for freedom in this land, or they can work in Liberia to save the souls of those who live in darkness and pursue freedom far from the shadow of American slavery."

A vein bulged in the forehead of Annie's suitor. "You are naïve to assume so many free Black people would wish to be removed from the only home they've ever known." Again, he cast a pointed look at Esther, her head bowed with her eyes on her largely untouched plate. "Most were born in the United States. They know nothing of Africa, of the ancestors who sold them into their lowly states as slaves."

The missionary crossed his arms, his food momentarily ignored as he sized up this surprise supper table adversary. "We are not forcefully removing anyone of any color from these shores to deliver them to another. We are simply providing a pathway for proud Black sons of the Heavenly Father to serve Him in a new and exciting way."

Jonas Edwards's deep sighs and frequent shifting in his chair made clear that rage bubbled beneath his skin, seeking an outlet he was unable to find. Sylvanus found the impotence utterly unappealing. He stole a glance at his sister. Her eyes darted between the two arguing men, her expression inscrutable.

"I know about your program." Edwards spat venom with every word. "I know what it does. It eliminates problems. It takes the people whose presence distresses those blinded by their unholy defense of slavery and removes them so neither those they offend, nor those they could inspire, will see them in their midst. The Southern slaveholders love this program. It solves a problem for them—the problem that when people begin to see those with dark skin behave in human ways—when the truth of common humanity is on display—slavery crumbles. If this is not foremost in your ministry, you are terribly misguided."

Sylvanus clenched and unclenched his hands beneath the table. He did not know John Seys well, but he'd listened to the man speak. He'd traveled with him and met one of the remarkable colored men he worked with. The missionary was honorable. All Jonas Edwards had going for him were his designs on Annie and an unfortunate nose.

"Thank you for this lively conversation, gentlemen, but I think it's been quite enough." Mayberry cut into the argument, earning him an appreciative look from his mother. "The ladies will grow tired of us."

Seys dipped his head in acknowledgment. "I do apologize, Mrs. Goheen. I fear I'm too easily engaged in such discussions. Mr. Edwards's concerns are echoed throughout the church, and it is important we continue to engage in the debate, but it's not necessary to do so at the supper table."

"Thank you, Reverend Seys." Sylvanus's mother turned her attention next to Edwards in obvious expectation, but when he opened his mouth to speak, it was with a vinegar that made Sylvanus's blood rise again.

"I disagree I'm afraid, with much of what you say. This is a crucial discussion, and it should be carried on everywhere and loudly until it is settled. The issue of abolition supersedes all others. Additionally, however, I believe Mayberry's assertion that such a conversation will bore the women is not only incorrect but insulting."

Mayberry's mouth dropped open, but a steadying touch from his wife stayed him.

Either Edwards did not notice his host's discomfort, or it didn't concern him. He plowed on. "Intelligent women engage frequently at more impassioned levels than we men when important issues arise. Their influence and partnership is invaluable."

He paused here in his speech. No one else said a word, waiting for the next audacious and insulting thing he might say about the family and its guests.

Jonas looked to Annie. His face softened as his lips curved into a smile Sylvanus didn't trust.

"In fact," Edwards said, "I have long wished for such a capable and intelligent partner. As we are all gathered here today, I'd like to ask Ann if she might be that partner. Miss Mary Ann Goheen, would you do me the honor of becoming my wife?"

The silence following this shocking question was all-consuming. Sylvanus's jumbled thoughts became a buzz. *What sort of man would ask the most intimate of questions in such an inappropriate way?* Edwards had placed his dear sister into a difficult situation, for after his abominable behavior, she must decline him.

Sylvanus studied her face and then all those around the table. Esther beamed at her friend, her joy catching him off guard. Elizabeth Goheen, too, appeared radiant and shared a disturbing look with Mariah. Perhaps they had not been as surprised by the question as Sylvanus had been.

As the eldest, Mayberry should have spoken up, should have reminded this troublesome Edwards that this was a conversation best held privately. Of course, a suitor would not have been expected to speak to Sylvanus about his intentions, but no one knew Annie better nor cared more strongly about her future than he. This was his moment. He should say something, add to the breaks in decorum, to the social chaos already created. He should come to Annie's rescue and had decided to do just that when she spoke.

"I will gladly become your wife."

Edwards stood and rounded the table toward her, reaching for her hand as she rose to meet him. "You have made me the happiest man."

Annie blushed, shy in this awkward moment as any fine lady should be but also as a woman drowning in the shadow of a looming mistake. Edwards, a smug sort of victory written on his face, slid his eyes from Annie toward Seys.

Sylvanus could not prevent this terrible turn in events, but he would not allow this man his triumphant moment. Pushing away from the table, he stood.

"Well, since this has become a night of big news, I have something I would like to share as well. Reverend Seys has asked me to consider joining the efforts of the Mission Society and I have decided to accept. I will use my medical skills and my enthusiasm for this noble effort to further the cause of colonization.

"As soon as possible, I will travel to Liberia."

9

Annie

Annie flitted from jubilation to grief in the space of each breath. Tonight, she had gained everything she wanted—a future with a worthy man, one who saw her neither as property nor burden, but as a partner in the most important of pursuits.

At the same time, she suffered a tremendous loss. With his announcement, Smee had not only committed his life to a dangerous mission at the edge of the world from which he might never return, but in doing so, he expressed his condemnation of her own choices and had declared his intention to cling to wrong thinking.

On what should have been the happiest night of her life, she was angry and hurt and sad.

"What you thinkin', Miss Annie?" Esther pulled on her nightgown and climbed into bed beside her.

Annie turned to her friend. "What *are* you thinking? And it's just Annie," she reminded her for what must have been the thousandth time. "Sisters don't address one other as 'Miss.'"

Esther threw up her hands. "That's the last thing you need to be worried 'bout, *Annie*. You've been pinin' over that man for more than a year and now he want you to be is wife."

Annie raised her eyebrows, never willing to let a teachable moment slip by.

Esther playfully cocked her head to the side. "He *wants* you to be his wife. You should be happy."

"I am," Annie insisted. "I want to be Jonas's wife, more than anything, but my brother is unhappy."

"Yes, he is, but the rest of your family is happy. They've been tryin' to marry you off for a long time."

Annie rolled her eyes. "Did you see the look on Mother's face? She's probably in her room crying for joy."

"She's not cryin' because you're getting married." Esther sat thoughtfully, propped against the head of the bed. "She's cryin' because her baby boy is movin' across the world."

"Mother doesn't spill tears over her sons. They are strong and capable and will change the world."

"I may not be a mama, but I had one once. Brothers, too. Mamas never stop worrying about their babies, especially not their youngest."

"Mother and Sylvanus don't have that kind of relationship."

"Oh, yes they do. You may not see it, but in your mama's heart, yes they do. She's sad he's leavin."

Annie wasn't so sure. She lay on her side and studied her friend, looking straight into her shining brown eyes. "Esther, you didn't say a word at supper."

"No one asked me to."

A lump formed in Annie's throat. "I'm sorry. Even at a Godly table where all are welcome, society's ill manners persist." She clasped the other woman's hand. "You know you are always invited to participate in the conversation."

"Yes, ma'am." She pushed out her feet and lay flat on the mattress, her eyes trained on the ceiling, her hands flat against the quilt.

Annie squeezed her hand.

"I am asking now. What do you think of colonization? Do you think it's a good idea, or like Jonas, do you think it sets back the movement to end slavery?"

The Black woman closed her eyes for a moment before answering. "I cannot imagine a day when slavery will end. I say if colored folks who got their freedom want to use it to go to Africa, then that's what having freedom is for. They should go."

"Would you ever want to move back to Africa?"

Her eyes flew open, her brow furrowed, and when she turned her face to Annie, she might have been looking into her soul. "I've never been to Africa in the first place, so I can't go back there. Thanks to your Jonas and by some miracle of God, this is my home.

"Freedom looks different to different folks."

Mother spoke little over the next few days, lost perhaps in her own form of grief. Annie played the role of the hostess and found that even under the weight of Jonas's misgivings and her best judgment, she liked John Seys. When he preached a sermon at their church, he did so with conviction. Pockets opened up as he won the congregation to his cause.

She recognized, even if her brother's drastic decision had been wrongly motivated, that John Seys believed with great conviction in his cause. She could respect him for that and would simply choose to pray for his deliverance from ignorance.

It remained true that Southern slaveholders rallied alike to the cause of colonization. Prominent abolitionists spoke out against the American Colonization Society and all it stood for.

Sadly, her own family was divided. Mayberry, living and preaching now in slave territory, spoke of the benefit of offering a way out of slave ownership for those Southerners opposed to the institution but trapped by statutes and societal expectation to continue engaging in it. These well-meaning people, he argued, could free their slaves and send them to Africa without opposition. Like John Seys, he believed the two movements could complement one another. John Wesley, however, agreed with Jonas that any system designed to remove free Blacks from American soil would only set back a far greater cause than individual liberty.

Away from home as they were, she could only guess what side of the argument her brothers Davis and William might fall on. The thought brought into sharp focus the even greater physical distance that would soon exist between her and Smee. In her nightmares, she saw him crossing the ocean, tossed by merciless waves and delivered into the hands of naked cannibals.

Smee stood steadfastly by his new mentor and would engage in little discussion of the subject. She feared his motivation came not from Christian calling, but from the draw of adventure and an opportunity to distinguish himself among his brothers. Or worse, to upstage her own happy news. She was frightened for him, for his impending journey, but also that she had lost the closeness they'd once shared.

For days, she prayed for a way to cautiously raise her concerns with him. She thought perhaps an opportunity had presented itself when she saw him enter the sitting room. She followed, pausing for a moment in the doorway. He wasn't alone as she had believed but was conversing with Reverend Seys.

Both men looked at her when she entered the room, the reverend laying aside a folded newspaper and standing to greet her. Smee observed no such ceremony.

"Annie." Smee's attention flicked toward her and away again. "I will write to the board today." He spared her barely another glance as he stood and fled the room, a gesture that made her heart ache.

"Miss Goheen, what a lovely morning it is."

"Yes, it is." She sat on the sofa.

Only after she settled did Seys regain his seat.

"My mother tells me you will be leaving tomorrow morning."

"I will. I have enjoyed your hospitality, but it's time for me to move on. I'm expected for a lecture series in New York next week and hope to be sailing soon after. I've been on leave for nearly two months. I fear my presence is much needed at the mission."

"And Sylvanus will be going with you?"

Seys studied her. "Only as far as New York for now. The mission board will interview him and review his qualifications. It will be up to them to make a final recommendation as to your brother's fitness for foreign mission work."

Annie's heart surged with hope. "You mean he may not be accepted?"

He shook his head. "It's difficult to say what the board will decide on any matter, but your brother is a strong candidate. As a physician, he also fills a desperate need for the Liberia mission. It helps that—"

"He has your endorsement."

Reverend Seys pursed his lips. "Miss Goheen, I know you are conflicted about colonization."

"I'm not." Her eyes met his with a challenge.

"I understand." He did not look away, but his expression held warmth. "You fear for your brother."

She answered him with the kind of silence that says much.

"I will miss your family's hospitality, Miss Goheen. I can see you share a great deal of love between you. I suspect you also trust one another. Sylvanus is a fine young man. He'll thrive in Liberia, and I promise I will look after him. He will be a member of my family as I have been a part of yours."

"Your family is in Liberia?"

"Our missionaries are a family, of course, but my wife and three of our children are there."

The thought of this man placing his own family into the hands of God an ocean away calmed her nerves somewhat. "Is it really safe enough?"

"Our mission house in Monrovia is well established, and we have a working relationship with the nearest native tribes. It is as safe for women as for men. In fact, two white women are training to work with us and will soon be teaching both missionary and native children."

"And is it a healthful environment?"

At this question, Reverend Seys leaned forward in his chair and took a little time before answering with what seemed a carefully crafted response.

"The native population is remarkably healthy. Emigrants and missionaries, we have found, do experience an adjustment period in the climate. Often newcomers fall ill early in their residency and may exhibit symptoms of fever and weakness. It comes and goes."

"And do people die from this illness?"

He swallowed hard. "What you must understand, Miss Goheen, is that those answering God's call into the mission field are doing so with glad hearts and willing spirits. Yes, some have died, but they have met their reward at the gates of Heaven with joy at the end of a race well run. There is risk in the work of the Lord."

Her heart pounded. She wanted to scream. "How can you ask so much of people? How can you ask it of your wife and children? Of my brother?"

He closed his eyes for the briefest of moments and clasped his hands before answering. "It is not I who ask, Miss Goheen, but God. My wife Hannah is as tenacious as you. You remind me of her—strong women, both of you. Sylvanus is strong, too. He brings many gifts to our mission."

"You overestimate us both."

"I don't think so. I believe your brother knows what he's facing, and I know he does so with a determined and glad heart. As for you, I just watched you connect yourself with an outspoken abolitionist. Make no mistake, you are also answering a call that will put you in jeopardy, yet you do so without hesitation because you know it is right. It's no different for those of us engaged in the project of colonization. It's no different for my wife."

Annie tried to picture her, this tenacious woman of the jungle with little children in tow. "Is she frightened?"

"I know she must be, though she wouldn't confess it to me. I wonder, Miss Goheen, as you two find yourselves in similar predicaments, would you be willing to correspond with her? She faces hardships and moments of doubt I'm sure she feels she cannot express to her family and closest friends back home. She doesn't want to give them further cause to worry. It would help her greatly to have a friend like you. Also, I imagine you'll find her willing to tell you the things your brother will not about how he is faring. What do you say?" One eyebrow raised. "Will you write?"

Annie smiled in spite of herself. This man had spoken calm and sense into her fears. They were not dispelled, but she could see why Smee would wish to follow John Seys across the ocean and into the unknown.

"I will write to her today."

The sunrise promised a beautiful fall day full of warmth not felt in the Goheen household where the mood was solemn. Having arisen early to see the travelers well fed and provisioned, Annie stifled a yawn as her baby brother finally caught her eye and approached her alone in the midst of gathering the breakfast dishes.

"Annie, might we talk?" He sat at the end of the table and invited her to take a chair as well.

"Shouldn't you be about to leave?"

"I have a few moments. Mother is peppering John with questions."

"That might be a long conversation." She sat across from him, her attempt at levity failing to calm her growing sorrow.

He hesitated, but when she offered no additional comment, he spoke. "I'm sorry if I've appeared distant on this visit."

"You've had much on your mind."

"I have, but then so have you. And I haven't been a good brother."

She didn't know what to say. His behavior had hurt her, but then perhaps she'd not been a good sister to him. She'd not said a word to him about his plans to travel halfway across the world, to die in a foreign land far from everyone who loved him. He must be frightened. She couldn't help picturing him as the often-ignored little boy who sought comfort in the arms of his sister when none was offered elsewhere.

"I—"

"No," he interrupted. "Please let me continue. I let the most important moment of your life slide past, consumed as I was with my own determined revelation. I want you to know that if Jonas Edwards is your choice, then I trust he is a fine and worthy man. Your happiness is all I wish for."

He studied her, his brow furrowed as if she were a fascinating specimen he couldn't identify. "Are you happy?"

"I am." The tension faded from her muscles and for the first time since Smee's return, Annie began to relax in his presence.

"I'm glad."

"Thank you for saying so. He was outspoken against colonization."

"Yes. He's not alone. It's a controversial movement I'm joining."

"Have you stopped to wonder why?" She could hear the pleading in her own voice, but he appeared utterly unaffected. "Could it be that it's wrong?"

He stared at her for a long moment, his sharp and serious eyes cutting into her. "Slavery is wrong. It's a poison in this nation, and though freedom is the treatment, liberty is the cure. There is no true liberty for Black men here. Not now. Possibly not ever. Maybe in Liberia, there is hope."

Tears trembled on Annie's lashes.

Smee reached across the table and took her hand. "It's difficult for me to imagine, too, but yes, I believe the road God wishes me to travel leads to Africa."

She tried a new approach. "You are abandoning your widowed mother."

"Our mother has sons enough to spare."

She sucked in a breath. "So that's it, then. You have a death wish." She would not look him in the eye, this young man who had changed little from the stubborn, precocious child he had been. "Or is it that you believe yourself invincible?"

"Annie," he said with a shake of his head. "Of course not. "

"It's wrong, Smee. I feel it in my bones." Her own honesty shocked her.

"It's liberty and a new beginning. It's a way forward for those who otherwise have none."

"And it's a step backward for those left behind in slavery."

"Then they will need you to fight for them. You and your Mr. Edwards." He stood and for the briefest moment moved as if to embrace her but stopped himself. "I'll miss you, Annie."

She backed away from him and looked long into the chiseled features, which in her heart belonged obscured in baby fat. "Will you?"

"Certainly."

Esther entered the room before she could respond. "Reverend Seys is asking after you, Mr. Sylvanus."

"Thank you, Esther. I'll join him right away." He clasped Annie's hands and locked eyes with her once more. "Be happy."

"I'll be happy when I know you're safe. Write to me?"

"I will."

"And before you sail you will come to my wedding?"

His only answer was a sad smile before he turned to walk out of the room.

She opened her mouth to call after him, to demand a response. It felt critical, somehow, that she receive it, but he was already gone. They'd had their moment of, if not understanding or reconciliation, then at least acknowledgment that they cared for one another. And for the time being, it would have to be enough.

Reverend Seys stood speaking to Mother and John Wesley as Annie emerged from the house. Mother wore a scowl, the brow crease above her nose a telltale sign of her unease. Esther had been right about Mother's fears over the loss of her youngest son to the wilds of the dark continent.

The missionary glanced up and beamed at Annie's approach. "Miss Goheen, I was hoping to speak to you again before I left. I have something for you, a token of my gratitude for your friendship." He handed her a folded sheet of stationary.

"Thank you, Reverend Seys. I wish you a safe journey and a happy reunion with Mrs. Seys and the children."

With a sharp intake of breath, Mother said, "Children? Your children are in Africa?"

"Yes. Three of them. A son and daughter remain here for schooling, but my wife really cannot bear to be without all of them."

"A mother's love is fierce," Mother admitted, her voice uncharacteristically meek. "Even crippling."

Annie's jaw loosened at her mother's vulnerable admission.

Reverend Seys clasped Mother's hand. "God will be with our children—mine and yours."

Mother turned her face away and swiped at her eyes with a clenched handkerchief as the missionary dropped her hand and climbed into the carriage. Smee followed behind him. John Wesley would take the two men to Columbia to catch the train to Philadelphia. Annie couldn't help but wonder if she'd ever see either of them again.

Without her consent, her baby brother had become a man. She already missed him—the boy he had been, the boy who had needed her. She waved as the carriage rolled down the road away from the farm. Only after it was out of site and Mother and Esther returned to the house did she remember to open the folded paper in her hands.

On it, in a neat hand was a poem:

Yes! I'll leave my name behind me
Worthless as that name may be;
Perhaps it may sometimes remind thee,
Of one you ne'er again may see!

But with that name—dear sister, let me
Leave on fervent prayer for thee;
For though I go—I'll ne'er forget thee
Where e'er my checkered lot may be.

May grace almighty e'er support thee,
Perfect love thy soul inflame
Religions charms forever court thee—
For thy heart—dwell Jesu's name!

May those so lov'd—kind heav'n spare thee,
Parents—Brothers—all bless'd;
And in the family above—there be
Forever in Eternal rest.

Columbia 24 Sept 1838—

Though Annie may not agree with his mission or his wooing of her brother to his cause, it was difficult to hold a grudge against a man who wrote her poetry.

She tucked the verse into her pocket and returned to the sitting room where she began penning a letter to Mrs. Hannah Seys, expressing her gratitude that she'd had the opportunity to meet the reverend and know her brother was joining a cause with such passion behind it.

It was all she could manage. Where had her baby brother, who once believed she knew everything, gone that this strange man with backward ideas had taken his place? But then it was natural, was it not, for a brother and sister to grow apart as they emerged into adulthood? She believed that, with conviction, for nearly ten seconds before her tears began to fall.

She thought then about writing to Jonas, hopeful that pouring out her anguish to him might help her to put it in perspective, but looking over the page in front of her, she hesitated, unsure of how to express it to him in a way he might understand. He'd been adamant that Smee was doing not only the wrong thing for his own family, but the way he spoke, her brother might even be betraying his own country and the cause of freedom.

She feared for both men. Jonas had returned to the South where his abolitionist activities made him a target for abuse. Smee rode swiftly to his first stop on his way to Liberia, half a world away.

She set aside her writing. Perhaps she would pen her letters another day.

10
Sylvanus

His eyes stung in the salty breeze as he watched the great ship move slowly out of the port. Only the cajoling of Sylvanus's old friend Garnet Wilson snapped him from the melancholy that had overtaken him.

"An early supper, then? And perhaps a whiskey?"

Sylvanus nodded. "I won't say no to the supper."

He followed Wilson into a hired carriage and allowed himself a moment to relax in the sanctuary from the wind and disappointment.

Wilson sat back with a sigh. "You'll be on your way soon enough."

He could only shake his head and wonder at his friend's ability to sense the source of his trouble.

"Sylvanus, you're the most talented physician I know. I mean it. This board will let you go."

"I'm by far not the most talented physician you know. And, yes, I think they will, but what am I to do in the meantime? Rest on my oars? How many people will die in Africa for lack of the care I can provide?"

His friend laughed. "Well, you're certainly the most arrogant physician I know. Even you won't cure all that ails an entire continent."

Sylvanus rolled his eyes. "You know what I mean. Monrovia. The mission. There's been so much loss."

"And there's sure to be more." Wilson waved a hand in front of his face as if he couldn't possibly be concerned about death on a far continent. "Look, are you even sure you want to do this? The last time we spoke about the future, you were resigned to taking over a practice in Middle of Nowhere, Pennsylvania. Then you hear one lecture and you're ready to board a ship bound for the other side of the world? It doesn't make a lot of sense."

"You sound like my mother."

"I just want you to think it through. It doesn't have to be Pennsylvania, but there are alternatives to Liberia."

"But why not Liberia? I'm needed there. I'm young. I don't have a family or commitments. I'm the ideal candidate."

"You're not the only young, uncommitted doctor in the world. Besides, you stick with me for a while, you might find yourself willing to be a little more committed. Evelyn's got a lot of friends."

He shook his head at his friend's reference to his high society fiancée. Both members of prominent families, Wilson and his bride-to-be had been practically betrothed for years, making it official once his medical training came to an end. Initially, Sylvanus suspected his friend might be rushing into marriage, but he couldn't deny the young lady's charms, nor the appeal of having a life so well laid out. Within a few months, the handsome young couple would wed, establish a home, and start filling it with beautiful babies.

Sylvanus would be lying to himself if he didn't admit such a future sounded nice, but he didn't mind lying to Wilson.

"You're trapped in a life already mapped out until your death as a fat old, retired physician with a shriveled wife, a sprawling home, and two dozen grandchildren."

The carriage stopped. Wilson grinned before stepping out. "You ask me, that's a fine picture."

"Well, I didn't ask you."

Sylvanus sat, a solitary figure on a lone, bare bench that served as the only furnishing in the cold hallway stretching between two office doors at the back of New York City's John Street Church. Across from him stood a third door leading into the choir loft and sanctuary altar, beyond which twenty-two men held in their hands the fate of the young physician.

After weeks of preparation and much waiting, and watching with a heavy heart as a ship sailed from sight bearing John Seys and George Brown into the horizon leading to Africa, at last he would receive the decision of the Missionary Board. Apprehension swirled in his unsettled stomach. He'd written to his family, to Annie and his mother and brothers about his growing determination to follow God's call to Liberia. Their letters to him spoke of the details of home and their wish for his good health, disappointment and fear creating silent etchings between lines of script.

Only his brother Davis wrote words of encouragement. His family largely seemed to feel as his old friend Garnet Wilson did. Wilson labored long hours in his burgeoning medical practice, healing where he could and comforting where he could not. It was important work which came with a fair bit of prestige, not to mention the pretty fiancée.

Sylvanus didn't know what his future might hold, an exciting thought, but frightening as well. He could have taken over Dr. Thompson's practice in Columbia, could have lived near his family and established one of his own. He still might, if the board declared him an unfit candidate for foreign missions. He felt ill at the thought.

The door to the choir loft opened with a sharp creak.

"Dr. Goheen, please join us." A man with a serious scowl who had introduced himself earlier as Reverend George Pittman beckoned him. Sylvanus followed through the door, down the steep steps from the loft, and around the back side of the altar, trying to slow the rapid pace of his heart.

At his escort's invitation, Sylvanus sat on a chair placed in front of the altar so that he faced the members of the mission board lined up in the pews. He studied the faces of these men who in this moment he could think of only as adversaries, each of them an ordained preacher, a man called by God to be a leader of souls. If anyone held the power to dissuade him from his current hopes, it was these men.

He disliked them.

"Dr. Goheen, we have all read your statements regarding your faith and desire to enter the mission field." The man who spoke wore a dark suit and a darker expression beneath thick eyebrows and wild hair.

Sylvanus did not breathe in this pregnant pause as he awaited the assessment of his answers to their probing questions. It was as if he were seeking ordination, which he most certainly was not. He felt no compulsion to the pulpit. He was a man of scientific inquiry, of applied medicine, and it was for this skillset he hoped God might make use of him.

"None among us doubts your sincerity."

The young physician let out his breath.

"You are a man of conviction, strong in your faith, and you possess a skill desperately needed by our African mission."

Finished with his piece, the speaker abruptly sat and exchanged glances with his colleagues, leaving Sylvanus to fear an upcoming shift.

A second man stood in the pews. He was a smaller, cheerier sort with eyes that smiled even as his mouth maintained a stern line. "Dr. Goheen," he said with a respectful deference, "I'm sure you sense hesitation in Reverend Wheeler's words. Please understand this comes not from your qualifications as a servant minister of God. You have impressed this committee, as you impressed Superintendent Seys. Our hesitation comes only from an understanding of the enormity of the task set before you.

"In the many years of the Liberian Mission, this society has lost nearly every white man it has sent into Africa. They understood the risks they undertook in the name of the Lord, but it is important you understand, Dr. Goheen, the land to which you wish to travel is the white man's graveyard.

"Your soul will be sustained by our Heavenly Father, but the devil may well attack your body. You will be a modern-day Job."

"Sir," Sylvanus responded, tamping rising panic, "is that not precisely why God would call a trained physician to this mission?"

Several heads nodded.

"Yes, the board believes as you do. We only wish to make certain you fully understand this commitment."

"I assure you I do." The words bespoke a boldness he did not fully feel, but the sentiment did not entirely originate from him. It arrived, as did his confidence, from a divine source, much larger than himself. He could no more resist it than his heart could avoid beating.

"And sir, are you willing to undergo training for a period of six months at the New York Hospital to supplement your medical education?"

"Is that necessary?" He nearly choked on disappointment. He heard in himself the attitude of a petulant child. Philadelphia was the heart of the medical field, the center of professional training. What he could possibly learn from another half year in New York, he couldn't fathom, and he told the arrogant reverend so, sparking a great deal of murmuring discussion among the board members.

The reverend hushed the crowd with a glare before he fixed his eyes back on Sylvanus. "We do not doubt your training. There is an expert, an outstanding physician, whose work with fever treatment, he feels has great potential against the African sickness that plagues our missionaries. We only wish for you to meet with him, learn what you can from him."

Sylvanus considered the words, the sting of the offensive implication of the insufficiency of his own training still fresh. Without enthusiasm, he nodded his willingness to comply.

The reverend took his seat, a satisfied grin on his face as his larger colleague, the original speaker, rose again to address the room.

"Then, if there is no one else wishing to address the good doctor..." He paused, but no one offered another word. "I am honored to announce the decision of the Missionary Society of the Methodist Episcopal Church to commission Dr. Sylvanus Goheen for service in its Liberian Mission.

"Congratulations, sir, and may God go with you."

11
Annie

"Annie, you have lost your mind. What can a freeborn man want with a dark-skinned slave girl like me?" Esther picked up a clump of dirt from the garden bed they'd been preparing for springtime planting and crushed it between her hands before letting it fall again.

Months had passed since Esther Smith first met Bennett Miller. Much to Annie's delight, the man had become smitten, and recently he had asked a serious question.

Annie, shovel in hand, shook her head. "He doesn't see you as a slave. He sees you as a person—as a beautiful, graceful woman with much love to share."

The corners of Esther's mouth turned up, but she shook her finger at Annie as if the compliment only served to further distress her. "He's a fool."

"You have caught his eye already. There's nothing you can do about it now." Annie pushed the shovel into unturned soil. "What did you think he was up to all those times he walked you home? A good man is in love with you. You can either be happy about it or break his heart."

"He is handsome." Esther's fingers worked the edge of her apron. "I don't know how to be a wife."

"I don't either," Annie assured her. "But if at my age I can accept Jonas and plan for a long life with him, then you can overlook the darkness in your past and do the same with Bennett. You're a free woman, and free women get to love whomever they wish."

"I'm scared." Esther said it so quietly Annie could barely hear her. "Every day I'm scared they'll find me, snatch me back, and I'll lose all of this."

Annie dropped the shovel, draped her arm around her dearest friend, and gave her a squeeze. "I'd never let that happen. Neither would Bennett. We both love you. You and I will be brides together. I can't imagine a more wonderful blessing."

Esther's eyes widened and a smile blossomed.

Annie giggled. "What did you say when he asked?"

"I said I needed to think."

"That's a perfectly proper response."

"But he looked so hurt. His whole face went dark."

"I doubt it was so serious." Annie took Esther's hand in hers. "But if you don't want to be his wife, then refuse him. Don't get married on my account. You have the freedom to choose your own path."

A small beam of light broke through the cloud in Esther's expression. "Growing up, I never dreamed of loving a man, of having a home and a family. I knew I could never have those things."

"And now you can. If you want them." Annie swallowed a growing lump in her throat. The joy she felt at her own impending marriage expanded at the vision of Esther settled into a happy future with a good man.

"I do." Esther's voice dropped again to a whisper, and the words felt all the more precious for it.

"Good." Annie picked up the shovel. "Then tell that man of yours the good news. And let's plan our weddings."

When Elizabeth Goheen learned she would be the mother of two brides instead of one that spring, the delight on her face revealed more warmth than her daughter thought possible.

"It's wonderful news!" The older woman swept Esther into a hug and wasted no time before making plans. "You'll need a new dress, something beautiful, but practical. And then there are your linens to think of."

There would be no stopping this woman as her head filled with lists of tasks that tripped out of her mouth as fast as Annie could write them down. All she and Esther could do was what they were told, spending their evenings piecing and then quilting two matching wedding ring patterned quilts, one for the marriage beds of each new couple.

The days of early spring were pleasant ones at the Goheen home. Among Annie's brothers, only John Wesley remained full-time on the farm, giving the three women ample time to enjoy together as the warmth of summer approached.

Plans for the double wedding consumed all three of them, and Annie found it difficult at times to focus on her teaching with the date looming. The happy event had been set for early June, the soonest Jonas could both prepare a suitable home in Virginia and take care of enough loose ends with his business to travel again to Philadelphia, this time with the intention of returning home with a new bride.

Unwilling to separate from her dearest friend before they must, Esther had wished to wait until June for her own wedding. Bennett had reluctantly agreed.

Together, the three women stitched and planned and dreamed, enjoying their last days all together.

"How are your students coping with the news of your leaving, Annie?" Mother asked on a Sunday afternoon as she pinned the hem on what would be her daughter's wedding dress. At Mother's insistence, it was the most extravagant dress she'd ever owned: a deep blue gown with a slim, beribboned waist and large, wispy sleeves. It was of a style suitable for many social events to follow on the arm of her respected lawyer husband.

"Well enough, I suppose," Annie replied from the stool where she stood enduring the tugs of Esther and Mother working the fabric of her skirt. "The younger ones are sad. I think some of the older ones are relieved and hoping I might not be replaced."

Around several pins clinched between her lips, Esther asked, "Miss Elizabeth, didn't you teach at the school?"

"Yes," Mother replied. "I taught for several years after Mr. Goheen passed, long enough for Annie to grow into the role." Annie blushed when Mother added, "In truth, she's an abler teacher than I was."

"Would you ever do it again?" Esther asked.

"No, I don't think I'm what the community needs anymore. Back then it was a perfect solution. I'd had enough education to qualify, and I had farmland with no one to work it and six children to feed. I needed support from my neighbors, and they needed a teacher for their children."

"But you wanted to teach?" Annie asked a more personal question than she'd normally dare and held her breath waiting for an answer she wasn't sure would be forthcoming.

Mother smoothed her side of the skirt and stood. "Well, it was better than marrying Patrick Duncan."

Annie twisted to look at her, causing Esther to grunt in frustration as the hem slipped from her fingers. "Mr. Duncan asked you to marry him? He had to have been twenty years older than you."

"Yes, he was. And he did. I might have been the lucky widow Duncan with an army of stepchildren and probably several more of my own to raise." Mother looked both young ladies in the eyes before adding, "Not that children aren't a great blessing."

Annie's mind reeled at the revelation that she had narrowly escaped living with a crusty old stepfather whose yellow teeth and wild lion's mane of white hair used to frighten her in church. "But why would he ever think you'd take him seriously? Why would he even ask?"

"Because men are convinced women are incapable of wanting anything for themselves more than marriage. And, Annie, because your father had the foresight to leave the farm to me, which made me an attractive prospect for a wife.

"Who knows? I might have considered remarriage if there'd been anyone worth having, but it turns out, your father was beyond compare."

"He'd have married you for your farm?"

Mother fluffed the skirt of Annie's dress and bid her to straighten so Esther could finish pinning the front side. "Don't pretend naiveté, Mary Ann. Yes, like most men, Mr. Duncan would have married me for my land and for whatever guidance I might offer his children. Men can be maddeningly practical with their affections. I was fortunate in love the first time, as are both of you. You are marrying fine men who will cherish and care for you as you deserve."

Esther reached for Mother's hand. "Mr. Goheen sounds like a good man. I wish I'd known him."

"I wish that, too, Esther. You'd have liked each other."

Annie nearly missed the tender moment as memories simmered inside her. "There was so much tension," she said. "Back then."

Mother dropped Esther's hand and crouched again beside the last unpinned portion of the dark blue hem. "Yes, there was. My family thought I was a fool not to remarry, but when the teaching position became available, I recognized an opportunity. I could remain single, which I felt honored your father and could more thoroughly supervise the education of my sons while offering a useful skill to my daughter."

"But didn't you enjoy teaching? At least a little bit?"

"It wasn't about what I enjoyed. I cared for the students, and I appreciated the way the position allowed me to provide for my family, but I wouldn't choose to reenter the classroom now. Someone younger, with more energy, would be much better. I'm just an old widow lady with sons aplenty to care for me."

And maddeningly practical with her affections, Annie thought.

12

Sylvanus

An unseasonable chill bit at his ears as Sylvanus leaned against the outside of the hospital building and imagined the ocean spray. He shoved his cold hands deep into the pocket of his coat and longed for the looming warmth and the promise of his journey to Africa. He'd never felt more confident about his decision. Though the weeks of training had been difficult in many ways, he craved the challenge of a new environment, a new way of thinking.

"Dreaming of Africa?" Dr. Knowles stepped through the door and slid beside him.

"Of adventure," Sylvanus answered, knowing the man would consider his answer incorrect. "And warmth."

"I can't understand you, Goheen. Your enthusiasm has never wavered, even under the worst circumstances. You have seen the lowest American men and women can sink, and you remain determined to seek out people of this world who will sink lower still."

Sylvanus could not truthfully claim his enthusiasm had never wavered, but even in the worst moments of his training in New York, his resolve had only strengthened. Again and again, he observed the ravages of disease on the faces of entire families who in their grief lacked the strength to fight their own fiery battles. When he looked at them, he now envisioned the faces of Reverend and Mrs. Seys, their children, rosy cheeks consumed by the deadly flush of fever.

"You and I have a different opinion of humanity," Sylvanus said.

"Indeed, we do."

"If a man's life can be preserved, it ought to be. That is our solemn duty to our patients and to God."

Sylvanus knew Knowles must harbor many of the same thoughts, but his application of them differed greatly. The first lesson the more seasoned physician had taught his reluctant pupil was that death comes for all. Regardless of the tools employed, it was not a fight in which man could be ultimately victorious. The second lesson was that some fights aren't worth the effort.

"Yes," Knowles agreed, "but so much of life cannot be preserved, and we must wrestle with how much to interfere in God's plan."

"If God wishes a man to die, no skillful human physician will prevent it."

In the past nine weeks, the men had borne witness to numerous deaths—mothers and children, poor immigrants and well-heeled gentlemen. The two doled out treatment, the same to all. Dr. Knowles had become an authority in the area of fever treatment, rejecting the notion of bloodletting in favor of medicinal intervention. Patients under his care were subjected to a careful regimen of diaphoretics through the day and tinctures of caustic alkali and nitric acid at night. Like Dr. Thompson in Columbia, Dr. Knowles preferred to use opium sparingly and considered a patient's bowel regularity of utmost importance to health. He routinely ordered cold compresses for fever treatment, monitored sweating, and made occasional use of a newer fever medication made from the bark of the South American quina-quina tree and referred to as quinine.

Sylvanus saw firsthand the remarkable effectiveness of these treatments, miraculous healings in cases his colleagues would have assumed hopeless. Yet sometimes death arrived.

"I believe the same can be said of souls," Sylvanus continued. "If a soul can be saved, then every effort should be extended in the attempt to offer salvation. God is in charge of that as well, but I cannot in good conscience fail to try."

"You may be a better man than I, Goheen. I couldn't do what you're doing. I've seen the medical reports return from Liberia. The white man isn't built for Africa. I say we should ship as many Blacks there as we can, but I don't believe we should be risking white lives to do it."

Sylvanus had read the reports, too. His mere presence in Liberia would not save anyone in soul or in body. He would have to fight for each life, and some battles he would lose. He might even lose the struggle for his own life.

"I'm well aware of your opinion on this subject, but I cannot agree. There are no colored physicians to be found, none anyway who are willing to serve God's church in Liberia. Until such a physician can be discovered, I'll do whatever is in my power to further the opportunity for the gospel to spread and for Black men to thrive in a land that can provide them with opportunity. To thrust men and women who have lived their entire lives in this country into life on a new continent, to establish a colony among natives of that land without any spiritual or physical support would be neglecting our Christian duty."

"Noble speech. I wish you well. I really do."

"Thank you." Sylvanus rubbed his hands together to warm his chilled fingers.

Knowles withdrew a folded letter from the pocket of his coat and handed it to Sylvanus. "By the way, a letter arrived here for you today."

"Here?" He slipped his thumb under the unfamiliar seal and scanned the letter. Knowles stared at the ground, waiting.

"It's from the Missionary Society. I-I am to sail for Monrovia the first week of June from Philadelphia on the schooner *Charlotte Harper*," Sylvanus stammered. "I'm not prepared. I've not served here even three months. They told me six."

Knowles pointed to the letter trembling in his apprentice's hand. "Seems someone has all the confidence in you the Society requires. You're a competent physician, Dr. Goheen. A fool, perhaps, but as good a challenger to the sickness of Africa as you are ever likely to be."

Sylvanus savored the bitterness of the strong coffee as he sat across from his friend and roommate of the last three months. He was glad for the company as he waited for the train to Philadelphia, the first stop on his journey to Monrovia.

"What do you know of your traveling companions?" Wilson asked.

Sylvanus set his cup on the garish saucer with a sharp clink. "Little. Only that there will be two women, missionary teachers, a Mrs. Wilkins and a Miss Beers."

"A month on the ocean with no one to talk to but some weather-beaten sailors and a couple of old schoolmarms? Could be dull."

"Could also be longer than a month. But I'll make the best of it. I have books. And now I will have time to read them." Sylvanus studied his friend's curious expression, dripping as it was with skepticism. "I suspect there will be others traveling. The American Colonization Society is always sending reinforcements. There's sure to be someone interesting among them."

Wilson ran a thumb over the rim of his cup. "It's admirable, what you're doing. Though I don't know if I can agree with the politics of it."

"Has colonization once again fallen out of favor with the abolitionists in the upper crust of New York?"

"I don't know that it was ever in favor, but yes, the rantings against outweigh the support."

"And I am a villain?" Sylvanus asked. "My sister thinks so. Did I tell you she's marrying an abolitionist? In his eyes I am single-handedly maintaining the condition of slavery in the United States."

"You could never be a villain, my friend. I know your intentions are noble." Wilson leaned back in the rickety coffeehouse chair. "In fact," he continued, "I wish I could travel to Philadelphia with you and see you off. Mine could be the last face you see on the shores of America as you sail into the sunrise, never to be heard from again."

"How poetic," Sylvanus teased. "It is truly tragic it won't be your privilege to send me to my untimely death at sea. But don't worry yourself about it. My brother Davis is meeting me. His letter mentioned that if he can convince her, my sister may come along. One of them might even miss me. Either way, I'm sure they'll do enough waving to see me through."

"It gives me great joy to know you'll be in good hands in your last few days on the earth." Garnet Wilson leaned forward again and lifted his coffee cup in a toast. "To a heroic death on the bottom of the ocean."

Sylvanus raised his cup in answer. "Or in lieu of that, to the greatest feast Africa's cannibals have yet enjoyed."

13
Annie

By the last Saturday in May, the weather turned warm and the earth sighed with relief as the final dreary wisps of a cold spring drifted into oblivion. Annie hung fresh laundry to dry and sighed along with it, enjoying the fresh scent of the wisteria finally deigning to bloom.

The farm was at its most beautiful this time of year and she treasured the opportunity to enjoy it in the quiet of the afternoon—the fresh green of young leaves, the trill of familiar birdsong, the warmth of the high sun shining on the house that had been her home for twenty-nine years.

One week from today she would leave its protection, no longer only a daughter, a sister, but from then on, a wife. After the wedding, she and Jonas would travel to Philadelphia for a few days to see Smee off on his adventure, a gift Jonas agreed to give her despite his political disagreement with her brother. She loved her intended all the more for it. After the trip, she would return with him to Richmond, his helpmeet and someday, she hoped, the mother of his children.

She pictured her finished wedding gown beside another. Esther's dress was simpler but just as beautiful. She'd chosen a peach fabric that glowed against her dark skin. Mother designed a respectable Sunday dress to flatter the woman's petite frame, and Annie had prayed for the couple's happiness with every stitch.

The two marriages would be celebrated on the same day at the schoolhouse which featured a fresh coat of paint for the occasion. Bennet would have preferred to marry in the African Zion Methodist Church where he worshipped regularly and where Annie and Jonas had met that terrible, wonderful night of the riots, but in deference to his bride who longed to stand to honor their commitment to one another in the first place she'd ever felt free, he'd agreed to the arrangement.

Bennett was a man clearly smitten. In the months since Esther's engagement, her man had made a delightful nuisance of himself. His free moments found him inventing excuses to spend time with Esther. He brought her endless small tokens, from wildflowers to bits of ribbon. Under Mother's ever-keen watch, the two huddled together to share dreams of their future. Annie delighted to see it and longed for the near day when she and Jonas would enjoy a similar closeness.

Jonas's letters had taken a more familiar turn as the wedding day approached. He continued to write of serious things—of his work, both public and veiled—but now he also wrote of his great anticipation at their coming union. He was not one for verse, but she pictured him trapped at a desk in his law office, pouring his longing into even the most mundane reports of the weather in Richmond, a lover's wistfulness in every flick of the pen.

Soon they would vow to cherish one another and she would see his deepening love for her written on his heart and in his expression as plainly as Bennet's shining adoration for his Esther.

Just as she finished hanging the last piece of bedding, she spotted the figure of the besotted Black man walking up the road. Annie grinned as she called for Esther, who rounded the back side of the house.

His shoulders drooped at the sight of her, and he became like a cave collapsing in on itself.

Esther ran toward him but stopped at the subtle shake of his head.

"Miss Annie, it's you I've come to see."

"What is it?"

"Mr. Edwards sent coded word about three new arrivals coming up from Virginia in need of a safe haven. He was to bring them when he came for the wedding."

"I don't expect him for a few more days." When she'd last heard from Jonas, he had written that he would see her soon, that he looked forward to their wedding vows. He'd made no mention of any new arrivals to her, but that was not unusual. He would not commit such plans to paper.

Bennett would not meet her eyes. He pulled off his cap and sighed deeply.

"What are you saying?" Cold seeped into her limbs. "Has something delayed him?"

His eyes darted to Esther who had stopped halfway toward them across the yard. "A rumor reached us about a group of recaptured slaves at the Pennsylvania border. We sent a man to see."

"What did he find?" Annie's arms and legs began to tremble.

Bennett opened his mouth, but no sound escaped. Esther ran to her friend and wrapped her arms around her.

"I'm so sorry, Miss Annie." Tears gathered in Bennet's eyes. He cleared his throat. "They recaptured the runaways. They hanged the white man with them."

Annie heard the words, but she could not understand their meaning. She patted Esther's back in comfort, which only made the small woman cry harder. Bennett's cheeks now were moist and he wrung the hat in his hands.

"You don't think—" The words stuck in Annie's throat.

"I'm sorry." He stepped back and gave the women and their grief more space, and it was this action, this moment of seeing an honorable man step away that caught Annie in the web of anguish woven delicately around her. Her heart ached—a physical ache that expanded through her chest, making it difficult to breathe.

"Jonas isn't due up north until just before the wedding." She shook her head. "It couldn't have been him."

But she knew it was.

She couldn't move, might never move again. She would remain in this spot in front of her family home, held by her dear friend, pitied by the man who had brought news of tragedy. She longed to retreat into the shelter of the house but could not imagine how to get there, how to get anywhere but here, in this single terrible moment.

14
Sylvanus

A survey of his fellow passengers did little to assuage Sylvanus's fears that it could indeed be a long voyage to Africa. The party of adventurers, meeting for the first time at Philadelphia's Pine Street Presbyterian Church, consisted of nine, including an insipid mill builder named Thomas who contributed so little to the conversation he might have vanished into the wall of the church without attracting the notice of his fellows.

Beside him stood the humorless Mr. William Pandeville, sent by the Education Society for Liberia to begin a manual labor school at Bassa Cove, southeast of Monrovia on the Liberian coast. A Miss Annesley was bound for the same settlement, as were the only noteworthy gentlemen among the group. The most promising companion of any interest to Sylvanus, Reverend John Matthias, traveled with his wife and was sent by the American Colonization Society to assume governorship of the area. Dr. Wesley Johnson, whose waxy skin and gaunt features made Sylvanus suspect the man might be ill himself, would serve as assistant physician to the settlement.

Their journeys would end differently from those of the Methodist missionaries bound for the city of Monrovia. Sylvanus would be accompanied to his final destination only by the teachers Mrs. Ann Wilkins and Miss Lydia Beers, charming enough creatures, he supposed, particularly Miss Beers whose sharp eyes held a twinkle of mischief when she smiled.

In various degrees of anticipation, the nine sat and turned their attention to the man who had gathered them. Captain O. Curtis, of the schooner *Charlotte Harper*, introduced himself as such, his hands clasped together in front of his well-fed belly. He was not a tall man, but the silver in his hair served to highlight the confidence in his demeanor that lent him authority, as did his deep baritone which must inspire obedience from all in his command.

"Thank you for meeting with me today. The crew of the *Charlotte Harper* will have her readied in a few days' time. Weather permitting, we'll set sail out of New Castle on Friday."

He launched into a lengthy description of the ship, details lost on Sylvanus, and then proceeded to drone on about his own extensive experience on the sea. Frustratingly lacking from his speech was information about Liberia itself.

"How long can we expect the voyage to last?" Miss Beers injected the question Sylvanus most wanted to ask. He'd heard tales of months-long crossings and hoped for reassurance.

"Difficult to say, Miss. With favorable winds, I have made the crossing to Liberia in as little as three weeks, but I wouldn't rely on less than a month.

"*Charlotte Harper* will be carrying supplies for Bassa Cove, but she's a comfortable enough ship to call home for a while. Of course, some of you may find the sea disagreeable to your stomachs at first."

Dr. Johnson coughed into his hand. Captain Curtis's eyes widened as he took in the sight of the sickly man before turning his attention directly to Miss Beers. "I trust you're all of hardy constitution if your societies are sending you to Africa. You've nothing to fear from the passage."

He leaned back on his heels and twiddled his thumbs. "If there aren't any more questions, I must be off. I've business to see to in this city and will meet you all in New Castle by week's end. You'll no doubt find the accommodations in Philadelphia more comfortable. There's a daily steamer to New Castle when you're ready. Please make sure your things are sent to the ship in a timely manner."

The passengers looked at one another as if expecting someone else to voice the myriad of questions drifting, nebulous, though their heads. No one spoke up, and the captain hurried out the church doors.

"Well," said Governor Matthias, "Our Captain Curtis is somewhat short on charm." He clapped his thighs and stood. "It's been a pleasure to meet everyone. Mrs. Matthias and I would be glad to enjoy supper with all of you and get to know you better. Perhaps we can make some plans to catch this steamer for New Castle. What do you say, Mr. Thomas? Dr. Goheen?"

Sylvanus flushed with pleasure at being singled out. He was briefly tempted to accept the invitation, wondering briefly if Miss Beers would be joining them. He cleared the thought with a shake of his head. "I would be honored, Governor Matthias, but I'm otherwise obligated this evening. My brother works in finance in the city, and my sister will have just arrived with her new husband. I'm to meet them for a heartfelt and teary goodbye."

The governor's face fell, but he quickly recovered his mirth. "We'll miss your company, but there's no greater gift than family. Treasure every moment, Dr. Goheen. It will be a long time until any of us gets another such chance."

The door of Davis's office opened at Sylvanus's approach and his brother spilled onto the street, his expression too glum for the occasion.

"You haven't seen me in four months," Sylvanus complained. "A decent brother might at least pretend to be pleased."

The comment yielded not so much as a crack in his brother's uncharacteristically stony visage. The corners of his mouth drooped, but his arm reached for the half-embrace of well-acquainted men.

Sylvanus stepped back from him, into the shade cast by the awning of the next building on the block. "You look as if someone has died."

In the tension that followed, he could almost see the shape of his words drifting into the ether. He watched Davis's attempt to collect enough strength to deliver what must be terrible news, his breathing slow and deep enough to imply intention.

"Is it Mother?" Sylvanus's mouth became dry at the thought.

"No." Davis shook his head. "No, Mother is well. It's Jonas."

Sylvanus searched his memory for the name, ashamed of the time it took his thoughts to land on the man who by now should be his sister's husband. "What of Jonas?"

"Days before the wedding, he was the victim of a lynching."

"What? Why?"

"He was transporting escaped slaves to the north. He was found out and overtaken."

The impact of the words settled like lead in Sylvanus's stomach. Killing a man for doing right in the eyes of God, this should have caused him outrage, and it did, but nothing outweighed the emotion closing his throat as he conjured the image of Annie, awaiting her groom and receiving this terrible news instead. He longed to see her, to comfort her if he could.

"Is she in Philadelphia?"

"No. She couldn't manage. I'm sorry. It was all such a shock."

"She must be devastated."

Davis's countenance was pale enough Sylvanus should have noticed, but the tension in his brother's face loosened as he spoke. "She's a strong woman, our Annie, but yes, this has been difficult to bear these last few days. I only arrived back in the city myself this morning."

"I should go to her. I can be to Columbia and back in time to sail."

Davis shook his head. "If you go home, will you have the heart to return? In her grief, our sister might ask you to stay. Could you deny her? The Mission Society is relying on you and your skills. There's nothing to be done for Annie outside of prayer."

Sylvanus stifled his inclination to protest. There was wisdom in the words. As a physician he'd been a frequent observer of grief, but rarely had it come this close to him. He longed to sit in silence with Annie, to gather a part of her burden onto himself, but Davis was right to discourage him. God's call pushed him toward Monrovia. Annie mightn't even want her Smee at her side. Their parting, though friendly, had been uneasy. He had not become the man she'd dreamed he would be. Instead, he was a disappointment to her, an embarrassment.

"I'll send a note, of course."

"I'll see she gets it." Davis squeezed his shoulder. "She will appreciate it, Sy. No matter how she feels about Africa, she loves you. Mother, too. You know that."

Sylvanus cleared his throat. "Yes, but thank you for saying so."

The brothers walked on in silence. The exercise worked feeling back into Sylvanus's limbs, and the bustling street around them that had faded from his awareness moments before began to reemerge and demand a forceful lifting of the mood.

"I also know I'm hungry," Sylvanus said. "Where is my brother taking me for supper tonight?"

At last Davis cracked a smile. "Am I buying, then?"

"I'm going to Africa for only God knows how long to eat only God knows what kind of food. I think the least you can do is fill my belly with good American fare before I go."

Thursday afternoon found the Goheen brothers stepping off a steamer in Wilmington into a misty drizzle echoing the mood descending on them.

"Not much of a town, is it?" Davis said.

Sylvanus took in the sight of dilapidated buildings and streets dotted with encroaching tufts of grass and silently agreed. He crossed the road to negotiate the hiring of a hack to deliver them to New Castle, carrying with him great hope they would discover a more picturesque community at the end of their journey, one which he could burn into his memory as the last American town he would set eyes on in a long while.

Fortunately, New Castle offered just what he hoped. Old and beautiful, several churches stood proudly alongside the town's neatly maintained municipal building. The brothers walked past it to find a promising public house with a sign advertising lodging.

"Shall we?" Davis reached for the door. The moment it cracked open, a blurry collection of white and black fur rubbed past them into the space and scuttled happily around the small collection of tables, the intrusion eliciting a frustrated growl from a portly man with impressive mutton chops who stood wiping down the bar.

"You're a menace, you little scrapper!"

The words flew like daggers at the oversized terrier which sat directly beneath the center of table closest to the brothers and cocked its head to one side as if it intended to listen. The mongrel was white with black splotches and had mismatched floppy ears. The black of his left ear drooped to encircle the corresponding eye, and Sylvanus could have sworn the creature smiled at the man who now approached them, his hand outstretched.

Davis clasped the extended hand.

"What can I do for you gentlemen?" the man said, shaking his head, which wiggled the enormous jowls beneath the mutton chops.

The dog answered with a happy yip.

"Bah!" The proprietor fired a look beneath the table. "You, I'll deal with later." He looked back to Davis. "Name's Mitchum."

"Davis Goheen," Davis said. "And my brother Sylvanus."

"You fellas need a drink?"

"A room, please, if you've got one," Sylvanus replied.

Mitchum's eyes scanned Sylvanus. "Yes sir. I have a room. Just for tonight?"

Davis replied, "Yes, please. My brother sets sail in the morning for Africa."

"Africa? In that case, I better get you gentlemen a drink as well."

"He's a missionary."

Mitchum exhaled and offered a curt nod. "Coffee then."

Davis sat and Sylvanus slid into the chair across from him at the near table as the proprietor waddled off to retrieve coffee. The dog leaned into Sylvanus's leg and received a gentle pat for his efforts. For his, Sylvanus got a sloppy lick on the hand.

"Well, little brother, are you ready for your great adventure across the world?"

"Would it upset you if I confess I'm terrified?"

At these words, the dog laid his head across Sylvanus's knee. Sylvanus patted the furry head and slid his fingers over one warm, silky ear to a burr at the base. He began to gently untangle it.

"I'd be shocked if you weren't. Truth be told, I'm scared for you myself." Davis leaned against the back of the chair. "But God is in this, and He'll protect you."

Sylvanus took a long breath. The burr came free in his fingers, and he flicked it to the floor. He debated confiding his true fears to his brother, his fear it had been his own stubbornness and not God's will that had pushed him onto this path leading to almost certain death on a distant continent. Instead, he said, "Yes. God will go with me."

"Now I can confess my jealousy. And also tell you how extremely proud I am."

If Sylvanus weren't mistaken, he saw moisture gathering in the corner of his brother's eyes, a moment of true emotion he might capture in his memories—he, the youngest brother of a noisy and successful brood, had become the object of jealousy and genuine pride. The arrival of Mitchum with two steaming cups of coffee saved Sylvanus from the need to respond.

He reached for his cup and a wet nose bumped against his other hand, worming its way in for another pat. Sylvanus laughed. "Who is this little fella?"

"Bah!" Mitchum said again. The joy on the man's face didn't match the disdain in his voice. "Just a mongrel I made the unfortunate mistake of feeding. He's a friendly little scrapper, but a nuisance."

"Does he have a name?"

"Not one I know of."

The dog perked, as if he knew he was under discussion. His warm brown eyes gazed at Sylvanus from beneath wiggling brows. A name dropped into Sylvanus's mind as clearly as if it had been spoken aloud.

"Hector. I think his name should be Hector."

"Hector it is, Mr. Goheen." The man rubbed his chin and bent to get a better look at the dog, which had settled at Sylvanus's feet to happily engage in licking a front paw. "Seems you've made a friend. Want to take him with you?"

"To Africa? Wouldn't you miss him?" Sylvanus regretted asking the question the moment it left his lips. His mind whispered a hasty prayer the answer would be no.

"Never been my dog. Besides, there's a dozen more like him on the streets."

Davis arched an eyebrow at his brother. "You would have to clear it with Captain Curtis, of course."

Mitchum reached down and scratched Hector's ears. "Oh, I know that old seadog. Been sailing out of here for years. He won't mind. A ship needs a dog."

Sylvanus gave Davis a satisfied grin. The sweet animal at his feet could be nothing other than a sign from God. He would not sail alone into the unknown. He couldn't agree with Mitchum more.

"A ship needs a dog."

15
Annie

The day of the wedding had dawned drizzly and cool, reflecting Annie's mood. Out of consideration for the bereaved, the happy couple had delayed their own wedding, but Annie couldn't expect Esther and Bennett to wait any longer. More precisely, she wouldn't ask it of them, because she knew they would oblige.

What should have taken place with two brides and two grooms in the tree grove beside the church and school had been moved to the African Zion Methodist Church, and Esther commanded all the attention.

"She's radiant," Mother whispered beside Annie.

"She is," Annie replied. "The peach dress was a good choice."

"A bride is always beautiful on her wedding day." Mother grabbed Annie's hand and squeezed. "Bennett is beside himself with joy. They make a handsome couple."

As the preacher pronounced them man and wife before the small collection of witnesses, an uncomfortable knot tightened in Annie's chest. "I think I need to leave," she said.

Mother turned to her sharply. "You will do no such thing."

"I—"

"This is a celebration of Esther's life, of her freedom and her future. A celebration, need I remind you, made possible by the efforts of your Jonas."

Annie stared at her feet and let the reprimand sink into her.

"Lord knows this is a difficult day for you," Mother continued, "but you dishonor his memory if you don't face it with poise." She handed her daughter an embroidered handkerchief. "Now, lift your chin and congratulate your friend. There will be time for sadness later."

Annie took the handkerchief and hoped her tears might give the impression of overwhelmed tenderness as she followed the small crowd outside the church to share a celebration meal served by some of the ladies from the Hill.

Annie and Mother had offered to contribute but Bennett wouldn't hear of it, insisting they had done enough. His kind concern over her feelings exhausted Annie as much as Mother's rebuke had done.

Mother stood speaking with her sons, two of whom had made it to the wedding. Busy with life as a family man and circuit rider, Mayberry had expressed his regrets he could not make the journey. Davis had returned to Philadelphia as the lone sendoff party for Smee, who likely sailed this same day toward the shore of dark Africa and his certain doom. The thought descended on Annie, deepening the melancholy already oppressing her spirit even as she watched Mother, William, and John Wesley laugh together.

Esther settled on the bench beside her and hooked an arm through hers, snapping Annie back into the celebratory moment. "Your face is too sad for a wedding."

Annie forced herself to smile at her friend. "You make a beautiful, perfect bride. Bennett is a lucky man."

Esther beamed for a moment before a shadow fell across her expression. "You should have gone with Davis, said goodbye to your brother."

Annie shook her head. "I wouldn't miss this celebration. I couldn't."

Esther cleared her throat. "I wanted this to be a happy day for both of us."

Annie patted her friend's hand. "And so it is. I wish you so much love and light."

"I'm the lucky one—to have him and to have you, to have a life like this." She laid her head on Annie's shoulder. "You can be sad. We won't mind, Bennett and me. We're sad, too. Jonas was a good man."

"He was." Annie exhaled rapidly as if to clear the air of smoke. "But I am well enough, and today is not about me and my sorrows."

"No. It's about love and family." Esther raised her head and looked Annie in the eyes. This tiny, confident bride was far removed from the escaped slave girl who not so long ago wouldn't have met Annie's gaze. Her heart really did swell with joy. "And if you need to, you go right ahead and cry. God will find you even in the worst of it."

Tears pricked the corners of Annie's eyes. "You really think so?"

"I know it. God saw me to Jonas and to you, and He'll see you through this. You watch for Him." Esther smiled and stood to return to her guests and her new husband, who waited at the other side of the church yard and hadn't taken his eyes off his bride.

Annie pondered the wise words of her fortunate friend and prayed they might be true.

16
Sylvanus

Davis escorted Sylvanus to the wharf the next morning, Hector loping happily beside them. The large ship loomed offshore, waiting and ominous with sailors scurrying about, their features indistinguishable from Sylvanus's vantage point on land.

Governor and Mrs. Matthias waited, in conversation with a lanky sailor whose gaze took the measure of the two brothers. He extended a weathered hand to Davis. "You must be Dr. Goheen. I'm Mr. Kennedy, first mate of the *Charlotte Harper*. You're the final passenger I'm expecting."

Davis shook the first mate's hand. "I'm afraid I'm only Mr. Goheen, sir, the proud brother of the good doctor."

Mr. Kennedy turned to Sylvanus and blinked before reaching out a determined hand. "You're younger than I expected."

Sylvanus swallowed a sharp retort and instead acknowledged the first mate with pretend enthusiasm, while viewing his brother with a more critical eye. The two of them shared a number of features, though perhaps Davis's edges were a little more roughened, his skin more leathered, his hair thinner, none of which, in Sylvanus's assessment, made him appear any wiser.

Hector barked once, begging for an introduction. Sylvanus obliged. "Mr. Kennedy, this is Hector, a recently acquired friend. Might he be allowed to board with us?"

The first mate dropped to a knee to address his response to the dog himself, along with a generous scratch behind both ears. "You look to be a sound fella. As long as you keep your maw away from the chickens, we'd be honored to have you aboard."

Sylvanus's annoyance at being confused with his brother vanished at the man's warm reception of the little dog, whose tail wagged fiercely, eliciting smiles from the Matthiases as well.

"It's a pleasure to see you again Governor Matthias. Mrs. Matthias."

"We are to share close quarters for a month or more, Doctor. I insist you call me William."

Sylvanus flushed at the easy acquisition of an ally among the intrepid travelers. "Only if you will call me Sylvanus, of course."

A mouse of a woman, Mrs. Matthias stood dutifully and silently by her husband's side. Sylvanus's thoughts drifted briefly to his sister, to the image of her standing beside her Mr. Edwards, a shadow without agency to speak her mind. Guilt trembled through him at his relief she would not yet face such a fate.

"Mr. Goheen," William said. "It's kind of you to see your brother off. Tell me, what do you make of this great journey we're all about to undertake?"

"I believe it is noble, sir. And I will pray for God's protection over all of you."

The governor spoke his thanks to Davis as Mr. Kennedy motioned for them all to follow him to a waiting boat.

Sylvanus turned to follow but stopped when he felt Davis's touch upon his arm.

"Be well, Sy. We will think of you often. All of us."

Sylvanus gave a solemn nod and embraced his elder brother. He was afraid to speak, frightened of the emotion that might pour from him. Instead, he only whispered. "Take care of Mother. And Annie. Tell her how sorry I am. Truly."

Davis released him, cleared his throat and said, "She would not doubt it, but I will tell her."

Deep melancholy gripped Sylvanus when he left Davis behind and climbed onto the boat. His mind became a jumble of tangled thoughts, of headlines his family might read: *Storm Sunk Vessel and All Aboard Lost, She Went Down in the Night, Cause Unknown,* or *She Happened in with a Pirate Who Murdered All Aboard.* What would his mother think then of her youngest son sacrificed to the sea in the name of God? How would Annie cope with another great loss? And if the voyage delivered him successfully to the coast of Africa, did it not contain more to be feared than did all the dangers of the deep?

Hector, unsteady on the boat, leaned into his chosen master, trembling enough to offer little comfort. Sylvanus's fears mounted in rhythm with the splashing of the oars. The *Charlotte Harper* awaited them. With two masts and numerous sails, the schooner was indisputably substantial, a fortress of protection upon a dangerous sea. He removed his handkerchief from his pocket and waved it toward the wharf where Davis remained, his own raised handkerchief fluttering a sorrowful goodbye snatched away by the wind.

A large swell tossed the ship from side to side. Sylvanus stumbled and would have fallen had he not been caught on the arm by the conveniently placed William Matthias.

"Careful. You'll send us all rolling across the deck in a pile." William released his grip and patted Sylvanus on the back. "Looking a little peaked."

Sylvanus wrapped his arms around himself, though it did nothing to calm his roiling stomach. Four days had passed since Captain Curtis shouted "Raise the mud hook!" and they had begun their journey out of the Delaware Bay and into the open sea. Most of the passengers had not been on deck since they'd gathered to share the few spyglasses among them and catch the last glimmer of land they would see for weeks.

Since then, they had become a sorry bunch, unable to swallow more than a spoonful or two of arrowroot and cornmeal gruel, thinned to almost nothing, before retching. Only Mr. Panderville seemed as unaffected as the well-seasoned seamen.

"What's your secret, Panderville?" William asked, a noticeable pallor to his complexion.

He and Sylvanus had ventured abovedeck to attempt a prayer meeting. All the others remained too ill to join, including the physician, Johnson. Sylvanus was ungraciously and secretly pleased to see the man suffer worse than himself. Younger by at least a decade, with more recent training and apparently a stronger constitution, Sylvanus had convinced himself he must also be a better physician than his Bassa Cove counterpart. It was a boost of confidence he sorely needed.

Panderville, nearly as fresh and neat as the first day they all met, grinned at his companions. "I eat," he said. "I never let my stomach complain of emptiness before I fill it up again with a hearty meal. There you have it, the great secret."

Sylvanus groaned inwardly at the thought, adding, "I don't believe that's an option for us lesser mortals."

"No indeed," William agreed.

Panderville shrugged. "Perhaps I'm just better suited for sea life. I might have missed my calling."

"Nothing for it but to get it done," said a gruff voice approaching them from behind. Hector yipped happily as Captain Curtis came into view. The little mongrel was discerning in his choice of companions. He'd become fast friends with the captain, first mate, and most of the passengers, but remained wary of the sailors with rougher manners, though the cook and cabin boy, who were always good for a few small scraps, were favorites as well.

"You'll all find your sea legs soon enough," the captain said. He drew up beside them and held a glass to his eye. He scanned for a moment, then stopped with a whispered curse.

"Kennedy!" he bellowed. The first mate appeared beside him and took the glass.

"Thirty degrees," the captain said.

Sylvanus and William exchanged a nervous glance with Panderville who retrieved a glass of his own from his coat pocket, raised it to his eye, and focused on the same area the first mate now examined. Sylvanus scanned as well but could distinguish nothing more than distant haze.

"There's a ship!" Delight lit Panderville's face. He lowered the glass and handed it off to Sylvanus to take a turn squinting into the distant blue.

"It's a ship, all right," said Captain Curtis, less enthusiastically. "But could you see its colors?"

The grin slid from Panderville's face as did the healthful glow of his cheeks. "What do you suspect?" The wary question slammed a lump into Sylvanus's throat.

Sylvanus studied the horizon for several seconds before he spotted it. Even through the glass, he might as likely have spotted a leviathan as a ship. He'd no hope of discerning waving colors. He passed the glass to Matthias, who did not raise it.

"What I suspect doesn't matter nearly so much as what is. We'll know soon enough. If she's a Spaniard, we'll see the black flag."

"Spaniard?" Matthias pulled up the glass with a shaking hand. "Do you mean the ship might carry pirates?"

Sylvanus's throat clogged with fear, for a moment overwhelming his nausea. Only one thought took up residence in his mind, thrumming along to the rhythm of the blood rushing in his ears.

This is the end of all here.

Mr. Kennedy remained glued to his glass. Several minutes passed without sound beyond the occasional slap of a sail against its rigging. Sweat trickled down Sylvanus's temple, pricked against his collar, soaked his back. Beside him, William Matthias stared toward the horizon with an open mouth and furrowed brow. Despite Mr. Panderville's lack of seasickness, the man leaned against the ship railing, staring down at the blue swirls below as if he, too, might lose the contents of his stomach to the sea.

The concerning vessel had drawn considerably closer to their own ship as Sylvanus could now, with his naked eye, perceive its shape—not that of a leviathan, yet no less frightening.

At last, Mr. Kennedy lowered his glass and with a cheer slapped his palm on the fence rail. "I see the flag. They are Portuguese," he said, causing Sylvanus to wonder if this information were somehow less alarming. The first mate explained, "Lazy fellows. Cowards, all of them. There never was danger from any Portuguese. They don't fight if they can run."

Sylvanus glanced at William, who remained as uneasy in his demeanor as he. Not having lived more than the last week of his life upon the ocean, Sylvanus's experiences could not confirm the validity of the first mate's assessment. Only when the captain lowered his own glass to express his agreement did the tightness in his throat begin to ease.

Captain Curtis patted Mr. Panderville's curved back. "Nothing to fear, sirs. I don't believe they mean us harm. I'll use the speaking trumpet when they draw nearer. They'll be wondering about us as well."

"Yes," said the governor. "Because to them we might be a pirate vessel full of missionaries. Sheep in wolves' clothing, if you will."

Sylvanus smiled at the joke but couldn't give himself over to frivolity while a nagging question demanded voice. "Would they not wait until they are closer to advertise ill intent?"

The first mate shook his head and the captain responded. "They're already close enough to be a problem we'd have to deal with. If we haven't seen the black by now, they're not planning to fly it. We'll pass by without incident." He nudged Mr. Kennedy in the ribs and pointed to the three passengers. "You can all feel free to write in your letters about your narrow escape from black-hearted pirates."

The *Charlotte Harper* featured nine conveniently sized berths with nine-foot ceilings and enough peace that all the passengers, including Sylvanus, spent a great deal of their time inside writing and reading. It would have been dishonest for Sylvanus to say he enjoyed life on the vast sea, but he gleaned comfort from the familiar acts.

But by the time an eerie calm settled over them on day seventeen of the journey, leaving the sails limp and useless, the walls had begun to close in. He'd sifted once again through each of his medical texts, taken stock of supplies and worried over the effects upon them of a long stint upon the sea, written countless pages to the family and friends he'd left behind, and brushed up on his own spiritual practices, in which he'd fallen embarrassingly lax in the previous year and a half.

Now that all aboard were cautiously venturing to satisfy meager appetites, Sylvanus spent more time in conversation with each of them, including the crew who regaled him with tales of ceremonial tributes to Neptune offered on voyages across the Equator and of daring escapes from great monsters of the deep. As much as he scanned for evidence of such creatures, the most dangerous thing he spotted were the bluebottle jellyfish, which drifted across the surface of the water, promising a swift death to any fish unlucky enough to cross their paths. They'd also been known to kill men foolish enough to molest them. Still, their beauty hardly inspired terror.

He didn't discover anything of particular biological interest to him until the wind picked up again four days after the initial lull. With the sails bulging and stars twinkling against a dark, clear sky, Mr. Kennedy called all of the passengers to the deck with the promise of a spectacular view.

"The sea is on fire!" Lydia Beers gasped in surprise and placed her hand on Sylvanus's arm, sparking in him a tingle of pleasure.

Sylvanus's own mouth gaped. Her description was apt. Light danced beneath the rolling sea water like a thousand tiny blue flames licking at the surface, becoming a mass threatening to burst through to the sky.

"Phosphorescence of the sea," he whispered more to himself than to those who gathered around him. "Is it insects?"

"Not likely," Mr. Kennedy on his other side answered the question Sylvanus hadn't intentionally asked aloud. "But whatever it is, it's caused trouble. I know of an English vessel once nearly got caught in an eddie trying to get a closer look."

"It's beautiful." Lydia voiced the only appropriate response. As she spoke, she removed her hand from Sylvanus's sleeve and folded her hands in front of her narrow waist. "Thank you for showing this to us, Mr. Kennedy. God has been hard at work in this place. The more we approach Africa, the more I glimpse His hand and our eventual success."

"Are we close?" Sylvanus asked.

The first mate gripped the ship railing and looked up the sky before answering. "Captain Curtis estimates about three hundred miles. The coloration of the ocean is changing from blue to a murkier brown. Land isn't far."

Governor Matthias's cautious chuckle emerged from behind Sylvanus. "Not too close?" he asked. "I hope we're not going to become shipwrecked."

Mr. Kennedy turned to face him, his back to the glowing ocean. "Not to worry, Governor. There're a number of islands in this part. We'll pass close to some. If we're lucky, we'll see mountains and volcanoes, but this ship knows what she's about. We'll get you to your destination safe enough. It's the welcome I'd be more worried about."

Sylvanus barely had time to register the ominous words before a dull thud broke through the quiet of the night. Mr. Kennedy slid off toward the sound holding his lantern high. In the light which spilled from it, two flopping fish writhed on the deck.

"Excellent," said Mr. Kennedy. "The fish are flying tonight. Cook'll make an excellent breakfast of this."

17
Annie

"What will you do now?"

In the weeks since Esther's wedding, this had been Mother's question every day. The two crouched together by the kitchen garden, harvesting vegetables and pulling weeds. It was not in Mother's nature to let a quiet moment like this pass without broaching the subject.

Two months Jonas had been gone. Two months since a feeble-minded mob filled with hearts full of evil had strung up her beloved.

Annie rarely lasted longer than a few hours without tears finding their way down her cheeks. She hadn't known Jonas well, she argued with herself. She'd known him most through his wonderful actions, touted in his letters. He was the man who'd brought Esther into her life and provided her with the excitement of planning a wedding and a future, with children, home, love, and purpose.

She didn't know which she grieved for more—Jonas or the life she had imagined they'd lead together. If she were honest, it was probably the latter, and the notion shamed her. Not once had she responded to her mother's pressing question, but perhaps it was time she should.

"What do you suggest?" Annie said.

If Mother was shocked to receive a response, she hid it well.

"Davis has accepted a more prestigious position at the bank. He's decided to rent a house and he could use company."

Annie pulled a beet from the ground. "My brother is a grown man. I'm sure he can take care of himself."

"Yes, he can, but it's nice to have family around. He asked me if I might consider sparing you."

"Davis asked you if I could come keep house for him in Philadelphia?"

"Well, I think you are misrepresenting his intention. We just discussed the possibility, how it might help if you changed your routine for a while."

Annie yanked so hard on the next greens, they ripped off in her hand, leaving the root vegetable behind for her to dig out. "The two of you decided to discuss it, without including me, asking me what I might want?"

"I'm talking to you about it now." Mother stood and wiped her hands together to loosen the dirt. "The opportunity has arisen recently. We haven't meant to keep it from you. You've just not been willing to talk about your future."

Annie couldn't look at her. "I don't know, Mother." She sighed as she tossed aside a clump of garden soil. "Jonas and I had such plans for our future working side by side. I don't know who I am without him."

"That, my dear, is utter nonsense."

"Pardon me?"

Elizabeth bent and reached out to take her daughter's chin between two soiled fingers. "My daughter does not need any man, even a good man like Jonas Edwards, in order to make an impression upon the world. I know of no stronger nor more capable woman."

Annie was on the verge of expressing a heartfelt thank you when her mother dropped her hand and continued. "I'm sure there is much to do in Philadelphia to help further the cause you and Jonas espoused. You'll find kindred spirits there. And who knows? You might even find another worthy man."

The burst of confidence Annie had felt under her mother's praise vanished, to be replaced by indignance. "Mother, I'm not touring the country for a husband."

"Do you want children and a home?"

Heat rose up her neck. The brief reprieve was at an end. "Yes, Mother. I do."

"And do you know of a man in Columbia, Pennsylvania who can give you children and a home of your own?"

"No."

"Then perhaps you should start packing."

Over the next several days, Annie organized her affairs for an impending move to Philadelphia. Though her heart had not yet conformed to the idea of leaving home, she dared not mope anymore. Part of her feared her mother might load her onto a stagecoach to be sent out west as a mail order bride for a frontiersman. She was glad to set the unpleasant thought aside when the mail arrived.

She spotted a letter from Hannah Seys postmarked from Monrovia. Delighted, she also discovered a slim and weather-beaten package, posted from Cape Verde, Africa and addressed to her from S. M. E. Goheen. She hadn't heard from her brother in some time and had only written him a brief note expressing her sorrow at being unable to attend his sendoff. She'd had no way of knowing when, or even if, it would reach him, and she hadn't felt greatly inclined to write since Jonas's death.

She couldn't imagine how Smee received her tragic news and hadn't cared to ask Davis when he'd hand-delivered an obligatory note of condolence. Perhaps it was with no small amount of satisfaction—a sickening and uncharitable thought. In some ways, Sylvanus's departure for Africa had made her pain easier to bear, even though she missed him terribly.

She smiled at how he had chosen to write his name. Others always referred to him as Sylvanus, but in formal documentation, he had chosen his initials that recalled the childhood nickname she'd given him.

Annie opened the letter from Mrs. Seys first.

To my dear friend Miss Ann Goheen,

I pray this letter finds you well and in good spirits as your wedding rapidly approaches, if it has not already come and gone. I wish to express to you how meaningful this correspondence has become to me. Monrovia is a lonely place. I am surrounded by missionaries, who are so single-mindedly focused, there is little diversion from the more difficult aspects of our lives. My brothers in mission teach and preach and I primarily care for the mission children, including my own. More often than not I am engaged in a great deal of sick care as well.

Though the native children are of healthy constitutions, the mission children are ill almost from the moment they arrive on the shores of Africa. They come in need of constant care, as do their parents. I do my best for them, but this land seems a death sentence for us all in the end.

I do not say this to frighten you. I am certain when your brother arrives, his own knowledge of health and disease will do much to protect him and us all. I anxiously await his arrival as more than half of those lying sick at the mission house, I can do nothing to help. I am at the end of my skills and have watched many, including two of my own children, succumb to death.

I do not despair, however, for I know the Lord is good. He is watching over us, guiding our steps and busies Himself in all of our tragedy to fulfilling the purposes of His glory.

I thank you again for your letters and your friendship. I look forward to the day when we might meet face-to-face, either on earth or in heaven.

Your sister in Christ,
Hannah Seys

Annie longed for this distant friend she knew only in her heart, a mother strong enough to bury a child and remain faithful in the face of such pain. This was a friend who might hear of Annie's sorrow, of her loss, and teach her to bear it bravely and use it for good.

Hannah was the one person with whom Annie felt she could be completely honest, only because they were separated by an ocean. She might have been angry with anyone else who suggested the danger Smee would face on his foolish mission, for that's what it was. She would not betray the memory of Jonas by embracing colonization.

But with Hannah Seys, she felt a deep kinship. The woman was, after all, only supporting her husband the way Annie would have done for Jonas, and even did to the point of arguing with the one person in the world she might have loved most before him. The wife of John Seys did not have an easy life. She struggled, both physically in the climate of Africa which tormented her constitution, but also with doubts about the purpose of their mission and her place within it.

Whatever she thought about the Liberia mission itself, Annie admired Hannah.

She sat down to compose a reply, struggling to find just the right way to communicate the news of Jonas's death and her loneliness in the weeks that followed. There on the page she found release for her warring emotions, giving voice to her grief and her guilt over experiencing relief in the freedom from commitment to a man who had a contentious relationship with her family. These were the things she could not share with her mother, and certainly not with Esther, so flush with the excitement of love and new marriage. With Hannah Seys she could express honestly her heartache, cushioned from judgment by an ocean.

It wasn't until after she had finished with her letter, and the accompanying tears, she thought again of the package that had arrived for her from Smee. She sliced through the strings binding the wrapping together. Inside was a leather book, ornately designed with raised patterns on the edges. Attractive, certainly, but with no title identifying it. Opening it, she discovered a title page bearing the words:

ALBUM

Presented
to
Ann Goheen
By
S. M. E. Goheen

Her name and his were penned in his hand. She flipped through the pages. All remained blank except for this. She turned the book over. It was merely a journal—a fine journal he had chosen for her. Tucked beneath it in the package was a folded piece of paper.

Dear Annie,

Words cannot express the great sorrow with which I write to you. The life you had wanted slipped away and I am not there to offer whatever comfort I might give. Our Atlantic crossing was not without its trials, but the weather bodes well for the remainder of our journey from a brief stop on the island of Costa Verde to the Port of Monrovia. I regret I was forced to leave for Africa's shore without a formal goodbye. I miss you, my dear sister. I pray daily for God's peace in your life and for the healing of your heartache. I know our great Creator has much in store for you, as He does for me. Do not forget me, though I travel to the ends of the earth in His name. Care for our brothers and our mother as only you can. Please also pray for me, that my skilled hands may give comfort and my soul may provide sanctuary. Fill the pages of this journal with the crying out of your soul, as though you are pouring it out not only to God, but also to me.

Your Loving Brother,
Smee

The sincerity of his condolences struck her heart. It only occurred to her after reading through the letter three times that he would by now be in Monrovia, established in his mission alongside Hannah. In the space of such a short time, she had lost the two men who meant most to her in the world. She refolded the letter and tucked it inside the album.

18
Sylvanus

Sweat slicked the back of Sylvanus's neck at the approach of the African shore. Hector panted beside him in the slats of shade offered by the deck railings. The dog had been a remarkably good sport on the journey, barking at sea birds, chasing the flying fish that flopped onto the deck, and even happily taking the occasional swim in the ocean with a rope tied about his middle for safety. In many ways the dog had fared much better than his master.

Their brief stop in Cape Verde to restock supplies and post letters had been a welcome respite from the rolling ocean, but Sylvanus's stomach did not care for the remaining six days of the journey to Monrovia, and even the smells of fresh pork roast wafting from the galley left him weak with queasiness. It was with a subdued sense of anticipation that he stood in the heavy sea air and absorbed his first view of Liberia.

The captain and crew guided the large vessel into an expansive port, past the decaying shell of a ship, its mast laying upon the surface of the water.

"Is this a dangerous harbor?" Sylvanus asked William Matthias, his constant companion and always a rich source of information, though from whence it came, Sylvanus didn't always know. Thorough research before accepting a governorship, he supposed, or the right questions asked at the right time.

"More so than it seems, I'm told. Mr. Kennedy says there's a difficult sandbar. It causes trouble for some of the less experienced captains."

"Explains the shipwreck."

William gripped the railing of the ship and leaned against it as if to get a closer look. "Could be."

"More likely an abandoned slaver." The explanation came from Mr. Kennedy himself, walking up behind them with a spyglass in his hands.

Sylvanus's eyes grew wide. The transatlantic slave trade had been illegal for nearly thirty years. He knew that hadn't stopped all exportation from Africa, but he'd believed the practice reduced to little more than a trickle. To see evidence of it here, on the edge of an American colony, caused a chill in his bones despite the warmth of the day.

"There's still demand," Mr. Kennedy said with a sigh. "And as long as that is so, there'll be traders willing to take big risks for great reward."

The thought turned Sylvanus's stomach, but he also swelled with pride at the triumph of humanity represented in the remains of the terrible vessel before him, slowly degrading into the ocean, unable to complete its monstrous mission. He stood at the entrance to a second front in the struggle to end slavery.

"No one reclaims such ships?" he asked. "They're just left to rot in the sea?"

"Not worth the trouble." The first mate lowered the glass and looked Sylvanus in the eyes. "Lot of souls packed into those boats. Not all of them make it off."

William leaned back as he turned to look at the first mate, his hands gripping the rail so he resembled a listing ship himself, tethered only by his arms.

The first mate's words settled over Sylvanus like the ocean mist. In the silence that passed only a moment, he could almost hear the waling of those souls, the ones freed from a fate worse than death by death itself.

Mr. Kennedy raised the spyglass again and scanned the water between ship and shore, then lowered it with a stiff nod. "Hear this, my young friends. There's more that lurks on this Dark Continent than the lost souls you plan to claim for your God."

Sylvanus exchanged a glance with William whose eyes betrayed concern his smirk attempted to hide.

The old sailor was already walking away when he added, "There's places here you don't want to go; spirits you don't want to meet."

William stood, released the railing, and cleared his throat. Hector whined between the two men, and Sylvanus reached to scratch behind the dog's ears.

He didn't place stock in Mr. Kennedy's warning, not really. Sailors traded superstitions between them, but he could not entirely discount the earnestness in the first mate's claim.

In that moment, Sylvanus Goheen wanted to go home.

Lydia Beers, with her round face and warm smile, was young and enthusiastic and seemed to have taken it upon herself to keep his mind distracted with cheerful discussions of her hopes for the students she would meet, the young minds she would mold. Only a few years older, but more experienced in the ways of the world, Mrs. Wilkins possessed a calmer, more even temperament. Together, the two ladies eased Sylvanus's own anxieties somewhat.

He couldn't have said he enjoyed being on the ship, but with Liberia's coastline in sight and the tingle of anticipation at the beginning of a new challenge, he could appreciate the vast expanse of the water, the lush land beyond it, and the breathtaking view of an equatorial sunrise.

"So beautiful," Lydia commented when the news of the first good glimpse of Monrovia enticed the ladies to join the gentlemen on the deck.

As grateful as he was to see it, beautiful might not be the first word Sylvanus would have chosen to describe the sight. The sun could not penetrate the thick blanket of fog sitting atop a stretch of ugly barracks along the coast, interspersed with free-standing shacks. Off to the west stood a row of proud houses with expansive front porches, as if the large plantation homes of the Southern United States had been lifted and deposited in the wilds of Africa. They stood in sharp contrast to the neighboring structures, reminiscent perhaps of slave quarters.

The mansions' incongruous presence in this alien land served to accentuate to Sylvanus the absurdity of transplanting the West into Africa, a thought that had him tugging at his tight collar while taking in the sight of scantily clad natives moving breezily about their business among their lighter skinned counterparts who fanned themselves in dark-colored frock coats.

Beyond the carcass of the slave ship, the large sandbar at Monrovia's Harbor necessitated more caution from the captain than any obstacle he had previously faced on this journey, and a slow, tedious approach to the coast provided the missionaries plenty of time to assess their new home.

Monrovia sat nestled on the shore, its houses and buildings built on a steep slope that mimicked another wave raising from the ocean. Wide roads of hardpacked dirt crisscrossed the town, but on them Sylvanus observed little activity.

"There are no carriages," he said with growing discomfort. "No horses."

Once again, William had the answer to the implied question. "Horses fare even more poorly than humans in the tropical West African climate."

Sylvanus stared across the water at his new home, so foreign, any romantic notion of adventure at risk of being swept aside by the realization that this was a land entirely apart from Pennsylvania. The air felt different with its thick, warm moisture, its odors of salt and decay mixed with the sweetness rising from the flowering trees lining empty roads.

William seemed to read his mind. "The place will feel like home before you know it."

Sylvanus couldn't believe the statement might be true. He would not miss much about life aboard the *Charlotte Harper*, but he dreaded parting ways with William Matthias.

"Those of us in Bassa will not be far away, and we will welcome your prayers and your letters."

Sylvanus responded to the man who had become a reliable friend with a firm handshake. "You will have both. Perhaps once we are settled here, even a visit might be arranged."

"I'd like that." Warmth beyond the moist heat of the coastal air radiated from the sincere emotion in the governor's eyes. Hector barked once, drawing William's attention, which came with a smile and pat. "I'll miss you too, Hector."

Their goodbyes drew to a close with the approach of canoes piloted by indigenous people, dark-skinned and well-muscled. Two wore loin cloths; the other half dozen were entirely naked. Each face bore blue lines tattooed from the peak of the forehead and down the bridge of the nose. The captain referred to them as *Kru* and greeted them with simple English.

"These men will take the Methodist missionaries and supplies ashore," he said to the passengers.

"Oh, good heavens, they aren't wearing a stitch of clothing!" A bright blush rose on the neck of Ann Wilkins and for a moment she looked as if she might faint. Sylvanus thought to offer his arm but was saved the embarrassment by the admirably self-possessed Lydia Beers who grabbed the older woman's hand. Both stared determinedly down at their feet.

Sylvanus shook his head at William, their departure from one another now imminent, and with Hector at his heels, he pushed past the women to allow the naked *Kru* men to help him onto their boat. At an encouraging nudge from Lydia, Mrs. Wilkins summoned enough courage to follow his lead.

A single envoy sent from the governor's office had been present to greet the new arrivals. The thickset Black man asked whether any settlers from America had arrived on the ship. When he discovered only the presence of three white missionaries, he'd had little to say to them, acknowledging them with no more than a head jiggle in the direction they now walked, up a rising pathway toward the mission house.

Lydia pressed on ahead, enthusiastically pointing out tropical fruit trees and butterflies to Mrs. Wilkins barely keeping up beside her. Sylvanus envied her captivation. He longed for the desire to study the strange flora, but for now it was all he could manage just to keep moving forward.

Ahead of them stood a small stone church and an impressive two-story house with a wrap-around porch and, between the two structures, the mission house itself. Sylvanus might have called it more of a complex, as it consisted of two parts that each seemed to belong to different structures mashed together to make a single, awkward building. The windows stood open wide to the ocean breeze.

The three missionaries paused to take in the sight of their new home. Compared to the two buildings beside it, the house was plain and serviceable with an unremarkable roofline rising above the straight rows of an orchard just beyond. Sylvanus had just thought to explore the variety of fruits when Hector began to growl a warning and Mrs. Wilkins screamed.

"Oh—" Lydia shrieked in answer while Sylvanus dropped to his knees to snatch his dog by the scruff and scrambled to glimpse what had frightened them—the largest snake he'd ever seen not four feet from the path.

"Ladies," he said, mustering a calm he did not feel as he stroked Hector in an attempt to soothe the wriggling and snapping dog. "Be as still as you can manage."

Some six paces away, he studied the long reptile. He knew nothing of the snakes he might find in Liberia, but those in Pennsylvania he knew well, having spent much of his childhood determining whether he might use them to torment his siblings.

The buff coloring and roundish head shape did not suggest venom, nor did the creature's lack of aggressive action toward them.

Lydia crouched beside him and clutched his arm. He could feel her violent trembling and fought the urge to wrap a comforting arm around her. Instead, Sylvanus patted her hand and stood up, clutching his wriggling dog, and sorted through his knowledge of snakes. Though significantly larger, this one's general appearance and demeanor compared best to the rat snake, a constrictor, fairly harmless to humans despite its lethality to rodents.

He was about to proclaim as much when the group was approached from behind by a white woman with a slight but sturdy build supporting a rounded belly, which revealed the cause of her waddling gait. "You don't need to worry too much about the little ones."

Lydia dropped Sylvanus's arm as the two of them turned toward the stranger.

Mrs. Wilkins, too, joined them in staring open-mouthed at her.

"Little one?" Mrs. Wilkins asked. "It's easily twelve feet long."

The woman smiled pleasantly. She wore a simple drab dress and carried a basket of small brown fruits resembling something between an apple and a potato. "I've seen many larger than that. They won't hurt you as long as you leave them be. But I would keep a close watch on the dog."

She set down her basket and stretched a hand toward them in greeting.

"You must be the new missionaries. My name is Hannah Seys. Superintendent Seys is my husband. He's away at Cape Palmas with our oldest son." She shook each of their hands in turn and carefully leaned forward to pat the top of Hector's head, eliciting a cheerful tail wag in response. "I'm assuming you are Miss Beers and Mrs. Wilkins. It is certainly a pleasure to welcome two new ladies into the colony. And, of course, Dr. Goheen. I've heard much about you."

"And I you." Sylvanus felt the warmth in her welcome and liked her as immediately as he had her husband.

Mrs. Seys picked up her basket once again, placed her free hand on the fabric stretched over her pregnant belly, and encouraged the group to continue toward the house. "That's only a python. It squeezes its prey, but it's not likely to get ambitious enough to try to make a meal of you. However, it's wise to give it a wide berth, as is the case with any snake you find in the colony. Many of them are much more dangerous."

Sylvanus, buoyed at last by the prospect of exploring a new environment, commented, "I would like to know as much about the local fauna as possible."

They reached the front of the mission house. Mrs. Seys climbed the three steps up to the unadorned wooden door and pushed it open as she answered, "You'll find much of interest to learn here, Dr. Goheen, but first, allow me to show you your new home."

Sylvanus did not ask whether Hector was welcome but ushered him inside where presumably there were no large snakes. Hannah didn't so much as blink at the inclusion of the dog in the party as they stepped through the door.

They entered an expansive kitchen featuring a long wooden table at its center, a large cupboard along the far wall, and a wide cast-iron stovetop. Tacked up pots and pans lined the wall above the stove, and more chairs than Sylvanus could quickly count were pushed up against the opposite wall where two big windows let in a great deal of light and air. Two Black women sat at the table working dough with strong fingers. The older of the two had a lighter complexion and appeared to be teaching the younger, whose face was nearly as dark as coal.

"This is Mrs. Amelia Jones." Mrs. Seys indicated the older woman who stood, wiped her hands on her long apron, and nodded to the missionaries with a broad smile. "She is part of our emigrant population from Mississippi. She helps prepare meals for missionaries, students, and others who may have cause to dine here from time to time."

Mrs. Seys stepped toward the younger woman and bid her to stand. The girl, who couldn't have been more than fourteen, offered the missionaries an awkward curtsy. Sylvanus feared she might fall.

"This," their hostess explained, "is Emma. She is one of our young natives from our Sunday school program. We do our best to teach them English and Scripture, of course, but also skills. We have had only a few students at the Mission House so far. We've been so anxious for you ladies to arrive and expand the program."

Lydia and Mrs. Wilkins exchanged grins.

"And this is where you will hold lessons." Mrs. Seys placed her basket of fruit on the table with a little huff and led the three new-comers through a doorway on the other side of the kitchen windows. "Watch your step. The floor is a little uneven."

Despite the warning, the slight step down threw off Sylvanus's balance. He placed a hand on the wall to catch himself. The room they entered was the addition he'd seen from the outside of the house—a simple space with rows of wooden benches and tables. A podium and slate stood on an elevated platform on the other end of the room. Good sized windows lined the walls with shutters opened wide, though it did nothing to cut the stifling heat and humidity, nor the musty odor of damp wood.

The ladies peppered their guide with questions, but Sylvanus tuned them out. He sat on one of the benches. Beside him, Hector dropped to the floor, his ears flopping forward as he rested his head on his front paws. Sylvanus longed to stretch out as well. Fatigue threatened to overtake him. He'd have liked to be shown his sleeping quarters where he hoped he could shake loose his lingering uneasiness.

Mrs. Seys kept on, winded though her speech seemed to make her in her late stage of pregnancy. "This classroom doubles as a mission meeting hall and occasionally hosts colony events as well."

She pointed through the windows to the stately house beyond them. "Of course, there are more classrooms in the seminary building next door. Shall we move on?"

Sylvanus ordered his reluctant muscles to follow the women once again into the kitchen and this time out the opposite side of the room where another doorway led to a hall, as Lydia Beers asked yet another question. How she remained in any condition to absorb so much information, Sylvanus couldn't imagine.

"What is this fruit?"

Mrs. Seys smiled. "We call them star apples. Dr. Goheen might find them useful. They are good for fighting indigestion."

She'd likely meant to imply that as a doctor he would be interested in any aid this native fruit might offer his patients. For now, however, his more immediate concern was his own unsettled stomach. He considered eating one.

"They're also quite tasty. Our own orchard, which you may have noticed as you approached, contains oranges, papayas, and paw paws, but there are many native fruits it does not," Mrs. Seys continued. "I'd have been down to meet you directly off the ship except I was approached by a colonist wishing to trade for sugar from the mission store."

At their blank looks, she explained, "The superintendent began a small mission store as a way to both track goods brought into the colony for use by the mission and to settle accounts within the colony when cash is not always on hand."

"Is money a problem for the mission?" Lydia asked.

"No. The Mission Board is faithful, but not always timely. It's an efficient way to smooth out the bumps in our mission budget."

In the hallway were three doorways. One formed the entrance to a staircase. To the right of it, a well-furnished sitting room, and to the left, a wide room filled with rows of cots. A fireplace stood at the far end, a smoldering fire releasing whiffs of smoke into the already stifling room. Two of the cots held patients, adult males, both Black, with the strong builds of farmers.

One of them opened his eyes. His brow was beaded with sweat, though he shivered beneath a blanket. The skin of both men glowed with an internal fiery heat. Sylvanus did not need to approach either to see their misery. Thoughts of his own discomfort slid to the back of his mind as he stripped off his coat and rolled up his shirtsleeves. He crossed to a water-filled basin. Beside it sat a stack of clean rags. He removed the first and soaked it. The water was tepid at best, but he mopped the nearest man's forehead with it anyway. The patient blinked his eyes shut as the water dripped across his flaming skin.

"African sickness?" Sylvanus asked Mrs. Seys who, along with the other women, had grown deathly silent when they'd entered the room.

Mrs. Seys nodded.

"What can you tell me about it?"

She sighed and grabbed a wet cloth herself, sliding behind him to mop the brow of the other patient. The two teachers joined her efforts by supplying refreshed cloths to both Sylvanus and Hannah Seys.

"African fever is the blight of both white and Black, young and old here. It doesn't seem to affect the natives much. They have the constitutions for this climate." She touched the shoulder of the open-eyed man and her own eyes filled with sympathy. "Some of our Black missionaries fare better, but nearly all of us have succumbed to its symptoms at some point."

"Who treats them?"

"I do. Mostly." She sagged at the admission and Sylvanus noticed anew the dark shadows beneath her eyes. He'd attributed their appearance to the exhaustion of her condition, but he could see now a fuller picture of the burden she'd been bearing.

"I use a mustard poultice on the feet to help the fever break. We have quinine sent to us by the Mission Board that's supposed to be useful for treating fever, but none of us has experience with the dosing and I don't know how helpful it's been."

"Have you been ill, as well?" he asked her, adopting the soft voice he used when beside the beds of dying men.

She shrugged and sagged onto one of the empty cots. "Not as ill as some. I am tired, though that may have more to do with this." She patted her swollen middle. "I spend most of my days nursing the sick. We really are so grateful to have you here."

Sylvanus looked into her expressive gray eyes and found a depth of fatigue and sorrow that tugged at his heart.

"I've been doing the best I can to nurse the sick through their bouts when I am not ill with it myself, but I lack your expertise."

Sylvanus surveyed the patients. "May I ask why you keep it so warm in here?"

"They alternate between hot and chilled. The chill is much worse, in my experience. It is agonizing to be unable to oneself warm, and so we maintain the fire." She paused to take a few shallow breaths. "We keep water boiling as well. We can clean rags swiftly or make coffee or tea for patients as they need rapid warming and feel up to trying to keep something down. It gives us the advantage, too, that we can quickly clean wounds. This is not a hospital, of course, but the natives and mission families alike have discovered we have certain resources and at least a small amount of knowledge here."

"Are there no other doctors?" Sylvanus's breaths grew inadequate. He'd not been informed he would be the only source of medical care in the whole of Monrovia. Had he known this would be the case, he'd never have boarded the schooner and would now be comfortably situated in Columbia.

Mrs. Seys blanched at his response but answered, "There is a colonial physician, Dr. Bacon. He works with an emigrant apprentice. Together they see to the colonists when they first arrive and later to their needs as he is able."

"Is he often not able?"

"He is overwhelmed. And his success rate is," Mrs. Seys paused for an uncomfortable beat. "Not impressive."

"Not impressive," Sylvanus repeated.

"And he will not treat the natives, who occasionally come to us. He may be less reliable than the native witch doctors anyway. We, I hope, are not."

Sylvanus conjured pictures of wild dance rituals and chants which called upon demons, endangering the souls of sick men whose eternal salvation was far more important than their bodily health. He said, with much more confidence than he felt, "Well, now you have a real and competent doctor. I'll do my best to see to the health needs of the mission and anyone else God sends our way."

Sylvanus felt the weight of the words coming from his lips. There were people here in need of healing, and he was now their best hope for it.

19
Annie

Mother received the news of Annie's imminent departure with a distressing stoicism, but then it was she who had recommended her daughter scour the countryside for a husband. Esther had managed to shed tears, but beyond them Annie could see a contentment that precluded any real sorrow at the departure of a friend, even one as dear as a sister.

Their lack of grief at saying goodbye confirmed she'd made the right decision. Philadelphia was not far, but in the bustle of city streets, she might push aside her loneliness for a time and throw herself into new and important endeavors.

She'd expressed this hope to her brother Davis when she'd agreed to stay with him for a while. How long she'd be in the city, she couldn't have said, but he'd been pleased enough to welcome her.

Two years older than her own twenty-nine years, Davis had settled into a prestigious banking position. He'd always been good with figures. In short order he'd gained a great deal of respect from his employers. The ordered environment of Philadelphia suited him and he'd settled in, taking a small house with room enough to provide a home for the grieving sister who shared his plain looks.

And, most importantly to Annie, he'd been supportive of her desire to join the abolitionist cause in the city, directing her to the meeting place of the Philadelphia Female Anti-Slavery Society. She could almost feel Jonas smiling as she pushed open the door to a room containing at least fifty women, both Black and white, interacting freely with one another.

Most engaged others in animated conversation. Some wore smiles. One did not. A slender blonde with a furrowed brow and the pinched gaze of an irritated schoolmarm approached Annie through the crowd as resolutely as Moses marching confidently through the Red Sea.

"I've not seen you before." It was not a question, though upon closer inspection, it seemed the woman's demeanor was more cautious than unfriendly.

"I hope I'm in the right place." Annie folded her hands tightly at her waist. "My name is Ann Goheen. I'm looking for the Anti-Slavery Society. I've recently arrived in the city and would like to join your efforts."

The woman's expression relaxed, and though her lips did not curl into a smile, her eyes softened with relief and pleasure. "I apologize for my brash manners. Not everyone who walks through our doors is friendly to our cause. My name is Mrs. Catharine Turner. And you are most welcome, Miss Goheen, assuming you share our belief in the inherent equal worth of every man and woman regardless of color, are willing to support our cause financially as you are able and participate in our boycott of Southern slave products such as cotton and sugar."

The thought of boycotting sugar lent a slight, embarrassing pause to Annie's enthusiasm, but in the conviction of Mrs. Turner's words, she found the strength to nod her assent.

"Very well. I will introduce you to my sisters in the noble fight. Our president, Mrs. Lucretia Mott, will want to greet you after the meeting. You've found us on a good night, as well. We have the newest writings of William Lloyd Garrison to be read aloud, and we have much to discuss of petitions."

The organized format of the meeting, the sheer numbers of those involved, and the mention of one of the most important names in the abolition movement all sent a thrill through Annie. "I'm eager to get started."

Here she felt a sense of purpose and belonging she'd not possessed in months. She claimed a seat beside a gray-haired woman whose straight back and silent attention to the front of the room labeled her as a leader among a class of warrior women. Annie's heart fluttered with joy at being one of them.

A stern-faced woman stood before the seated abolitionists and called the meeting to order, causing a swift hush.

"Welcome to all of you. It's wonderful to see new faces among us this evening. My name is Mary Grew and I serve as Corresponding Secretary for the Society. I have a letter from our founder Mr. William Lloyd Garrison that I will read for the consideration and edification of us all."

Annie allowed the words of the formidable Garrison to wash over her, lost in their power as he, through the strong voice of Mary Grew, deftly wove together Scriptural truth and sound logic to paint a clear picture of the evils of human slavery and, to further his point, the dark purposes of The American Colonization Society. Her stomach churned.

The woman beside her nodded along as Garrison's letter described the "colonization scheme" as "inadequate in its design, injurious in its operation, and contrary to sound principle."

The condemning words of this giant among abolitionists continued to roll over her in sickening waves.

"The more scrupulously I examine its pretensions," Garrison had written, "the stronger is my conviction of its sinfulness."

The arguments raised by the letter against colonization echoed many of the same Jonas had once fired at the unflappable John Seys, a man Annie truly held in great esteem, and at her own brother, a young and impressionable man barely old enough to be making his way in a world so far from his home. She believed their intentions were good, that the missionary's desire to shine God's light on the continent of Africa was noble, but she could not accept colonization as a worthy pathway to accomplishing their goal.

Sylvanus had argued that Black men could not currently access the benefits of freedom in the United States, even when documentation ensuring such freedom was attained, but Garrison's reason suggested otherwise.

"My Bible assures me," Mary Grew read on. "that the day is coming when even the 'wolf shall dwell with the lamb, and the leopard shall lie down with the kid, and the wolf and the young lion and the fatling together;' and if this be possible, I see no cause why those of the same species—God's rational creatures—fellow countrymen, in truth, cannot dwell in harmony together."

Misguided at best, at worst lost to a foreign land where he had no business ever being, her brother was wrong in his thinking. She could see no way to justify the choices he'd made. The brief respite, the distraction from grief which the society meeting had offered her splintered like broken glass.

When the reading ended, she clapped just as those around her did. Others dabbed at their eyes with handkerchiefs, fierce women reacting with raw emotion to the inspiring words which condemned the ideals of her brother. Tears did not accompany her sorrow. Too deeply imbedded was her anguish for it to surface in this public space, surrounded by women whose opinions of her meant more than she might admit even to herself.

She feared they would label her an imposter were they to discover she was the sister of a champion of colonization and the regular correspondent of one of its great defenders.

Mary Grew sat, granting Annie a brief reprieve from her anxiety, and Lucretia Mott took her place at the front of the room. A short woman of slight build, Mrs. Mott's vivacious mannerisms and bold speech commanded greater attention than even the recitation of Mr. Garrison's eloquent words, and she easily shifted the attention of the room to a new consideration.

Mott spoke with conviction about the real actions of women in seeking an end to slavery, about the schools set up for people of color, about the activities of those smuggling escaped slaves toward freedom in the north, and about the many petitions sent to Washington from the lionesses in this room.

"The Congress of this United States may demand our silence with their vindictive gag orders, but they'll not receive it. No, my friends, we will only grow louder and more troublesome. We will flood them with our demands until they cannot but listen."

Mott lifted a stack of pages, edges dancing as she shook her clasped hand. "This, ladies, is our new crusade. This petition demands the right of a full jury trial to any alleged escaped slave, just as our Constitution demands for every citizen of this nation. To deny our colored brothers and sisters this most basic right is an abomination.

"Get out there, sisters. Pave the streets of this city with righteous speech and gather as many signatures as you can. We will not be silent, because God is not silent. He insists upon righteous action. So must we."

A sea of women's voices cheered the words. Annie stood with the rest to applaud, her rejuvenated heart swelling nearly to bursting with conviction and purpose, for a moment eclipsing the part of that tender organ which was bruised and aching with despair.

Gladly she received several pages that included their call to action and space for signatures and had gathered herself to leave the meeting hall when she heard her name.

"Miss Goheen, I'd like to you to meet Mrs. Lucretia Mott." Catharine Turner approached her through the dispelling crowd, the beaming Mrs. Mott in tow.

"It's wonderful to meet you, Mrs. Mott."

"Likewise, my dear."

Annie might have thought to find her breathless after her intense speech, but instead the woman seemed refreshed by this recent experience, ebullient with the joy of it—a trait Annie had recognized in only a few preachers.

"You spoke very well."

"Thank you." Mrs. Mott received the compliment by humbly bowing her head. "It is not difficult to speak with conviction about that which God has placed upon all our hearts."

"Indeed," added Mrs. Turner. "Miss Goheen has arrived in the city quite recently and is anxious to join our cause."

"What has brought you to Philadelphia?"

Annie opened her mouth to speak but hesitated as the pain of her recent loss flooded her mind. "I-I lost someone dear," she said. "My betrothed was killed. I have come to Philadelphia to live with my brother and try to mend my heart."

Mrs. Mott's smile drooped and her head dipped. "I'm sorry to hear it."

"Thank you. He was an abolitionist, a crusader attacked for his moral actions in escorting men of color to their God-given freedom."

Mrs. Mott clasped her hands together and Annie warmed in the glow of pride and sympathy emanating from her, only briefly pausing to wonder if the same would extend to her grief over the loss of Smee to a futile mission in a hostile land—a loss that in many ways felt sharper and less resolved.

"There is no rest in our work, but here your heart will find healing. Many good men have given their lives to this worthy struggle, and I suspect many more will be called to do so. You honor his memory by the work you will do here with us."

Annie pulled back and blew out a slow breath. "I long for that, Mrs. Mott."

"You must call me Lucretia."

"And please, I'm Catharine. May we call you Ann?"

"Yes, of course."

Catharine draped an arm around Annie. "Well then, Ann, let's gather some signatures."

20
Sylvanus

Sylvanus awoke in a puddle of sweat, disoriented on his first morning in Monrovia, and on each morning the first week after his arrival. The dull gray sky and determined rain did little to lighten the overwhelming sense of foreboding in the place.

But on the ninth day of his service in Monrovia, the dawn penetrated both the literal clouds and those residing in the young physician's heart.

"Good morning, Amelia." Sylvanus stepped into the kitchen to find the woman busy even with few diners about. "Where's your helper this morning?"

Amelia pulled a cup from a cabinet above her, poured coffee, and handed it to Sylvanus, her expression dark. "Her family took her."

"Took her?" He sipped the steaming brew. "Why would they do that?"

"Because, Dr. Goheen, these natives do what they want without regard for anyone else."

"Mrs. Jones, that is unkind." The subtle reprimand, bold and resonant, commanded attention and tugged at Sylvanus's memory, lightening his heart.

He turned to find the long-absent John Seys seated beside two Black missionaries. Amos Herring had been in the mission house since Sylvanus's arrival. His muscles bulged despite his recent bout of sickness and in all ways, he appeared much improved. Across from Seys and Herring sat a newcomer to the house who was the same man whose powerful sermon delivered to a packed church in Philadelphia had inspired Sylvanus to pursue the missionary field in the first place. He smiled in recognition of George Brown.

"I'm sorry, Reverend." Mrs. Jones placed a plate with a thick slice of bread and an egg on the table and motioned for Sylvanus to sit as she continued her complaint. "But it's true."

"There are cultural differences at play we do not fully understand."

"I understand just fine." The woman was growing agitated, and Sylvanus wondered if, as a physician, he should intervene. Instead, he remained a fascinated observer. "That poor little girl has been given a taste of civilized life and now she's been dragged back into the jungle where unspeakable things will happen to her."

"Calm down, Mrs. Jones."

There was a sharp edge of authority in the superintendent's tone. Sylvanus didn't know a great deal about women, but in his experience, telling them to calm down rarely helped them do so. In demonstration of his silent observation, the cook swiped at a tear rolling down her left cheek. "You don't know what they do to them."

The man's next words held a tender note. "I understand your concern. Emma's life will not be easy, nor will it look like what you hoped for her, but she is in God's hands. Thanks to your guidance, she knows it."

Sylvanus slipped into the seat at his breakfast plate and the conversation shifted.

Seys smiled at him. "Welcome to Africa, my friend. I trust you had a good journey?"

"I don't know about good. My constitution proved less amenable to the sea than I had hoped, but I'm here in one piece thanks to the grace of God."

"Each of us is here by the grace of God," said George.

Reverend Seys nodded his appreciation. "Mr. Herring tells me you wasted no time getting to work. He seems fit as can be."

"Amos is a strong man. He'll do well as long as he keeps to his doctor's advice to eat only light meals and stay out of the night air."

The large Black man shook his head at the superintendent. "Eating light is never a problem given our inconsistent supplies, but I keep explaining to the good doctor that out in the mission settlements, the night comes for you."

"Indeed," Seys agreed. "I'm just glad to see you on your feet again, Amos. And Sylvanus, my wife has not stopped singing your praises since we arrived here last night."

Sylvanus blushed. "Mrs. Seys is a diligent nurse and has been a considerable help."

"She is a wonder, but lacks expertise, as we all do. Do you have the supplies you need?"

Sylvanus gave the superintendent a rundown of the supplies he'd brought with him. Most had shipped well, with the exception of a single broken glass funnel. A third of his iron had turned blue but might be useful made into a tincture with mercury. He'd failed to bring nitric ether.

"I can get you nitric ether," Seys assured him. "In the meantime, have you met the colonial physician Dr. Bacon?"

"I've not yet had the pleasure." Given Hannah's scathing review, he doubted it would be much of a pleasure at all.

Seys drained his coffee cup. "You should introduce yourself. I'm sure he'd welcome your help at the barracks. A boatful of emigrants arrived a few days before you did. He'll have his hands full."

"Is it mainly the acclimatization fever that grips them?"

"It is by far the worst of it." Seys placed his empty cup on the table. "By now I'm sure you've observed it strikes Black men the same as the white, regardless of what you may have heard in America." He pointed to Amos, who had just handed his cleaned plate to Mrs. Jones. "You've experienced that firsthand."

"The emigrants have a hard time when they first arrive," Amos explained, taking over for the superintendent. "The colonial government gives them six months of room and board before they are expected to provide for themselves. Many are not yet recovered when the time is up. We try to help when we can and usually have the cooperation of the local government, though the ACS agent Ashmun sometimes grumbles about it."

"Why would he do that?" Sylvanus asked.

Seys swallowed and said, "For the same reason politicians do anything, I expect, Dr. Goheen—for the love of their own power."

Silence provided the opportunity for the implication of this statement to penetrate fully. All was not well, it seemed, in the Colony of Liberia, between the ACS-established government and its missionary partners.

"What can you tell me of the natives?" Sylvanus finally asked, now eager to learn from the superintendent all he might share about this new life.

Seys pursed his lips and glanced to the missionaries beside him before answering.

"They're tribal but can be roughly divided into two main cultural groups. Around Monrovia, you'll find mainly the Bassa. They speak Kwa, as do the Dei to the north and the Cru to the south. They answer to kings, but their governmental structure is only loosely connected and so they can be tricky to negotiate with. Even so, some of our mission outposts have made good inroads with them. Brother Brown has had much success at Heddington."

George Brown, his head bowed in a show of humility, clasped his hands on the table. Sylvanus gave it a moment to see if the missionary might elaborate. He did not.

"And the other group?"

"The Mel-speaking tribes of the Mende people. These you will find toward the interior. They are more organized and send their people to a kind of warrior initiation school, which is what likely happened to our young Emma."

"They'll mutilate her, I'm telling you. Destroy the flesh that would make her a woman." Mrs. Jones had given the impression she wasn't listening, but clearly the loss of the girl troubled her enough even to raise such an indelicate subject in mixed company, and over breakfast.

If what she claimed was true, Sylvanus could understand why. He looked to John, to the two missionaries, for some evidence of her exaggeration. They offered none.

Instead, George Brown explained, "It's difficult to know what exactly transpires in the Devil Bush. Outsiders are not allowed in. All we know for certain is that many of the Mende are often less open to Christianity than the more hospitable Bassa tribes. They keep their secrets."

"Are they violent?" Questions streamed through Sylvanus's head, but this seemed the most important. Were these men, to whom he would attempt to bring the light of Christ, whose wounds he might tend, in their hearts true savages engaging in human sacrifice and cannibalism?

George scratched at his chin and did not answer as promptly as Sylvanus would have

liked. "Generally, no."

Amos spoke next. "You want to be careful, though. There is lingering resentment toward the emigrant community. The natives want our trade, and they'll accept the educational opportunities for their children—"

"But they don't want to give the emigrants a speck more land." The thought was completed by George Brown.

Amos added, "And they don't want our God."

"I disagree with you, Amos." George spoke more forcefully this time, as a man weary of a well-worn conversation. "They do not yet know God. His power is as transformative on this Dark Continent as it is on the American frontier."

Brown locked eyes with Sylvanus, his next words directed exclusively to the group's new physician. "But there is an evil spirit in this land. It has a firm hold on the hearts of the people and will not easily let go. If you've never come face to face with the Devil, Dr. Goheen, you soon will."

The morning was already a hot one, but Sylvanus hardly cared, so relieved was he to see the bright sunlight. He returned to his room only long enough to grab his medical bag and a dose of quinine to combat the dull ache in his limbs, which he attributed to the damp environment. He considered opening the slat window overlooking the orchard to catch a few rays of the long absent sun, but prudence gained the advantage. The rains would return, perhaps within the hour, and with them would come disease. As missionary physician, perhaps the only man with significant medical skill in all of Monrovia, he could not afford to take chances.

Despite the warmth of the day, he donned his cloak, tucked an umbrella under his arm, and took his time strolling down the path leading toward the coast and the ugly barracks, referred to locally as the longhouse, where the colonial government temporarily stashed its newest citizens like so many crates of cargo.

Fruit trees lined the street, their branches burdened with bright oranges and lumpy brown tamarinds reminiscent of overlarge peapods. Beyond them stood small houses of brick, stone, and weatherboard, most of them on stilts to better catch the constant breezes which blew both inland and out to sea, alternating every twelve hours. In the distance, Sylvanus saw the roofs of some of the larger public buildings, including both the Baptist and Presbyterian churches, and the unyielding Fort Norris perched in the center of town.

By the time he reached the longhouse, the determined clouds had rolled back into the sky working as hard to dampen his spirit as was the stale odor of sickness awaiting him at the door of the barracks. Approximately eighty feet in length, the building was divided into eight apartments filled with the sick and dying.

A tall light-skinned Black man with drooping jowls and untamed whiskers stepped out of the shadow of the closest apartment doorway to greet him. "Sir," said the man, confusion laced with his words. "May I help you?"

There were few white men in the colony. As far as Sylvanus knew, only he, Dr. Bacon, and the recently returned Reverend Seys fit that description. If one counted fourteen-year-old Jacobus Seys who had traveled with his father, the total came to only four. Sylvanus's keen awareness of this imbalance filled him with an uncomfortable anxiety.

"My name is Dr. Goheen."

The man's posture straightened, and he appeared to light from within. "You're the Methodist doctor."

"Yes." Sylvanus's heartrate slowed. "I hoped to find Dr. Bacon here and to offer my assistance if he could use it."

"He can use it." The man wiped his left hand on his loose trousers and offered it to Sylvanus who shook it. "I'm Dr. Proud, Dr. Bacon's assistant and apprentice."

"I'm pleased to meet you."

"The pleasure is mine, Dr. Goheen. Let me show you what we're facing."

Sylvanus followed Dr. Proud through the doorway from which he had stepped. Four sets of stacked bunks lined the walls of the small apartment that included few amenities. Against the only bit of wall not obscured by the bunks was a dry washbasin and a wood-burning stove with a spider web stretching from cooking surface to floor. Three of the bunks contained occupants, only one of whom looked up when the two physicians entered the room.

"Thirty-six emigrants arrived in early July. Fourteen have died."

"Fourteen." Sylvanus repeated in disbelief, sure he had not heard the man correctly. The number was staggering. When Dr. Proud did not correct him, Sylvanus asked, "All with the same symptoms?"

The Black doctor shook his head. "Not always the same symptoms, but most respond favorably to opium, which Dr. Bacon prescribes liberally."

"If most respond well to treatment, then how exactly have you managed to lose fourteen patients?"

The question was rude, but Sylvanus was incredulous that such significant losses could be claimed so casually. At best it was simply offensive to the practice of medicine; at worst, gross malfeasance.

Dr. Proud's weary features turned to stone. "With all due respect, sir, you've only just arrived. Dr. Bacon is a skilled physician and an excellent teacher. This is an unhealthful and dangerous land."

Sylvanus had not meant to come across as confrontational or difficult. He regretted discouraging the Black physician, the very type of learned man necessary for the success of the colonization effort, but he suspected the famed Dr. Bacon had little skill to offer either his patients or his pupil. Sylvanus left his unkind thoughts unspoken while silently thanking God for his own exposure to the lessons of Dr. Knowles and the wisdom of mission board for requiring the training that might do some good for these patients.

Aloud, he pretended humility. "I apologize. You must know more of practicing medicine in Liberia than I. I'd like to review your active cases if I might."

Dr. Bacon offered a sidelong glance and a stiff nod, his meaning clear. The two men were not yet reconciled, but help would be accepted.

Sylvanus spent the next several hours in the close conditions of the longhouse, visiting patient after patient. Few of the remaining emigrants could claim complete health, though not all of the ill suffered from the tenacious fever of acclimatization sickness. Rather Sylvanus found himself treating numerous sequelae, the fallout from pre-emigration diseases with which he was all too familiar.

Under the supervision, and he hoped careful observation, of Dr Proud, Sylvanus administered diaphoretics and magnesium carbonate for fever and minor illnesses of the liver and stomach. He offered no opium and advised patients on maintaining a light diet through their convalescence, instructing them to pay careful attention to their bowels. For one woman who had long suffered with a cutaneous ulcer on her foot, Sylvanus painted the hard edges with caustic kali, applied a dressing, and instructed the woman to follow up with him in a week's time, eliciting an exasperated grunt from Dr. Proud.

With a new confidence, Sylvanus determined to finish his visit by administering smallpox vaccines to the youngest of the longhouse occupants and made his way back through the now rainy afternoon to retrieve the supply stored in the mission house.

He was twenty yards away when he heard his name shouted from the direction of the seminary.

"Dr. Gohun! Dr. Gohun! Quick, quick!" A native child ran to him through the orchard. He'd seen the boy before, among the students taught by Mrs. Wilkins and Miss Beers. When he reached Sylvanus just outside the mission house, the boy panted his message between deep gulps. "Miss Say baby comin."

Sylvanus hastily followed the boy next door and up the stairs where the superintendent and his family had rooms. Lydia Beers met them at the top of the stairs.

"Thank Heavens you're here. Thank you, Gartee." She dismissed the boy to return to his duties and showed Sylvanus to a closed door behind which a woman groaned.

"How long has she been laboring?" he asked.

"Jacobus came to the mission house to get help an hour ago, but I think she has progressed rapidly. This will be her ninth birthing."

"Has the midwife been summoned?"

Lydia pursed her lips and shook her head. "I think the governor has gotten to her. She doesn't want to help us. Her response was something like, 'You have a doctor now. Let him do it. I'm busy.'"

"Charming." Sylvanus pushed open the door to the bedroom. Mrs. Wilkins, looking about ready to swoon herself, stood beside the bed, holding the hand of Mrs. Seys whose sweaty red skin and wild gray eyes exuded pain and exhaustion.

"Dr. Goheen!" Mrs. Wilkins exclaimed. "I know nothing about delivering babies."

Sylvanus looked to Lydia who only shook her head.

"Very well."

Mrs. Seys groaned again and her back arched. Each new contraction arrived on the heels of the last.

"Mrs. Seys," he said. "I'm going to see what's going on, but I think you are nearly to the conclusion. Lydia, find a clean blanket for baby. Mrs. Wilkins, stay strong for her. Keep hold of her hand."

The two women did as they were told, and Sylvanus moved to the end of the bed to see what already appeared to be a crowning head. Relief flooded him as he took in the welcome sight of a healthy birth in progress.

"I don't think you need me at all, Hannah. You've done most of the hard work already. Just give a strong push at your next contraction."

The woman responded with an almost imperceptible nod, and then an animal growl as she pushed with all her might. Lydia hustled back into the room, an embroidered baby quilt in hand, just as Sylvanus scooped a baby girl with lungs as powerful as her mother's.

"A girl!" Lydia squealed. "She's perfect, Hannah. Absolutely perfect."

Sylvanus smiled at the babe. "She is," he agreed. He nodded to Lydia who held out blanket-covered arms to receive the little one so he could rummage in his bag. Soon the cord was cut and placenta deftly delivered.

It had been quite a day for Monrovia's newest doctor, culminating with the arrival of the littlest member of the mission family now busy rooting for her first feed, safe in the arms of her smiling mother.

21
Annie

"And how was your day as a soldier of the Female Anti-Slavery Society?" Davis asked as he helped Annie to clear the supper from the table.

"I wish you wouldn't tease. It's a serious organization, filled with good women fighting an important battle." It had been three months since Annie had joined the ranks of the Society and in that time, she'd found purpose like she'd never known before. This was more than teaching a few Black children to read. She was a part of an organized force pushing against the institution of slavery itself.

"So I hear." Davis sat and pulled some pages from the satchel at the foot of his chair. "I suppose you haven't mentioned your youngest brother off to recolonize Africa, a proper enemy to righteousness?"

She rolled her eyes. "I have not."

Annie had appreciated living with her older brother again for these weeks, getting to know him as an adult, but there were times he chose to be as exasperating as when they were children. "But just what do you hear?"

Davis dropped the papers to the table and rubbed at his eyes. "Don't misunderstand me, Annie. I appreciate this is helping you cope with your loss. There's no question it's been good for you. I still can't see how getting people to sign a petition that will never be read is helpful to your cause."

"To my cause?" She draped the wet dishcloth across her bucket of heated water, wiped her hands on her apron, and sat across from him. "Is this not your cause, too?"

"You know that's not what I meant. Yes, slavery should end. I signed your damned petition, didn't I?"

"There's no need to swear." Annie looked at her brother with fresh eyes. He was tired, more so than usual. There was a tension in his face she hadn't seen before, and his cheeks sagged. "Are you unwell?"

He looked down at the table, at the papers displaying columns of numbers. "I'm well." "You're not."

He raised his blue eyes to meet her concerned gaze. Were it not for the shadow of whiskers indicative of a long day, she might have been looking at her own reflection. Davis possessed the same long nose, the same narrow chin that she did, and when he laughed, a shallow dimple appeared on his left cheek, as it did on hers. If only he wore it now, she could shake the sense of foreboding enveloping her.

"I have some news I need to discuss with you," he said.

Annie folded her hands. "What news?"

"I've been offered a position as the chief financial officer of an institution, a college."

Relieved, she let out a breath. "That sounds like good news. Why do you look ill?"

"It is good news. It's a good opportunity for me, but I would have to relocate."

"I see." Annie began wringing her hands and her head swam. Philadelphia was not her home but it had become her sanctuary; the women of the Anti-Slavery Society, her dear friends. "Where will you be going?"

"The college is in Illinois."

Annie's chest tightened.

"It's a young institution, only established six years ago. They need financial expertise—expertise I possess."

"In Illinois?"

He nodded. "It's the first college of its kind in the entire state."

"But why you? Surely there's someone else who could go. You've barely begun in the position you have here."

"It's a Methodist school. I was approached through the church. There's no one as qualified as I am." The next words he spoke so softly she strained to hear them. "Or as willing."

"You're as bad as Smee."

Now he did smile, his dimple popping into his cheek, daring her to smack it off of him.

"Maybe he's inspired me. He can't be the only adventurer in the family." He frowned, a reflection of the dismay he must have observed on her own face at his mention of the parallel. "Illinois is not Liberia."

She stood and grabbed the dishcloth, flinging water to the floor with a snap. "It might as well be. Have you considered Mother? Mayberry left her for New York and has a family of his own. Smee left for the other side of the world where he'll probably be eaten by cannibals. It's only a matter of time before William and John Wesley strike out as well. And I'll be the one left. Alone. Alone with Mother."

"Calm down, Annie. It's not all that bad. If you know anything about our mother at all, then you know she can fend for herself. You could come with me."

"To Illinois?"

"Yes. Please, come with me."

"I can't." Annie said the words before she even thought about whether or not they were true. Her brother's forehead crinkled forming a ridge above his nose. "I'm trying to determine what reason you might have for refusing my invitation. You can't remain in

Philadelphia, a single woman alone. Even a fierce warrior of the Female Anti-Slavery Society wouldn't be so bold. Your teaching position has been filled. You've no students awaiting your return. To hear you tell it, there are no eligible bachelors you might consider in Columbia. What is holding you here?"

Annie's mouth opened with a response she couldn't articulate. Davis wasn't wrong. Still, he was infuriating. In the space created by her own silence, she allowed herself to consider the possibility, to picture herself at the edge of civilization, surrounded by hostile natives and wild men hardened by the toil of carving a life out of new land. She could not envision herself among them, so far from the civilization of the east.

More sternly this time, she said, "I can't."

"Yes, you can, Annie." He stood and fixed her with the same unyielding stare that, when they were younger, meant he was itching for a fight. "Illinois isn't the wild west. It's a state, as civilized as Pennsylvania. It's a comfortable place to make a home."

"You haven't been there."

"I've been reading about it and corresponding with the college. The town is growing, likely in need of qualified teachers." He dropped his gaze to the abandoned papers strewn across the table. "And there aren't as many sophisticated ladies there as there are men who want to marry them."

A flash of anger replaced any sympathy she might at the prospect of seeing him travel alone to the edge of the civilized world. She turned away, hiding the color rising in her cheeks.

"Well then, dear brother, you should marry yourself a fine lady and drag her with you to Illinois. I am not a bride to be bartered, and you are a grown man. If you need your sister to take care of you, then perhaps you shouldn't go either."

"Do you regret your decision?" Mother asked the moment the stagecoach was out of sight, Davis and his dreams of adventure aboard with only two bags of worldly possessions and no sister to accompany him to his new home in Illinois.

Annie hesitated but shook her head. "No. This is Davis's great adventure, not mine. I'm grateful to have had time with him these past few months, though. I never noticed before how alike he and Smee can be. I shouldn't be surprised he jumped at an opportunity to run away from home."

"Yes," Mother agreed, turning back to the carriage where William stood calming the horses with apple slices and whispers. "Of all my children, you and Sylvanus have always been the closest, but he and Davis have always been the most alike, and the most like your father."

"And I've always been your favorite," William chimed in.

Mother smiled at the familiar jest. "I love all my children." She reached behind her, took Annie's hand in hers and squeezed. "I'm glad you didn't decide to run away, too."

William held out his hand to see their mother into the carriage and then offered the same to Annie, a playful scowl on his face when she took his arm. She giggled.

As soon as she was settled, William hoisted himself into the driver's seat and slapped the reins. The carriage rolled forward and Mother said to Annie, "There's another person who will be happy you've come back home. Esther is expecting a baby."

"Already?" Annie smiled with her lips, but the joy did not reach her eyes. It had been difficult watching her friend marry when she should have been a bride at the same time. She'd thought it might yet be a while before she faced the reality that she'd lost more than a husband, but also the opportunity for a family of her own to nurture. This sad realization plagued her thoughts until William drove the carriage onto their lane. The moment Annie saw the home that should have brought her respite and comfort, she instead felt a twinge of regret she wasn't on her way to Illinois.

Four days after they saw Davis off for his great adventure in the West, two letters arrived from Liberia. The first was a brief account from Smee. He had reached Monrovia safely and found himself thrust into a medical crisis. The way he wrote, she got the impression most white men and women dropped dead the moment they touched foot on African soil, and so she was relieved to discover the second letter had come from Hannah Seys.

To Miss Ann Goheen—

I must as always express my great gratitude at your willingness to write to me. Your letters of home, or nearly home for me, provide a beautiful distraction from the troubles around me. We are so grateful your brother has arrived, and I believe his work has already begun to improve the general health of the mission. My ministrations of comfort in the throes of African sickness can only do so much, but in his skilled hands I believe we will fare better.

I was especially grateful for his calm medical expertise recently. Not two weeks after his arrival, your brother did me and my family a great service. He oversaw the birth of my ninth child, a daughter we have named Maria. I have previously lost children, beginning with my oldest boy, a sickly child who died on our journey from the West Indies where we married, to the United States. Two other dear ones rest in African soil.

I don't tell you this so you will grieve for me, but to demonstrate for you how much I treasure your brother's presence in this place, which is often bleak. I have witnessed much death and can admit to you, my dear friend, that I feared this birth as none of my others before it. We have one local midwife, a colored emigrant who has become wary of administering medical aid to the missionaries as the relationship between the ACS and local government officials grows more strained.

But God was with me and with Maria, who is healthy and strong, on that wonderful day, and His Holy Spirit attended me with love and care in the person of Sylvanus. You should be proud of him and of the work he does here for the Glory of our Heavenly Father.

I pray you and your family are well, as I also pray for the day I might greet you in person.

Hannah Seys
Monrovia, 1837

Annie shook her head. "I do not understand men at all."

"Who does?" Esther sat across from her on the porch steps.

Annie laughed. "I wish you'd come inside and sit in a chair."

Esther's growing belly already overwhelmed her petite frame, but she moved as if nothing had changed in the five months of her pregnancy. "I like the cool out here." She patted her baby bulge.

Annie set the letter from Hannah on the step beside her and smiled at her friend. She wanted to be gracious enough to sympathize with Esther's discomfort, but no matter how fervently she prayed for relief, jealousy lingered.

"What does your brother have to say?"

Esther's question brought Annie back into the moment. Remorse stabbed at her. "He writes of terrible things. Disease and death and savages. If I only had his words on which to judge I'd be convinced I'd never see him again. I almost don't dare share his letters with Mother."

"Menfolk tell tales."

Annie wished she could share her friend's confidence. She sighed. "It might really be that terrible, but why he won't share the beautiful things with me, I couldn't explain. He delivered a healthy baby to Hannah Seys."

"The superintendent's wife?" Esther snatched up Hannah's letter and began to fan herself.

"Yes. And my brother didn't even mention it."

"I suppose men don't think much about birthing babies." One of Esther's hands returned to her abdomen.

"Are you frightened, Esther?"

"Me? No. I've seen birth, even helped with it before. And I've seen a lot worse, too. Besides," she closed her eyes and continued to fan with one hand as the other continued to move back and forth across her belly. "I've got you to help me through."

Emotion swelled in Annie's throat, and she swallowed hard against it. "Yes, you do. And Mother and Bennett. You and your baby are so loved."

Annie gently patted her friend's back and nearly choked on the heartache that threatened to break her.

22
Sylvanus

Sylvanus moved through the oppressive stuffiness of the mission house with purpose and the knowledge that his skills were indispensable for the mission. It was a burden he'd not felt entirely prepared to carry, but he did find himself growing into the role. He'd toiled over the sickbeds of the greatest missionaries of God and led them back from the edge of death like the Savior calling forth Lazarus. He had bandaged wounds, soothed aches, and even safely delivered the superintendent's child. Still, he feared the day his knowledge would prove insufficient.

Sylvanus climbed the stairs and knocked on the door of the room dedicated to mother and child. The Seys family rooms were part of the seminary building, but when the superintendent recently departed to Heddington with George Brown, Sylvanus had insisted on moving Hannah closer to himself and his medical supplies. She had been ill after the birth of her babe and had yet to recover her strength as fully as he'd have liked.

The child, Maria, thrived in her first weeks of life, suckling greedily and howling out her tiny complaints while her mother fought fevers and chills, summoning barely enough strength to feed her greedy babe.

"How is our patient, Jacobus?"

Hannah's eldest son stood when addressed. He'd been her most diligent nurse during these long, hot days when the mission's busy women taught and cared for a large collection of native and missionary children. Jacobus was a devout and serious young man who at fifteen stood nearly as tall as his father, and who possessed a curiosity about the world that rivaled Sylvanus's at the same age.

The young man set aside the book in which he had been engrossed and motioned for the conversation to move to the hallway. "She and the baby are both resting finally," he said, quietly closing the door behind them.

Sylvanus examined the boy more closely. His usually bright, curious eyes were dull. Fatigue settled in dark circles beneath them. "How long have you been here? Did none of the women relieve you?"

"They offered." He shrugged. "The baby was fussy. Mother fought fever and chills through the night and complained of stabbing pain in her head. I couldn't leave. I'm good at calming Maria and I think Mother feels better knowing I'm here."

Sylvanus placed a hand on the young man's arm. "I'm sure she does. She's fortunate to have a son so dedicated to her."

He nearly choked on the words, for he meant them. He'd never been such a son. Sylvanus had moved half a world away from his mother despite her apprehension. Jacobus Seys traded long, carefree hours as a student of the world and of nature to soothe his baby sister and mop his mother's fevered brow.

"You should get some rest while you can. I'll send one of the women to sit with them."

The boy glanced at the closed door as if skeptical.

"Son, you will be no good to them if you don't take care to maintain your own health."

Jacobus swiped at his nose and grimaced in response.

Sylvanus added, "I don't want your father to return to find you sick, too. My reputation would be left in tatters."

The boy eased into a lopsided grin. "You win, Dr. Goheen. Send one of the women in and I'll go get some sleep." He stepped into the hallway before turning back, his expression somber. "You'll wake me if she worsens or asks for me?"

Sylvanus looked toward the blanketed outline of the sleeping Hannah Seys and to the bassinette beside her. "Yes, I will retrieve you if your patient needs you, Dr. Seys."

"Dr. Seys." Jacobus nodded. "I like the sound of that."

Sylvanus watched the young man shuffle off down the stairs and chuckled. There was a spark of something in Jacobus Seys—of scientific curiosity and a love of humanity—perhaps the same kind of spark Sylvanus's mentor had once seen in him. He'd have to see if it could be fanned into a flame.

The mission house, normally a busy hub of much activity, stood fairly quiet in the late afternoon. When the morning rain passed, the young class meeting led by Mrs. Wilkins had gone outside to the orchard to enjoy the breeze as they worked on their letters.

Sylvanus found he liked the young students, once they were reasonably civilized. The native children often arrived at their doorstep naked and without a single English word, but with the proper attention were soon properly attired and could manage the niceties of civil conversation.

He generally only interacted with them during worship, but at the suggestion of Lydia, had noticed curious glances at his work as he toiled to bring about better outcomes for his patients. He was tolerant of the children, even indulging those bold enough to ask him questions, in part, he realized, because such patience elicited warm looks from their pretty teacher.

The people he found it most difficult to abide were the adult natives who frequented the mission house asking for "dash" or gifts. If they could provide the mission with something, some information or contact it needed, then they would receive it as food or a bolt of fabric. Some of the missionaries had resorted to luring the natives to church service with such gifts, a practice he thought both wasteful and fruitless.

Sylvanus found Abigail, a dark-skinned emigrant woman who helped with the housework, and asked her to attend to Hannah Seys.

With the superintendent gone and a low patient load, the house was almost too quiet. Sylvanus was on the verge of sitting down to write a letter home when a ruckus outside the house called his attention. He glanced out the front window of the sitting room and could see the students and their teacher in a neat circle among the trees. The commotion was not coming from them.

"What is all that?" Jacobus asked from the kitchen table where he'd not made it past an inviting basket of bread. Fed and distracted, he had bounced back to alertness as only the young can do.

"I don't know." Sylvanus crossed from window to kitchen door to discover the source of the disruption.

"Doctor, Doctor!" several natives, black as night shouted and moved toward Sylvanus in a group, carrying with them another man who dripped blood into the dirt. Sylvanus jumped into action, waving the men through the door to the patient room. He indicated with his best hand signals to place the man on the cot nearest the entrance and accepted several clean cloths from Jacobus.

Sylvanus examined the injury carefully, hollering for water. Jacobus signaled to one of the native men and together they brought him the entire basin of warm water. Sylvanus dunked one of the rags and wrung it out over the side of the writhing man, whose abdomen stood open wide with a single long slice from sternum to naval.

"What happened?" he asked as he worked to staunch the bleeding, pressing rag after rag against the gaping wound. Several answers came rushing at him at once, but not one of them arrived in a language Sylvanus could understand.

"It doesn't matter," he tried to explain. "I need more hands." Jacobus stepped up, but Sylvanus waved him off. "You are supposed to be resting!"

He pointed to a tall, slender man in only a loose pair of trousers, which was more than some of his companions wore. "You!" Sylvanus grabbed him by both hands and pulled him toward the wounded man. The reluctant assistant took a minute before he seemed to understand what Sylvanus wanted him to do. Revulsion registered on his drawn face, and he raised his hands and backed toward the door.

Jacobus leaned in again and this time Sylvanus did not stop him as the young man took over holding pressure against the wound. With well-practiced hands Sylvanus threaded a long, curved needle with catgut string and went to work, weaving it in and out of the screaming patient's skin.

The procedure took what felt to Sylvanus like hours. His back was stiff and as the adrenaline left his body, he collapsed onto a chair. He finally convinced Jacobus to leave. The men who had brought him the patient left soon after. Only one remained and took a seat beside both Sylvanus and the cot.

The patient slept fitfully. Sylvanus watched the rise and fall of his chest and prayed God might spare him, though he knew it was unlikely. The man had lost so much blood, a lot of which now slicked the mission house floor from kitchen to cot. It covered Sylvanus, too, no longer the civilized one when he looked at the native beside him who wore some type of wrap covering both his manhood and half of his chest. Sylvanus gazed at him for a full minute.

And then the man spoke. "He will not live."

The comment surprised Sylvanus, as did the careful and unbroken English.

Sylvanus took a deep breath of putrid air that carried hints of the bitter tang of blood. "I think he will not," he replied, then added, "but the human body can sometimes surprise. God heals where he chooses. All we can do is put forward our best efforts and pray that it be His will this man is saved."

Several seconds passed in silence before the native man responded. "Your god, he could save this man?"

"Yes, He could. It remains to be seen whether or not He will. I have done what I can. Is he important to you?"

"He is the headman. He is important, but he is a bad man. He will not live." The man spoke with stunning conviction.

"What is your name?" Sylvanus asked.

"My English name is Robert. My African name, a white man could not say."

Sylvanus wouldn't argue. Robert suited him.

"Will you continue to sit with him, Robert? Watch over him?"

The man nodded, and Sylvanus rose from his chair. "I'm going to try to clean myself up." He walked through the kitchen, careful not to slip in the blood.

"Were you able to save him?" Jacobus sat at the kitchen table, his head resting on his arms.

Sylvanus held back the reprimand on his tongue. The boy should be in bed, would be if not for an insatiable curiosity Sylvanus grudgingly admired.

"He lives for now. One of his own people is sitting with him. I doubt he will survive the night. He lost far too much blood."

"Could I have done something differently?"

"No," Sylvanus said, shocked to see how upset the young man had become. "Of course not. He arrived at our doorstep with a serious injury. You and I did everything we could, exactly as we should have. I could not have helped at all without your assistance."

Exhaustion painted Jacobus's features, exhaustion that Sylvanus had begun to feel seep into his own bones.

"I was just going to wash up and check on your mother. Go get some sleep. Now."

"Yes, sir." The young man rubbed his face with both hands. "Mother is doing better. The fever has cooled, and she is sweating."

"Good. That's good. She'll be on her feet taking charge of all of us again before long."

"I have no doubt."

"Off you go."

Sylvanus watched him trudge out through the front door and then stepped outside himself and walked to the pump, stripping off his soiled shirt as he went. He'd have been more discreet at home, but here in the wilds of Africa, surrounded by the darkness of night which he was usually careful to avoid, he seemed constantly overdressed anyway.

The cool water refreshed him, but it wouldn't wash away the knowledge that he had probably just lost his first patient in Africa.

The fever set in later that night. Sylvanus and Robert took turns cooling the patient's brow with compresses, but Sylvanus knew, and suspected Robert did as well, they fought against an enemy they could not defeat. The headman slipped away before dawn broke. Robert left shortly after, and with the sun came a wailing like Sylvanus had never heard.

A large crowd of native Africans in various states of dress stood at the kitchen door of the mission house. Their shouts and cries were wild and somehow ancient, infused with a grief almost palpable and so uniquely human, Sylvanus nearly wept at the sound.

"We've come for the body." Robert pushed his way through the front of the crowd. Both Ann Wilkins and Lydia Beers rushed into the kitchen to see what the ruckus was all about, but Sylvanus waved them back.

"Just you, Robert," he said. "I will help you."

Sylvanus moved aside to let the lean African through the door. Robert said a few words to the people closest to him, and though their excitement did not waver, nor their wailing decrease, they made no move to follow him.

Lydia grabbed Sylvanus by the elbow, her eyes wide with fear. He reassured her with a pat on the arm, leaned his head toward hers, and whispered, "All will be well."

She bit her bottom lip but did not argue with him. She nodded once. Her trust emboldened him and added to his determination to protect her.

The mourners were wild in their communal grief, but he did not sense particular danger from them. They were all men as far as he could see, perhaps all the men from Robert's tribe.

Sylvanus and Robert worked together in tandem with little need to communicate verbally. The body had been washed and wrapped in a clean sheet, leaving only the need for each man to grab an end of the corpse and carry it together back through the kitchen, an action that earned them a well-deserved look of disgust from Mrs. Wilkins.

Outside, the noise grew louder when the gathered men caught sight of the grisly package. From within their gathering was produced a long pole. Someone took over Sylvanus's end of the burden and he stepped back, watching as they swiftly secured each end of the sheet to the pole. Two of the men then hoisted the pole onto their shoulders and as the crowd divided for them, they marched through the middle, bearing their deceased headman like a field-dressed deer on a triumphant return from a successful hunt.

The procession fell out, moving behind the bizarre trophy as the noise continued, now accompanied by a series of grotesque movements, some primitive form of dance. Sylvanus couldn't tear his attention from it, and without a word to the women in the house, he followed.

His mind filled with memories of funeral processions in the United States. His father's he couldn't remember, but as a physician's apprentice, he had attended several. Though more solemn, the grieving process might have been similar in some ways. The Africans, it seemed, expressed verbally what was only felt as internal suffering at an American funeral.

He followed them away from the Mission House and away from Monrovia, along the St. Paul River, leaving behind civilization and pushing their way into the bush. For miles he trailed them and though he did not join in with the expressions of grief, no one questioned his presence. He wondered how the large group of men continued to have the energy to keep up their fuss, as he grew tired just in the walking.

At last, they stopped at a shallow pit on the outskirts of what looked to be a settlement of small huts. Without further comment, the pallbearers dropped the corpse into the pit and Robert emerged once again to unroll the sheet, exposing the headman to view.

The corpse didn't look a good deal worse for its hike stretched on a pole. The headman's legs and arms were now splayed, and he lay naked for all the world to see. Blood and bodily juices seeped from his wound. Sylvanus looked aside, uncomfortable with what struck him as a violent and irreverent exposure of the dead.

Robert clasped an offered hand and hoisted himself up out of the pit. Then he made his way toward Sylvanus with a ghastly grin across his face.

"Will you bury him here?"

"No, Doctor," Robert said, clearly amused at Sylvanus's question. "We bury him tomorrow in the Devil Bush." The man pointed west, toward thick woods. "Today we leave his body open, so his soul may go."

"The Devil Bush?" He knew the term, but not the meaning of it.

Robert nodded. "That bush is where the devil makes his home. It is where the dead go to live. We will place him there."

Sylvanus nodded as though he understood, but the concepts these foreign men espoused were utterly strange to him. He tried to see how Christ could fit into the lives of those who believed the devil was their only connection to the spirit world, and he wondered if this devil of which Robert spoke was, in fact, the Devil of Christianity. He gazed toward the dense woods, unnaturally dark in the bright daylight as if a gray mist hung over them even in the height of the afternoon.

As he watched, the nearest trees rustled. A breeze swept over him, hot and moist like the breath of a beast. Sylvanus's skin tingled and he shivered as he stepped closer to the edge of the woods, unable to shake the sensation that he'd been watched, evaluated, and found wanting.

"You don't want to be going there, Doctor." Robert placed a hand on his shoulder. "Not a Christian man like you."

The words snapped Sylvanus back to himself. He had no wish to argue Robert's point. Something sinister lurked in those trees.

"You be getting home now." Robert pointed toward the river. I have a boat. I'll take you."

"Thank you," Sylvanus muttered. He stepped after his gracious guide, infected by the sensation that something from the bush watched him, even followed him, settling over him like the same dense fog he'd observed in the bush itself.

Sylvanus climbed into the boat, dizzy with all he had witnessed. He could not shake off the cold that overwhelmed him, seeping into his bones as he stared into the Devil Bush, and another set of shivers traveled up his spine. He pulled his arms around himself.

"What is wrong, Doctor?" Robert's expression became grave, his obsidian features etched with concern.

"Nothing at all. I think my nerves have just gotten the better of me, is all." Sylvanus said the words, but he didn't believe them. The bone-chilling cold had settled on him like a blanket of ice, holding his terror close. "Tell me, have you been in the Devil's Bush?"

"I have for palaver, but it is not a place to go."

Palaver was a word Sylvanus did know, had even used himself. It was a meeting of sorts. The churches at their outer mission establishments held "God palaver" for the natives in which missionaries did their best to translate the Western concepts of Father, Son, and Holy Spirit in a way that could be understood by devil-worshipping savages. Their tales made Sylvanus grateful for his medical training, which saved him from frequent engagements with such activity, though certainly he hoped and prayed for their success. For if the great experiment of the colony of Liberia were to succeed, even the land itself must be won for God.

"What's in there?"

"The Devil and his spirits."

At Robert's ominous words, Sylvanus began to shiver again and this time he could not suppress it. His African companion looked on him with pity as he dropped on his side into the bottom of the boat where he lay shaking.

"I will get you home, Doctor."

The sweats hit him as the edge of Monrovia came into view. He couldn't be sure how he had managed the hundred yards to the mission house but knew he had relied heavily on Robert who practically dragged him to their destination. About the next many hours, he remembered little—images mostly of Lydia bringing him damp cloths for his head, trying to spoon broth into him, wiping his chin and rubbing his back when he couldn't hold it down. Jacobus, too, sat beside his bed, reading aloud from Swift's *Gulliver's Travels*.

Three days passed before his head had begun to clear, though it pounded desperately as if his brain might be clawing its way out of his skull. "Lydia," he whispered as she walked into the room with a tray holding a steaming bowl.

"Doctor Goheen," she greeted him. "You gave us a fright, but I think you are through the worst of it for now."

"African sickness?" He knew the pieces fit. His symptoms, the ice flowing in his veins, had nothing to do with evil spirit from the Devil Bush. He had succumbed after all to the great sickness of all white men and many of the Black missionaries and emigrants as well. And he had survived his first bout with it, which he thought a good sign that his constitution would allow him to continue to serve this dark continent.

Lydia's complexion darkened. A tear streaked down her cheek.

"My dear lady, are you unwell?" He couldn't abide seeing a woman cry. Sylvanus had been raised by a woman who never cried to the best of his knowledge and a sister who remained stoic in nearly every circumstances. He'd not been equipped to handle female tears.

"It's nothing." She waved away his concern and brought him the bowl containing a thin, brown broth. He accepted it from her, feeling now strong enough to at least feed himself, though his head spun when he sat up and he wondered if he'd be able to do anything else.

"Can you manage?"

"Yes," he assured her, instilling his voice with more confidence than he truthfully possessed. "I am mending nicely thanks, I am quite certain, to your diligent ministrations."

"It's not been only my doing. You've been well looked after. Mrs. Wilkins has been here much of the time, and Jacobus."

Sylvanus leaned forward at Lydia's request, and she tucked a rolled blanket behind him. It offered welcome relief from the tension in his back. She had good instincts for patient care. He'd noticed as much at the birth of Hannah's baby, too.

"You make a fine nurse."

Lydia lowered herself into the chair beside his sickbed and sighed. "Hannah would do better, I'm sure."

Sylvanus swallowed some broth. It was warm and rich, and it slid easily down his throat. It was comforting, as was the presence of the woman beside him. She was warm, too, and agreeable and hardworking and pleasant to behold. Lydia was sturdy and reliable and competent, features Sylvanus found a great deal more attractive than a shapely waist and rosy cheeks, though she did possess such features. And full lips as well that were moving, saying something he'd not heard.

"...She has so little energy. Between you and me, I think the superintendent is right."

"Hannah, you mean."

Lydia smiled and stood. "I think I'd better let you rest."

"No," he said sharply.

She regained her seat, her smile hardening a touch.

"I apologize," he was quick to add. "My mind is still adrift. What were you saying about the superintendent? About Mrs. Seys? Is she still unwell?"

"Reverend Seys wants to send her to the United States to recover her strength."

"This upsets her." He could read as much in Lydia's expression, the worry in the light furrows of her brow that told him more. "It upsets you as well."

"Yes, Dr. Goheen. It does." She threw up an exasperated hand and Sylvanus felt a pang of undeserved guilt. "It is difficult for a woman. We throw our hearts, our energy, and even our health into our life's work, and a man can take it away as if it were all for nothing."

Sylvanus set aside his bowl and swiveled his body so that he faced her more fully. "I hardly believe it is John's intention to hurt her."

Lydia's shoulders dropped. "No, of course it isn't. But she has given so much. She's even buried two children on African soil. Did you know that?"

He had not.

"She'll rest. She'll recover her strength. She'll be back."

Lydia's eyes had grown watery, but she nodded and sniffed. "Yes, I think that's true, but I also know she sees it as banishment, a punishment for her weakness."

Sylvanus wanted to reach out and capture her in his arms but remembered himself in the last moment. He was sick in bed, weakened from days of fever, and not at his best. If there would ever be a time for holding Lydia, this was not it.

He settled for saying, "It's not weakness to need rest."

Reverend Seys returned only a few hours later filled with joyful news from the settlement of Heddington where George Brown had brought more than a hundred souls out of the darkness of savage Africa and into the light of Christ Jesus.

"You should see it," he said to Sylvanus. His vigilant nurses had not allowed the doctor to return to normal activity, demanding he spend at least this day in bed. He was grateful to them but also anxious to get back to work.

"He has them all dressed in appropriate clothing and though the language they use is a broken sort of English, they listen to Brother Brown's counsel. God is at work."

"That's wonderful news."

"It is. It's news I will share with the Mission Board in person when I travel there next month."

"You're going to America?" Sylvanus tried to hide his disappointment.

"This is the life of a superintendent. I oversee the great work the missionaries under me are doing and I make certain they continue to have the funds they need. It requires a lot of travel and speaking."

"I thought the mission store brought in enough money to sustain us."

"It does, but it is only as successful as the goods that come into it. To ensure we continue to receive those goods, I will have to beg. Also, I would like to accompany Hannah and the children."

"You'll all go?"

"I think it would be easier for her, though Jacobus has expressed a strong desire to stay, and I am inclined to allow it. He's become a great admirer of you."

"And I of him," Sylvanus said. "Would you have time to look in at Columbia?"

"To see your kind family? I'd consider it a great honor to do so, and I know Hannah would appreciate the opportunity to meet your sister in person. You know they correspond regularly?"

"I did know. Your wife hears from my sister far more than I do. I'm jealous."

"Women do need one another, after all," John said. "I rarely think they need us at all."

23
Annie

Annie couldn't contain her enthusiasm at the prospect of seeing her friend despite the fact that her mother's patience had worn thin.

"For goodness sake, you are a woman grown, and giddy as a schoolgirl in braids."

"Mother, Hannah Seys is one of my most intimate friends and I have never even met her. I'm so antsy I might burst. And you would be, too, even a woman as old as you."

Annie's hands flew to her mouth, but Mother only laughed. Over the past few years, they had almost grown to be friends more than mother and daughter.

"My daughter, the most disrespectful, excitable, old maid in the county."

Even well-deserved, the comment stung. "Oh, Mother."

John and Hannah Seys arrived the precise day they said they would, and it turned out to be a beautiful, sunny summer afternoon. With them traveled four of their children, including the baby Maria whose chubby cheeks and shining eyes enchanted them both. One daughter, fourteen-year-old Mary, remained with her grandmother in Connecticut, recovering from an illness. Their eldest son remained in Africa with Smee.

Mother pulled aside Reverend Seys to pepper him with questions, giving Annie some much anticipated time to speak with Hannah.

"We should take a picnic out to the pond." Annie wiggled her nose at the babe in her friend's arms. Little Maria cooed back at her, causing a flutter in her heart and a familiar yearning. Esther's dear boy, only recently born, had the same effect on her.

"A picnic sounds wonderful, doesn't it, children?" Hannah Seys addressed her brood, which ranged in age from eight months to twelve years. She shifted the baby on her hip and shooed the lot of them outside.

Annie smiled to see the two boys shoving one another in their rush to escape the tedium of the adults, their four-year-old sister Jane trotting happily in their wake. It might have been an image from her own childhood when she and her brothers were the ones rushed from the house so the grownups might have some peace. She smiled.

"I can't tell you how wonderful it is to lay eyes on you, my friend," Hannah said as she watched her children go.

"I was delighted to receive your letter, and so glad you could make the time to come see us while you're in the country."

"Your brother sent us here specially, a command we were happy to oblige. He's sent a letter." Annie took a folded note from her and set it on a side table. She would read it with Mother later, but they would learn little from it. Her brother had been a less than faithful writer of letters home, and the few they received rarely contained much information. He filled the pages instead with religious platitudes, unskilled poetry, and terror. She longed for more, her heart aching with the memory of their unsatisfying parting. She feared there was much he'd never tell her. Such a long way their relationship had fallen from when they were young and as close as any siblings could be.

"How is my brother, really? He writes so little." As she spoke, Annie invited Hannah to sit and then settled on the sofa across from her.

"He is well." She bounced the baby on her knee. The little girl squealed with delight.

This was the babe Smee had delivered into the world. The thought warmed Annie through.

"Truly?" She missed her brother so much she felt physical pain in the pit of her stomach.

"Yes, truly. He struggled with a bout of African sickness but came through it as well as anyone. And he's been busy revolutionizing the treatment of our sick. He has more energy than all of us put together, I think, and a great deal of adventurous spirit. I've never known such a curious person. Nearly every day he sets out purposely to either observe the culture of the natives or examine and collect samples of the local flora and fauna. Our Jacobus trails behind him, enamored."

"That sounds like Smee."

Hannah's eyebrows raised at the nickname. She glanced over her shoulder toward Elizabeth and John, then leaned close. "I suspect, too, that he may have found love."

Annie's lip quirked into a skeptical smirk. "Really?" She'd never known her youngest brother to show romantic interest in anyone, though several young ladies had attempted to catch his eye. "Who is she?"

Hannah grinned. "One of the missionary teachers, Lydia Beers. They cross the Atlantic on the same ship. She's lovely and energetic and as committed to the mission as he."

"That's wonderful news." Annie was sure her expression did not match the words that formed her response to this new information which settled into her brain like a distracting hum. Smee's letters contained no reference to this Lydia, a fact that felt to Annie as nothing short of betrayal. Once she had hoped for him to find a good match, an energetic and dedicated woman that might serve as an anchor for his wandering spirit, one that would maintain him securely at home where he belonged. She had not considered he might discover his mooring in Africa.

"You're close, aren't you?" Hannah studied her companion, her brow wrinkled.

Annie shrugged, not entirely sure she wanted to discuss her brother any longer. "We were."

"And you're not now?" Hannah persisted despite the signals Annie tried to send that she'd rather switch topics. "Is it because he went to Liberia?"

"In part. It's difficult to be involved in his life when there's an ocean between us. But there's more to it."

"You don't have to tell me."

"I know." The truth was that once she'd received permission to stop, the idea of putting words to her thoughts about her brother became all at once more appealing. She couldn't speak to her mother or brothers about him. Their own feelings about his mission, his absence, about the awkwardness of their relationships with him obscured her own emotions. "It feels good to talk about it. It is a weight on my soul."

"By all means, please continue."

The happy sound of the Seys children drifted through the window as they ran through the trees, laughing and chasing one another.

"Smee didn't care for my intended."

"Jonas?"

"Yes." Annie's throat clogged with the threat of tears that, after so many months, surprised her in some moments. Though Esther had named her son after him, Annie had not spoken about her ebbing grief over Jonas in a long while, yet it remained difficult to mention him. "He was a good man."

"I've no doubt of that. John has spoken highly of him."

The comment stabbed at Annie's her heart with embarrassment, as she knew the feeling had not been mutual.

"He was a man of deep convictions and he and Smee did not agree on many important things."

"Such as?"

"I'm not sure I should say."

"Jonas was not supportive of the work of the Colonization Society?"

Annie nodded. "Did Reverend Seys tell you?"

"No. He only said my dear friend in America had found herself a staunch and enthusiastic abolitionist in whom he saw a great deal to respect. I assumed the rest. Many abolitionists do not appreciate the work we are trying to do."

Truer words, Annie couldn't have spoken.

"He is a gracious man, your husband. Smee could not abide with someone disagreeing so vehemently with his efforts."

"Your brother is a young man. He'll grow more patient with time."

"I think that's unlikely. Especially if what you say is true." She pictured him with a pretty missionary teacher hanging on his arm, whispering misguided encouragement. She felt his loss more keenly than ever. "But you're gracious, too. You don't think poorly of me loving a man who so opposed your ministry?"

"I'm frustrated we colonizationists and abolitionists can't come together better. We are, after all, two sides to the same coin. We want an end for slavery as much as anyone. We see its genesis in the slave ships prowling our coast, and in the fighting and kidnapping among native tribes. Being in the part of the world where the slavery process begins, we are positioned to intervene and stop it from happening in the first place."

Smee had made a similar point in one of his early letters to her. She could not pretend to understand the problem of slavery from the African perspective. All she knew was that American slaveholders who were not boldly confronted with their sins saw little reason to repent of them.

Hannah continued, "We also believe a free person should be able to decide how he wants to pursue life, liberty, and happiness. An abolitionist could not argue against that."

Annie frowned. She thought highly of this woman and wanted desperately for her to understand her wrong thinking.

"I believe you have a beautiful heart engaged in a pursuit of God, my friend, but I can't agree with you. Ultimately, of course, all free people should be able to choose whether they wish to live their lives here in America or whether they wish instead to pursue life in another land. But we have not yet achieved such a lofty goal. This is not a nation in which all people are free, and until it is, our efforts must not be diverted. If there is no market for slavery here, then the slave ships will stop coming."

The baby squirmed and fussed, and Hannah placed her on the floor where the appeased little girl began to crawl and explore.

"I admire your fervor. It is determined people such as you that God will use to end the horror of slavery. I'm certain of it. Obviously, we don't agree entirely on the means to that end. I can't in good conscience support the restriction of freedom for those who already have it. And neither can your brother."

Annie felt a tug on her skirt as Maria pulled against her in an attempt to stand. The baby had not yet mastered the skill and she fell to her diapered bottom with a frustrated *oof!*

Annie chuckled fondly at the effort and sighed. "I suppose we will never agree."

"But we can love one another. I value your friendship, Annie." Hannah stood and bent to help the little girl stand, supporting the child around her chubby middle. "May I call you Annie? It's how your brother refers to you."

"Yes, of course you may. I value your friendship as well and admire the way you've thrown your life into a new land, an entirely foreign people."

"I have." Hannah's gaze dropped to the wispy curls that topped her daughter's head and she scooped her up. "But if am honest, I have grown weary. I've buried many friends and dear ones in foreign soil. I constantly nurse my sick children as they succumb to the climate of a land that seems determined to shake us off. As disappointed as I was to leave, a part of me was relieved to travel with my husband back to America this time."

Hannah's confession of weariness was shocking in light of her recent words defending colonization. Annie's heart soared to hear a small hint of doubt, and perhaps a slightly renewed hope that the call to Africa may not last forever.

"How long will you remain in the United States?"

"I don't know for certain. John will return soon. The mission needs him, and he'll be accompanied by new missionary recruits as well as a new wave of emigrants. I'm considering staying in Connecticut with my mother and children for a while. I don't wish to be separated from my husband, but I've grown weak since this last pregnancy. My constitution needs rest, and I live in constant fear of losing more of the people I love to a foreign land."

The fatigue in Hannah's voice settled over Annie. It was exhaustion of the soul, which she had herself come to know. All her life she'd cared for others. First her brothers, her students, Esther. Jonas. Her breath caught as the name formed again in her mind, the shape of it filling her with longing and sorrow and regret. Was this what Hannah Seys felt when her husband set out into the world following God's call, when he brought his family from a plantation in the West Indies and committed the body of a beloved son to the raging sea? This was the plight of a woman—called to love and nurture and grieve.

Annie didn't understand the full depth of her friend's sorrows but knew what it was to need rest.

For three days, Annie relished the chaos of a full house with children in every room and a crowd at every meal. The Seys family made for cheerful guests. William regaled them all with animated readings each night and John Wesley was always ready with tasks and encouragement for the young boys during the days. Mother, too, seemed to loosen, long held stress draining from her as she slipped treats to the Seys children and snuggled little Maria.

The revelry came to a halt with the arrival of a letter addressed to Reverend and Mrs. Seys from a Mrs. Osborn in Connecticut—Hannah's mother. John read it first and handed it to his wife, his face ashen.

Hannah only cried and when Annie inquired about the cause of their suffering, her friend handed her the brief letter.

"I'm afraid we must cut our visit short, Mrs. Goheen." John was the first to recover himself enough to speak and he turned his attention to Mother—the only person in the room who did not yet know the contents of the note. "Our daughter Mary's illness has grown serious. It's unclear whether she will live."

Annie set the letter on the side table and reached for Hannah to embrace her, willing her own strength to help shore up her friend beneath this new sorrow.

Reverend and Mrs. Seys left that afternoon to make their way northeast. At Mother's suggestion, all but the baby stayed behind in Pennsylvania to ease some of the travel burden from their parents, a prospect that pleased Annie, though a gloom had fallen over their time together.

"When will Mother and Father come back?" Henry asked. Nine years old and sharp as a hawk, he'd rapidly become Annie's favorite.

She mussed his dark hair and shook her head. "I'm sure they'll write as soon as they have news. Until then, we will just have to be patient."

The boy frowned. "I think being patient is about the worst thing there is."

"I can't disagree with you, young man."

They waited a week for the letter to arrive, bearing the news they all dreaded.

To the Goheen Family,

It is with the heaviest of hearts and from the depth of grief that I write to you. The Lord has seen it fitting to take my Mary home. She succumbed to cholera, of which there has been a terrible outbreak here. She was a beautiful young lady with a heart for service and she knew the Lord as her Savior. I know we will meet again one day in Heaven. For now, I am so grateful my other children are well. My heart is comforted knowing they reside in your care.

It is from this place of gratitude and with sincere affection, I feel I must ask you for a favor. The Lord has made it clear to me in this hour of grief that I cannot be separated from my husband. I must not neglect my duty to be his helpmeet, but so can I also not bear to subject my youngest children to the harsh clime of Africa. John will sail again soon, after a brief lecture series. My mother remains weakened by the disease which still holds this community hostage. I will seek to offer her what comfort I can. Then I will return to Monrovia with Maria.

My dear friend, might I prevail upon you to take in, for a brief time, my other three, as I fear bringing them here where so many lives have already been lost. You were born to be a mother, and I know God has gifted you with a unique ability to love all children and nurture them in a Christian home. There is no one I would trust more. If you are agreeable to this request, I will come to you as soon as I am able to bid farewell to Jane, Henry, and Cornelius.

With a Full and Grateful Heart,
Hannah Seys

Annie handed the letter to her mother.

"That's a lot to ask," Mother said after scanning the words.

"She lost her daughter—in Connecticut, where she was safe with her grandmother. She's brought children through terrible sickness in a foreign land and then when she thought they were safe, they weren't."

"She's asking you—she's asking us—to raise three children."

"Only until their grandmother is fully recovered."

"If she fully recovers," Mother argued.

Annie bowed her head in agreement. "If she fully recovers."

Elizabeth Goheen pursed her lips. "Do you want to raise another woman's children? Because Hannah's right. They could not do better."

Conflict raged inside Annie's heart. Already she felt keenly the pain of living without a family of her own every time she was with Esther and Bennet and their sweet baby boy. To care for the Seys children would be to perform a sacred service for a dear friend, but it could also become an amplification of the pain and longing she had felt for so long.

"I cannot say no," she whispered.

Mother reached for Annie's hand.

"You can say no, my daughter," she whispered. "But you won't."

24
Sylvanus

Two weeks after the native funeral, Sylvanus stepped out of the mission house to enjoy the glow of a gorgeous sunset and spotted several figures approaching through the tree grove. He counted three silhouettes of walking men, their progress slowed by a fourth, small figure among them. The fourth companion moved strangely and appeared to be bound by a tether.

His chest burned with a flash of anger, wrenching an otherwise peaceful moment from him. The still-thriving slave trade among many of the indigenous tribes along Liberia's coast was an open secret, but he'd not seen it displayed so boldly in Monrovia. How, he raged, could the curse of slavery end in America when it could not be stopped here at its beginning?

"Hey," he yelled, rapidly walking toward the group that sauntered his direction. "What is the meaning of this?"

The men waved back to him as if his greeting were the friendliest thing they'd ever heard. He could not hear their response, but they made no attempt to avoid him. Rather, they altered their path to better intercept his.

His heart pounded. Sylvanus was brave and certain in his convictions, but he had no wish to entangle himself in a physical altercation with three large native Africans. He thought to turn back to the mission house where two other missionaries prepared for an evening church meeting. John Seys and his family had departed for the United States on tour, leaving the mission to fend for itself under the direction of men he knew to be faithful and dedicated. He could not pretend they were warriors, but he would welcome their assistance.

But then something made Sylvanus pause, to look again at the approaching figures. The small one was wider and stockier than the others, its proportions oddly distorted. It piqued his curiosity and tickled the scientist in him. He stopped, staring, as the group drew closer, and it occurred to him why the picture was so odd.

He laughed.

The short figure did not appear quite human, because it wasn't, in fact, human at all. It was some sort of primate with long, brown hair and an awkward gate. This was not an unfortunate young human in chains. It was an animal. Relief flooded him and he smiled in greeting as the group drew closer to him.

"Doctor." A large, friendly grin played across the face of the man who addressed him, who was now close enough for Sylvanus to identify as Robert, the tall African who'd sat beside him holding vigil over his headman in the last hours of his life.

"Robert. How are you, sir?" Sylvanus reached out to shake his hand. "What brings you here this evening?"

The animal stood on two legs looking at him with large, thoughtful eyes.

"We bring a dash. To thank you."

"To thank me? What did I do to deserve thanks?"

"You cared for our headman as you would a white man. You tied him together. You stood by his side."

"But I didn't save him." Sylvanus spoke to the men but kept his eyes on the primate, an orangutan if he wasn't mistaken, though he'd have liked to have a better look in a brighter light. A female, probably, powerful and apparently entirely docile.

"The devil decided he would die. No way to save him. But you treated him well." Robert gave a signal to one of the other men, the one who held the end of the rope tied to the orangutan. He handed it to Sylvanus, who made no move to accept it.

"I don't understand."

"She is a gift, Doctor."

"But she's an orangutan."

All three men nodded and again held out the end of the rope toward him again. This time Sylvanus took it.

"We know you collect and study our plants and our animals of the bush."

Sylvanus was too stunned to speak for a moment. He had in fact spent a great deal of time engaged in collection, cataloguing all kinds of specimens to ship back to the United States, determined to add to the understanding of natural history among scholars there, but this didn't make any sense. He'd seen primates and thought it likely many existed here that he'd not yet identified, but to the best of his knowledge, and of the general knowledge of Africa, such as he had studied, the continent did not naturally contain orangutans.

"How did you get her?"

Robert flashed a toothy grin. "The headman traded for her."

"But where did she come from? She doesn't belong here."

"She was a baby, found with her mother. The mother made good food. Baby made a good pet. She was the headman's. She is yours now."

Robert clapped him on the back and spoke some words to his companions that Sylvanus couldn't understand. They all began to walk away, leaving Sylvanus holding onto a rope tied to an orangutan as out of place and as far from home as he was.

"Wait!" He tried to flag them down, but he couldn't run after them unless his ape friend was also willing to do so. As strong as he knew she was, he feared he would not be able to take her anywhere she didn't wish to go. Her serene expression suggested she was in no hurry to go anywhere at all.

The Africans were well within earshot but didn't even slow as Sylvanus called after them, demonstrating the famous selective hearing so many of the missionaries complained about. It was no use. He looked down at the orangutan, who stared up at him. She wasn't especially large, though her belly protruded over her substantial feet. Even when she stood, she barely reached much more than two feet in height, making Sylvanus suspect she was quite young. He'd read about such creatures, seen sketches, but he'd never encountered one.

"Well, it seems we might be stuck with one another." Sylvanus shook his head. He was attempting to carry on a conversation with an animal who clearly couldn't understand what he said. But when the orangutan reached for him and took his hand in hers, he wondered. Her palm was velvety against his, not rough as he would have expected, and when she stood to step closer to him, he didn't feel threatened by her strength, but rather comforted. It seemed as though she offered friendship.

She began to walk in the direction from which he had come, back toward the mission house, and he fell into step with her, grasping the end of the rope in his other hand even while fairly certain he didn't need to. She had chosen him. He didn't know exactly why, but a kinship had passed between the two of them.

"You are a long way from home, my friend," he said as they ambled on together. She looked at him when he spoke. "How does an Asian primate find herself in Western Africa?"

She didn't come forward with any answers and he could think of none until they reached the kitchen door of the Mission House where Lydia stepped out, Hector at her heels. A low growl rumbled from the terrier's throat.

"What is that?" Lydia shrieked, shrinking back from Sylvanus and his new friend.

"It's an orangutan, one of the great apes. And it shouldn't be here."

"It definitely should not."

"It was a gift," he said. The creature had pulled up short of Lydia and studied her with earnest eyes. Hector gave up his growling and approached cautiously, his nose twitching.

"The headman with the knife wound from a few weeks ago, she evidently belonged to him, and his tribesmen brought her to me to thank me for my service to him."

"To thank you? And you accepted?" Lydia tensed as the orangutan reached its hand toward the dog who sniffed its large fingers.

"I don't think I had a choice. Have you spent much time trying to reason with Africans who barely speak your language?"

At this she laughed, and the animal moved closer to her, leaning into her slightly so its fur touched the tips of the woman's fingers. "I see your point." She pulled her hand away from the creature and clutched at the high neckline of her dress. "Is it dangerous?"

Sylvanus thought for a moment. "I don't think so, but I don't know her well yet. I will keep her contained or tied outside for now, until I have a chance to observe her more fully."

"She'll be living here, then?"

By now the orangutan had laid her head up against Lydia's leg, as though recognizing her as a mother-like figure, something she must sorely miss. Hector sat, content by the larger animal's side. Lydia did not move away, frozen, it seemed, in her anxiety.

"This is not her native home. I don't know how she came to be here, but she's an Asian ape, and this isn't where she belongs. I think I'll have to keep her. I fear she wouldn't survive on her own in Liberia."

Lydia looked down at the ape now almost clinging to her like a child. "She is rather dear, I suppose. Does she have a name?"

"I guess we'd better give her one." Sylvanus thought for a moment. "I read an article not too long back, written by a British naturalist, about an orangutan in the London Zoological Garden that took tea with him, very civilized."

"You're joking. It took tea? Like a gentleman?"

"Like a lady, I would think. The creature's name was Lady Jane. Jenny for short."

Lydia released a nervous puff. Timidly she stroked the top of the orangutan's head. Hector whined and wriggled with jealousy. "I don't think your new friend is quite as proper as a lady. But I suppose she could be a Jenny."

Sylvanus looked at the orangutan now leaning into Lydia with closed eyes, as calm and blissful as he could imagine a wild creature ever appearing.

"I think she likes it," he said. "Jenny it is. It seems the mission house has a new pet."

"Well," Lydia said with a sigh, "I'm sure the children will love her. If it's safe for her to be around them."

"She seems docile. The men who gave her to me said she lost her mother when she was small. I don't know how an Asian ape comes to be an orphan in Western Africa, but all of us here are far away from where we started. Perhaps this will be a good home for her after all."

He reached down, moving slowly, and grabbed Jenny's hand. She opened her eyes at his touch and if he could have believed her capable, he might have thought she smiled at him as they walked together into the house.

25
Annie

"How does a mother bid farewell to her small children?" Annie had been pondering the question since the moment Hannah Seys left with her infant to begin the trek back to Africa. She'd given her friend privacy as she spoke with the older three children and could not imagine what words one might share in this heartbreaking situation. Annie had been a teacher and a sister and caregiver to many children, but she could not fathom what might comfort in this situation.

Her own mother answered the question as they sat together in the parlor, the young ones finally snuggled into bed. At four-year-old Jane's request and big brother Cornelius's insistence, all three slept together in the room Annie once shared with her own youngest brothers. She couldn't blame them for wanting to remain close to one another, but her heart went out especially to Cornelius who shouldered as much of the burden of grief as he could for the others.

"I'm sure she told them she loves them." Elizabeth looked up from the book she read in the lamplight. "She explained to them that it was because she loves them that she's leaving, even though they can't possibly understand. And she reassured them they would see their sister in Heaven one day."

"Empty words."

"Important ones."

"What will I say to them?"

Mother closed her book and set it on her lap. "You will say that you love their mother, and you love them, and you are honored she has trusted you to care for them. You will promise to do your best. And when they cry, you will wipe their tears."

Annie bit her lip. "What if they ask whether their mother is ever coming back? People die in Africa. All the time, people die."

"John and Hannah believe they are following God's call. Whatever happens is going to happen. Their fate is in God's hands. And the fate of their children, at least for a time, has been trusted to yours."

The incorporation of three grieving children into the life of the Goheen farm took some adjustment, but Cornelius was a good help. William had recently returned from his seminary studies in Baltimore, and he took a special interest in the boys. Cornelius was captivated by him. He and his brother Henry happily helped with chores around the farm. Then, after only a week of this routine, Cornelius asked Annie if they both might attend school.

"Your grandmother will send for you soon."

"She could." Cornelius shrugged. "But Henry needs to meet other boys. And Mother wouldn't want us to neglect our studies."

The wisdom of a child's words struck her. She'd assumed the children would wish for this temporary home to continue to feel fleeting, but establishing a normal routine likely would be helpful to all of them.

"I'll speak to the teacher. I'm sure she'll be glad to have you join the class."

Annie liked the school's newest teacher, recruited from the other side of the state in anticipation of Annie's ill-fated wedding. Miss Pepin's bright smiles and youthful exuberance demanded the attention her students and sparked in Annie a hint of yearning for her days in the classroom, before she'd known the heartache of losing the man she loved. Perhaps one day she would explore that longing and determine what to do with her complicated emotions. Today she would simply be grateful the new teacher possessed a gentleness that might be a balm to the Seys children's dear little souls.

Jane was a different matter. The four year old was a doll with dark curls, long lashes, soft baby skin, and soulful blue eyes that only thinly veiled pain and confusion so intense it made Annie shudder. In the absence of her brothers during the school day, she refused to leave Annie's side. When Elizabeth tried to coax the girl away, she cried, hot tears streaming down her cherubic cheeks. And though she had demonstrated an impressive vocabulary for one so young in the presence of her parents, in their absence, the little girl would say nothing at all.

"Janie, dear," Annie spoke softly as she carried her home from walking with the boys to school. "What would you like to do with this beautiful day?"

Jane's arms tightened around Annie's neck, but she gave no other indication she'd even heard the question.

"Miss Elizabeth would like some help making bread, I'm sure. And maybe we can visit Esther and the baby when William goes into town later. Would you like that?"

Still no response. Annie stopped and set her down gently. Kneeling, she stood the little girl in front of her. She reached for a curl and drew it between her fingers. "Sweetheart, I know you miss your mama. I miss her, too. She's my dear friend."

The child stared into Annie's eyes and she felt herself judged, as though Jane was deciding the worth of Annie as a guardian, perhaps even the worth of her soul. She wondered how she measured up.

245

The little girl swiped at her nose, a perfectly childlike gesture, which offered hope in an innocence not entirely lost to the trauma of grief over the death of a big sister and saying goodbye to a mother and father who, half a world away, might as well have joined her.

Annie smiled as warmly as she could, chucked the girl's chin, and swept her up again into her arms. Jane Seys, without uttering a word, hugged her fiercely back.

Esther stepped through the door of her neat cabin to greet them as William lifted Jane from the carriage and offered Annie a hand. He placed the little girl on the ground and playfully mussed her curls. "I'll be back to get you lovelies after I finish my business. Shouldn't be more than an hour."

"Thank you, William." The rote response served as an adequate dismissal, but Annie's attention had been captured by the gaunt appearance of the small Black woman in the doorway to the cabin. She snatched Jane's hand and rushed toward Esther.

"What's wrong? You look a mess."

Esther wiped her hands on her long apron, worrying imaginary dirt into its dingy creases.

She welcomed them inside with a flick of her kerchiefed head. Only two rooms, the cabin wasn't a grand space, but on previous visits Annie had delighted in the obvious pleasure the new bride and now mother took in creating a warm and inviting home. Delicately constructed doilies had graced the center of the sturdy table and the small stand beside the fireplace, which served as exalted resting space for a family Bible Mother had presented to Esther when she married. Now the doilies were absent, as was the Bible.

"Esther, tell me," Annie said, "why do you look so miserable?"

A tear slipped down Esther's cheek. She shook her head and reached for a newspaper sitting atop the table, handing it to Annie.

She took it, a copy of the *Columbia Spy* from several days past. Her gaze dropped to the words on the folded page beneath a headline touting the resolution of a town hall gathering of Columbia's citizens. She began to read, the words twisting her stomach into a knot.

> *Resolved, that a committee be appointed whose duty it shall be to communicate with that portion of those colored person who hold property in this borough and ascertain if possible if they would be willing to depose of the same at a fair valuation and it shall be the duty of the said committee to advise the colored persons in said borough to refuse receiving any colored persons from other places as residents among them.*

"What is this?" Annie asked in disbelief.

"Bennet says there's been more unrest at the lumberyards. The whites don't want us here. There's been attacks at yard and here on the hill. A porch was tore down in the middle of the night and gardens set ablaze." Esther had begun to shake.

Annie guided her into a chair. "There's been unrest before, riots even," she said. "I've been caught up in them myself."

Esther shook her head and exhaled a shaky breath. "Not like this. They're after Stephen Smith."

"The man who owns the lumberyards?"

"The *colored* man that owns the lumberyards," Esther said. "The one who employs most of us, including Bennett."

A baby's soft whimper drifted from the adjoining room. Esther's head drooped and she pushed against the chair as if to rise. Before she could fully gather the strength to do so, little Jane, her eyes round and bright, slipped through the doorway. The fussing stopped and the women could soon hear the scraping of the cradle against the floor as it rocked back and forth under the determined hand of a young caregiver.

Esther sunk back into her chair, the exhaustion of new motherhood etched in thin lines and dark circles around her eyes.

Annie pictured the sad little girl beyond the doorway, rocking the baby to sleep, dreaming as she likely was of the babe in her own family, whose coos and giggles the big sister must be missing. A flicker of a memory tugged at the edges of Annie's thoughts recalling an indescribable emotional swell touched off by the weight of a squirming sixteen-month-old Smee in her arms, acting to displace some of the grief she'd experienced at the loss of her father.

She smiled at Esther. "Janie will see to him. You look exhausted."

"I am. He barely slept last night. Too much sorrow in the house."

Annie patted her hand and turned to the paper to continue reading.

> *Resolved, that the citizens of this borough be requested in case of the discovery of any fugitive slaves within our bounds to cooperate and assist in returning them to their lawful owners.*

Annie sucked in a sharp breath, the realization of what these words must mean to Esther, the fear they must have evoked. "You don't think you're in danger?"

Esther wiped at her tear-dampened cheeks with her fingers. "Bennett does."

"But Jonas said no one was looking for you, that your former masters—those people—that his heirs weren't going to come after you."

"He might be right. But there's no stopping an angry white man from snatching me up and selling me down south anyway. They know Bennett. He was born free. He's been here all his life. I'm new. Where they gonna think I came from?"

"You'll move back to the farm then. You and Bennett and Baby Jonas. You'll live away from town where no one is going to care who you are."

"Annie, I love you, but the farm can't be my home anymore."

Annie's heart raced, angry thuds against her chest. "Home is with the people you love and who love you. We're your family."

Esther drew a deep breath, closed her eyes, and placed the fingertips of one hand on her forehead. "You've been good to me. You took me in when I had no place to go and I am grateful, but we aren't family. You're white, Annie. I'm not. Nothing can ever change that. I've lived things you can't imagine."

Annie opened her mouth to protest but held her tongue when Esther raised a hand to stop her.

"I'm glad you can't." She dropped her hand to her lap. "I see it every time I close my eyes—the wild, angry stare of a man so enraged he'd whip a mama senseless in front of her little girl. I've seen and felt unspeakable things."

"Oh, Esther." Annie's chest tightened. Her throat clogged with emotion.

"What happened to her and to me isn't your fault, but you can't solve it, either. Men like that breathe down my neck every minute I stay here. I have to do what's best for my family. Bennett and Jonas are my family."

Annie digested the words in silence for a moment, struggling to accept the sense of them even as she recognized their truth. If Esther were to live her life as a free woman with her husband and son, she could not do so as a guest in someone else's home. And, it seemed, she could not do it in Columbia, Pennsylvania.

"There's nothing right about any of this," Annie whispered. "Where will you go?"

"North," Esther said with a shrug. "Bennett has some connections. We'll go north until we find a place we can settle."

"I don't want you to have to leave your home."

"It's like you said. Home is with my family."

There was no point in arguing. Annie sniffed and willed away her tears. The doilies and Bible were already packed away, with who knows what else. Esther would leave her, and soon.

From the other room came a purposeful cry. Little Jane poked her head around the door frame. "Baby is hungry."

Annie was almost too lost in this fresh wave of grief to notice the first words the little girl had spoken since the departure of her mother and baby sister.

"She speaks," Esther said with surprise. The young mother raised her eyebrows at Annie and dipped into the other room to retrieve the fussy infant.

Jane crossed the room and climbed up in Annie's lap to lean against her surrogate mother's chest. Annie stroked the little girl's tangled hair and let her gaze fall back to the abandoned newspaper on the table.

There she saw the words that sent a chill through her veins.

Resolved, that the Colonization Society ought to be supported by all the citizens favorable to the removal of the Blacks from the country.

She whispered the words aloud as she read them again. These were her neighbors, the people she spoke with in town, worshipped with on Sundays. They had been her brother's patients, had bought produce from their farm, had shared meals when they grieved.

Columbia had functioned well for years as a free society of both white and Black, but now her fellow white citizens were ready to take this unholy action, to join in league with the devil and move against their colored neighbors.

And they claimed the Colonization Society as their ally.

26
Sylvanus

The John Seys had Sylvanus met disembarking at the Monrovia harbor was not the confident superintendent who had left the mission months earlier. This man sagged as though gravity had begun acting on him with a greater ferocity than before, pulling him into himself and, if he weren't careful, into the ground on which he stood.

Emotion choked the physician as he took in the appearance of his long-absent friend, so much so that initially he barely registered the tall white stranger beside him or the new crop of emigrants shuffling off the gangway around him. Exhausted by their journey, the emigrants made a sad picture. Sylvanus could imagine the hopefulness shining in their eyes as they boarded a ship bound for Africa, a return to the land of their ancestors, and a chance at living a free life away from those who thought them lesser. Upon arrival, however, that light was gone.

Many of them were already sick from the tossing of the sea and facing weeks or months of acclimatization illness, stuffed into the cramped and poorly constructed temporary barracks along the coastline. Six months of government support would be too little for most to find their bearings. Liberia offered a new start for the free Black men from America, but that didn't always translate into as much opportunity as Sylvanus had hoped.

He avoided their eyes as they shuffled off, carrying carpetbags of meager possessions, to be greeted and sorted by waiting government liaisons. Instead, he focused on the two white men.

"You look shaken, John. Was it a difficult journey?"

"The journey was fine. The visit home took its toll." Seys began lumbering toward the path leading to the mission house.

The silent newcomer fell in behind, his skin so pale he was nearly green, his eyes darting from one foreign sight to the next. He might have been the image of Sylvanus himself arriving in Monrovia for the first time, awash with seasickness and anxiety.

Reverend Seys looked between the two of them and apologized. "Dr. Sylvanus Goheen, this is Walter Jayne. He joins our mission as a printer."

"We need a printer?"

Walter Jayne's mouth drooped at the corners.

The superintendent only said, "We have much to discuss, but it will wait for prayer meeting tonight when I can address everyone."

Sylvanus nodded his understanding, the extent of the reverend's fatigue clear to him. As he fell in beside the printer and followed the weary superintendent, Sylvanus's thoughts drifted back to the memory of his own arrival in Monrovia, of stepping into another world from the one he had left in the United States—a world that soon filled him with a wonder of discovery recaptured from childhood when the hills of Pennsylvania still held mystery for a young boy with imagination.

John stopped short, causing Sylvanus to stumble in order not to collide with him.

"What on earth?"

The superintendent pointed toward the paw paw trees a few paces ahead of them, the edge of the mission's orchard. A large creature emerged from behind the first row of trees next to the mission house.

John gasped.

An odd squeak escaped the throat of jumpy Walter Jayne as the man slid behind the other two.

"That," Sylvanus said in the most reassuring tone he could muster, "is Jenny."

"H-huge m-monkey." Walter's jaw quivered as he spoke.

"She's an ape," Sylvanus said. "An orangutan, to be precise."

Seys backed away from the orangutan slowly. "She looks right at home."

"She's on a chain."

John's posture loosened at Sylvanus's assurance. "And she wouldn't hurt anyone anyway," Sylvanus continued. "She's just enjoying some outside time. She was a gift."

"A gift?" John raised an eyebrow.

"You'll find you've missed quite a bit around here, John."

Sylvanus walked ahead of his stunned companions toward Jenny who greeted his return by stretching a long arm toward him. He reached into his pocket and pulled out the key to the collar at her neck, which supported a chain attached to a loop on a line stretching between the kitchen door on the side of the house and a large orange tree. The setup gave Jenny most of the yard in which to roam but kept her from wandering too far into the orchard and away from the safety of the house.

Sylvanus placed the key into the orangutan's large palm and watched as she spun it deftly with her fingers and fitted it into the keyhole on her collar. After she did so, she sat patiently as Sylvanus turned the key to open the collar. Then he slipped the key back into his pocket, held his furry friend's hand, and said to John and Walter, "Welcome home."

The superintendent was allowed little time to settle back in before he received the onslaught of questions, requests, and urgent needs from an active mission that had limped along for months without its leader. Sylvanus had much to discuss with him as well but left him to it for now.

He strolled through town, Hector loping by his side on what had turned out to be a beautiful sunny afternoon. Under the guise of social visits, he checked in on the handful of colony patients currently under his care.

A new governor had taken office in the superintendent's absence. Thomas Buchanan had been serving as an administrator in Grand Bassa where he'd worked closely with Sylvanus's old friend William Matthias, but now had been named as the replacement for the recently deceased Colonial Agent Jehudi Ashmun. Buchanan became the first man to bear the title of Governor of Liberia, an honor bestowed upon him by the American Colonization Society in an attempt to provide the colony with a more autonomous government structure, or at least the feel of it.

Sylvanus knew little about the man outside of one brief encounter in which Buchanan had made it clear that, even more so than his predecessor, he wished for colonial patients to be treated by colonial physicians. Sylvanus had nearly laughed at the thought, assuming the governor to be joking given the remarkable lack of medical skill among the small population of Monrovia's medical personnel. Yet the man had been earnest.

Buchanan's admonition hadn't swayed Sylvanus's conviction to treat all those who sought his aid, but it had made him more cautious. He was not one to be intimidated, but this new government put him on edge, and he was anxious to discuss his concerns with John.

Spirits had been running high at the mission house since the first whisper of the superintendent's imminent return, the walls themselves seeming to buzz with a new energy of anticipation and a sense that change was coming. Despite his deflated demeanor,

John Seys did not disappoint. At the evening meeting and devotion time, he approached the pulpit with important news for a dozen present missionaries, three representatives of the governor, and a handful of native students.

"On my recent trip to America, I was given the opportunity to address the board on behalf of the Liberia mission and I have some good news. After expressing in person the woes I had written about on numerous occasions, they have finally been made to understand the difficulty of delays in both financial support and much needed supplies. They have given us the means and permission to proceed with construction of both a saw mill and sugar mill in White Plains."

A spattering of applause broke out in the room. Sylvanus joined in, as did the new printer beside him. The emigrant representatives sat stiff in their straight-backed chairs.

Seys continued. "I would also like to welcome Walter Jayne to the mission staff."

The tall man popped briefly to his feet and gave the room a half-hearted wave.

"He is here to help us begin a biweekly newspaper we're going to call *Africa's Luminary* with the aim of keeping both our community and our supporters abroad better informed about our ministry goals and successes."

Again, Sylvanus looked to the rigid expressions of the governor's men. Their lack of enthusiasm for the newspaper project caught Sylvanus's attention for only the briefest of moments before the reverend's next words filled his heart with sorrow for his friend.

"On a more personal note, I'd like to ask for your prayers for my family. Mrs. Seys and I lost our beautiful daughter Mary to typhoid fever. She had remained with her grandmother to attend school in the United States and never set foot on this continent, but she was beloved and had professed a love for Jesus and a strong hope in salvation. We her family do rest assured in our eventual reunion in glory."

Sylvanus watched the tears gather on John's lashes. Though they did not fall, the grief of a father was palpable. All remained silent except for the trill of insects gathering to sing in the dusk beyond the open windows, a sober dirge filling the empty spaces of the room.

"You are all part of our family now, as well, and even though you did not know Mary, I know you share in our grief. Your love is felt, and I thank you for it. Mrs. Seys remained behind to see our other children settled. Her mother was weakened through illness as well, and so we thought it best to place the children in temporary care—to that of our own Dr. Goheen's family."

Sylvanus lifted his moist eyes in surprise. He had not received a letter from home in months, and without the presence of Hannah Seys and her correspondence with Annie, he'd known nothing of how life in Pennsylvania fared for his family.

"I received word of the arrangement just prior to boarding my ship and was assured my wife would be following close behind with the baby. Please also join me in praying for their safe journey."

Sylvanus barely heard the superintendent's closing remarks, his mind swirling with thoughts of home, which he'd been keeping largely at bay. Annie was angry with him, he knew. Angry with him for leaving in her time of need, angry for involving himself in colonization, an effort she believed immoral. But now she was caring for the children of the man responsible for his leaving. Perhaps there was hope they could come to an understanding, an opportunity to disagree in approach but to come together in love and mission. Clearly his sister had grown closer to Hannah Seys than he'd been aware. He knew they'd written letters, but to be raising the woman's children?

There was no one better. Annie had practically raised him when his grief-stricken mother could not. The Seys children were fortunate to have her. Oh, how he missed her.

The next day, Reverend Seys summoned Sylvanus to one of the meeting rooms on the first floor of the seminary, which he'd identified as the new office of the printer Walter Jayne.

Curious, Sylvanus arrived early to find Jayne bent over an open crate, equipment spread across the floor around him. If it were possible, the man looked even more haggard than he had while unfolding himself from the Kru-piloted canoe in the harbor.

Sylvanus knocked on the doorframe. "Did you sleep at all?"

Jayne, finally induced to look up from his work, shook his head.

"I'm sure your work is important, but as the mission physician, I must insist you get plenty of rest. The environment here is unfriendly to new arrivals. You risk your health."

"From what I understand," said the man as he continued to rummage through the crate, "I'll be ill sooner than later. I don't want my press in the hands of anyone else. I will oversee its unpacking and construction before I am confined to bed."

The rejection of his professional advice hit a nerve deep inside Sylvanus and intensified his unfavorable first impression of the printer. His fellow missionaries did not question Sylvanus's judgment. They had been recruited for their skills at sharing the Gospel with those in need of it; he had been recruited to see to their health as they did so. They appreciated his expertise as he respected theirs. Jayne, on the other hand, was in Monrovia because of his skill at the press, an occupation requiring long hours in a small room by one-self. Sylvanus hoped what the printer lacked in social grace, he made up for in talent.

Jayne lay aside his search inside the crate and dropped back on his haunches. He looked up at Sylvanus. "Are you to be my editor then?"

"Your editor?" Sylvanus said, taken aback. "I'm not a newspaper man."

Jayne studied him, piercing him with bloodshot eyes, which on better days must appear as gray as the coastal sky. "Perhaps you sell yourself short, Dr. Goheen. Reverend Seys tells me you've an in-quisitive mind, a good grasp of the issues affecting Monrovia and the mission, and the opportunity to interact daily with people from all kinds of backgrounds and with all kinds of goals. That is the mark of a newspaper man. I'm just a printer. It's the men with pas-sion for the mission who can put together a newspaper people want to read, the kind that sells papers back home where the money to support this mission comes from."

"He's not wrong." John appeared in the doorway, significantly more put together than the previous day when Sylvanus had met him at the port, though no less weary. "But perhaps Walter did, as they say, steal my thunder."

"You want me to serve as the editor of the *Liminary?*" Sylvanus couldn't make sense of the request. He'd assumed the superinten-dent would be filling the role of editor himself. If not, then any of the field missionaries—all men who primarily preached and taught, great communicators each of them—would be a more logi-cal choice.

"There is no one I trust more." John stepped fully into the room and sat on the corner of an unopened crate. "The Mission Board has brought to my attention that Governor Buchanan is unhappy with the state of our mission. He has raised numerous complaints with the American Colonization Society and has shown no restraint in his criticisms of me."

"The man is a snake," Jayne added.

The superintendent nodded in agreement, a shockingly causal mockery of the colonial governor of Liberia but not at all unwelcome to Sylvanus. Perhaps his initial assessment of the printer had been rushed.

The governor had struck him as a small-minded and anxious man, afraid of losing what little power he possessed. Sylvanus was relieved he might be free to say so.

"So, you wish to use the newspaper as a mouthpiece against the governor?"

Seys tapped on a piece of iron frame leaned against the wall beside the crate on which he sat. "I'll tell you this: I am not going to simply allow the governor to spread rumors about our mission without any form of defense. Have you seen him moving against us? He's quite clever."

The superintendent surely referred to the subtle jabs at holding local meetings in mission buildings, which the *Liberia Herald* suggested was a grab for power by the missionaries rather than a practical solution to the simple problem of space. Then, too, were the occasional editorials discouraging Monrovia's citizens from seeking assistance, even medically, from the mission rather than from colonial agencies. And, of course, there were expressions of concern of the mission's financial footing, which in many ways was far more stable than that of the colonial government.

"I have seen it," Sylvanus said. "I know he would like nothing better than to charge duties on the mission supplies."

Jayne coughed, barely covering a laugh at a statement he clearly believed inadequate.

"I'm afraid it's more insidious than that," John said, looking between the two men. "I believe he is laying the groundwork to charge us of much greater offenses. He's communicated as much with the Board. He has essentially accused me of engaging in unlawful trade."

Sylvanus shook his head, incredulous. "You've done no such thing, John. Everyone knows it. Mission goods aren't taxable when used for the mission's purposes."

Jayne pounded on the crate beside him. "What everyone knows is the message they hear—the one they read about. All it takes is a deft hand on a good story to convince the mob, regardless of the truth."

John held up a hand to block the tirade threatening to spill from Walter's quivering lips. Any traces of apprehension at arriving in Africa had fallen away now that the printer had sought solace with his press.

"Governor Buchanan seems to think my corruption knows no bounds. He believes I am somehow a threat to his new position, perhaps to the success of the colony. The air is heavy with greed and plotting, my friend. We need to be ready. *You* need to be ready, for the coming attack."

"I will help however I can."

"Then take over the primary editorial duties of the *Luminary*. I will assist you, but it's best if I am not the sole editor. When Buchanan's accusations come screaming through the pages of the *Liberia Herald*—"

"That rag they have the nerve to call journalism," Walter muttered through clenched teeth.

John smirked. "When it happens, we will have a way to stand up for our rights and responsibilities given to us by God."

Sylvanus had never heard the superintendent speak so harshly or with such conviction about anything but the Grace of Christ. He liked this new fire he saw. He would do his part in the upcoming battle for the soul of Liberia.

"I'll do it."

"You will be brilliant." John stood and clapped him on the back. "You'll be in good hands with Walter.

Another three weeks passed before Hannah arrived. Sylvanus had been attending the ill most of the day. Three of his sick beds were currently occupied by recent emigrants to the colony. Governor Buchanan's rules would not allow him to care for the sick in the barracks, but he would not turn away those who sought his help at the mission house. He'd treated several natives as well for minor wounds and offered care and advice to a few of the missionaries. It had been a long day, one he was glad to see draw to a close with the happy arrival.

If only it had been happy. John was gone to White Plains to oversee the beginnings of construction on the new lumber and sugar mills and wasn't present to greet his wife who had arrived bone tired wearing a mother's grief as a shroud.

Baby Maria was unrecognizable to Sylvanus, transformed as she was from a squalling, red-faced infant into a chubby-cheeked cherub squirming against her mother's hip, petitioning for the opportunity to crawl about. Hannah was about to oblige her when Jenny entered the room behind a delighted Lydia. The mother's eyes grew wide, and she clung tightly to her daughter as introductions and explanations were given.

Jacobus, fresh from cleaning up evidence of the day's work in the infirmary, entered behind the orangutan, completing a subdued welcoming party in the mission house kitchen. At the sight of him, Hannah's face lit, and she shifted the baby so she might embrace her son with one arm.

"You've grown!" she exclaimed.

The boy really had grown a great deal in his mother's absence, perhaps as dramatically as his baby sister had. Jacobus was a young man at a time of life when only a few months may make an astonishing difference. Hannah had left behind a boy at least two inches shorter and returned to find a man as tall and strong and serious as his father.

"Oh, Maria has grown so much, too!" Lydia reached for the squirming baby and Hannah surrendered her with a smile that did not reach her eyes.

The sight of Lydia with a babe in her arms evoked a thrill Sylvanus did his best to ignore as he clasped Hannah's hand. "Welcome back."

She dropped his hands and hugged him. "It's good to see you, Sylvanus. Your sister sends her love."

"Does she?" He tried to imagine Annie saying those words, actually asking her friend to deliver a message of love to him. His throat tightened at the realization he couldn't quite conjure the image.

Hannah tilted her head to one side. "Well, of course she does."

"John tells me Annie has taken in your middle children."

"For a time. My mother was unwell after we lost Mary. I have no doubt she will recover, but your mother and sister both agreed without hesitation to care for my children. I can't express to you how much of a blessing they've been."

Sylvanus swallowed an unbidden rise of jealousy. This woman had grown as close as a sister to Annie through only the exchange of a few letters and perhaps a shared anxiety about Africa, despite the same political differences that kept he and Annie so far apart.

He turned away as Lydia swept the superintendent's wife into conversation about the baby and focused instead on Jacobus, who had stepped slyly away from his mother to sneak a piece of fruit from a bowl in the center of the table.

"Hungry?" Sylvanus asked the young man.

"Always," Jacobus replied with a sheepish grin.

"I think you've grown a foot since your mother last saw you."

His cheeks flushed with pleasure. "Maybe not a foot, but did you notice I'm as tall as Father now?"

The question made Sylvanus's breath catch for the briefest of moments. A boy wanted nothing more than to be like his father.

27
Annie

Two letters arrived the same day and each tugged at Annie's heart. The first came from Monrovia and bore Smee's unmistakable scrawl. Annie scanned the unusually lengthy note with widening eyes.

"Oh, children," Annie said, "you'll want to hear this. My brother Dr. Goheen has sent a letter from Africa and he has some exciting news."

Cornelius and Henry had just crashed through the doorway into the kitchen. After school, they helped William with farm chores and had only just washed up. They'd be anxious for supper, but the contents of the letter would make for lively table conversation. Jane looked up from her seat at the table where Annie had put her to work snapping string beans.

"Is it about Mother and Father?" Cornelius gasped as Henry shoved him in the gut on his way to take a seat at the table.

"Henry!" Annie exclaimed. "Slow down. Supper will be served soon. There's no need to run through the house like an animal. You could have hurt someone."

The freckled boy glanced at his brother. "Sorry, Cornelius."

Cornelius barely acknowledged the apology with a grunt, his attention focused already on the letter in Annie's hand. "Does it say anything about our parents?"

"It does not. Your mother might not have arrived yet even now, and your father probably hadn't at the time the letter was sent." She bid him sit at the table beside his brother and sister, offering her mother, who continued to cook, a glance of apology as Annie stepped toward the children. "Do you remember when I showed you Africa in the atlas?"

The boys nodded. Jane continued to snap.

"It takes nearly a month for a ship to cross the great ocean expanse between here and Liberia on the western coast of the African continent. It takes the same length of time to carry a letter as well, and then it has to find itself from a port city to our little town in Pennsylvania. So how long ago do you think my brother wrote us this letter?"

Cornelius barely hesitated before saying, "Six weeks."

Annie smiled, marveling at the boy's fast intelligence. "You are close. According to the date on the top of the letter, it was written six weeks and two days ago."

"But what's so exciting?" Impatient, Henry squirmed in his seat.

Jane dropped her latest bean halves into the bowl and stared, awaiting the wonderful news, whatever it may be.

"He has a new friend." Annie paused, catching the eye of each member of her small audience. "Dr. Goheen has taken in an orangutan as a pet."

"What's that?" It was little Jane who had spoken, garnering even the attention of Elizabeth Goheen, who raised her eyebrows as she stirred a pot at the cooktop.

"Boys, have you ever heard of an orangutan?"

They both shook their heads.

"According to the letter, it's a type of ape, like a monkey, but larger and without a tail."

"Is it hairy?" Henry asked.

"Yes." Annie reveled for a moment in the enthusiasm of each of them, not formally her pupils, but reminding her so of her days in the classroom. "He says she, for his orangutan is a female, has long red-brown fur covering her entire body. He says she has big, brown eyes and large feet and that she balances on a rope stretched between an orange tree and the house where they live."

"It lives with him?" Cornelius's question dripped skepticism.

"Oh yes. She's quite friendly. Her name is Jenny, and she follows him around. If one of the ladies gives her a dust cloth, she even helps with the housework. Just imagine!"

"I could use one of those," said Annie's mother. "Maybe she'd help cook supper."

Annie was too pleased with herself to be bothered by her mother's jab, which just made Henry giggle.

"Maybe she'd chop wood, too," the oldest boy added.

"Well," Annie said, "she might. He describes her as strong and highly intelligent. She walks on her hind legs just like a person, with long arms to help her balance. He sent a sketch."

Annie placed the drawing on the table in front of the children. Her brother had always been skilled at recording the things he saw in nature, and she had often lamented that the same steady hand did not carry to his penmanship. The accuracy of this sketch she could only imagine, having never seen an orangutan herself.

"It's labeled 'Asian Orangutan.'" Henry pointed to the words along the side of the drawing. "What's it doing in Africa?"

"Good observation, Henry. Dr. Goheen mentioned that in the letter as well." Annie scanned the page again. "He received her as a gift from some natives and has no idea how she is so far from home. She's displaced from her family."

"Like us," said Cornelius.

Annie drew a sharp breath. The parallel Cornelius had astutely drawn hadn't occurred to her until this moment, and she began to regret making such a point of the charming letter.

"Yes, well, I suppose that's true," she said, attempting to recover her composure with a soft smile. "And like you, Jenny has found herself in the care of a good friend who loves her."

She let the thought linger and, she hoped, embed itself into the hearts of Hannah's children. "Now, let's see what else we know about Jenny. She is nearly two-and-a-half feet tall and about four years old."

"Like me!" The excitement in little Jane's voice lifted Annie's spirits like nothing else could and she laughed.

"Yes, like you." She walked around the end of the table, crouched in front of the little girl's seat, and touched her gently on the nose. "But you, my dear, are taller, and, I dare say, much smarter than an orangutan."

Jane threw her arms around Annie's neck and squeezed her tightly. For just this moment she would not consider the second letter which had arrived from Mrs. Mary Osborn, mother of Hannah Seys, and grandmother of Cornelius, Henry, and Jane. The second message carried the happy news that the cholera scare had subsided and with it, the expectation that Mrs. Osborn would retrieve her grandchildren soon. Judging by the wording, the woman was likely already on her way and would arrive within the week.

Annie would soon lose the responsibility of care for the children she had just come to love.

Mrs. Mary Osborn was perhaps even more formidable than Annie's own mother. A short, prim woman, neatly attired but with no frivolous adornments, she did not strike Annie as the warm grandmother she'd pictured coming to collect Hannah's children. For Elizabeth Goheen, the two grandchildren Mayberry and his wife had now provided her had seemed to transform her into a softer version of herself. Mary Osborn's experience with grand-parenthood had perhaps not yielded the same results.

Cornelius, of course, had already spent time in his grand-mother's care, having been left with her previously, along with his now deceased sister, to attend school. For Henry and Jane, the ex-perience of living with Grandmother Mary was a thrilling, un-known proposition. The enthusiasm of the children upon seeing their grandmother again was inversely proportional to their age. Annie couldn't help but notice that Cornelius gave his grandmother only a stiff kiss on her cheek in greeting.

Mrs. Osborn joined the family for a light luncheon, after which William would accompany the whole family into town to catch the train to Philadelphia where further travel arrangements awaited them.

"Mrs. Goheen, your home appears efficient. Has this farm been in your family for a long time?"

Annie directed the children to double check their things were packed and ready to go. Then she busied herself clearing the table as the two older women talked.

"Thank you. We've been on this land since my children were young. I lost my husband when my youngest was only a babe. I'm not sure what I would have done without my older children, espe-cially Mary Ann."

Annie blushed as she offered a cup of coffee to their guest.

"No thank you, Miss Goheen. I do not imbibe stimulating bever-ages."

She sobered at the stiffness in the woman's reply.

Elizabeth took a long sip from her own cup before saying, "We certainly have enjoyed having your grandchildren with us—intelli-gent and polite children. You should be proud."

"I am, and thank you." Annie longed to hear more warmth in the words. "They have endured a lot, all of them, with their parents traipsing off to Africa. For their sakes one can only hope the dreadful experiment comes to an end soon."

"Do you think it will?" Annie hated that she found hope in the words, that she wished to engage her more, this woman who would be taking the children away from her. She pushed aside her reluctance and sat, giving Mrs. Osborn her full attention.

Mrs. Osborn paused for a moment before saying, "I think there is trouble between the mission and the colonial government. My son-in-law's tone on his recent trip to America was one of uncharacteristic worry. He met with the mission board and had little to say after. It's unlike him not to share information. He's a confident man, perhaps to a fault."

"That has been my observation as well," added Mother.

"He was shaken after his meeting. And he was insistent Hannah join him in Monrovia, as well, claimed it would bolster confidence in his leadership if his wife were with him. I wonder if the whole mission might be teetering on a thin edge."

In Annie's heart, a flicker of hope began to take hold. Perhaps America was coming to see the light and colonization would soon be at an end. As the pressure from the free Black population increased in the United States without its Liberian release valve, perhaps the cause of abolition could finally capture the hearts and minds of even those stubborn Southern slaveholders. And perhaps Smee would return from his African adventure.

This was a small consolation Annie could grasp as she hugged the children goodbye and packed them off to return to a life with a stern grandmother.

The notion was enough to sustain her for three days after the children's departure, before a deep melancholy wormed its way into her heart. At the breakfast table she attempted to commiserate with William who she knew must also miss the Seys children.

"You've got to take hold of some joy," he said.

Frustrated though she was at his refusal to feed her grief, he was right.

"I don't even know where to begin," Annie replied.

William sopped up the last smear of gravy from his plate, swallowed, and said, "You know, Mother and I had some ideas."

"You and Mother discuss me when I'm not here?"

A smirk played across her brother's face. "Would you rather we talk about you right in front of you? Because we will."

Annie shook her head, but she smiled. It was the first true contentment she'd felt since saying goodbye to Hannah's children. The family of her birth, this pack of brothers that had protected and encouraged her throughout her life had always lent her strength when she could summon none and provided her with unwavering affection and easy comfort. Though they were scattered, among far-flung states and even continents, she loved each of them for it.

"I know you will," she replied. "You are relentless."

She fixed her mother, sitting as always like a queen at the head of the table, in a narrow-eyed gaze. "And just what have you two decided I should do?"

"Isn't it obvious?" said Mother. "You should go to Illinois with your brother."

"Pardon me?" Annie had long thought the subject dismissed and didn't wish to revisit it now. "Davis left months ago, or had you forgotten?"

"With me," William said. "Davis wrote to me of an opportunity to invest in a large parcel of rich farmland in Illinois. This farm won't sustain both John Wesley and me once we have families of our own to support."

"Do either you or John Wesley have plans to start a family sometime soon?" she asked.

William blushed and pushed his chair back from the table. "I met someone, Annie."

She studied her handsome brother. He possessed the same wavy, dark hair as all the Goheen men, the same prominent cheekbones and strong chin, the sun-kissed complexion and well-formed muscles of a farmer. He looked dependable, determined, and honest.

"When? Who? Do I know her?"

"Her name is Susan. I met her in Baltimore. We've been writing." His eyes lit as he spoke, and Annie had to admit he looked like the perfect frontier husband for a woman named Susan.

"She wants this, too? To get married and move to Illinois?" Annie had no right to be upset by William's news, and she wasn't really. Except that the thought of another brother leaving, of another happily married couple, was more than she wanted to consider. Her anxiety rose as this new information pounded through her head.

"Calm down, Mary Ann." Her mother's commanding voice brought her back to herself. "They want to begin a fresh life in a new place."

"You sound as if you want them to go."

Elizabeth rolled her eyes at her daughter in that exasperated way only a mother could. "I support William in his decision, but it's not for me to approve or not. He's a grown man and he has already committed. He'd like for you to go with him."

Across the table from her, William nodded his agreement. The overwhelming love Annie had felt for her family only moments before evaporated into a mist of betrayal.

"Why didn't you tell me about all of this?"

Elizabeth explained, "You had the Seys children. You wouldn't have left them. Now they're safely back with their grandmother and you're free to go. Esther's gone. There's nothing for you here."

"You speak as if this decision has already been made. What if I don't want to go?" She sounded like a whining child, but she didn't care. They had ambushed her.

"Annie," William said, "no one is forcing you to go anywhere. I know it's frightening to move so far from the home you've always known, but I would love to have you with us. You and Susan will become fast friends. I know it."

Mother added, "You might even find a husband."

Of course, this was the point. They believed her broken and incomplete and she was to be a mail order bride after all, delivered by stagecoach to whatever ill-mannered frontiersman would have her. Her stomach bubbled with disappointment.

"Mother, I think that ship might have sailed by now, don't you?"

"You're a young enough woman. You should be raising your own children and not someone else's."

"I love Hannah's children as if they are my own."

Elizabeth patted her arm. "But they're not your own. You have always been a wonderful mother to any child who has needed you, and now God calls you on to a new opportunity where you may yet have children of your own."

"Why on earth would you equate moving a thousand miles away from the home I have always known with finding a husband and raising children? Illinois might as well be the end of the earth for all I know about it."

"Davis is there. He's working at a college. There must be people and civilization. It can't be all Indians."

She narrowed her eyes in suspicion at her mother. "What has Davis told you?"

"He did send me one letter I didn't share with you."

"And what did it say, Mother?"

"He suggested he had perhaps found you a good match."

"So that's it, then. You want me to go so you can get me married off to a complete stranger."

William laughed. Annie shot him a dark look.

"Davis says he is of the finest character."

"Oh, does he? And how am I to trust Davis's judgment? He probably just wants to lure me to Illinois so I can keep house for him."

"Your brother is a man of fine character, too, or have you forgotten? He wants the best for you. We all do. And the best thing for you to do is to find some peace and happiness."

Her head had begun to ache. The two of them had worked together to trap them, and Davis had helped.

"And what does my brother suggest makes this man so perfect for me?" The question came from between clenched teeth and might have been uttered in a growl she was so frustrated.

"He didn't say perfect. He said suitable."

"Oh, well, then, I will lower my expectations."

"Stop acting like a child." Mother stood and carried her empty plate to the wash basin. William reached across the table for Annie's plate to stack on top of his.

"Is he handsome?" Annie batted her eyes and hugged herself tight like a lovelorn child. Her mother didn't take the bait.

"He's respectable."

William added, "Strangely enough, Davis didn't comment on the man's handsomeness."

Elizabeth followed up in a dry tone. "He's a widower, with another woman's children for you to raise. You should like that part. And he's a founding board member of McKendree College where your brother is serving."

Annie pushed back from the table with a huff. "He sounds like a dream."

Mother grumbled. "Mary Ann Goheen, it's time for you to grow up."

28
Sylvanus

Editing the *Luminary* proved more satisfying than Sylvanus had anticipated. John and Walter ironed out the details—the subscription rate of two dollars per year, the frequency of publication, which was an easy pace of every other Friday, and the rough makeup of the paper itself.

Walter used his publishing contacts to develop relationships with other mission efforts throughout the world and news agencies able to provide him with stories of great interest. The pages also included more light-hearted offerings such as fables and poems. Sylvanus, or those he cajoled, contributed pieces on the natural science and culture of Liberia. He imagined family back home, gathered about the fireplace to read of the Devil bush and the greegree men performing strange rites late into the night.

There was always space devoted to the goings-on of their own Liberian mission stations, promoting successes whenever possible for those benefactors in the United States. Such stories also served to increase the esteem of Reverend Seys in a community increasingly bombarded by the accusations of Governor Buchanan and his allies.

Sylvanus wrote with passion about the mission, and with the help of his bright young apprentice, Jacobus, managed the health of the missionaries with enough efficiency to borrow days here or there to visit each of the mission stations.

Heddington was his favorite. Twelve miles beyond Caldwell up the St. Paul's River to the north of Monrovia, a trip to Heddington required either a treacherous hike or an uncomfortable, though amusing, ride atop a chair suspended on long poles and borne by the strong natives whose surer footsteps more easily traversed the dense jungle.

Once arrived, one would be greeted with much loud celebration by kings Bango, Peter, and Tom, whose enthusiasm for the Gospel induced them to gather their respective villages within a short radius of the long palaver building and frame two-story mission house established by the particularly gifted George Brown.

Brother Brown's Philadelphia sermon many years earlier had sparked a fire for mission within the heart of a young physician and since then, his indomitable spirit had subdued savage natures with the message of Jesus Christ. Heddington represented for Sylvanus, and through him for the readers of *Africa's Luminary*, the triumph of God and of the missionary effort on the Dark Continent.

And so the news of its destruction arrived as a shock while Sylvanus examined the ulcerated foot of *Liberia Herald* editor Hilary Teague.

"I was sorry to hear of the battle at Heddington." Teague winced when the caustic mixture of potash and nitric acid contacted the hardened edges of the ulcer and just grazed the tender surrounding skin.

Sylvanus looked up from his work with a start. Though their roles as rival editors, and Teague's particular loyalty to the colonial government, made the two men natural enemies, they had brokered a tentative truce weeks before when the newspaper man appealed to Sylvanus for help. Treated previously by a string of colonial physicians, each less well trained than the last, Hilary Teague suffered with a voraciously spreading cutaneous ulcer. What had begun on his Achilles heel had spread to the side and front of his foot.

The injury was unsurprising. Such blights affected at least ten percent of the colonial and missionary population, often indicating a tendency toward uncleanliness. Teague's ulcer had proven as stubborn as the man himself. Sylvanus nearly enjoyed the discomfort that mingled with the smugness on the man's face.

"What battle?" he asked, reluctant to reveal his ignorance. He painted more chemical onto the wound.

"I thought you'd have received word from your man there. Brown, is it?"

Sylvanus turned away from his gloating patient to retrieve the dressing materials from Jacobus, watching from behind him. The young man's eyebrows arched. Sylvanus responded with a subtle headshake before turning back to Teague.

"My sources from the jungle tell me the Kru slaver Gatumba waged a vicious attack on the settlement." The sting of the acid now barely registered in the man's rejuvenated demeanor. "They say he wants Brown's head."

Sylvanus dropped his gaze to the bandages he held loosely in his trembling fingers. He tried to focus on the construction of a splint, to push aside a clawing fear. George Brown had been the most effective of their missionaries. His success had made the slave trade more difficult in the region.

"Is George—"

"No." Teague crossed his arms casually. "I heard they defended themselves well. The mission house took damage. The natives suffered losses and scattered some, but Brown's household was largely intact, I believe."

Sylvanus released a breath. His deft hands began to work—the hands of a surgeon, and now an editor who had been scooped. He finished the splint and lowered his patient's foot to the floor.

"The slavers will always discover a formidable opponent among Liberia's missionaries and an immovable fortress in God Almighty." Sylvanus wished he could feel as certain as he sounded.

"Let's hope you're right, Dr. Goheen." Surprising sincerity had crept into Teague's words. Despite their differences, both editors wanted a peaceful Liberia where emigrants and natives could both thrive. The vision could never be realized without defeat of the slavers who still prowled the coastline and plundered the remaining strong backs of already weakened tribes.

Sylvanus's mind formulated a brief prayer for the safety of George Brown and the Heddington mission station.

"Eat a sensible diet. Keep this splint clean and dry." He patted Teague's bandaged leg. "If your foot swells excessively or the ulcer spreads, let me or young Mr. Seys here know right away."

As quickly as he moved, Sylvanus might have been carried by wings to the seminary and the office of Walter Jayne, rather than by the swift strides that delighted Hector the dog as he weaved around his master's feet.

At Sylvanus's knock, the printer looked up from his work poring over long pages of type. "What can I do for you, Doc?"

"Have you news of Heddington?"

The editor's eyes narrowed. "A messenger arrived a few hours ago for John. He was short on details, though. What have you heard?"

Sylvanus relayed Hilary Teague's scant information.

Walter frowned. "Not much more than we got. Apparently, the station was pinned down by gunfire, or at least the threat of it, for a couple of days."

Panic flooded back into Sylvanus. He'd felt safe in Liberia. Even comfortable. He knew there were slavers at work along the coast to the south and that native tribes warred with one another, but it had never occurred to him the missionaries themselves might fall under attack. They were men of God. Should that not afford them some level of security?

"Where's the superintendent?"

Walter leaned back from his desk. "He left to see Buchanan and was told he'd find him in Bassa Cove. So that's where he went."

Sylvanus's heart caught in his throat. At best, John would be several days traveling to petition the governor for help—help Buchanan might prove unwilling to offer to the mission he saw as a threat to the stability of the colony. The notion was ridiculous, but paranoia rarely lost to common sense.

"What does he think will the governor do?" Sylvanus asked, incredulous.

"Doc, he has a militia. We don't."

"It doesn't matter." His volume overwhelmed the small space. "John has consistently argued that the government should stay out of mission affairs. We've written the damning editorials ourselves. We've all but condemned Buchanan. He won't help. Why would he help?"

"The governor's always crusaded against the slavers." Walter rubbed his eyes with ink-stained fingers. "But you might be right. Heddington is ours. He might not see the value in using militia resources in its defense."

"I'll go."

Walter's brow creased. "Are you a soldier, then?"

"No." He crossed his arms in defiance. "I'm a physician. I can treat the wounded, organize their removal, offer whatever assistance I can."

"What if you encounter Gatumba?"

Sylvanus shoved aside the fear the question invoked, displacing it with unearned courage.

"Then he'll wish I hadn't."

Just after dawn the next morning, Sylvanus boarded a long canoe piloted by two dark-skinned natives with only a handful of English words between them. He did not typically mind silence, but as the hours stretched, filled with only the quiet paddle strokes, the drone of insects, and the skittering of monkeys through the trees along the banks of the St. Paul, he'd have appreciated a distraction from his worry.

He didn't know what he would find at Heddington or whether he'd be merely helpless at the scene of destruction, a concern that had plagued him since the moment he'd pulled aside his young assistant to provide instructions for his absence.

Sylvanus had taken Jacobus under his wing in much the same way as his old friend Dr. Thompson had done for him back home in Pennsylvania. As a young man, Sylvanus possessed little confidence in his own potential, and it had been a gift to glimpse a future in the enthusiasm of a mentor.

He'd hoped to provide similar guidance to the oldest Seys boy and took a great deal of pride in the eagerness the young man demonstrated.

"Deliver this to Dr. Proud at the longhouse." Sylvanus had handed the young man a bottle containing an opium tincture he'd prepared that morning. "Tell him if he uses it sparingly it may offer relief to the woman I consulted on yesterday."

Jacobus swirled the liquid and slipped the bottle in his pocket.

"Stress the *sparingly*."

"Yes, sir."

"And be subtle. Proud may accept our help, but only if it doesn't bring him trouble from the governor's men."

"I know." Jacobus rolled his eyes in a rare show of frustration.

Sylvanus appraised the capable young man. "You're responsible for general health advice and triage only. Direct anything more complicated than you can comfortably manage to Dr. Proud. But only if the situation cannot await my return. Lord knows what good he'll do them."

Sylvanus would not be gone long. He would assess the Heddington situation, treat the injured as well as he could, and return with the mission's survivors. He might even beat John back to Monrovia.

Had he not been there before, Sylvanus might have wondered when his guides delivered him safely to the edge of the cleared land whether it was, in fact, an established settlement and not a pile of long-abandoned ruins. The cassava and potatoes that once stood neatly in rowed fields were now no more than burned husks, the ash of which coated the soil.

In the dimming evening light, he made out the dark silhouettes of men digging into the ground at the edges of the jungle, presumably to bury the dead whose putrid stench fouled the air for miles around the once ordered village. On his first visit, Sylvanus had been celebrated by kings. This time, he was greeted by ghosts.

Warily he passed the scorched bones of the palaver building where George Brown's native congregants worshipped *Grippau*, their peculiar name for God, and wailed with joy at the preacher's powerful words of salvation through Christ.

Beyond these remains, the mission house stood defiant, untouched by fire but scarred by bullet holes and the jagged teeth of broken windows. Sylvanus stepped onto the porch and followed a trail of dried blood, remnants surely of a dragged corpse on its way to a final resting place at the jungle's edge.

He knocked before letting himself into the dark front room without awaiting a response. He called out a greeting, identifying himself as a doctor just arrived from Monrovia.

"Doctor, come." The voice beckoned him forward and obediently he crossed the room, his boots grinding glass shards with each step, until he reached the shadow of a figure belonging to the voice. It was a boy, initially obscured by the gathering darkness. Sylvanus identified him as one of the many young native students Brown had welcomed into his home, patiently teaching them English and Christianity as well as American dress, mannerisms, and customs. No missionary had been more effective in this effort than Brother Brown had been. He loved these children and poured into them as he would his own. At least one of them had rewarded his efforts by remaining by his side as the battle raged.

"Where is Brother Brown?" Sylvanus asked. The lad seized his hand and led him down a dark hallway, at the end of which the soft yellow light of an oil lamp spilled beneath a door.

The boy pushed his way into the room. In the light, Sylvanus could see him better. The whites of his curious eyes shined bright against his dark skin, and his face cracked into a wide grin as Sylvanus studied him. Standing there in a collared shirt, unbuttoned waistcoat, and trousers, he could have been one of the Black children on the Hill in Columbia.

"Dr. Goheen. Is that you?"

Sylvanus looked beyond the child to a high bed frame beside which stood a nightstand and the steadily burning oil lamp. Atop the mattress was George Brown, whole and if not well, at least alive.

Sylvanus hurried to his side. "George, are you hurt?"

"No. I'm not hurt." His answer came accompanied by a raspy chuckle fading into a cough. "The Lord saw fit to spare me from a thousand raining bullets only to lay me low again with the fever."

Sylvanus placed a hand on George's forehead, so hot it might have sizzled when touched. He lowered his medical bag to the floor beside the bed and dropped to his knees to rummage its contents. He withdrew a small vial containing a tincture of quinine.

He uncorked and handed the vial to George. "Swallow this, my friend. We'll have you on your feet again in no time, ready to make the trip back to Monrovia."

George took the vial and drained the contents. "I can't go to Monrovia right now."

"What do you mean? You can't stay here. You were attacked. The station is nearly destroyed."

Brown closed his eyes. "Did you come alone, Doctor?"

"Yes," Sylvanus leaned back on his heels, marveling at the man's stubbornness. "As soon as I heard the news of the attack."

"And what of Reverend Seys? The militia?"

Sylvanus paused. He didn't want to cast John in a poor light with one of his most successful missionaries, and he feared anything he might say would do so. "Reverend Seys went to petition Governor Buchanan for aid."

George nodded slowly, his head barely moving from its cushioned resting place. His eyes did not open. "Tell me," he said, "do you think Reverend Seys has a cordial enough relationship with the governor to receive a sympathetic response?"

"I'm not sure." But he was sure. The two men would not find a way to cooperate in this nor in any other matter.

Brown didn't respond for a full minute, and Sylvanus began to suspect the man had drifted into a fevered sleep when at last his eyes flew open. "Thank you for coming, Dr. Goheen. All will be well. God protected this mission station. He drove away our enemy like the Midianites before Gabriel's sword. Some in my congregation gave their lives in His service. Some scattered. Some will come back together to rebuild. I'll be here with them when they do, testifying to the glory of our Heavenly Father in this place."

"What if the attackers return? You can't believe you're safe here."

"God never promised following His will would be safe. This is where I belong." George's eyes slowly opened to fix Sylvanus in a penetrating stare. "Where do you belong, Dr. Goheen?"

Brown's question swirled through Sylvanus's mind, mingling there with the man's earnest prayers for a safe return journey to Monrovia and an easing of tensions between the governor and the superintendent.

The missionary's fever had broken by the next morning and, though weak, his health was much improved. He possessed a strength not so much of body, but of undeniable spirit.

Where George was faithful and brave, humble and honest, Sylvanus began to suspect himself of insincerity and cowardice, arrogance and deceitfulness. For the first time since arriving in Africa, perhaps since agreeing to serve the mission, Sylvanus found himself crying out to God, to ask him where he needed to be and what sort of man he was to become.

His journey down the St. Paul became the single most profound moment he'd ever spent with God. John Wesley—the original John Wesley—would have called it a strange warming of the heart. That God was moving in this place, he had no doubt.

God had revealed to Sylvanus the evil of Heddington not because George Brown needed rescuing, but because a frightened and confused physician needed to learn something—something he'd been too arrogant to see—that it was only through the grace of God he could hope to influence the evil underpinnings of this world. While Sylvanus attempted to control life and death with tinctures and dietary advice, George Brown stared down demons with the confidence of God Almighty.

The sun dropped below the jungle treetops while Sylvanus walked up the path to the mission house where lights blazed in welcome. Only when he drew even with the front edge of the orchard did he recognize that something was wrong.

Windows had been thrown open to catch the breeze—a breeze which should have carried songs of praise and the payers of evening vespers, but instead brought to him the sounds of sorrow, of tears and disbelief. With hurried steps, he rushed into the house and followed the sounds to a gathering in the infirmary. There in their midst was a sight that broke him.

Upon one of the cots lay a lifeless figure, tinged blue at the lips and as pale as the sheet upon which he was laid out. Sylvanus's knees gave out beneath him at the sight there of Jacobus Seys.

29
Annie

The long trek across the country was an arduous one and included canal, railroad, and stagecoach, the last of which carried the three travelers on the final leg of their journey toward the town of Lebanon, Illinois, thirty miles east of St. Louis.

Still sullen from her reluctant acceptance of her brother's invitation and ever cognizant of the newness of his marriage, Annie had tried to give the couple space as they traveled. Now, clattering down the rough western road, she did her best to block out their flirting and reviewed the letters she hoped to post once they reached their destination.

To Cornelius, Henry, and Jane Seys, by now well established in their grandmother's home, she'd written descriptions of the Allegheny Mountains, the rolling hills of Ohio, the vast plains of Indiana and Illinois. She'd spent hours composing a letter to Hannah as well, sharing her complicated feelings about seeing the children go and beginning a new chapter of her own story as well. By the time her friend received such a letter, Annie would be a lady of the frontier. It was perhaps not as exotic a locale as Monrovia, but she was on an adventure of her own, even if it was without a great deal of enthusiasm. In that, she had to admit, she felt some pride.

"What are you working on so diligently?" Susan Beale, now Goheen, leaned toward Annie, her eyes shining and hopeful. William slouched, somehow asleep against the side of the bouncing coach.

"Just looking over the letters I'll be posting once we get to civilization again," Annie said. "I want to add something more about the prairie grass to the children."

Susan arched an eyebrow. "I bet those boys would be more interested in hearing about the wild Indians that fired arrows at our wagon as we passed by. Or the howling cayotes threatening our safety on the trail. Or the highway robbers that held up this stagecoach."

Annie laughed. "We've had a very different trip."

Susan shrugged. "Well, your brother tells me the Seys children have pretty good imaginations. I don't think they'd mind if you spiced up the tale a little bit. It's a shame they had to leave before the wedding. I'd like to have met them." She folded her hands on her lap and looked out the window. "I suppose the prairie grass is pretty."

"It is," Annie said. "And William is the storyteller. He should write his own account. We can mail them together. I'm sure the children would like that."

Susan's face broke into a wide grin. "It's going to be wonderful, isn't it? A new state. A new home." She reached for Annie's hand. "A whole new everything."

"I suppose it is." Annie reflected on all she'd left behind and discovered only the ghosts of all she'd lost—Esther and Bennett, the Seys children, her teaching career, Jonas. She envied Susan's optimism and felt a stab of desire to share it.

"A whole new everything," she agreed.

The town of Lebanon was charming with its tree lined streets and neat homes, its citizens a collection of serious but quirky characters. The Mermaid House Hotel greeted them first. The two-story, red-sided inn was kept by an old sailor who swore he'd had encounters with mermaids on his journeys. He enchanted Annie and Susan with ridiculous stories while William arranged for transportation of their trunks to Davis's home.

Much to Mother's chagrin, Davis remained unmarried, but he rented a large, comfortable home and had been wise enough to hire domestic help. His position as chief financial officer at the college gave him little time for household chores.

The housekeeper, Mrs. Lowe, was plump and kind and organized. She kept Davis well-fed and on task, which came as a relief to Annie. As much as she bristled at the idea of being dragged to Illinois to find a husband, she also did not wish to be thought of as the spinster housekeeper for her crusty bachelor of a brother. Perhaps once she was settled, she could tutor or even return to the classroom. The house stood only a few blocks from McKendree College which was quaint and beautiful, housed in two large brick buildings.

William talked of setting to work right away, looking for farm labor to hold him over until he could find a plot of land to purchase and establish a homestead for himself and Susan, but in the meantime, the four of them would be perfectly comfortable here.

"Family," Davis addressed them as he walked into the sitting room where Annie sat writing in her diary and the newlyweds huddled together by the fire. William read to his bride from an open book as she gazed lovingly at him. "I hate to do this on the day of your arrival, but I have an important supper tonight at the college." Davis was dazzling in a fresh, dark suit, clean-shaven and his hair recently trimmed.

"You cut a handsome figure when you want to," Annie said.

"If you didn't sound so surprised, I might be flattered." He kissed her cheek. "William and Susan, how would you enjoy some time alone and a dinner for two? Mrs. Lowe is an excellent cook."

"Sounds good," William answered for them both.

"What am I to do?" Annie smirked. "Hide in a wardrobe?"

"Actually," Davis said, "I had hoped you might join me. I'd like to introduce you to my colleagues. Have you a nicer dress?"

Annie shivered at the thought of what colleagues she might be likely to meet and looked down at the faded gingham she wore. It was as drab as she felt herself to be, recently arrived after her long trip.

"You should wear the blue one." Susan piped up from the corner. "It will bring out your pretty eyes. Elegant."

The dress was elegant, designed for an elegant event on the arm of a man who never saw her wear it, but Susan was right. It would make a good match to Davis's attire and would be suitable for meeting anyone else who might enjoy seeing the way it brought out her pretty eyes, a notion that made her stomach hurt.

"Yes, I have a nicer dress," she admitted. "May I ask a follow-up question about these colleagues of yours?"

William closed his book and stood, a half-cocked smile on his lips. "I assume this banquet will include an eligible bachelor for our dear sister."

"There might be one or two." Davis did not look at Annie as he said this, casting his attention instead onto William and Susan. "But if you must know, I tire of going to these tedious banquets alone. It would be nice to have some company and to show people that even a poor-mannered bookkeeper may be related to grace and charm."

Annie appreciated his praise but was not fooled by it. "You're already planning to pawn me off on any eligible man you know?"

"Mother would have his head if he didn't at least try." William's grin revealed a shallow dimple on his cheek.

Susan playfully slapped her husband's arm. "Leave her alone."

Davis straightened his waistcoat. "I'm not trying to marry you off to any old bachelor who comes along." He lowered his voice and added, "But perhaps a particular widower who might enjoy the company of a capable woman."

"And I'm so capable." Annie tried not to feel hurt by her brother's words, which he probably did intend as a compliment, but even a single woman in her thirties might rather be described in other, less practical ways.

Susan jumped to her rescue. "Certainly capable, but also more lovely than words could describe."

The flattery from her pretty young sister-in-law did more to bolster Annie's confidence than she'd care to admit. She would put on her blue dress and survey what her new town may have to offer, but she wouldn't let her irritating brother off easy either.

"Very well, Davis. Susan says I'm lovely and we all know I'm charming. And I suppose we are related. I will put on a more acceptable dress and accompany you to your banquet to show you in your best light."

"Thank you, Annie," Davis said. "I apologize. I did not mean to offend you. I really do think you might get along well with the man I'm thinking of. He's a little older and has children already—serious sort, though far from humorless, and would unlikely have his head turned by a young, fresh face."

"Thank you for that stunning compliment," she answered dryly, rolling her eyes toward William whose snort of laughter earned him swift reprimand from his wife.

"You're older than I am, Davis," Annie pointed out. "Perhaps there's a practical woman without a young fresh face waiting for you, too."

He shrugged. "As long as she enjoys a good joke. I don't mind finding out."

The supper meeting was held in a large banquet hall in the main building of the college, and it was crowded. Men and women, all well-dressed and well-mannered, milled about engaging in lively conversations. Annie felt out of sorts at first, but Davis proved to be a good escort and introduced her around so she might converse with any number of those in attendance, none of whom seemed to be the widower of which he had hinted.

Annie scanned the crowd, trying to spot the man she was evidently destined to spend the rest of her life with. When she found no one who fit the description, her thudding heart began to slow and she settled into the comfort of an easy evening out, thinking that was perhaps the end of her family's ridiculous crusade to see her become a bride.

Davis, however, did not drop the subject and once they were settled at their table, he addressed the other diners. "Has anyone seen the good Reverend Akers this evening? I was hoping to discuss something with him."

If Annie could have slid under the table she might have done so, such was her mortification at her brother's words and the knowing smiles shared by their fellow banquet guests.

A gentleman across the table answered. "I was under the impression he was coming, but I haven't seen him."

"Nor have I," said one of the ladies. "But he is not unlikely to allow himself to be caught up with a spiritual matter when his alternative is a formal banquet."

There was chuckling around the table.

Davis grabbed Annie's hand beneath the table and squeezed it. "I do hope to see him soon."

At this, Annie blushed and wished she hadn't, sure everyone at the table must have noticed and guessed she was the business to be discussed. When no one seemed to pay her any extra attention, however, her cheeks cooled. They were most of the way through the main course by the time the door opened at the far end of the hall and a large, somewhat clumsy figure burst through it.

"Ah, there he is." Davis waved to the newcomer who ambled toward the table. Annie took in the sight of him, which was frankly dreadful. His suit was a mess, rumpled and dirty as though he'd just ridden miles and miles on horseback, which she supposed he probably had.

Davis stood and shook hands with the stranger before guiding him to the only empty seat at the table, to the left of Annie. "I'm glad you could join us, Reverend Akers."

"Thank you, Reverend Goheen. I thought I might not make it, and perhaps I shouldn't have come. I'm a frightful mess, but I only just came into town. The Burroughs family lost an infant. I stayed with them to perform the baptism and bury the poor lad. I feared by the time I arrived here I would miss supper if I were to clean up first, and I am awfully hungry."

"Think nothing of it. We were all discussing earlier what we thought could have been the important business keeping you away, and we never doubted for a moment you were here in spirit."

"Indeed, I was. Your friendly greetings and warm smiles were all I could think of as I rode the last ten miles." At this the Reverend Akers looked directly at Annie. His eyes were blue, bright and keenly intelligent, and also soft and filled with the kind of compassion that would make a man risk missing an important meeting to spend a few extra moments comforting the grieving mother of a deceased infant. Her first impression of him as a rude barbarian of a man began to recede, and her heart thawed slightly to this gentle giant with deep laugh lines etched at the corners of his eyes.

"Reverend Peter Akers," Davis said, "may I introduce my sister Miss Mary Ann Goheen, just arrived from Pennsylvania."

"Welcome to the west, Miss Goheen." His entire face softened as he locked eyes with her, as though the stress of his journey and the difficulty which proceeded it no longer mattered once he found himself in her presence. "I hope you'll find much happiness here."

Deep skin creases framed his mouth, suggesting his tendency to laugh heartily and often. Annie cleared her throat and glanced down at the table, chastising herself for evaluating him. He'd have towered over Jonas in stature, her brothers as well. His dark, thick hair was windblown from travel, and he smelled of horses and sweat. Still, she could see in him traces of the strength she'd so admired in all the men who had been most important to her.

"Thank you, Reverend," she replied.

Davis saved her from formulating more of a reply by asking, "Tell me, Peter, how fares the Ebenezer project?" Then he added as a side to Annie, "Reverend Akers has recently begun a manual labor school for Indians."

"Are there many Indians in the area?" Annie had little knowledge of and no experience with Indians. The acknowledgment that she now lived in their near vicinity stabbed her heart with fear.

Davis squeezed her hand, a brotherly gesture which calmed her, but it was Reverend Akers who answered her question. "There are fewer now. Recent conflict has pushed most of them west of the Mississippi River."

"What kind of conflict?"

"War, Miss Goheen," Akers said. "War waged by our United States government against a people forcibly displaced from the land they once called home."

"I see," she said, stiffening at what felt like a chastisement in his tone. "And would you have us all live together in blissful harmony?" Annie's sarcastic comment sounded harsh even to her own ears, and she braced for a biting comeback.

Instead, the reverend's words echoed the gentleness permeating from his presence. "Is it such a terrible dream to believe all God's children might live together in peace?"

Annie's mouth dropped open at the words she herself had so often spoken while arguing against the colonization movement in which her family was so dearly invested.

"Is that practical?" She could almost hear Smee asking the same question of her.

Peter Akers actually laughed, a rich sort of chuckle originating from deep within a man who clearly laughed often. "It is most definitely not. But that problem, Miss Goheen, is what we hope to rectify with Ebenezer School."

"Meaning what, exactly?" Davis asked, injecting a surprisingly unwelcome reminder to Annie of his presence.

"Our mission is not only to teach practical skills—learning through labor, if you will—but also to instruct in Biblical truths and principles of mission."

"You're training missionaries, then. Indian missionaries?" A tingle ran through Annie, a hint of an excitement she found herself hoping she might catch.

Akers nodded. "We are, for those who wish for it. I'm hopeful the more we share our cultural values and our devotion to Christ, the easier it will become to live together."

"And it's not just Indians you teach, correct?" Davis inserted himself once again. Annie fought a strong urge to push him off his chair.

"We have three Indians currently, as well as two other serious missionary students, and we have our first female student as well. There's talk we may even soon become a school for young children."

"You're growing fast," Davis said.

Akers tipped his head in a slight bow. "The glory goes to God, my friend. He's planted us and He will see us flourish if it is His will."

Davis nodded. "I'd love to see the school sometime."

"You'd be welcome to visit."

"And," Davis added with a glance at Annie, "my sister has experience in the education of young children. For years she taught at the schoolhouse where we grew up in rural Pennsylvania."

"Is that so?" The appraising look Peter Akers now gave to Annie made her heartrate increase once again. "Of course, we'd love to receive a visit from you both."

Annie felt a jab in her side from her brother's elbow, followed by a sideways glimpse of a devilish wink that made her scowl at him, but with less conviction than she had originally intended.

30
Sylvanus

Sylvanus drew his hand across the coarse skin on the back of his neck where sweat mingled with the salt in the air to form a gritty slime he could never fully wash off. A physician's hands should be soft instruments for carefully palpating a distended belly, prodding a swollen joint, or comforting a fevered brow. They should be capable and strong and sure.

Sylvanus looked at his hands. He could not make sense of his own calloused fingers, stained with the dirt of the grave he'd helped a grieving father to dig in the harsh coastal soil of a foreign land. These hands that should save had instead abandoned.

Sent on an errand by Dr. Proud, inappropriately assigned, to collect herbs of no medicinal value Sylvanus could determine, Jacobus had apparently lost his footing and drowned in the Mesurado River. There had been no hands nearby to rescue him, no physician to nurse him back to health. In an instant, all the potential and promise of a Godly and intelligent young man had been washed away.

Hours passed before two Kru men found the swollen corpse caught against the bank. They carried it to the mission house and claimed no knowledge of how a capable swimmer had succumbed to the river. Sylvanus had wondered if perhaps they'd borne some responsibility in the boy's death, but John, possibly because grief clouded his judgment, refused to entertain the idea.

Sylvanus stood at the fresh mound of dirt. The rest of the missionary family had gone. Lydia had wrapped the sobbing Hannah in her arms and attempted to catch Sylvanus's attention as the missionaries began the solemn descent from the graveyard. Sylvanus refused to meet her gaze. He wished to reveal his vulnerability to her even less than he wished to return to the mission house where a fog of melancholy displaced previously inextinguishable optimism and raised doubt the mood might ever shift again.

John Seys had left even earlier than his wife. Before the last syllables of eulogy faded from the heavy air, the stony-faced superintendent turned down the hill, his shoulders sagging in defeat as if he wore a thick and onerous cloak.

It would rain soon. Sylvanus's skin anticipated the kiss of the gentle, swirling drops that whispered along one's body. He missed the purposeful rainfall of Pennsylvania that washed and cleansed and refreshed. Monrovia's more constant precipitation carried the briny sea, the faint scent of fish. It coated, enveloped, suffocated.

"God, why?"

Sylvanus knew some people spoke to God aloud in this way—people of more faith than he. People like his eldest brothers, both seminary-trained and serving in the land where God had called them. Or like Annie whose certainty in pursuing home and family he found astounding. Even his mother's determined strength had been an answer to a natural call, one she had filled with grace and force.

He laughed joylessly at the thought.

He'd been called once. Dr. Thompson filled his head with knowledge and his heart with longing to heal, to cure, to conquer death.

But to do such was not the realm of man.

"What are we doing here?"

He found a strange sort of comfort in the sound of his own voice, high on this forsaken hill of graves. Great men lay beneath it, thousands of miles from where their lives had begun. Sylvanus examined the markers. The more recent ones were carved stone; others merely wooden crosses, splintered and slick with decay, faintly proclaiming the names Barton, Cox, Stocker, Wright, and so many more. Some stood alone; others marked the resting places of missionary couples, of their children. Above the newest grave stood a freshly carved name, Jacobus O. Seys, with the dates 1824-1839.

"He should be alive," Sylvanus shouted. "They should all be alive."

Jacobus should have left with his parents, should never have stayed with Sylvanus to follow false dreams. He should be there now, safe in America. He could have lived in Columbia with Sylvanus's own family as his younger siblings had done. He could have met Dr. Thompson, a worthier mentor, a man whose competent hands saved.

If Sylvanus hadn't been so eager to rush off to rescue a missionary who hadn't desired rescuing, the young man beneath the ground might be talking to him now, answering his questions, unlike the obstinately silent Almighty.

He studied the names again, each in turn. Such men and women, like him, had come to Liberia to spread the Gospel, to establish a home for God's people displaced by the sin of slavery, to Christianize the darkest, most degraded of Adam's fallen race. It was good, what they did. He knew it was good.

But then he thought of the wretched emigrants, newly arrived and stashed in the longhouse, shivering with fever and bewilderment. Along the coast he could see the large plantation-style houses occupied by Monrovia's upper crust, early emigrants who had found success in trade and used it to rise above their neighbors. Often these wealthy Monrovians took servants from the native population who understood little of the exploitation under which they suffered. Oppression had once again found a way to flourish.

And what of those Africans just beginning to glimpse the light of Christ, who were now slaughtered and scattered in Heddington? Were they better off because the *white Black men*, as the emigrants were called, had come to live among them? Were their lives improved because so many white men now lay in the African dirt?

Sylvanus didn't know the answers to such questions, and as the raindrops began to whirl and mix with his tears, he wasn't certain he possessed the strength to ask.

John Seys had as little success at convincing Governor Buchanan to send military aid to Heddington as Sylvanus had at delivering aid himself. Only at the superintendent's insistence did George Brown reluctantly agree weeks later to remove to Monrovia, and he was anxious to return. The forceful Black preacher knocked on the door of the superintendent's office moments after Sylvanus had answered a summons himself.

"Brother George," John said. His smile did not reach his eyes, beneath which hung dark circles of grief and too little rest. "Have a seat. What can I do for you?"

Two chairs stood in front of the desk. Sylvanus occupied one.

George Brown remained standing in the doorway, twisting his hat in his hands. The man did not hesitate to state his purpose. "I need to know when I might go back to Heddington."

"There are rumors of continued danger." John folded his hands on his desk and leaned back in his chair. "I can't put you and the future of the ministry at risk."

"With all due respect," George began in a tone which conveyed little respect, "I have children at home. I need to get back to them."

"Native children," John replied with a sigh. "They survived before you came and will survive in your absence. I will not send my missionaries into harm's way."

"They are God's children." George made a fist by his side, lacking only a pulpit to strike. "And I am His servant. Not yours."

Sylvanus fought back his rising temper. He had never heard anyone speak to John in such a manner. The superintendent was patient, slow to anger, and open to the ideas of others but could not be accustomed to disrespect from subordinates. And this from a Black man.

Sylvanus sucked in sharp breath, a chastisement for the unbidden and ungracious thought, which brought a flush to his cheeks he hoped neither of his companions noticed. Next to John, George had been the one most responsible for inspiring him to come to Liberia. The man's passion for the mission had built its most successful remote station out of inhospitable jungle and at times outright hostile natives. Surely he, too, was deserving of Sylvanus's respect.

A vein throbbed visibly in John's temple, but his words came out slow and even.

"I understand, George, I do. No man appreciates your passion for this ministry more than I do, but I cannot authorize your return." He looked down at his desk and shuffled a stack of papers awaiting his attention. "In fact, I'm not sure how long I'll be authorizing anyone to do anything."

Neither of the other two men responded to this strange admission. John cleared his throat, took the paper from the top of the stack, and handed it to Sylvanus.

"This is a court summons," Sylvanus said, stunned. "I don't understand."

"The governor has made an accusation against the mission." John shook his head. "Against me, really."

"An accusation of what?" George asked from the doorway where he remained standing.

John's weary eyes shifted slowly from George to Sylvanus. "Counterfeiting. The governor has accused me of counterfeiting."

"Preposterous." Sylvanus stood, as his indignation rose, his brow deeply creased. "How does he think he can justify such a charge?"

"The promissory notes from the mission store sometimes get traded for services or even other goods."

George Brown stepped into the room and claimed the empty seat, nodding. "He might have a point. I've heard the complaints of emigrants. Liberian currency is unstable. They prefer the Methodist notes when they can get them."

"But to suggest we are intentionally undermining the currency system?" Sylvanus shook his head. "We are missionaries!"

"Missionaries who are engaged in trade," Brown rebutted.

"Only for the purposes of mission. It's not legitimate trade for profit."

"That's not how Buchanan sees it." John took the page back from Sylvanus and dropped it on his desk. "He insists on collecting duties on our incoming supplies—duties that are not owed. I have refused him."

"As you should!" Sylvanus's voice rose once again, too large for the small office.

"We must render unto Caesar what is Caesar's," George said.

"Not if Caesar has no legal right to collect," Sylvanus snapped.

"Sometimes the Kingdom of God is furthered most by standing down from a conflict." George Brown touched a finger to the side of his nose. "In the book of Romans, it says, 'If it be possible, as much as lieth in you, live peaceably with all men.'"

"You can't be serious," Sylvanus said. He looked to John, to see how the man would react to having Scripture thrown in his face in the midst of a clear injustice.

Several moments passed in silence as John seemed to mull over the words. At last, he pushed back his chair and stood. "I appreciate St. Paul's words, but we must stand in opposition to the governor's misguided vengeance. Brother Brown, perhaps you are right. It could be just the time for a return to Heddington."

The Black man's mouth opened as if he wished to respond, but then closed again in what Sylvanus took to be both concern and relief.

"Sylvanus," John continued, "you and I should find Walter Jayne. This will be a battle waged with the printed word before the reading public."

Sylvanus sat on the top porch step of the seminary and leaned against a tall pillar. He'd spent a long afternoon strategizing with John and Walter about the series of editorials he would write defending the superintendent and attacking Governor Buchannan and his allies.

He closed his eyes and took several deep breaths.

"Are you unwell, Dr. Goheen?"

He opened his eyes to find Lydia Beers standing over him, her feet planted on the bottom step, her eyes round and curious.

Sylvanus sat up straight. "Lydia."

Her eyebrows arched at his use of her first name, something he was usually careful not to do when they were alone. As she was the only unmarried woman among the missionaries, Sylvanus had been careful to maintain a respectful formality between the two of them, though he never thought of her as Miss Beers. And he did think of her, more often than he'd care to admit.

Sylvanus swept a sweaty clump of hair off his forehead. He was disheveled after spending several hours in a stuffy office with only frustrated men for company.

"I startled you." She joined him on the top step and sat, arranging her skirts about herself. "I apologize."

"No. No need. I'm tired is all."

"And I disturbed your rest." Her voice was light and playful. It reminded him of a butterfly on the breeze. She smelled good, too, like the orange blossoms that scented the air beside the mission house.

"I think if I want a good rest, the seminary stairs are not likely the best place to get it." He smirked. "Can I help you with something?"

She clasped her hands together. "Well, it's not an urgent request, but I have a student, Andrew. He's the son of a headman in the interior and has not been with us long. I'm afraid he doesn't speak much English, but he has a sore on his leg that has me worried. Could you find time to check him over?"

"Of course."

"I do appreciate it." She pursed her lips and made no move to stand.

"Something else on your mind?" he asked.

"I hope I'm not overstepping." She dropped her gaze to her lap. "You have been uncharacteristically melancholy of late. It's been a heavy time, but is there more? Are you missing home?"

That she'd noticed his mood surprised and pleased him, but he did not like to think he'd worried her. "No, it's not that." He paused. It could be partly that, but he didn't know how to explain his mix of emotions to her.

"I guess I'm feeling helpless, like things are spinning out of control. First the attack on Heddington. Then Jacobus." His voice hitched when he spoke the young man's name and Lydia's hand caught his. Neither of them moved to let go.

"Now the superintendent is in trouble, and I don't know if I can help."

Lydia's brow furrowed. "Are these problems that you alone must solve?"

Sylvanus studied her face, her clear eyes, her plump rosy cheeks, the hint of a smile on her lips even in the midst of a serious conversation. "Not entirely," he admitted.

She really did smile then, the skin around her eyes crinkling with a joy he wished he could capture.

"How do you do it?" he asked.

She tilted her head to one side. "What is it that I do?"

"You are unfailingly optimistic."

"I am no such thing."

"You're more optimistic than I am. Trouble slides off of you."

Lydia placed her hands flat against the floorboards of the porch and shifted her weight. "I think it's because I am grateful. Every day I wake up in Monrovia and see the faces of my silly, sometimes uncivilized but promising students, and I feel thankful that I can be here in this place. I'm a part of something that feels important. You're a part of it, too."

He heard the truth of her words. She spoke of the reason he'd come to Liberia in the first place, not because he expected it to be a utopia but because he knew he could play an important part in what it might become. His chest swelled with admiration for this wonderful woman who'd not forgotten and who had reminded him.

"Thank you, Lydia."

"Well," she said, dropping his hand as she moved to stand. "You're welcome, Sylvanus."

31
Annie

Annie didn't see Reverend Akers again for several months after Davis's shameful insistence that the two of them be thrown together. She was reluctant to ask her brother about the man, lest she be forced to endure a tremendous amount of teasing.

But she did think of him.

After three weeks she finally gave in to the impulse to ask as she and Davis sat over breakfast.

"Whatever became of the preacher you introduced me to?" She injected as much casual air into the question as possible. Davis's wide grin suggested she had failed.

"Peter has a home a few miles north of Jacksonville."

Annie flinched at the easy use of the reverend's given name—Peter, the rock upon which Christ's church was built. A strong and serious name, indicative perhaps of a strong and serious nature.

"You know him well, then?"

Davis set down his fork. "Well enough. He served for a while as the president of McKendree. Earlier in his career he was a financial officer at a college in Kentucky. He was a help to me when I was learning about my position here. A few years ago, he requested a circuit appointment and started his Indian school. His passion for education is rivaled only by his power in the pulpit."

"Reverend Akers sounds impressive." Annie stared down at her plate, burying the embarrassment of her last statement.

"He is. Now when he's not traveling his circuit, he spends his time at Ebenezer. It's where his children live. He lost his wife about a year ago." He paused, but when she made no comment, he continued. "Since he doesn't currently have an active role in the daily operations of McKendree, he makes it to board meetings when he must."

"And so it was at a board meeting you decided we were meant to be together? This impressive man with how many children? And no wife to care for them?"

Davis laughed. "He spoke forcefully." Her brother dabbed to corners of his mouth, laid his napkin at the side of his plate, and pushed back from the table. "I don't know how many children. I've heard him mention both sons and daughters.

"Don't fight it, dear sister. I saw the gleam in your eye when he entered the room covered in muck and smelling like a horse. He cleans up well, too."

"I'm glad to know you find him so dashing."

He stood. "Peter's a good man. You could do a lot worse." The pointed look he gave her suggested he thought she had. Annie was aware of her mother's concerns about Jonas, and Smee had certainly not been his biggest fan based solely on their political differences, but it cut her to know the whole family might have had reservations about her choice in husband. And it bothered her to think of them conspiring now to match her with a man of their choosing rather than hers.

But despite her misgivings, she had liked Peter Akers. He wasn't especially handsome, but he was tall and carried himself with nobility. At the dinner to which he had arrived late and disheveled, he had also regaled the table with funny stories from the road. When he laughed it was with a joy genuine enough, and others laughed with him.

Perhaps her family did know her well enough to choose her husband, assuming Peter Akers had any desire to be chosen.

"Enough about Peter Akers." Annie stood to clear their plates from the table. "How is your love life, brother?"

Davis ducked the question. "Best be off. It'll be busy in the office today." He cleared his dishes from the table and took them to the washbasin to soak. "What's on your schedule?"

Annie marveled at his ability to change the subject so easily and silently chastised herself for her failure to do likewise when the subject lit on her own embarrassment.

"I'll spend my day ensconced in sisterly affection at William's house." The newlyweds had rented a small farmhouse at the edge of town and Susan had kept happily busy establishing a comfortable home for them.

"You like her, don't you?" Davis asked.

Annie considered the question. William's Susan was surprising, but she possessed a certain charm. Younger than Annie by more than a decade, Susan's kind and playful spirit never flagged. Her heart was light and she was generally content, even in the face of a challenging pregnancy in a new place far from the home of her childhood. Annie admired her greatly.

"Yes. I do. Very much." She narrowed her eyes at her brother. "Do you not?"

"I would never have thought William might choose someone like her. Frankly, I'm amazed Mayberry had the insight to introduce them."

Annie couldn't deny the stolid nature of her eldest brother whose crusted edges had grown even harder through marriage and fatherhood. It was difficult to picture him playing at matchmaker. "Perhaps it was his wife's doing?"

Davis picked up the satchel awaiting him by the door. "Regardless, I think Susan is William's perfect match. Family can often see what we ourselves might miss."

The next time Annie saw him, Reverend Akers showed up on a chilly Sunday evening for a special prayer service held at the McKendree chapel. This time, he appeared to have had an opportunity to clean himself up. In a fresh suit of clothes and a clerical collar, he cut a reasonably handsome figure.

He delivered a sermon nearly forty-five minutes long, though it felt as if it could have been only ten minutes, so captivating was his intellect. Watching him, Annie got the distinct impression that it was not he who spoke, but rather it was the Spirit of God speaking through him. The tenor of his voice changed, commanding the listener, but not in a coercive way. It was invitational, but she also felt she had no other option than to hang on every word. She marveled at the sensation that rather than listening to a preacher, she might have been eavesdropping on a conversation between a man and his Creator.

When the service was over and he had shaken hands with most of the congregation, Reverend Akers approached her. She stood next to the pew alongside Davis who was engaged in a deep conversation with one of the McKendree administrators. At first, she assumed Reverend Akers approached the men, but it was her to whom he spoke.

"Miss Goheen, it's a pleasure to see you here tonight. Do you attend prayer service often?"

"I have not yet missed one since my arrival. It's good to see you again, Reverend Akers. You delivered a powerful sermon."

"Ah, thank you. Credit, of course, must be given to the Holy Spirit. I am but His vessel."

She'd known few men who so smoothly entwined humility with strength. Even Jonas had often failed to do so, aware as he was of the crucial role he played in his cause. But then Jonas had been younger than the man who stood before her now. Perhaps with time, his self-importance would have mellowed. A pang of regret followed the thought.

The preacher looked at his shoes—sturdy, scuffed boots not quite fitting the rest of his attire. His next words carried less confidence. "I wonder, Miss Goheen, if you might be joining your brother in Jacksonville later this spring?"

Annie knew little of Davis's daily work and nothing of any upcoming plans for travel. "I'm afraid I don't know to what you're referring, Reverend."

His eyebrows arched and he cleared his throat. "I apologize if I've overstepped. There is a planning meeting to discuss the possibility of beginning a women's college in Jacksonville. I had thought you might have some insight to offer."

"Because I'm a woman?" Annie enjoyed watching the blush creep into his cheeks.

"No."

She tilted her head and smiled. The reverend's weight shifted.

"Well, yes," he said. "You are a woman, obviously. But I was thinking of your experience in education."

"You believe experience teaching in a rural one-room schoolhouse lends me special knowledge of women's colleges?" Now she was being coy, perhaps even cruel and couldn't have explained why. In truth she was flattered and secretly hoped Davis, engaged as he was in another conversation, was catching at least a hint of this one.

"In fact, yes." Reverend Akers appeared more composed in his next response, a remarkable recovery from a moment of awkwardness, displaying admirable conversational dexterity. "This nation, it's great leaders and thinkers, survive only as long as we have strong, educated wives and mothers to support and prepare them."

"Reverend Akers, forgive me, but I am neither a wife nor a mother." She relished the power she held to push him off balance. Though her response visibly shook him, he did not succumb to the pull of gravity.

"From what Davis tells of you, you have a generous spirit and have often stood in the role of teacher, mother, and at times even helpmeet to those God has place in your life. I suspect you have a great deal to offer in the consideration of women's education." He cleared his throat again and glanced toward Davis and the other administrators. "And one never knows what plans God may yet have in store."

Annie could not think how to respond. His words, disguised as spiritual counsel, might as well have been a proposal, or at least a hint of one to come. The blood drained from her face and she felt a bit faint.

"Are you unwell, Miss Goheen?" Reverend Akers reached to catch her elbow in his grasp. His firm touch brought Annie to her senses as Davis turned from his conversation in time to glimpse the interaction.

The hint of a smile played across Davis's lips. Before he could interject, she wrenched her arm from the reverend's grip, which gave way easily, mumbled an excuse, and turned to make her way toward a group of women in the far corner, most of whom she could not even name if pressed.

She remained at the periphery of the gathered ladies, one ear trained on the conversation she'd escaped. Reverend Akers addressed her brother who had given the man his rapt attention.

"I would welcome Miss Goheen's opinion."

"I have no doubt she would be glad to give it."

She tensed, listening to Davis make her sound like some overbearing monster and found herself a little short of breath when it occurred to her that she cared very much what Peter Akers thought of her.

32
Sylvanus

Sylvanus's heart filled with dread as he read the message handed to him in the infirmary by John. It had been delivered by the schooner *Emperor*, arrived in the Bay of Monrovia the previous afternoon.

The first week of January 1840 had brought mild weather to his West African home, and after the unforgiving wet weather of the previous months, Sylvanus found hints of optimism returning to the mission family and to his own mind.

Grief and sickness, though pervasive, did give way at times to joy in the work God had set before him. He'd found pleasure, too, in his growing admiration for Lydia and in his editorial duties. While a handful of the Methodist missionaries had adopted George Brown's neutral viewpoint on their superintendent's legal troubles, Sylvanus's own persuasive work in the *Luminary* swayed most diligent readers to John's point of view.

The long-awaited letter he now held stressed the mission board's confidence in the character of Reverend John Seys and urged the ending of a lawsuit it deemed frivolous and an antagonism that could not serve the interests of the colony's citizens.

It also said in order to speed a resolution of a regrettable conflict, the board voluntarily consented to an immediate recall of both Superintendent Seys and the assistant editor of *Africa's Luminary*, Dr. Sylvanus Goheen.

"I don't understand," Sylvanus said as he read over the letter for the third time.

John sat on the edge of an empty cot and waited for the physician to look up from his reading. When he did, the superintendent's piercing gaze met his and they were moist with emotion.

"Why do this?" Sylvanus demanded. He slammed the page on the table beside him, causing the tinkling of several glass tincture bottles. "It doesn't make sense. The lawsuit has no merit. It's nearly at an end. They claim to support you and yet—"

"Yet they have made a difficult and correct decision for the purpose of the mission." John stood and placed a brotherly hand on Sylvanus's arm. "I'm sorry you got caught up in all of this. You've been a blessing to the people here—missionaries, emigrants, and natives alike. And you've been an indispensable friend to me."

Sylvanus wrenched his arm loose from John's grip and shook his head. "No. You can't just give up. You're the superintendent. Without you, there is no mission."

"I appreciate your fervor, my friend. I do. In many ways such passion from my missionary colleagues has sustained me these last many months. But I have been arrogant."

Sylvanus opened his mouth to protest. John held up a hand to stop him.

"It's true." John crossed his arms. His chin dipped. "I've been a good manager of mission funds and goals, which has enabled us to grow, but I fear somewhere in the midst of those pursuits, I managed to lose sight of our primary function, which has always been to win souls. I have not allowed our singular missional purpose to be my guide above all others."

"You'll surrender, then. Without a fight." The muscles in Sylvanus's jaw clenched as he fought against the urge to yell sense at the man before him.

"The board is filled with faithful, prayerful men. If they believe it's time for me to step down, then I will trust them." He moved toward Sylvanus, who sidestepped to avoid him. "You should trust them, too."

Sylvanus slid past the nearest cot and walked toward the open window. Beyond it stood the orchard where several of Lydia's young students played during their noontime recess from lessons. Above the gnarled branches he could see the steeple of the church next door. A deep breath brought with it the now familiar tickle of salty sea air. Liberian air.

He felt the pressure of welling tears and the tingle of reddening flesh. He heard John's footsteps leaving the room. And he felt the absence when he was gone.

"I can't believe it." Lydia had made the same comment a half dozen times in the twenty minutes since Sylvanus had entered the kitchen and found her seated at the long table with Hannah. He stood in the doorway and listened to them talk.

Maria, now a robust and curious two year old, had wandered past him to greet Jenny tethered to her line outside. The orangutan was gentle with the little girl, reaching out a hand to steady her when she stumbled on the uneven ground. Though Sylvanus would not leave the two unsupervised, he'd come to trust Jenny, and she had become a favorite among the household. As distant from her native Asia as he was from America she had, like him, made Monrovia her own comfortable home.

He chewed at his lip and wondered what would become of his displaced furry friend. Without the work that had defined his professional life, without this mission, he didn't honestly know what would become of him, either.

"When do you leave?" Lydia directed the question to Sylvanus as Hannah rose from the table and rushed through the door to retrieve her daughter, now laughing at the antics of Jenny who swung lazily by one long arm from the rope while her other hand and both large feet dragged against the dusty earth.

For a moment he couldn't answer but only absorbed the sadness in her gaze until he was dizzy with it.

"I expect us to catch the next available ship headed to America." His stomach churned at the thought of the voyage across the rolling Atlantic and at leaving the woman who deflated at his words.

Lydia sighed. "It's unfair. I don't know how we'll get along without all of you—the superintendent's strong leadership, Hannah's motherly presence, your medical expertise." She shook her head. "Not one of us would be alive without your steady guidance."

He turned from the sight of Hannah, Maria swept into her arms, exchanging pleasantries with Jenny as one might with any lady. The orangutan held Hannah's gaze and one might imagine Jenny understood every word, so eerily human was her expression.

"That's not true." He stepped toward Lydia and sat across from her, placing his cup and then resting his elbows on the table, his hands folded.

"Another physician will take my place." He nearly choked on the words at the notion of his replacement, caring for these patients who had become dear friends and allies in the adventure of a lifetime. He would miss them. He would miss Monrovia—the hot, heavy air, the smiling and shamelessly naked natives expecting and offering gifts at every turn. His heart would ache at the absence of the haunting territorial cries of primates in the mornings and the hinge-door squeal of scampering guinea fowls as he walked through town.

Lydia reached across the table and squeezed his forearm, her cheeks pink with emotion. "They may send another physician, Dr. Goheen, but he will never replace you in our hearts."

"And what about in your heart?" His throat clamped tight at the shock of his own daring, but he could not regret the question. Their time grew too short for subtlety.

Lydia pulled back her hand. Her eyes shifted to Hannah and Maria still happily engaged outside with Jenny. She brought her hand to her forehead, and when she lowered it again to look at him, he could feel the pounding of his heart.

"If you are asking me whether I will miss you, of course I will."

"That's not really what I'm asking, Lydia."

"It's not?" The question came out barely above a whisper.

He shook his head. "You could return to America with me."

"Oh." She brought the back of her hand to her mouth and Sylvanus thought she might be sick, but then she smiled, one of those wonderful, joyful smiles that lit her face and brought crinkles to the corners of her eyes. "Are you asking me to marry you?"

The sound of the question he'd only implied coming from her lips caused his mouth to go dry, but his heart also fluttered at the acknowledgment of it, of this thing between them that had grown since the moment they'd both stepped onto African soil—when she had become enamored with this land and its people, and he had become enamored with her.

"Yes," he said with a grin that she returned.

Then the light faded from her countenance. It was subtle, but he saw the moment it happened.

"A part of me wants more than anything to say yes." Her voice wavered.

"Then say yes." He exhaled quickly and turned his gaze to the ceiling, as if his refusal to look at her might prevent what he knew was coming next. "What's to stop us?"

"You're a good man, Sylvanus. I care about you a great deal and I don't doubt we would be happy together, but I can't leave the mission, my students. I'm needed here."

"*I'm* needed here." His response was loud enough that Hannah glanced into the kitchen, her concern evident. He sounded petulant even to his own ears. "I'm sorry. I don't mean—"

"You're upset. I understand. But your world is a large place." She bit her lip and reached once again for him. He slid his arm out of her reach.

"My world is small," she said. "And it is in Liberia."

The *Susan Elizabeth* arrived just three weeks later with a small crop of emigrants and supplies for the colony from New York where it planned to return. John arranged for passage for himself, his wife and daughter, Sylvanus and, despite the captain's misgivings, for Jenny.

"I can't leave her," Sylvanus explained. He'd hoped to ship her to London, where she might be safely housed in the London's zoological garden in the company of the Jenny for whom she'd been named, the orangutan who once enjoyed tea with the naturalist Charles Darwin. He could not burden the missionaries with her care, and he feared the natives might eat her as they had her mother.

"I'll take her with us and find a home for her at the earliest opportunity. Surely there are menageries that would welcome her."

John hadn't opposed the plan, as Jenny would be a welcome distraction for Maria on the long voyage, and the captain was made amenable once offered a larger sum and the promise the animal would spend most of her time in a cage.

Sylvanus also made the difficult decision to leave Hector behind with Lydia. He'd no way of knowing the dog's age, but over the last two years the animal's energy had waned, suggesting his puppy days were long behind him. Another ocean voyage would be difficult for the terrier who'd ingratiated himself to the mission family and served well as protector, barking alarms and intimidating curious wildlife. The dog would serve, too, as a token of Sylvanus's affection for all of them, and for Lydia in particular. Unlike his master, Hector was still welcome in his colonial home.

33
Annie

Jacksonville was a busy town with more than two thousand people, a thriving college of its own, and a bustling square. To Annie it was almost worth the long carriage ride to get there, which had given her a new appreciation for the rare appearances of Reverend Akers in Lebanon, a hundred miles to the south. She couldn't imagine traversing the rough roads for hours on horseback the way the Methodist circuit riders did with great frequency and little complaint.

Beautiful scenery smoothed the discomforts of the trip. Between wide open gaps of prairie, dense woods hugged the route she and Davis followed, the branches fresh with the early pale green promise of spring.

Davis secured them comfortable rooms at the Heslep Tavern on State Street, a long, shaded road lined with large elm trees pointing the way to a dignified courthouse and into the heart of town. Once settled in, they strolled together arm in arm, Davis more effusive than normal, apparently at ease away from the stresses of his office at the college.

"This is a wonderful idea." he'd said. "I'm so glad to have you with me, and better still that it was Peter's suggestion. He's taken with you, I think."

Annie had not allowed further conjecture on the subject and instead focused on her qualifications as a strong, intelligent woman whose insights into the new school would be valuable.

Unfortunately, many of the other attendees, perhaps those who did not believe as fervently the old adage "Great men have great mothers and good men have good mothers" did not crave her presence in their committee meetings. Annie chose not to let their poor attitudes dampen her spirits as she spent the morning making what suggestions she could about curriculum. Then, when the men dismissed her to pore over financial matters, she took advantage of her free time to explore the booming town, with its sturdy brick architecture reminiscent of cities in the eastern states.

Davis returned to the hotel in the late afternoon bearing an invitation Annie would not admit to him she had been highly anticipating.

"We've been invited to Ebenezer for a tour and supper," her brother told her before filling her in on the details of his meeting. It had not gone as smoothly as hoped. The site of a potential women's college had been hotly debated, as had the financial burden on the Methodist Conference and the perceived need for such a project to begin with.

"But Peter is tenacious when he has a worthy goal in his sights. He was impressed by your input, and if I were a betting man, I would wager on his eventual triumph in almost any matter."

"Mm." Annie heard little of her brother's report after the dinner invitation, preoccupied as she was with thoughts of the man who had issued it. She nodded along with Davis as her mind spun the possibilities of the evening and the wish that she could discuss it with Esther or her mother. Even Susan might have been a welcome source of female companionship. Her sister-in-law had wished her good luck with a knowing wink before the trip.

"Are you listening to me?" Davis asked, his expression conveying feigned hurt before he broke into a grin. "Or perhaps you are considering other fine virtues of our dear Reverend Akers."

Annie turned her back on her brother so he would not see her blush.

About four miles north of Jacksonville, Ebenezer Manual Labor School looked to Annie like any other large family farm. With the exception of the welcome they received from a young man with a braid of silky, black hair and skin like red clay, it might have been at home in Pennsylvania. Their carriage passed recently plowed fields as they approached what appeared to be a church or schoolhouse. Behind the fields stood a large frame house.

There on the porch waited the only Indian Annie had ever seen up close.

"Welcome to Ebenezer." He shook Davis's outstretched hand and tipped his head gracefully to Annie. "My name is George Copway. I am a student here. Reverend Akers is at the main house. He and the children will join us shortly. Please, come in."

Annie attempted to hide her surprise at his eloquent speech, ashamed of how unexpected it was to her. News in the east, especially during the recent conflict known commonly as the Blackhawk War, painted Indians as violent savages who could barely speak. This Mr. Copway was certainly a challenge to her preconceptions.

He led them into a spare but functional sitting room, where he introduced them to two other Indian students, young men named John and Peter, though Annie suspected these had not been their given names at birth. These young men greeted them as graciously as had their fellow.

George invited them to make themselves comfortable before asking Davis, "Was it a productive meeting today, Reverend Goheen?"

"Well," Davis blew out a puff of air. "I believe there were solid points made, perhaps a framework for eventual success. Did Reverend Akers have much to say on the subject?"

"We've not had time to converse with him yet. He only returned two hours ago and has spent his time with the children. He's been away more than here for the last two weeks. I'm sure he's missed them as much as they have missed him."

Annie silently added the descriptor of loving and attentive father to her growing list of the circuit rider's fine qualities. She didn't have much time to ponder them before the man himself entered the house, followed by seven children ranging in age from a practically fully-grown young lady to a squirming toddler held fast in her arms.

"Reverend and Miss Goheen," Peter Akers said after they all filed in. "May I present my children: daughters Mary, Sarah, Nancy, and Cynthia." Each of the girls curtseyed when her name was called, including the eldest Mary who held the littlest boy.

"And this is George." Reverend Akers squeezed the shoulder of the tallest boy. "Followed by Joshua and Little Robert."

Davis clapped his hands together. "Wonderful to meet all of you in person. Your father speaks well of you all. And quite often."

Annie, too, greeted the children, gratified to see them return her smile, even Robert who giggled in delight as she scrunched her nose at him. They made a fine brood and Annie's heart went out to all seven of them. She knew what it was to come from a large family of siblings left by death and bereavement to largely care for one another.

Though her mother had never remarried, Annie sometimes wondered how their family might have been different if she had—to have two parents to lean on and support one another, to have love and time enough to spare for the constant needs of the children in their home. Until this moment, she might not have known she longed for it. Now she could see the desire, played out on the faces of the Akers children, particularly the eldest on whose shoulders much of the burden must fall in the midst of their father's busy career.

Supper was served at a long table in the school dormitory where they had gathered and where, Annie was shocked to learn, food had been prepared by the Indian students themselves.

"This is a working farm and home. We study together, work together, and live together as family."

"I've several other students as well who live in and around Jacksonville," Reverend Akers explained. "But only our three Indian friends remain here full-time, as their tribes have been forced to the other side of the Mississippi."

"What do you study?" Annie addressed her question to the young Indian John who sat beside her and displayed impeccable table manners.

"Law and theology mostly, as well as agriculture techniques. My hope is one day to return as a teacher and missionary to my people."

"An admirable goal," she said. *And an uncomfortable parallel*, she thought.

When, after supper, Reverend Akers asked Annie if she might like to walk the grounds with him, a plan to which Davis agreed and gracefully declined to join, she nervously accepted.

"Reverend Akers," she began as they walked down the lane rounding what she now knew to be the schoolhouse, "I admire what you're attempting to do here, to smooth the way for the Indians by educating some of their own in our more civilized ways."

"I wish you might feel comfortable calling me Peter."

She tipped her head to hide any evidence of her delight before nodding her consent. "And then you must call me Ann." She shrugged. "Or Annie, if you like."

Peter smiled openly at the suggestion. "The American Indians are a tribal people, but I would hesitate to call them uncivilized. Their culture is not organized the same way as ours. That's why it's often difficult for us to understand one another. In general, they have been ill-treated because our differences have made them vulnerable to exploitation. My hope is that I might help by giving them a taste of our culture as well as educating them in practical skills and enable them to make their way in this new landscape of their home."

"My brother is attempting to do something similar. My youngest brother," she clarified. "Sylvanus is a missionary with the Methodist Conference in Liberia."

"Oh yes," he said. "Davis has mentioned him. He's proud of his adventurous little brother." Peter stopped walking at the edge of a tree-lined pond Annie hadn't noticed on her earlier approach to the house.

"You know," he said thoughtfully, "in some ways it is certainly similar, but the African task includes more layers of difficulty. Here there are white interlopers, now generations in, on a land that once belonged exclusively to the Indians. In Africa, the experiment is in its infant stage and the interlopers are a formerly enslaved people themselves, in many cases grossly undereducated and now urgently thrust into the position of the oppressor. It's difficult to know how such people will respond. And, of course, it's impossible to know how a previously unstudied culture will receive such pressure."

Annie's heart fluttered. "You believe colonization is a foolish idea?"

"I wouldn't go so far as to say so." He gazed out over the pond for a moment before he continued. "I simply meant it should be pursued with great care, which I'm sure your brother and his fellow missionaries well understand."

To read Smee's letters, as filled as they often seemed with self-praise and lofty ambitions, she wasn't convinced, but then she supposed he probably did not share with her the more tedious or difficult aspects of his Liberian life.

Peter concluded, "I'm grateful men of God have taken up the call to be present in what must be a tumultuous upheaval on a foreign continent. What better, more level-headed arbiters could be wanted than those whose primary concern isn't to conquer but rather to spread the light of Christ?"

"I've never thought of it in that way, but I suspect you're right." She stopped walking and appraised him with wide eyes. "I might as well confess to you I have never been in favor of colonization, nor of my brother's role in it. I believe Mr. Garrison and the abolitionists are correct when they suggest that removal of free Blacks from the United States only serves to harm their noble cause."

"You are an abolitionist then?" Peter turned to look at her and she attempted to read his expression.

"Yes, I believe I am." She glanced away from him. "Are you not?"

The corners of his mouth quirked downward in the faintest frown, and he started to walk again. She fell in beside him.

"I abhor the practice of human slavery," he said, "but I resist the label. Abolitionists, in my experience, are a stiff and unyielding lot. They espouse a just cause, but in doing so often discount the humanity of those they argue against."

"How so?"

"I was raised in Virginia and spent the early part of my career in Kentucky, both slave states and both home to many wonderful people whom I love, many of whom would have no pathway out of slave ownership if not for the possibility of colonization. Evil rarely exists without also the presence of good."

His words troubled her, and her blood began to rise despite the growing chill of the evening. "But what of the humanity of enslaved people? Even reluctant southern slaveholders seem to have failed to account for it. Do you not believe slavery is evil and must come to an immediate end?"

"Please don't misunderstand me, Annie." His words were steady and sure, and the sound of her familiar name on his lips worked to melt her indignance. "With my entire heart, I do believe slavery must and will come to a swift end in the United States. I have spoken such words from the pulpit because God has laid them upon my heart. Still, I fear the violence ahead. I think it unwise to rush headlong into a conflict from which this nation will not soon recover. We are on the brink."

Annie wrapped her arms around herself to stave off the chill from the breeze coming off the water.

"You're cold," Peter noted. "We should return to the dormitory. The sun will soon set. I'm sure Davis would prefer to be back to town before the hour grows too late."

His thoughtfulness touched her, as did his calm demeanor in the midst of disagreement. This was a man who listened and considered, even when an opinion offered came from a woman.

"I want to thank you, Annie," he began as they started up the lane to the dormitory. "For your visit and for engaging with me in such stimulating conversation. I hope we can continue to speak on this and other matters. With Davis's permission, and yours, I would appreciate the opportunity to call on you again."

Annie smiled. He was a challenging man but, she believed, also a good man.

"I would like, Peter, and if I may speak for him, I suspect Davis will have even less objection than I."

34
Sylvanus

Sylvanus sat on the same lonely bench in the cold hallway behind the chancel of John Street Church where he'd awaited his opportunity to prove his fitness for foreign mission. The moments bookended a grand adventure—two and a half years of professional and spiritual growth in the midst of struggle, sorrow, and death.

But there were triumphs, too—patients he'd pulled from the grip of disease, fascinating scientific collections, spiritual awakening. God had been with him in Africa, had guided his exertions against darkness and obscurity. As unlikely as it might seem, Monrovia had become his home, a place where he'd been an integral part of a burgeoning society. He had more to give. He'd do anything for the opportunity to go back.

John Seys emerged from the door to the left of the choir loft. The creek of its hinges transported Sylvanus to his previous visit and all the nervous anticipation he'd once felt, now replaced by dread the moment he saw the sullen expression on John's face.

"Sylvanus, they're ready for you." The man who was once a superintendent motioned for Sylvanus to follow him back through the door, down the familiar stairs, and around the altar to face the gathered members of the Mission Board.

Sylvanus counted only thirteen stern-faced men seated in the front pews of the spacious sanctuary, far fewer than had evaluated him on his previous visit, fewer opportunities to sway a decision he feared was already made.

He closed his eyes and swallowed.

"Dr. Goheen, welcome back." Sylvanus found the light greeting oddly cheery for such a somber occasion. It came from a short man in a dark suit whose familiar face was pudgier than Sylvanus remembered. He sifted through his memories for the man's name but could not recall it. Their previous encounter seemed a lifetime ago.

"Thank you," Sylvanus said. He sat in a chair beside John, both facing their adversaries.

The short man remained standing, turning his head and smiling toward his colleagues. He clasped his hands together and cleared his throat. "Please know that your service to this mission has been exemplary. We would like to extend our sincere gratitude for the difficult work you have accomplished in maintaining the health of so many of our missionaries."

"If you appreciate my work, then why did you recall me?"

John fidgeted beside Sylvanus, but he didn't care to heed his former mentor's caution. These men needed to hear of his anger at their unjust decision. They needed to consider the lives they might have spared had they left him in Africa, of the lives surely lost because he wasn't there, of his own life interrupted by an aching heart.

A murmur passed among the observing board members. The short representative cleared his throat again before answering.

"It is our hope that you can see this recall not as a punishment for a job well done, but as a necessary step toward healing of a damaged relationship with the colonial government."

"Yes, that's the explanation I was given," Sylvanus said, his heart beating faster as his fury grew. "But I fail to see how the board can willingly sacrifice missionary lives to soothe the hurt feelings of Governor Buchanan."

"Now, Dr. Goheen—"

John Seys interrupted before the sputtering man could formulate his response. "Please excuse my colleague, gentlemen. He's disappointed, as we all are, that his time in Liberia could not have continued. There was much fruit produced and more harvest yet to come."

Sylvanus opened his mouth to build on the words, but John forged on, stealing away the chance. "We know this decision was made prayerfully and with great care toward the future of the mission. We humbly thank you for the difficult hours you have each spent in coming to this decision regarding our time of service. We look forward to the challenge of serving the Lord in new capacities."

The mollified board members nodded in acknowledgment of John's careful words and began to stand as if the business at hand were now settled and the meeting adjourned.

Sylvanus was not so easily appeased. "I won't be going back, then?" he asked, his voice rising above the general rustle of fourteen men shuffling about, reaching for hats and gloves. None of the board members acknowledged him. Instead, it was John Seys who answered.

"I did appeal the decision." He stood and invited Sylvanus to do the same. "I made your case as clearly as I could."

Sylvanus pursed his lips. Thoughts of Lydia flashed into his mind, his longing to return to her, but his anger could not find a hold on his longtime friend. "I know you did."

"They'd already made their decision." John shrugged. "They want an expeditious, peaceful resolution and they believe they can accomplish it by cleaning house at the *Luminary*. Speaking up in my defense sealed your fate, I'm afraid."

"I don't blame you, John. I'll always be your defender." Sylvanus's head dropped and he rubbed his forehead with his hand. "I just don't know what comes next."

John put an arm around Sylvanus. "Thank you, my friend." His words fluttered with emotion.

The two men began to follow the board members as they filed toward the doors at the back of the sanctuary.

"As for what you should do," John said with a lightness Sylvanus had rarely seen. "Have you considered that you have an orangutan? Perhaps you could be a showman."

"Oh, I didn't tell you. Jenny is on a ship to London." He did not regret the arrangement made shortly after his arrival in New York, but he would miss his furry friend more than he cared admit. "I expect she'll be having tea with Queen Victoria in a month or so."

"I think I might miss the old girl." They emerged from the church and squinted in the sunlight flooding the city street.

"What about you?" Sylvanus asked him. "What will you do?"

"I'll join Hannah and the children in Connecticut, pursue a domestic appointment for a while, see what may come of it."

"Would you ever go back?"

"Into the foreign mission field?" John paused, his head tilted to the left, as if to more fully examine the question. "I will not hesitate to go where God leads. For now, however, I'm grateful to have less responsibility, to spend more time with those I love the most. In fact, my friend, you might want to think about doing that as well."

Sylvanus stopped walking. "Those I love the most?" Logically he knew John did not refer to Lydia. They'd not spoken of the attachment Sylvanus had formed or had wished to form.

"Your family," John replied, his easy manner suggesting he'd failed to observe the tension in his companion. "Have you even written to your mother?"

Sylvanus shook his head and continued to walk. "I wrote to her from Liberia. She should know I am returning to the United States." Sheepishly he added, "I have not sent word of our arrival."

"Then I recommend you go home. Let them fawn over you and assure themselves you're alive and unharmed."

"I've never known my mother to fawn." He crossed his arms and tried to picture Elizabeth Goheen, excited to see the return of her failed son who had been officially exiled, expelled from a foreign land, a disgrace to the Goheen name. Inwardly, he shuddered.

Anticipating a return to the farm of his childhood filled his heart with more fear than had the prospect of sailing across the Atlantic.

In his absence, Columbia had changed in those subtle ways hometowns shift when one is gone for an extended period. If pressed, Sylvanus could not have precisely identified the differences, but on the short walk from the train station to the livery, he felt as if he were looking at a mere reflection of a place he once knew. The colors from his childhood memory stood faded, the imposing buildings had grown weaker and less impressive with the weathering of time.

There were a few differences he could note. Some of the businesses had changed hands and now featured unfamiliar signs and window displays. Dr. Thompson's shingle had been replaced. The building remained a medical office, now featuring the name of Dr. August Rhodes. Sylvanus searched his memory for the man and discovered only a momentary twinge of regret the sign didn't proclaim his own name.

When the farm came into view at last it, too, was disorienting. Spring tulips popped up along the side of the house where he never recalled them having been planted before. The narrow front porch featured several new, unpainted boards along the bottom. The kitchen garden stood untilled, surprising for the time of year, and it took up less space than he remembered from his youth.

The strangest sight of all, however, was that of his mother, who stepped onto the front porch at the approach of his rented carriage.

She'd not changed a great deal in appearance—perhaps with just few more strands of white in the hair pulled back into a neat bun at the nape of her neck and a slight increase to the bend in her back. These years had been kind to her in a way Sylvanus knew they had not been as forgiving of him. He was thinner, for one, after suffering periods of insufficient food and bouts of illness in Africa, followed by weeks of seasickness on the rolling ocean swells. He wondered how he must appear to her, how he might compare to his brothers, well-fed and successful in their various careers.

His concerns fell away in a moment because with the grace of a much younger woman, his mother flew from the porch to greet him, her arms wide and a smile on her face, out of place on her regal features.

"My boy." She embraced him. He was surprised at her strength, undiminished in all these years from when he was small. She held him fiercely and, if he weren't mistaken, she was crying.

After a long, awkward moment, she loosened her hold and pushed back from him, her hands still clasping his arms as she looked him over. Her lashes were moist, her eyes red. Warmth spread through Sylvanus. His mother was happy to see him.

"I only received your letter a week ago. I hadn't dared hope I'd see you so soon." The joy never faded from her eyes as she spoke, and she didn't let go of him.

"We boarded a ship not long after I sent the letter with another headed down the coast. I'd have been here sooner, but I had to meet with the Mission Board in New York."

She dropped his arms and took another step back. A shadow fell across her features and the mother he remembered emerged. "What did they have to say for themselves?"

Sylvanus was taken aback at her tone, at the way her thin eyebrows bunched together. The sight made him sputter before he answered. "They remain convinced the recall was necessary to the future success of the mission."

"Cowards," she huffed. "Men of God allowing themselves to be pushed around by a power-grubbing politician. It's disgraceful."

If a strong wind had risen, Sylvanus would have been knocked off his feet, such was his surprise at her disgust of the unfortunate situation. That she had followed along with his plight at all came as a shock, and the surprise must have been written on his face because the previous softness returned to hers.

"I do read the *Luminary*." She brushed away his confusion with a wave of her hand. "You haven't exactly been diligent in your letter writing, and when a son is the editor of an international newspaper, his mother reads what he writes."

His cheeks reddened. Of course, he knew his family subscribed to the paper, had even thought at times how a particular article might be especially appreciated by Annie or Davis or John Wesley. Just never Mother. It had never occurred to him that she might read his articles, even scour the words for hints of his state of mind, of his well-being. Such action demonstrated love. He was touched.

"Thank you," he said. "For reading. And for caring."

At twenty-seven years of age, standing a good five inches taller than her, Sylvanus didn't even feel the absurdity of the gesture as his mother reach up to cup his cheek. "I'm proud of you, you know."

He hadn't known. A lump formed in his throat.

"And," she added, "I'm glad you're home."

John Wesley was happy to see him, too, when he returned home later in the early evening. The two caught up while Mother cooked a feast, insisting Sylvanus needed fattening.

"I can't believe Annie actually went to Illinois." He shook his head. "To find a husband? Really?"

He knew she'd done it because she'd written to Hannah Seys about the journey, and he'd felt a sting of resentment over her failure to write to him of her plans.

"Don't tell her that's what she's done." John Wesley smirked. "She'd deny it, and you'd never hear the end of it."

"Probably true." Sylvanus thought of his proper sister and her well-ordered life, derailed by the violent death of a fiancé. She had always been unflinching in her beliefs and immovable in her opinions. He missed her tremendously. "Anyway, I'd have thought she'd have better luck in a place like Philadelphia than on the rough and tumble frontier. What sort of husband is she meant to discover there?"

"I don't know," John Wesley admitted. "But Davis insists there's a prospect. A circuit rider. Rough and tumble for sure."

"A preacher," Sylvanus said. "She always wanted to marry a preacher."

John Wesley shrugged. "True, but our sister is stubborn, and the whole thing might just be wishful thinking on Davis's part. At least they all seem to be settling into Illinois."

"Thinking of heading west yourself?" Sylvanus joked, and then wished he hadn't when his brother didn't answer right away. If John Wesley left, too, it would only be him left with Mother, a thought that didn't thrill him. He had no desire to farm, nor did he wish to compete for patients in a town the size of Columbia. He didn't know what the future held for him, but whatever it was, he was convinced it wouldn't be on the family farm.

"Not to Illinois," replied John Wesley.

The answer sounded ominous.

"Are you thinking of going somewhere else?"

"Mother didn't tell you."

"Tell me what?" Sylvanus asked, genuinely nervous.

"Uncle Leon made an offer on the land."

Sylvanus wasn't sure he'd heard correctly. His entire life his mother had fought to keep the farm for her children who might continue to carve a living from it.

"Will she accept?"

"She already has. Mayberry and Mariah have invited her to live with them in Baltimore. She wants to be with her grandchildren."

"And what about you?" Sylvanus searched his brother's face for a hint of uncertainty or concern. He didn't find it. "What do you want to do?"

"I'm going with her. I've a head for business, not farming. Baltimore holds opportunity I'm not going to find here. And if I don't leave, Mother never will. She's getting older, Sy. It'd be nice if she didn't have to work so hard."

Sylvanus couldn't deny the logic, even as the sad ramification sank in. His childhood home would soon be gone, to become instead a home to generations of cousins. It would take him time to adjust to the notion.

"You could come, too. I'm sure Baltimore has need of a new physician."

"No." He didn't know what made him speak so emphatically, but he was certain in his response. He didn't belong in Baltimore, felt no desire even to visit the place. He longed for something else, and he'd known it long before he identified the drive. He'd left a part of his heart on the west coast of Africa. What remained longed for America's west, on the rough and tumble frontier. Illinois would be a good place to start.

35
Annie

Davis walked through the door just as Annie set the table with the supper Mrs. Lowes had helped prepare. The delicious aroma of roasted pork, cornbread, and beans from the thriving kitchen garden did little to chase away her brother's melancholy.

"What's the matter with you?" she asked.

He waved off her concern as he dropped into a chair at the table. "The board meeting today didn't go as well as I'd hoped."

"You look as if you've a dark cloud following you."

"It's nothing," he said, inviting her to sit. "The college has run into some unanticipated financial and staffing issues. It's nothing we can't handle."

Financial issues sounded important to Annie, but Davis's dismissive comments convinced her she would get little information from him, and his foul mood could not dampen her cheerful one. Tomorrow she would spend the afternoon with Peter, and she had at long last heard news directly from her youngest brother.

"Perhaps this will lighten your mood," she said after he'd asked a dispassionate blessing over the food. "We have received a letter from Smee."

Davis's head raised and one corner of his mouth quirked upward, though a full grin failed to bloom. "What does he have to say?"

Annie retrieved the brief letter from her apron pocket and read it aloud:

To my brothers and dear sister—

From the burning rays of Africa's inhospitable clime your brother has returned to this continent, to the home of our birth to be received in love by Mother and John Wesley, on their way soon to Baltimore. As they depart, so must I, and it is to the mysterious frontier of Illinois I feel called. I pray this note finds you all well and I long for the near day of our reunion.

Your loving brother,
S.M.E. Goheen
Columbia, Pennsylvania
April 26, 1839

Davis shook his head. "Always had a flare for the dramatic, our little brother."

"Yes," Annie said with a giggle. "But he's home. And he's coming here."

Knowing this filled her with an intense desire to set things right between them. She believed she had forgiven him for breaking her heart by going to Liberia. She'd found a peace, too, in the space between abolition and colonization, a slice of gray Peter had helped her to discover. It remained her determined belief that slavery must be swiftly and decisively abolished, but she had begun to understand freedom to be a fragile dream, not yet fully realized even among free men of color in the United States. It was all more complicated than she had imagined.

That's what she would tell Smee—not that he had been correct, but that perhaps neither of them had been. She would hope when she finally saw him again in the flesh, hugged him tightly, and let him know, *really* know, that she had missed him, it would be enough to soothe the strain in their relationship.

The day was settling into a thing of beauty with bright sunshine and the hint of spring flowers in the breeze, a promise of the summer soon to come. Annie dressed with care as Susan, *Lady's Godey Book* in hand, supervised.

"Oh, how I envy your tiny waist," said Susan. She tugged at Annie's skirt, a pale green silk overlaid with pink roses. It hadn't been Annie's choice. She'd have favored blue as she always did, but Susan had been insistent, and miserably pregnant at the time, so Annie had accepted her advice.

Her sister-in-law was a far better seamstress than Annie had ever been and possessed a good eye for color and fashion as well. She was glad she'd listened. The color both pulled out the rosiness in her cheeks and toned down the brassiness in her walnut brown hair. The bodice of the dress featured a high neckline, tight sleeves, and modest pleats gathered to the waist. It highlighted her best features—her smooth, ivory complexion and her narrow waist that evidently elicited envy.

"You'll be slimmer than me before you know it," Annie said.

Slight of build and only twenty-one years old, Susan had been ill every day of her pregnancy and had been swollen and miserable from its earliest stages. Since delivering a thriving baby boy named Wilbur, she'd experienced what Annie viewed as a steady recovery. Susan saw it differently.

"You're kind to say so, but I doubt it." Susan stepped back and appraised Annie with a smile. "You'll see one day. Peter will take one look at you in this dress and sweep you into the church to marry you. Then you can ruin your figure with babies, too."

Annie could hardly imagine having children of her own, or even the possibility of marriage, but she had to admit she cut a fine figure in the dress specially designed by her optimistic sister-in-law. And even the serious-minded Reverend Akers could hardly miss noticing.

"Peter has plenty of children already. I doubt he's anxious for more."

"A good man can always make room for more children in his life," Susan said. "Especially when is gaining a perfect wife and a perfect mother for those he already has."

"Perfect?"

Susan stood before her and pinned a fallen piece of Annie's hair into place.

"Yes," she said with a satisfied nod. "Perfect."

For this visit to Lebanon, Peter had brought his children with him, as the town had been their home when he served as McKendree's first president. While he attended his board meeting, the children visited with family friends. Today, Annie would join Peter and the children for a picnic.

She placed the final dishes into the basket, covered it with a quilt, and turned to a well-timed knock at the door.

"Well, hello," she said at the sight of six-year-old Cynthia, with a head full of wild blonde tresses and a smile that demonstrated her delight at being named designated door knocker. "How wonderful to see you all."

In each of the children, neatly dressed and fresh, she could see pieces of their father shining out at her. Twelve-year-old George must have resembled his mother in large part but possessed the mirror image of his father's long nose. Mary, at sixteen, had the air of a young lady only recently come into the blush of her beauty. She projected a stern Akers nobility. Little two-year-old Robert, his hand firmly clamped in his father's large paw, perhaps resembled Peter the most—the shape of his ears, sticking out a little bit too far beneath fine wisps of hair yet to fill in fully. The shape of his eyes, too, as he stared in wonderment at her, appeared identical to the curve of Peter's eyes as she met them and found the same sense of wonderment there.

His warm smile at seeing her served to soften the hard edges the circuit had etched into his face and her breath caught. "It's wonderful to see you, too, Annie. Are you ready to go?"

Peter let go of the little boy's hand to reach for the basket and when he did, Robert reached toward Annie, who happily scooped him up and settled him on her hip.

Davis's house sat on the northwest part of town, only a few blocks from the college where the happy gathering found a grassy lawn upon which to set their feast. The children chattered about the joy of returning to Lebanon, finding familiar faces and playing beloved old games. Annie listened, astonished that their childhood so wonderfully echoed her own in Pennsylvania, eight hundred miles away.

Peter said little during the meal, but remained attentive to every word from his children, laughing heartily at all the right moments and smiling when Cynthia climbed unbidden into Annie's lap.

After everyone had finished eating, Peter suggested a game of tag to the five middle children and Mary assumed the responsibility of watching over Robert, too little to participate and just big enough to get himself hurt in the attempt. As the children scattered, Peter turned to Annie.

"I'm pleased you could join us today."

She felt herself blush. "The pleasure has been mine. Your family is darling, really."

"Thank you for saying so." He leaned back on one arm and gazed in the direction of the game of tag. Joshua tumbled into George's legs and both boys sprawled on the grass. Peter sighed. "They're not always so well mannered."

"They are children." Annie chuckled. "I think you've done a marvelous job with them, especially considering how busy you are. It's no easy task."

"Well," he said. "I have a lot of help. And Mary is a blessing."

"Yes, she is."

He pursed his lips. "I rely on her too much, really. It's not fair to her. She's had to grow up quickly."

Annie could relate and she told Peter so.

He smiled. "To hear Davis tell of it, you were a force to be reckoned with, even to your eldest brothers."

Annie pulled a long piece of grass from beside the quilt and worked it with her fingers. "When my father died, my mother changed—not her personality, but her focus. She never broke under the pressure of raising us by herself, but it bent her. Her light dimmed."

"And you helped brighten her."

Annie bit her lip. "I wanted to. I don't know if I did, but her light has returned in recent years."

"I'm certain you are largely responsible." He sat up straight and turned to face her. "Just as I'm certain you bring light to my life and to the lives of my children."

The blood drained from her cheeks, and she barely felt it when he took her hand in his.

"I wrote to your mother," he said. "Did you know?"

She shook her head. Her breaths grew shallow.

"I spoke with Davis as well and shared my intentions. Now I'd like to share them with you."

The noise of the playing children and the birdsong in the trees all seemed to stop. She shivered.

"Annie, I believe God has brought us together, brought this family together. I know you to be a humble servant of the Lord with a heart full of love for family and ministry. My children have grown to love you, as have I. I would be honored if you would consider becoming my wife."

36
Sylvanus

Sylvanus drew a deep breath as he walked, bag in hand and brow damp with sweat, toward the frame house with its expansive porch. He'd been directed to the dwelling place of McKendree College's chief financial officer Reverend Davis Goheen and his spinster sister. He had nearly scoffed on Annie's behalf at the description.

Even as the sun began to set, the Illinois heat in the middle of July was a force unto itself, more intense than Monrovia where the breeze to and from the Atlantic maintained mild evenings and the humidity had the decency to develop into rain. The memory of Pennsylvania summers couldn't compare either to this sticky sensation of trudging through soup.

In the shade of the porch sat two women in animated conversation. Beside them were two men, wise enough to have shed their coats. From this distance he could not determine the figures' identities, but their laughter carried with it a certain note that transported him to the farm, to his childhood.

He shaded his eyes with his free hand and squinted toward the house. "Annie?" he called.

At her answering squeal, all the tension of travel and the anticipation of this moment of reunion melted from him. He ran the last distance to the house, dropped his bag and pulled her into a hug.

"I can't believe you're here," she mumbled into his shoulder before pushing him away. "It's too hot for hugging, but oh, how I have missed you." She punched him playfully on the arm and beckoned him to the porch.

He walked beside her and with his free hand pulled a letter from his coat pocket to hand to her. "Mother wanted me to deliver this to you. It's from Esther and Bennett. They are safe and happy."

Annie slid it from his hand, clutched it to her chest, and seemed to glow. "Thank you."

When they got to the porch, the second woman rose as if to greet him. He didn't recognize her—slight of build, but with a ferocious, scrutinizing gaze yielding at last to a stiff nod. "He looks a bit like Mayberry, I think. And Davis, he's got your cleft chin."

"Our father had the same chin," Davis confirmed, emerging from the porch, a smiling William behind him. His two brothers took turns with a firm handshake and slap on the back from each.

"Sylvanus Goheen," William said, "meet Susan Goheen, my wife."

"It's a pleasure," Sylvanus said. He swallowed. Life had marched on while he'd been away.

It came as a surprise when Susan moved toward him, setting aside the lace she'd been sewing, and gathered him into suffocating hug as enthusiastic as the one he'd received from Annie. "The pleasure is mine. Welcome home."

She released him with a grin that Sylvanus returned before he dropped his bag on the porch and sat on the top step.

"Tell us about Africa," Annie urged.

"You don't want to hear about it," he said. "Disease, death, political nonsense. It's not exactly a utopia. As you predicted."

"There's no utopia on this side of heaven," Annie said. Her tone lacked any trace of the gloating and condescension he'd expected. "The only thing I predicted was that my little brother would work hard to save lives and serve God. I'm certain you did both."

"I tried." He paused, but the silence only grew as his audience awaited more. "It turns out freedom and liberty are tricky things to hold onto."

He studied their faces, each expectant and welcoming and so full of love he almost couldn't catch his breath. "But that's quite a tale, best saved for another day when I'm not so travel weary."

"There's no rush," said Davis. "You're here to stay, I assume?"

Sylvanus wasn't entirely sure how to answer the question. He'd attempted and failed to think beyond reuniting with his family in Illinois. "I'm here for now."

Undaunted by the noncommittal response, Davis said, "Because your arrival is perfect, if you don't have further plans, you might solve a problem for me."

"Oh?"

"The college is in need of a qualified professor in the natural sciences. I could put in a good word for you."

A sense of peace expanded in Sylvanus's chest, and he made a show of removing his coat to expose his sweat-soaked shirt in hopes his siblings might not see the moisture at the corners of his eyes.

"I think I'd like that," he said before spying the silky fabric in his sister's hands. "What are you ladies working on?"

It was Susan who answered. "Annie's wedding dress."

Sylvanus didn't hide his delight, his lips spreading into a wide grin. "You're getting married, Annie? To this preacher I heard so much about?"

She sighed, but her easy smile told him all he needed to know. "Yes, to the preacher you've heard so much about. Peter's a good man."

"I'm sure he is." His words were sincere. Any concern he'd once had that she'd choose poorly was gone. "You've waited a long time for this and suffered a great deal. I'm sorry for it."

"It wasn't your fault Jonas died."

"No." He shook his head. "But I regret not being there to help comfort you when it happened, just as I regret not trusting you more."

"Thank you for saying so." Annie swiped at a tear on her cheek. "God has used my misfortune for good."

He chimed in with an "amen."

"But Sylvanus?" She leaned down to him from her chair and looked him right in the eyes. "This time I'd like you to come to my wedding."

He stared right back at her, unflinching.

"My dear sister, I wouldn't miss it."

Author's Note

This book began where I wish they all did, in the false-bottom drawer of a lawyer cabinet. After my grandmother passed away quite a few years ago and the furniture had been divvied up among her descendants, it was my aunt who stumbled on a diary, long forgotten and tucked away, from the late 1830s, that once belonged to Ann Goheen, the sister of my grandfather's great grandfather.

That alone is a treasure, but as we examined it, we discovered in its unfortunately sparse pages, an unfolding story of love and family, devotion and grief, and just a hint of political history. Annie (as I later discovered her family called her) eventually became the wife of Reverend Peter Akers, a name that history remembers as the prophetic voice that touched Abraham Lincoln deeply and started him thinking about the role he might eventually play in bringing about an end to American slavery. There's plenty about Akers in the historical record, but not surprisingly, little about Annie who was described in his obituary notice (which admittedly she may have written) as "the perfect wife."

Annie was Peter's third wife and the two did not marry until 1846 when she was thirty-nine years old. I moved up that timeline a few years for the sake of story, but more or less maintained the proper ages of Peter's children. Peter and Annie did have one son together, who did not survive to adulthood.

Because she didn't marry until very late for the era, and because single women were generally written about even less than their married counterparts, much of Annie's story was difficult to track down beyond the few scraps in her diary and an occasional mention of her in writings about or by her brothers. Much of her story that appears in this book is invented, including her dashed marriage hopes with the fictional Jonas Edwards and her friendship with the imagined Esther. Her relationship with the Seys family, however, is real. She corresponded regularly with Mrs. Ann Seys (whose name I changed to Hannah to avoid confusion on the page), and she did briefly care for some of the Seys children in her family's Pennsylvania home. The couple later named a daughter Ann Goheen Seys.

But what intrigued me most about Annie's diary, and led me to the extensive research that eventually became this book, was that it had been presented to her by her youngest brother, Dr. S. M. E. Goheen, upon his departure to Liberia as a missionary physician with the Methodist Episcopal Church.

Sylvanus left a bit more of a record, as did the American Colonization Society. Though it is a piece of history that is not well-remembered in the United States today, the ACS was established in 1817 with the goal of founding the colony of Liberia in which free Blacks could develop a nation of their own. Supporters of the venture included well-intentioned missionary organizations seeking to evangelize Africa, generational slaveholders wanting to extricate themselves from the practice, southern slaveholders determined to maintain the institution, and even some abolitionists, both white and Black.

The colonization effort made for some strange bedfellows, generated a great deal of controversy in its time, and set up a complicated political history that, two hundred years later, continues to have far-reaching ramifications for what became the nation of Liberia.

Sylvanus Goheen had a very small part to play in a complex story. I have done my best to use accurate dates and details for his travel to and from Africa and most of the events of the novel that take place in Liberia did occur, though not all directly involve nor come from accounts written by Sylvanus himself. Most of the missionary and colonial names used in the novel are those of people who were there, but in many cases those names have been used in at least somewhat fictional ways and should be read that way.

Hector the dog was real, as was the story of how Sylvanus came to travel with him. Also, though I was unable to determine her ultimate fate, Jenny the orangutan was given to Sylvanus by indigenous people in Liberia and she did return with him to the United States. I have made a little bit of a leap in sending her to London. The London Zoo had an orangutan named Jenny who became the subject of an article by Charles Darwin in which he described having tea with her. The dates guarantee that the two orangutans cannot be the same, but London's original Jenny died shortly after Darwin's writings and she was replaced by a second female orangutan, also named Jenny, who arrived with a ship captain looking to be rid of her. She *could* have been Sylvanus's Jenny. And I like to think she was.

Whether the real Annie and Sylvanus had a falling out over conflicting political ideologies, I don't honestly know. Annie's diary is austere and practical, while Sylvanus's private writing reveals imagination and playfulness. His contributions to *Africa's Luminary* at times demonstrate a little impetuousness. I attempted to be as true to their characters as my information allowed, but I admit I hijacked their stories in order to present the historical controversy and to highlight the importance of family in the midst of heated political debate. I will have to hope that my great-great-great-great aunt and uncle can forgive me for any liberties I have taken.

Acknowledgements

This book has taken a long journey from found family diary through a sea of research and into the shape of a story, none of which could have been done without the assistance and enthusiasm of many, many, people. My gratitude begins with my Aunt Pat who insisted that Annie and Sylvanus's story make it into the world. Sadly, she passed away before the book was finished, but it truly would not exist without her encouragement. I am also extremely grateful to Michael Goheen, Doris Goheen, and Velma Finnern who each contributed to the family history research without which this story could not have been told. Early readers Ruth McClintock, Amy Houke, and Margery Reynolds offered invaluable feedback, as did the many brilliant writers of Coffee & Critique and the HNS Historical Novel Masterclass. A project like this requires a great deal of research and I could not have tackled it without the dedicated archivists at MacMurray College, the St. Charles City-County Library, the University of Wisconsin-Madison, and Drew University. I would especially like to thank Christopher Anderson at Yale's Divinity Library who went above and beyond to ensure that I could gain access to the personal writings of S. M. E. Goheen. No novel project is ever complete without the talented people who shine it up and make it beautiful. Thank you to Megan Harris, Jeanne Felfe, and Steven Varble for doing just that. And last, but certainly not least, thank you to my husband Paul and our two sons, my greatest cheerleaders.

About The Author

Sarah Angleton is the author of three historical novels, including companion novels *Gentleman of Misfortune* and *Smoke Rose to Heaven*. She is the writer behind the Practical Historian humor blog and the essay collection *Launching Sheep & Other Stories at the Intersection of History and Nonsense*, as well as the episodic dystopian thriller *Tiger Moth*, available to read on Kindle Vella. She lives near St. Louis with her husband, two sons, and one very loyal dog. Catch up with her at Sarah-Angleton.com.